Spectacular reviews for

Red Sorghum

"*Red Sorghum* creates the backdrop for mythic heroism and primitivist vitality through the exotically portrayed setting of Shandong's lush sorghum fields." —*The Boston Globe*

"[Yan's] style is vibrant, alternating between lyrical passages and an oddly conversational tone. This historical tale has a remarkable sense of immediacy and an impressive scope."

—*Los Angeles Times*

"Having read *Red Sorghum*, I believe Mo Yan deserves a place in world literature. His imagery is astounding, sensual and visceral. His story is electrifying and epic. I was amazed from the first page. It is unlike anything I've read coming out of China in past or recent times. I am convinced this book will successfully leap over the international boundaries that many translated works face. . . . This is an important work from an important writer."

—Amy Tan

"Mo Yan spares us nothing . . . *Red Sorghum* fixes our attention on a series of exquisite images . . . [as] he paints his pictures of a world in chaos, where every day is a struggle to preserve life, if not honor, and there is no safety even in death." —*New York Magazine*

"*Red Sorghum* is so unlike any other piece of contemporary Chinese literature that, were it not so clearly set in China, one might imagine it to be a product of another place and time. . . . With this work Mo Yan has helped his country find a new and powerfully convincing literary voice."

—Orville Schell

"A masterful translation . . . The appearance of *Red Sorghum* is an important event for English-language literature, one which bids well for the power and infl 21st century." *h*

"Yan tempers his brutal tal sm . . . A powerful new voice on ne late '20s and '30s."

PENGUIN BOOKS

RED SORGHUM

Mo Yan was born in 1956 and is a native of Shandong. The author of four novels, dozens of novellas, and many short stories, he has won virtually every national literary prize and is the most highly praised Chinese writer of his generation. Mo Yan is a member of the cultural affairs department of the People's Liberation Army. His novel *Song of Wild Garlic* will be published in 1995.

An acclaimed translator from the Chinese, **Howard Goldblatt** is the editor of *Modern Chinese Literature*. He teaches at the University of Colorado.

MO YAN

Red Sorghum

A NOVEL OF CHINA

Translated from the Chinese

by Howard Goldblatt

PENGUIN BOOKS

PENGUIN BOOKS
Published by the Penguin Group
Penguin Books USA Inc., 375 Hudson Street, New York, New York 10014, U.S.A.
Penguin Books Ltd, 27 Wrights Lane, London W8 5TZ, England
Penguin Books Australia Ltd, Ringwood, Victoria, Australia
Penguin Books Canada Ltd, 10 Alcorn Avenue, Toronto, Ontario, Canada M4V 3B2
Penguin Books (N.Z.) Ltd, 182–190 Wairau Road, Auckland 10, New Zealand

Penguin Books Ltd, Registered Offices: Harmondsworth, Middlesex, England

First published in the United States of America by Viking Penguin,
a division of Penguin Books USA Inc., 1993
Published in Penguin Books 1994

10

Translator's note

At the request of the author, this translation is based upon the Taipei Hong-fan Book Co. 1988 Chinese edition, which restores cuts made in the Mainland Chinese edition, published in 1987 by the People's Liberation Army Publishing House in Beijing. Some deletions have been made, with the author's approval, and minor inconsistencies, particularly in dates and ages, have been corrected.

Thanks to Joseph S. M. Lau, Haili Kong, Chu Chiyu, and Sandra Dijkstra for responding to my occasional cry for help. The translation was made possible in part by a grant from the National Endowment for the Arts, whose support is gratefully acknowledged.

THE LIBRARY OF CONGRESS HAS CATALOGUED THE HARDCOVER AS FOLLOWS:
Mo, Yan.
[Hung kao liang chia tsu. English]
Red sorghum: a family saga/by Mo Yan; translated from the Chinese by Howard Goldblatt.
p. cm.
ISBN 0-670-84402-0 (hc.)
ISBN 0 14 01.6854 0 (pbk.)
I. Title.
PL2886.01684H8613 1993
895.1′352—dc20 92-50396

Printed in the United States of America
Set in Weiss
Designed by Francesca Belanger

WITH THIS BOOK I respectfully invoke the heroic, aggrieved souls wandering in the boundless bright-red sorghum fields of my hometown. As your unfilial son, I am prepared to carve out my heart, marinate it in soy sauce, have it minced and placed in three bowls, and lay it out as an offering in a field of sorghum. Partake of it in good health!

CHAPTER ONE

Red Sorghum

1

THE NINTH DAY of the eighth lunar month, 1939. My father, a bandit's offspring who had passed his fifteenth birthday, was joining the forces of Commander Yu Zhan'ao, a man destined to become a legendary hero, to ambush a Japanese convoy on the Jiao-Ping highway. Grandma, a padded jacket over her shoulders, saw them to the edge of the village. "Stop here," Commander Yu ordered her. She stopped.

"Douguan, mind your foster-dad," she told my father. The sight of her large frame and the warm fragrance of her lined jacket chilled him. He shivered. His stomach growled.

Commander Yu patted him on the head and said, "Let's go, foster-son."

Heaven and earth were in turmoil, the view was blurred. By then the soldiers' muffled footsteps had moved far down the road. Father could still hear them, but a curtain of blue mist obscured the men themselves. Gripping tightly to Commander Yu's coat, he nearly flew down the path on churning legs. Grandma receded like a distant shore as the approaching sea of mist grew more tempestuous; holding on to Commander Yu was like clinging to the railing of a boat.

That was how Father rushed toward the uncarved granite marker that would rise above his grave in the bright-red sorghum fields of his hometown. A bare-assed little boy once led a white billy goat up to the weed-covered grave, and as it grazed in unhurried contentment, the boy pissed furiously on the grave and sang out: "The sorghum is red—the Japanese are coming—compatriots, get ready—fire your rifles and cannons—"

Someone said that the little goatherd was me, but I don't know. I had learned to love Northeast Gaomi Township with all my heart, and to hate it with unbridled fury. I didn't realize until I'd grown up that Northeast Gaomi Township is easily the most beautiful and most repulsive, most unusual and most common, most sacred and most corrupt, most heroic and most bastardly, hardest-drinking and hardest-loving place in the world. The people of my father's generation who lived there ate sorghum out of preference, planting as much of it as they could. In late autumn, during the eighth lunar month, vast stretches of red sorghum shimmered like a sea of blood. Tall and dense, it reeked of glory; cold and graceful, it promised enchantment; passionate and loving, it was tumultuous.

The autumn winds are cold and bleak, the sun's rays intense. White clouds, full and round, float in the tile-blue sky, casting full round purple shadows onto the sorghum fields below. Over decades that seem but a moment in time, lines of scarlet figures shuttled among the sorghum stalks to weave a vast human tapestry. They killed, they looted, and they defended their country in a valiant, stirring ballet that makes us unfilial descendants who now occupy the land pale by comparison. Surrounded by progress, I feel a nagging sense of our species' regression.

After leaving the village, the troops marched down a narrow dirt path, the tramping of their feet merging with the rustling of weeds. The heavy mist was strangely animated, kaleidoscopic. Tiny droplets of water pooled into large drops on Father's face; clumps of hair stuck to his forehead. He was used to the delicate peppermint aroma and the slightly sweet yet pungent odor of ripe sorghum wafting over from the sides of the path—nothing new there. But as they marched through the heavy mist, his nose detected a new, sickly-sweet odor, neither yellow nor red, blending with the smells of peppermint and sorghum to call up memories hidden deep in his soul.

Six days later, the fifteenth day of the eighth month, the night of the Mid-Autumn Festival. A bright round moon climbed slowly in the sky above the solemn, silent sorghum fields, bathing the tassels in its light until they shimmered like mercury. Among the chiseled flecks of moonlight Father caught a whiff of the same sickly odor, far stronger than anything you might smell today. Commander Yu was leading him by the hand through the sorghum, where three hundred fellow villagers, heads pillowed on their arms, were strewn across the ground, their fresh blood turning the black earth into a sticky muck that made walking slow and difficult. The smell took their breath away. A pack of corpse-eating dogs sat in the field staring at Father and Commander Yu with glinting eyes. Commander Yu drew his pistol and fired—a pair of eyes was extinguished. Another shot, another pair of eyes gone. The howling dogs scattered, then sat on their haunches once they were out of range, setting up a deafening chorus of angry barks as they gazed greedily, longingly at the corpses. The odor grew stronger.

"Jap dogs!" Commander Yu screamed. "Jap sons of bitches!" He emptied his pistol, scattering the dogs without a trace. "Let's go, son," he said. The two of them, one old and one young, threaded their way through the sorghum field, guided by the moon's rays. The odor saturating the field drenched Father's soul and would be his constant companion during the cruel months and years ahead.

Sorghum stems and leaves sizzled fiercely in the mist. The Black Water River, which flowed slowly through the swampy lowland, sang in the spreading mist, now loud, now soft, now far, now near. As they caught up with the troops, Father heard the tramping of feet and some coarse breathing fore and aft. The butt of a rifle noisily bumped someone else's. A foot crushed what sounded like a human bone. The man in front of Father coughed loudly. It was a familiar cough, calling to mind large ears that turned red with excitement. Large transparent ears covered with tiny blood vessels were the trademark of Wang Wenyi, a small man whose enlarged head was tucked down between his shoulders.

Father strained and squinted until his gaze bored through the mist: there was Wang Wenyi's head, jerking with each cough. Father thought back to when Wang was whipped on the parade ground, and how pitiful he had looked. He had just joined up with Commander Yu. Adjutant Ren ordered the recruits: Right face! Wang Wenyi stomped down joyfully, but where he intended to "face" was anyone's guess.

Adjutant Ren smacked him across the backside with his whip, forcing a yelp from between his parted lips: Ouch, mother of my children! The expression on his face could have been a cry, or could have been a laugh. Some kids sprawled atop the wall hooted gleefully.

Now Commander Yu kicked Wang Wenyi in the backside.

"Who said you could cough?"

"Commander Yu . . ." Wang Wenyi stifled a cough. "My throat itches. . . ."

"So what? If you give away our position, it's your head!"

"Yes, sir," Wang replied, as another coughing spell erupted.

Father sensed Commander Yu lurching forward to grab Wang Wenyi around the neck with both hands. Wang wheezed and gasped, but the coughing stopped.

Father also sensed Commander Yu's hands release Wang's neck; he even sensed the purple welts, like ripe grapes, left behind. Aggrieved gratitude filled Wang's deep-blue, frightened eyes.

The troops turned quickly into the sorghum, and Father knew instinctively that they were heading southeast. The dirt path was the only direct link between the Black Water River and the village. During the day it had a pale cast; the original black earth, the color of ebony, had been covered by the passage of countless animals: cloven hoofprints of oxen and goats, semicircular hoofprints of mules, horses, and donkeys; dried road apples left by horses, mules, and donkeys; wormy cow chips; and scattered goat pellets like little black beans. Father had taken this path so often that later on, as he suffered in the Japanese cinder pit, its image often flashed before his eyes. He never knew how many sexual comedies my grandma had performed on this dirt path, but I knew. And he never knew that her naked body, pure as glossy white jade, had lain on the black soil beneath the shadows of sorghum stalks, but I knew.

The surrounding mist grew more sluggish once they were in the sorghum field. The stalks screeched in secret resentment when the men and equipment bumped against them, sending large, mournful beads of water splashing to the ground. The water was ice-cold, clear and sparkling, and deliciously refreshing. Father looked up, and a large drop fell into his mouth. As the heavy curtain of mist parted gently, he watched the heads of sorghum stalks bend slowly down. The tough, pliable leaves, weighted down by the dew, sawed at his clothes and face. A breeze set the stalks above him rustling briefly; the gurgling of the Black Water River grew louder.

Father had gone swimming so often in the Black Water River that he seemed born to it. Grandma said that the sight of the river excited him more than the sight of his own mother. At the age of five, he could dive like a duckling, his little pink asshole bobbing above the surface, his feet sticking straight up. He knew that the muddy riverbed was black and shiny, and as spongy as soft tallow, and that the banks were covered with pale-green reeds and plantain the color of goose-down; coiling vines and stiff bone grass hugged the muddy ground, which was crisscrossed with the tracks of skittering crabs.

Autumn winds brought cool air, and wild geese flew through the sky heading south, their formation changing from a straight line one minute to a V the next. When the sorghum turned red, hordes of crabs the size of horse hooves scrambled onto the bank at night to search for food—fresh cow dung and the rotting carcasses of dead animals—among the clumps of river grass.

The sound of the river reminded Father of an autumn night during his childhood, when the foreman of our family business, Arhat Liu, named after Buddhist saints, took him crabbing on the riverbank. On that gray-purple night a golden breeze followed the course of the river. The sapphire-blue sky was deep and boundless, green-tinted stars shone brightly in the sky: the ladle of Ursa Major (signifying death), the basket of Sagittarius (representing life); Octans, the glass well, missing one of its tiles; the anxious Herd Boy (Altair), about to hang himself; the mournful Weaving Girl (Vega), about to drown herself in the river. . . . Uncle Arhat had been overseeing the work of the family distillery for decades, and Father scrambled to keep up with him as he would his own grandfather.

The weak light of the kerosene lamp bored a five-yard hole in the darkness. When water flowed into the halo of light, it was the cordial yellow of an overripe apricot. But cordial for only a fleeting moment, before it flowed on. In the surrounding darkness the water reflected a starry sky. Father and Uncle Arhat, rain capes over their shoulders, sat around the shaded lamp listening to the low gurgling of the river. Every so often they heard the excited screech of a fox calling to its mate in the sorghum fields beside the river. Father and Uncle Arhat sat quietly, listening with rapt respect to the whispered secrets of the land, as the smell of stinking river mud drifted over on the wind. Hordes of crabs attracted by the light skittered toward the lamp, where they formed a shifting, restless cloister. Father was so eager he nearly sprang to his feet, but Uncle Arhat held him by the shoulders.

"Take it easy! Greedy eaters never get the hot gruel." Holding his excitement in check, Father sat still. The crabs stopped as soon as they entered the ring of lamplight, and lined up head to tail, blotting out the ground. A greenish glint issued from their shells, as countless pairs of button eyes popped from deep sockets on little stems. Mouths hidden beneath sloping faces released frothy strings of brazenly colorful bubbles. The long fibers on Father's straw rain cape stood up. "Now!" Uncle Arhat shouted. Father sprang into action before the shout died out, snatching two corners of the tightly woven net they'd spread on the ground beforehand; they raised it in the air, scooping up a layer of crabs and revealing a clear spot of riverbank beneath them. Quickly tying the ends together and tossing the net to one side, they rushed back and lifted up another piece of netting with the same speed and skill. The heavy bundles seemed to hold hundreds, even thousands of crabs.

As Father followed the troops into the sorghum field, he moved sideways, crablike, overshooting the spaces between the stalks and bumping them hard, which caused them to sway and bend violently. Still gripping tightly to Commander Yu's coattail, he was pulled along, his feet barely touching the ground. But he was getting sleepy. His neck felt stiff, his eyes were growing dull and listless, and his only thought was that as long as he could tag along behind Uncle Arhat to the Black Water River he'd never come back empty-handed.

Father ate crab until he was sick of it, and so did Grandma. But even though they lost their appetite for it, they couldn't bear to throw the uneaten ones away. So Uncle Arhat minced the leftovers and ground them under the bean-curd millstone, then salted the crab paste, which they ate daily, until it finally went bad and became mulch for the poppies.

Apparently Grandma was an opium smoker, but wasn't addicted, which was why she had the complexion of a peach, a sunny disposition, and a clear mind. The crab-nourished poppies grew huge and fleshy, a mixture of pinks, reds, and whites that assailed your nostrils with their fragrance. The black soil of my hometown, always fertile, was especially productive, and the people who tilled it were especially decent, strong-willed, and ambitious. The white eels of the Black Water River, like plump sausages with tapered ends, foolishly swallowed every hook in sight.

Uncle Arhat had died the year before on the Jiao-Ping highway. His corpse, after being hacked to pieces, had been scattered around the area. As the skin was being stripped from his body, his flesh jumped and quivered, as if he were a huge skinned frog. Images of that corpse sent shivers up Father's spine. Then he thought back to a night some seven or eight years earlier, when Grandma, drunk at the time, had stood in the distillery yard beside a pile of sorghum leaves, her arms around Uncle Arhat's shoulders. "Uncle . . . don't leave," she pleaded. "If not for the sake of the monk, stay for the Buddha. If not for the sake of the fish, stay for the water. If not for my sake, stay for little Douguan. You can have me, if you want. . . . You're like my own father. . . ." Father watched him push her away and swagger into the shed to mix fodder for the two large black mules who, when we opened our distillery, made us the richest family in the village. Uncle Arhat didn't leave after all. Instead he became our foreman, right up to the day the Japanese confiscated our mules to work on the Jiao-Ping highway.

Now Father and the others could hear long-drawn-out brays from the mules they had left behind in the village. Wide-eyed with excitement, he could see nothing but the congealed yet nearly transparent mist that surrounded him. Erect stalks of sorghum formed dense barriers behind a wall of vapor. Each barrier led to another, seemingly endless. He had no idea how long they'd been in the field, for his mind was focused on the fertile river roaring in the distance, and on his memories. He wondered why they were in such a hurry to squeeze through this packed, dreamy ocean of sorghum. Suddenly he lost his bearings. He listened carefully for a sign from the river, and quickly determined that they were heading east-southeast, toward the river. Once he had a fix on their direction, he understood that they would be setting an ambush for the Japanese, that they would be killing people, just as they had killed the dogs. By heading east-southeast, they would soon reach the Jiao-Ping highway, which cut through the swampy lowland from north to south and linked the two counties of Jiao and Pingdu. Japanese and their running dogs, Chinese collaborators, had built the highway with the forced labor of local conscripts.

The sorghum was set in motion by the exhausted troops, whose heads and necks were soaked by the settling dew. Wang Wenyi was still coughing, even though he'd been the target of Commander Yu's continuing angry outbursts. Father sensed that the highway was just up ahead, its pale-yellow outline swaying in front of him. Imperceptibly tiny openings began to appear in the thick curtain of mist, and one dew-soaked ear of sorghum after another stared sadly at Father, who returned their devout gaze. It dawned on him that they were living spirits: their roots buried in the dark earth, they soaked up the energy of the sun and the essence of the moon; moistened by the rain and dew, they understood the ways of the heavens and the logic of the earth. The color of the sorghum suggested that the sun had already turned the obscured horizon a pathetic red.

Then something unexpected occurred. Father heard a shrill whistle, followed by a loud burst from up ahead.

"Who fired his weapon?" Commander Yu bellowed. "Who's the prick who did it?"

Father heard the bullet pierce the thick mist and pass through sorghum leaves and stalks, lopping off one of the heads. Everyone held his breath as the bullet screamed through the air and thudded to the ground. The sweet smell of gunpowder dissipated in the mist. Wang Wenyi screamed pitifully, "Commander—my head's gone—Commander—my head's gone—"

Commander Yu froze momentarily, then kicked Wang Wenyi. "You dumb fuck!" he growled. "How could you talk without a head?"

Commander Yu left my father standing there and went up to the head of the column. Wang Wenyi was still howling. Father pressed forward to catch a glimpse of the strange look on Wang's face. A dark-blue substance was flowing on his cheek. Father reached out to touch it; hot and sticky, it smelled a lot like the mud of the Black Water River, but fresher. It overwhelmed the smell of peppermint and the pungent sweetness of sorghum and awakened in Father's mind a memory that drew ever nearer: like beads, it strung together the mud of the Black Water River, the black earth beneath the sorghum, the eternally living past, and the unstoppable present. There are times when everything on earth spits out the stench of human blood.

"Uncle," Father said, "you're wounded."

"Douguan, is that you? Tell your old uncle if his head's still on his neck."

"It's there, Uncle, right where it's supposed to be. Except your ear's bleeding."

Wang Wenyi reached up to touch his ear and pulled back a bloody hand, yelping in alarm. Then he froze as if paralyzed. "Commander, I'm wounded! I'm wounded!"

Commander Yu came back to Wang, knelt down, and put his hands around Wang's neck. "Stop screaming or I'll throttle you!"

Wang Wenyi didn't dare make a sound.

"Where were you hit?" Commander Yu asked him.

"My ear . . ." Wang was weeping.

Commander Yu took a piece of white cloth from his waistband and tore it in two, then handed it to him. "Hold this over it, and no more noise. Stay in rank. You can bandage it when we reach the highway."

Commander Yu turned to Father. "Douguan," he barked. Father answered, and Commander Yu walked off holding him by the hand, followed by the whimpering Wang Wenyi.

The offending discharge had been the result of carelessness by the big fellow they called Mute, who was up front carrying a rake on his shoulder. The rifle slung over his back had gone off when he stumbled. Mute was one of Commander Yu's old bandit friends, a greenwood hero who had eaten fistcakes in the sorghum fields. One of his legs was shorter than the other—a prenatal injury—and he limped when he walked, but that didn't slow him down. Father was a little afraid of him.

At about dawn, the massive curtain of mist finally lifted, just as

Commander Yu and his troops emerged onto the Jiao-Ping highway. In my hometown, August is the misty season, possibly because there's so much swampy lowland. Once he stepped onto the highway, Father felt suddenly light and nimble; with extra spring in his step, he let go of Commander Yu's coat. Wang Wenyi, on the other hand, wore a crestfallen look as he held the cloth to his injured ear. Commander Yu crudely wrapped it for him, covering up half his head. Wang gnashed his teeth in pain.

"The heavens have smiled on you," Commander Yu said.

"My blood's all gone," Wang whimpered, "I can't go on!"

"Bullshit!" Commander Yu exclaimed. "It's no worse than a mosquito bite. You haven't forgotten your three sons, have you?"

Wang hung his head and mumbled, "No, I haven't forgotten."

The butt of the long-barreled fowling piece over his shoulder was the color of blood. A flat metal gunpowder pouch rested against his hip.

Remnants of the dissipating mist were scattered throughout the sorghum field. There were neither animal nor human footprints in the gravel, and the dense walls of sorghum on the deserted highway made the men feel that something ominous was in the air. Father knew all along that Commander Yu's troops numbered no more than forty—deaf, mute, and crippled included. But when they were quartered in the village, they had stirred things up so much, with chickens squawking and dogs yelping, that you'd have thought it was a garrison command.

Out on the highway, the soldiers huddled so closely together they looked like an inert snake. Their motley assortment of weapons included shotguns, fowling pieces, aging Hanyang rifles, plus a cannon that fired scale weights and was carried by two brothers, Fang Six and Fang Seven. Mute was toting a rake with twenty-six metal tines, as were three other soldiers. Father still didn't know what an ambush was, and even if he had, he wouldn't have known why anyone would take four rakes to the event.

2

I RETURNED TO NORTHEAST GAOMI TOWNSHIP to compile a family chronicle, focusing on the famous battle on the banks of the Black Water River that involved my father and ended with the death of a Jap general. An old woman of ninety-two sang to me, to the accompaniment of bamboo clappers: "Northeast Gaomi Township, so many men; at Black Water River the battle began; Commander Yu raised his hand, cannon fire to heaven; Jap souls scattered across the plain, ne'er to rise again; the beautiful champion of women, Dai Fenglian, ordered rakes for a barrier, the Jap attack broken . . ." The wizened old woman was as bald as a clay pot; the protruding tendons on her chapped hands were like strips of melon rind. She had survived the Mid-Autumn Festival massacre in '39 only because her ulcerated legs had made walking impossible, and her husband had hidden her in a yam cellar. The heavens had smiled on her. The Dai Fenglian in her clapper-song was my grandma. I listened with barely concealed excitement, for her tale proved that the strategy of stopping the Jap convoy with rakes had sprung from the mind of my own kin, a member of the weaker sex. No wonder my grandma is fêted as a trailblazer of the anti-Japanese resistance and a national hero.

At the mention of my grandma, the old woman grew expansive. Her narration was choppy and confused, like a shower of leaves at the mercy of the wind. She said that my grandma had the smallest feet of any woman in the village, and that no other distillery had the staying power of ours. The thread of her narrative evened out as she talked of the Jiao-Ping highway: "When the highway was extended this far . . . sorghum only waist-high. . . . Japs conscripted all able-bodied workers. . . . Working for the Japs, slacked off, sabotage . . . took your family's two big black mules . . . built a stone bridge over the Black Water River. . . . Arhat, your family's foreman . . . something fishy between him and your grandma, so everyone said . . . Aiyaya, when your grandma was young she sowed plenty of wild oats. . . . Your dad was a capable boy, killed his first man at fifteen, eight or nine out of every ten bastard kids turn out bad. . . . Arhat hamstrung the mule. . . . Japs caught him and skinned him alive. . . . Japs butchered people, shit in their pots, and pissed in their basins. I went for water once that year, guess what I found in my bucket, a human head with the pigtail still attached. . . ."

Arhat Liu played a significant role in my family's history, but there is no hard evidence that he had an affair with my grandma, and, to tell the truth, I don't believe it. I understood the logic of what the old clay-pot was saying, but it still embarrassed me. Since Uncle Arhat treated my father like a grandson, that would make me sort of his great-grandson; and if my great-granddad had an affair with my grandma, that's incest, isn't it? But that's hogwash, since my grandma was Uncle Arhat's boss, not his daughter-in-law, and their relationship was sealed by wages, not by blood. He was a faithful old hand who embellished the history of our family and brought it greater glory than it would have had otherwise. Whether my grandma ever loved him or whether he ever lay down beside her on the kang has nothing to do with morality. What if she *did* love him? I believe she could have done anything she desired, for she was a hero of the resistance, a trailblazer for sexual liberation, a model of women's independence.

In county records I discovered that in 1938, the twenty-seventh year of the Republic, four hundred thousand man-days were spent by local workers from Gaomi, Pingdu, and Jiao counties in the service of the Japanese army to build the Jiao-Ping highway. The agricultural loss was incalculable, and the villages bordering the highway were stripped clean of draft animals. It was then that Arhat Liu, a conscript himself, took a hoe to the legs of our captured mule. He was caught, and the next day the Japanese soldiers tied him to a tethering post, skinned him alive, and mutilated him in front of his compatriots. There was no fear in his eyes, and a stream of abuse poured from his mouth up until the moment he died.

3

SHE TOLD IT EXACTLY like it was. When construction of the Jiao-Ping highway reached our place, the sorghum in the fields was only waist-high. Except for a handful of tiny villages, two crossing rivers, and a few dozen winding dirt paths, the marshy plain, which measured sixty by seventy-odd li—or about twenty by twenty-five miles—was covered with sorghum that waved like an ocean of green. From our village we had a clear view of White Horse Mountain, an enormous rock formation on the northern edge of the plain. Peasants tending the sorghum looked up to see White Horse and down to see black soil that soaked up their sweat and filled their hearts with contentment. When they heard that the Japanese were building a highway across the plain, they grew restive, awaiting the calamity they knew was coming.

The Japanese said they would come, and they were as good as their word.

My father was sleeping when the Japs and their puppet soldiers came to our village to conscript peasant laborers and confiscate their mules and horses. He was awakened by a disturbance near the distillery. Grandma dragged him over to the compound as fast as her bamboo-shoot feet would carry her. Back then there were a dozen or so huge vats in the compound, each brimming with top-quality white liquor, the aroma of which hung over the entire village. Two khaki-clad Japanese soldiers with fixed bayonets stood there as a couple of black-clad Chinese, rifles slung over their backs, untied our two big black mules from a catalpa tree. Uncle Arhat kept trying to get to the shorter puppet soldier, who was untying the tethers, but the taller comrade forced him back with the muzzle of his rifle. Since Uncle Arhat was wearing only a thin shirt in the early-summer heat, his exposed chest already showed a welter of circular bruises.

"Brothers," he pleaded, "we can talk this over, we can talk it over."

"Get the hell out of here, you old bastard," the taller soldier barked.

"Those animals belong to the owner," Uncle Arhat said. "You can't take them."

The puppet soldier growled menacingly, "If I hear another word out of you, I'll shoot your little prick off!"

The Japanese soldiers stood there like clay statues, holding their rifles in front of them.

As Grandma and my father entered the compound, Uncle Arhat wailed, "They're taking our mules!"

"Sir," Grandma said, "we're good people."

The Japanese squinted and grinned at her.

The shorter puppet soldier freed the mules and tried to lead them away; but they raised their heads stubbornly and refused to budge. His buddy walked up and prodded one of them in the rump with his rifle; the angered animal pawed the ground with its rear hooves, its metal shoes glinting in the mud that sprayed the soldier in the face.

The tall soldier pointed his rifle at Uncle Arhat and bellowed, "Come over here and take these mules to the construction site, you old bastard!"

Uncle Arhat squatted on the ground without making a sound, so one of the Japanese soldiers walked up and waved his rifle in front of Uncle Arhat's face. *"Minliwala, yalalimin!"* he grunted. With the shiny bayonet glinting in front of his eyes, Uncle Arhat sat down. The soldier thrust his bayonet forward, opening a tiny hole in Uncle Arhat's shiny scalp.

Beginning to tremble, Grandma blurted out, "Do it, Uncle, take the mules for them."

The other Jap soldier edged up close to Grandma, and Father noticed how young and handsome he was, and how his dark eyes sparkled. But when he smiled, his lip curled to reveal yellow buck teeth. Grandma staggered over to Uncle Arhat, whose wound was oozing blood that spread across his scalp and down his face. The grinning Japanese soldiers drew closer. Grandma laid her hands on Uncle Arhat's scalp, then rubbed them on her face. Pulling her hair, she leaped to her feet like a madwoman, her mouth agape. She looked three parts human and seven parts demon. The startled Japanese soldiers froze.

"Sir," the tall puppet soldier said, "that woman's crazy."

One of the Jap soldiers mumbled something as he fired a shot over Grandma's head. She sat down hard and began to wail.

The tall puppet soldier used his rifle to prod Uncle Arhat, who got to his feet and took the tethers from the smaller soldier. The mules looked up; their legs trembled as they followed him out of the compound. The street was chaotic with mules, horses, oxen, and goats.

Grandma wasn't crazy. The minute the Japs and the puppet soldiers left, she removed the wooden lid from one of the wine vats and looked at her frightful, bloody reflection in the mirrorlike surface. Father watched the tears on her cheeks turn red. She washed her face in the wine, turning it red.

Like the mules he was leading, Uncle Arhat was forced to work on the road that was taking shape in the sorghum field. The highway on the southern bank of the Black Water River was nearly completed, and cars and trucks were driving up on the newly laid roadway with loads of stone and yellow gravel, which they dumped on the riverbank. Since there was only a single wooden span across the river, the Japanese had decided to build a large stone bridge. Vast areas of sorghum on both sides of the highway had been leveled, until the ground seemed covered by an enormous green blanket. In the field north of the river, where black soil had been laid on either side of the road, dozens of horses and mules were pulling stone rollers to level two enormous squares in the sea of sorghum. Men led the animals back and forth through the field, trampling the tender stalks, which had been bent double by the shod hooves, then flattening them with stone rollers turned dark green by the plant juices. The pungent aroma of green sorghum hung heavily over the construction site.

Uncle Arhat, who was sent to the southern bank of the river to haul rocks to the other side, reluctantly handed the mules over to an old geezer with festering eyes. The little wooden bridge swayed so violently it seemed about to topple as he crossed to the southern bank, where a Chinese overseer tapped him on the head with a purplish rattan whip and said, "Start lugging rocks to the other side." Uncle Arhat rubbed his eyes—the blood from his scalp wound had soaked his eyebrows. He picked up an average-sized rock and carried it to the other side, where the old geezer stood with the mules. "Use them sparingly," he said. "They belong to the family I work for." The old geezer lowered his head numbly, then turned and led the mules over to where teams of animals were working on the connecting road. The shiny rumps of the black mules reflected specks of sunlight. His head still bleeding, Uncle Arhat hunkered down, scooped up some black dirt, and rubbed it on the wound. A dull, heavy pain traveled all the way down to his toes.

Armed Jap and puppet soldiers stood on the fringes of the construction site; the overseer, whip in hand, roamed the site like a specter. The eyes of the frightened laborers rolled as they watched Uncle Arhat, his head a mass of blood and mud, pick up a rock and take a couple of steps. Suddenly he heard a crack behind him, followed by a drawn-out, stinging pain on his back. He dropped the rock and looked at the grinning overseer. "Your honor, if you have something to say, say it. Why hit me?"

Without a word, the grinning overseer flicked his whip in the air and wrapped it around Uncle Arhat's waist, all but cutting him in half. Two streams of hot, stinging tears oozed out of the corners of Uncle Arhat's eyes, and blood rushed to his head, which began to throb as though it might split open.

"Your honor!" Uncle Arhat protested.

His honor whipped him again.

"Your honor," Uncle Arhat said, "why are you hitting me?"

His honor flicked the whip and grinned until his eyes were mere slits: "Just giving you a taste, you son of a bitch."

Uncle Arhat choked off his sobs as his eyes pooled with tears. He bent over, picked up a large rock from the pile, and staggered with it toward the little bridge. The jagged edges dug deeply into his gut and his rib cage, but he didn't feel the pain.

The overseer stood rooted to the spot, whip in hand, and Uncle Arhat trembled with fear as he lugged the rock past his gaze. With the whip cutting into his neck he fell forward, landed on his knees, and hugged the rock to his chest. It tore the skin on his hands and left a deep gash in his chin. Stunned, he began to blubber like a baby; a purple tongue of flame licked out in the emptiness inside his skull.

He strained to pull his hands out from under the rock, stood up, and arched his back like a threatened, skinny old tomcat. Just then a middle-aged man, grinning from ear to ear, walked up. He took a pack of cigarettes out of his pocket and held one up to the overseer, who parted his lips to accept the offering, then waited for the man to light it for him.

"Revered one," the man said, "that stinking blockhead isn't worth getting angry over."

The overseer exhaled the smoke through his nose and said nothing. Uncle Arhat stared at the whip in his twitching yellowed fingers.

The middle-aged man stuffed the pack of cigarettes into the pocket of the overseer, who seemed not to notice; then, snorting lightly, he patted his pocket, turned, and walked away.

"Are you new here, elder brother?" the man asked.

Uncle Arhat said he was.

"You didn't give him anything to grease the skids?"

"Those mad dogs dragged me here against my will."

"Give him a little money or a pack of cigarettes. He doesn't hit the hard workers, and he doesn't hit the slackers. The only ones he hits are those who have eyes but won't see." ← interesting

All that morning, Uncle Arhat desperately lugged rocks, like a man without a soul. The scab on his scalp, baked by the sun, caused terrible pain as it dried and cracked. His hands were raw and bloody, and the stiffened gash on his chin made him drool. The purplish flame kept licking at the inside of his skull—sometimes strong, sometimes weak, but never dying out completely.

At noon a brown truck drove up the barely negotiable road. Dimly Uncle Arhat heard a shrill whistle and watched the laborers stumble up to the truck. He sat mindlessly on the ground, showing no interest in the truck. The middle-aged man walked over and pulled him to his feet. "Elder brother, come on, it's mealtime. Try some Japanese rice."

Uncle Arhat stood up and followed him.

Large buckets of snowy white rice were handed down from the truck, along with a basket of white ceramic bowls with blue floral patterns. A fat Chinese stood next to the baskets, handing bowls to the men as they filed past. A skinny Chinese stood beside the buckets, ladling rice. The laborers stood around the truck, wolfing down their food, bare hands serving as chopsticks.

The overseer walked up, whip in hand, the enigmatic grin still on his face. The flame in Uncle Arhat's skull blazed, illuminating thoughts of the hard morning that he had tried to cast off. Armed Japanese and puppet sentries walked up and stood around a galvanized-iron bucket to eat their lunch. A guard dog with a long snout and trimmed ears sat behind the bucket, its tongue lolling as it watched the laborers.

Uncle Arhat counted the dozen or so Japs and the dozen or so puppet soldiers standing around the bucket eating their lunch; the word "escape" flashed into his mind. *Escape!* If he could make it to the sorghum field, these fuckers wouldn't be able to catch him. The soles of his feet were hot and sweaty; the moment the idea to flee entered his mind, he grew fidgety and anxious. Something was hidden behind the calm, cold grin on the face of the overseer. Whatever it was, it made Uncle Arhat's thoughts grow muddled.

The fat Chinese took the bowls from the laborers before they were finished. They licked their lips and stared longingly at kernels of rice stuck to the sides of the buckets, but didn't dare move. A mule on the northern bank of the river brayed shrilly. Uncle Arhat recognized the familiar sound. Tethered to rolling stones beside the newly plowed roadbed, the listless mules nibbled stalks and leaves of sorghum that had been trampled into the earth.

That afternoon a man in his twenties darted into the sorghum field when he thought the overseer wasn't looking. A bullet followed his path of retreat. He lay motionless on the fringe of the field.

The brown truck drove up again as the sun was sinking in the west. Uncle Arhat's digestive system, used to sorghum, was intent on ridding itself of this mildewy white rice, but he forced the food past the knots in his throat. The thought of escape was stronger than ever; he longed to see his own compound, where the pungent odor of wine pervaded the air, in that village a dozen or so li away. The distillery hands had all fled with the arrival of the Japanese, and the wine cooker now stood cold. Even more he longed to see my grandma and my father. He hadn't forgotten the warmth and contentment she had bestowed upon him alongside the pile of sorghum leaves.

After dinner the laborers were herded into an enclosure of fir stakes covered with tarpaulins. Wires the thickness of mung beans had been strung between the stakes, and the gate was made of thick metal rods. The Jap and puppet soldiers were billeted in separate tents several yards away; the guard dog was tethered to the flap of the Jap tent. Two lanterns hung from a tall post at the entrance of the enclosure, around which soldiers took turns at sentry duty. Mules and horses were tethered to posts in a razed section of the sorghum field west of the enclosure.

The stench inside the enclosure was suffocating. Some of the men snored loudly; others got up to piss in a tin pail, raising a noisy liquid tattoo, like pearls falling onto a jade plate. The lanterns cast a pale light, under which the sentries' long shadows flickered.

As the night stretched on, the cold became unbearable, and Uncle Arhat couldn't sleep. With his thoughts focused on escape, he lay there not daring to move; eventually he fell into a muddled sleep. In his dream his head felt as though it were being carved by a sharp knife, while his hand felt seared as if he clasped a branding iron. He awoke covered in sweat; his pants were soaked with piss. The shrill crow of a rooster floated over from the distant village. The mules and horses pawed the ground and snorted. Stars winked slyly through holes in the tattered tarpaulin above him.

The man who had come to his aid that day quietly sat up. Even in the relative darkness of the enclosure, Uncle Arhat could see his blazing eyes, and could tell that he was no ordinary man. He lay there, watching silently.

As the man knelt in the enclosure opening, he raised his arms slowly and deliberately. Uncle Arhat's eyes were riveted on his back and his head, around which hung an aura of mystery. The man took a deep breath, cocked his head, and thrust out his hands, like arrows from a bow, to grab two metal rods. A green glare shot from his eyes, and seemed to crackle when it struck an object. The metal rods silently parted, admitting more light into the enclosure from the lanterns and overhead stars, and revealing the shoe of a sentry. Uncle Arhat saw a dark shadow dart out of the enclosure. The Jap sentry grunted, then, in the man's viselike grip, crumpled to the ground. The man picked up the Jap's rifle and slipped silently into the darkness.

It took Uncle Arhat a moment to realize what had happened. The middle-aged man had shown him the way to escape! Cautiously, he crawled out through the opening. The dead Jap lay on the ground, face up, one leg still twitching.

After crawling into the sorghum field, Uncle Arhat straightened up and followed the furrows, taking care not to bump the stalks and get them rustling. He found his way to the bank of the Black Water River, where the three stars—Rigel, Betelgeuse, and Bellatrix—hung directly overhead. A heavy predawn darkness had fallen around him. Stars glistened in the water. As he stood briefly on the riverbank, he shivered from the cold, his teeth chattered, and the ache in his chin spread to his cheeks and ears, finally merging with the throbbing pain in his festering scalp. The crisp air of freedom, filtered through the juices of the sorghum plants, entered his nostrils, his lungs, and his intestines. The ghostly light of the two lanterns shone weakly through the mist; the dark outline of the fir-stake enclosure was like an immense graveyard. Astonished at having gotten away so easily, he strode onto the rickety wooden bridge, above splashing fish and rippling water, as a shooting star split the heavens. It was as though nothing had happened. He was free to return to his village to let his wounds mend and to go on living. But as he was crossing the bridge, he heard the plaintive braying of a mule on the southern bank. He turned back for Grandma's mules. This decision would lead to a grand tragedy.

Horses and mules had been tied to a dozen or more tethering posts not far from the enclosure, in an area saturated with their foul-smelling urine. The horses were snorting and eating sorghum stalks; the mules were gnawing on the tethering posts and shitting loose stool. Uncle Arhat, stumbling three times for every step, stole in among them, where he smelled the welcome odor of our two big black mules and spotted their familiar shapes. Time to free his comrades in suffering. But the mules, strangers to the world of reason, greeted him with flying hooves.

"Black mules," Uncle Arhat mumbled, "black mules, we can run away together!" The irate mules pawed the earth to protect their territory from their master, who was unaware that the smell of his dried blood and new wounds had changed his identity to them. Confused and upset, he stepped forward, and was knocked down by a flying hoof. As he lay on the ground, his side started turning numb. The mule was still bucking and kicking, its steel-crescent shoes glinting like little moons. Uncle Arhat's hip swelled up painfully. He clambered to his feet, but fell back. As soon as he hit the ground, he struggled back up. A thin-voiced rooster in the village crowed once more, as the darkness began to give way to a glimmer of stars that illuminated the mules' rumps and eyeballs.

"Damned beasts!"

With anger rising in his heart, he stumbled around the area looking for a weapon. At the construction site of an irrigation ditch he found a sharp metal hoe. Now armed, he walked and cursed loudly, forgetting all about the men and their dog no more than a hundred paces distant. He felt free—fear is all that stands in the way of freedom.

A red solar halo crumbled as the sun rose in the east, and in the predawn light the sorghum was so still it seemed ready to burst. Uncle Arhat walked up to the mules, the rosy color of dawn in his eyes and bitter loathing in his heart. The mules stood calmly, motionlessly. Uncle Arhat raised his hoe, took aim on the hind leg of one of them, and swung with all his might. A cold shadow fell on the leg. The mule swayed sideways a couple of times, then straightened up, as a brutish, violent, stupefying, wrathful bray erupted from its head. The wounded animal then arched its rump, sending a shower of hot blood splashing down on Uncle Arhat's face. Seeing an opening, he swung at the other hind leg. A sigh escaped from the black mule as its rump settled earthward and it sat down hard, propped up by its forelegs, its neck jerked taut by the tether; it bleated to the blue-gray heavens through its gaping mouth. The hoe, pinned beneath its rump, jerked Uncle Arhat into a squatting position. Mustering all his strength, he managed to pull it free.

The second mule stood stupidly, eyeing its fallen comrade and braying piteously, as though pleading for its life. When Uncle Arhat approached, dragging his hoe behind him, the mule backed up until the tether seemed about to part and the post began to make cracking sounds. Dark-blue rays of light flowed from its fist-sized eyeballs.

"Scared? You damned beast! Where's your arrogance now? You evil, ungrateful, parasitic bastard! You ass-kissing, treacherous son of a bitch!"

As he spat out wrathful obscenities, he raised his hoe and swung at the animal's long, rectangular face. It missed, striking the tethering post. By twisting the handle up and down, back and forth, he finally managed to free the head from the wood. The mule struggled so violently that its rear legs arched like bows, its scrawny tail was noisily sweeping the ground. Uncle Arhat took careful aim at the animal's face—*crack*—the hoe landed smack on its broad forehead, emitting a resounding clang as metal struck bone, the reverberation passing through the wooden handle and stinging Uncle Arhat's arms. Not a sound emerged from the black mule's closed mouth. Its legs and hooves jerked and twitched furiously before it crashed to the ground like a capsized wall, snapping the tether in two, with one end hanging limply from the post and the other coiled beside the dead animal's head. Uncle Arhat watched quietly, his arms at his sides. The shiny wooden handle buried in the mule's head pointed to heaven at a jaunty angle.

A barking dog, human shouts, dawn. The curved outline of a blood-red sun rose above the sorghum field to the east, its rays shining down on the black hole of Uncle Arhat's open mouth.

4

THE TROOPS EMERGED onto the riverbank in a column, with the red sun, which had just broken through the mist, shining down on them. Like everyone else's, half of my father's face was red, the other half green; and, like everyone else, he was watching the mist break up over the Black Water River. A fourteen-arch stone bridge connected the southern and northern sections of the highway. The original wooden bridge remained in place to the west, although three or four spans had fallen into the river, leaving only the brown posts, which obstructed the flow of the white foam on top of the water. The reds and greens of the river poking through the dissipating mist were horrifyingly somber. From the dike, the view to the south was of an endless panorama of sorghum, level and smooth and still, a sea of deeply red, ripe faces. A collective body, united in a single magnanimous thought. Father was too young then to describe the sight in such flowery terms—that's my doing.

Sorghum and men waited for time's flower to bear fruit.

The highway stretched southward, a narrowing ribbon of road that was ultimately swallowed up by fields of sorghum. At its farthest point, where sorghum merged with the pale vault of heaven, the sunrise presented a bleak and solemn, yet stirring sight.

Gripped by curiosity, Father looked at the mesmerized guerrillas. Where were they from? Where were they going? Why were they setting an ambush? What would they do when it was over? In the deathly hush, the sound of water splashing over the bridge posts seemed louder and crisper than before. The mist, atomized by the sunlight, settled into the stream, turning the Black Water River from a deep red to a golden red, as though ablaze. A solitary, limp yellow water-plant floated by, its once fiery blooms hanging in withered pallor among the leafy grooves like silkworms. It's crab-catching season again! Father was reminded. The autumn winds are up, the air is chilled, a flock of wild geese is flying south. . . . Uncle Arhat shouts, "Now, Douguan, now!" The soft, spongy mud of the bank is covered with the elaborate patterns of skittering claws. Father could smell the delicate, fishy odor wafting over from the river.

"Take cover behind the dike, all of you," Commander Yu said. "Mute, set up your rakes."

Mute slipped some loops of wire off his shoulder and tied the four large rakes together, then grunted to his comrades to help him carry the chain of rakes over to the spot where the stone bridge and highway met.

"Take cover, men," Commander Yu ordered. "Stay down till the Jap convoy is on the bridge and Detachment Leader Leng's troops have cut off their line of retreat. Don't fire till I give the order; then cut those Jap bastards to pieces and let them feed the eels and crabs."

Commander Yu signaled to Mute, who nodded and led half the men into the sorghum field west of the highway to lie in ambush. Wang Wenyi followed Mute's troops to the west, but was sent back. "I want you here with me," Commander Yu said. "Scared?"

"No," Wang Wenyi said, even though he nodded spiritedly.

Commander Yu had the Fang brothers set up their cannon atop the dike, then turned to Bugler Liu. "Old Liu, as soon as we open fire, sound your horn for all you're worth. That scares the hell out of the Japs. Do you hear me?"

Bugler Liu was another of Commander Yu's longtime buddies, dating back from when he was a sedan bearer and Liu was a funeral musician. Now he held his horn like a rifle.

"I'm warning you guys," Commander Yu said to his men. "I'll shoot any one of you who turns chicken. We have to put on a good show for Leng and his men. Those bastards like to come on strong with their flags and bugles. Well, that's not my style. He thinks he can get us to join them, but I'll get *him* to join me instead."

As the men sat among the sorghum plants, Fang Six took out his pipe and tobacco and his steel and flint. The steel was black, the flint the deep red of a boiled chicken liver. The flint crackled as it struck the steel, sending sparks flying, great big sparks, one of which landed on the sorghum wick he was holding. As he blew on it, a wisp of white smoke curled upward, turning the wick red. He lit his pipe and took a deep puff. Commander Yu exhaled loudly and crinkled his nose. "Put that out," he said. "Do you think the Japs will cross the bridge if they smell smoke?" Fang Six took a couple of quick puffs before snuffing out his pipe and putting it away.

"Okay, you guys, flatten out on the slope so we'll be ready when the Japs come."

Nervousness set in as the troops lay on the slope, weapons in hand, knowing they would soon face a formidable enemy. Father lay alongside Commander Yu, who asked him, "Scared?"

"No!"

"Good," Commander Yu said. "You're your foster-dad's boy, all right! You'll be my dispatch orderly. Don't leave my side once it starts. I'll need you to convey orders."

Father nodded. His eyes were fastened greedily on the pistols stuck in Commander Yu's belt, one big, one small. The big one was a German automatic, the small one a French Browning. Each had an interesting history.

The word "Gun!" escaped from his mouth.

"You want a gun?"

Father nodded.

"Do you know how to use one?"

"Yes!"

Commander Yu took the Browning out of his belt and examined it carefully. It was well used, the enamel long gone. He pulled back the bolt, ejecting a copper-jacketed bullet, which he tossed in the air, caught, and shoved back into the chamber.

"Here!" he said, handing it over. "Use it the way I did."

Father took the pistol from him, and as he held it he thought back to a couple of nights earlier, when Commander Yu had used it to shatter a wine cup.

A crescent moon had climbed into the sky and was pressing down on withered branches. Father carried a jug and a brass key out to the distillery to get some wine for Grandma. He opened the gate. The compound was absolutely still, the mule pen pitch-black, the distillery suffused with the stench of fermenting grain. When he took the lid off one of the vats in the moonlight, he saw the reflection of his gaunt face in the mirrorlike surface of wine. His eyebrows were short, his lips thin; he was surprised by his own ugliness. He dunked the jug into the vat of wine, which gurgled as it filled. After lifting it out, he changed his mind and poured the wine back, recalling the vat in which Grandma had washed her bloody face. Now she was inside, drinking with Commander Yu and Detachment Leader Leng, who was getting pretty drunk, no match for the other two.

Father walked up to a second vat, the lid of which was held in place by a millstone. After putting his jug on the ground, he strained to remove the millstone, which rolled away and crashed up against yet another vat, punching a hole in the bottom, through which wine began to seep. Ignoring the leaky vat, he removed the lid from the one in front of him, and immediately smelled the blood of Uncle Arhat. The two faces, of Uncle Arhat and Grandma, appeared and reappeared in the wine vat. Father dunked the jug into the vat, filled it with blood-darkened wine, and carried it inside.

Candles burned brightly on the table, around which Commander Yu and Detachment Leader Leng were glaring at each other and breathing heavily. Grandma stood between them, her left hand resting on Leng's revolver, her right hand on Commander Yu's Browning pistol.

Father heard Grandma say, "Even if you can't agree, you mustn't abandon justice and honor. This isn't the time or place to fight. Take your fury out on the Japanese."

Commander Yu spat out angrily, "You can't scare me with the Wang regiment's flags and bugles, you prick. I'm king here. I ate fistcakes for ten years, and I don't give a damn about that fucking Big Claw Wang!"

Detachment Leader Leng sneered. "Elder Brother Zhan'ao, I've got your best interests at heart. So does Commander Wang. If you turn your cache of weapons over to us, we'll make you a battalion commander, and he'll provide rifles and pay. That's better than being a bandit."

"Who's a bandit? Who isn't a bandit? Anyone who fights the Japanese is a national hero. Last year I knocked off three Japanese sentries and inherited three automatic rifles. You're no bandit, but how many Japs have you killed? You haven't taken a hair off a single Jap's ass!"

Detachment Leader Leng sat down and lit a cigarette.

Father took advantage of the lull to hand the wine jug up to Grandma, whose face changed as she took it from him. Glaring at Father, she filled the three cups.

"Uncle Arhat's blood is in this wine," she said. "If you're honorable men you'll drink it, then go out and destroy the Jap convoy. After that, chickens can go their own way, dogs can go theirs. Well water and river water don't mix."

She picked up her cup and drank the wine down noisily.

Commander Yu held out his cup, threw back his head, and drained it.

Detachment Leader Leng followed suit, but put his cup down half full. "Commander Yu," he said, "I've had all I can handle. So long!"

With her hand still on his revolver, Grandma asked him, "Are you going to fight?"

"Don't beg!" Commander Yu snarled. "I'll fight, even if he doesn't."

"I'll fight," Detachment Leader Leng said.

Grandma let her hand drop, and Leng jammed his revolver back into its holster.

The pale skin around his nose was dotted with dozens of pockmarks. A heavy cartridge belt hung from his belt, which sagged when he holstered his revolver.

"Zhan'ao," Grandma said, "I'm entrusting Douguan to your care. Take him along the day after tomorrow."

Commander Yu looked at my father and smiled. "Have you got the balls, foster-son?"

Father stared scornfully at the hard yellow teeth showing between Commander Yu's parted lips. He didn't say a word.

Commander Yu picked up a wine cup and placed it on top of Father's head, then told him to stand in the doorway. He whipped out his Browning pistol and walked over to the corner.

Father watched Commander Yu take three long strides to the corner—three slow, measured steps. Grandma's face turned ashen. The corners of Detachment Leader Leng's mouth were curled in a contemptuous smile.

When he reached the corner, Commander Yu whirled around. Father watched him raise his arm, as a dark-red cast came over his black eyes. The Browning spat out a puff of white smoke. An explosion erupted above Father's head, and shards of shattered ceramic fell around him, one landing against his neck. He shrugged his shoulder, and it slid down into his pants. He didn't utter a sound. The blood had drained from Grandma's face. Detachment Leader Leng sat down hard on a stool. "Good shooting," he said after a moment.

"Good boy!" Commander Yu said proudly.

The Browning pistol in Father's hand seemed to weigh a ton.

"I don't have to show you," Commander Yu said. "You know how to shoot. Have Mute get his men ready."

Gripping his pistol tightly, Father darted through the sorghum field, crossed the highway, and ran up to Mute, who was sitting cross-legged on the ground, honing his saber knife with a shiny green stone. Some of his men were seated, others lying down.

"Get your men ready," Father said to him.

Mute looked at Father out of the corner of his eye, but kept honing his knife for another moment or so. Then he picked up a couple of sorghum leaves, wiped the stone residue from the blade, and plucked a stalk of grass to test its sharpness. It fell in two pieces the instant it touched the blade.

"Get your men ready," Father repeated.

Mute sheathed his knife and laid it on the ground beside him, his face creased in a savage grin. With one of his mammoth hands, he signaled Father to come closer.

"Uh! Uh!" he grunted.

Father shuffled forward and stopped a pace or so from Mute, who reached out, grabbed him by the sleeve, jerked him into his lap, and pinched his ear so hard that he grimaced. Father jammed his Browning pistol up into Mute's rib cage. Mute grabbed Father's nose and pinched it until tears came to his eyes. An eerie laugh burst from Mute's mouth.

The seated men laughed raucously.

"A lot like Commander Yu, isn't he?"

"Commander Yu's seed."

"Douguan, I miss your mom."

"Douguan, I feel like nibbling those date-topped buns of hers."

Father's embarrassment quickly turned to rage. Raising his pistol, he aimed it at the man wishfully thinking of date-topped buns, and pulled the trigger. The hammer clicked, but no bullet emerged.

The man, ashen-faced, jumped to his feet and wrenched the pistol away. Father, still enraged, threw himself on the man, clawing, kicking, biting.

Mute stood up, grabbed Father by the scruff of his neck, and flicked him away. He flew through the air and crashed into a thicket of sorghum stalks. A quick somersault and he was on his feet, railing and swearing as he charged Mute, who merely grunted a couple of times. The steely look in his eyes froze Father in his tracks. Mute picked up the pistol and pulled back the bolt; a bullet fell into his hand. Holding it in his fingers, he looked at the notch in the casing from the firing pin, and made some unintelligible hand signs to Father. Then he stuck the pistol into Father's belt and patted him on the shoulder.

"What were you doing over there?" Commander Yu asked.

Father was embarrassed. "They . . . they said they wanted to sleep with Mom."

"What did you say?" Commander Yu asked sternly.

Father wiped his eyes with his arm. "I shot him!"

"You shot somebody?"

"The gun misfired." Father handed Commander Yu the shiny dud.

Commander Yu took it from him, examined it, and gave it a casual flick. It described a beautiful arc before plopping into the river.

"Good boy!" Commander Yu said. "But use your gun on the Japanese first. After you've finished them off, anybody who says he wants to sleep with your mom, you shoot him in the gut. Not in the head, and not in the chest. Remember, in the gut."

Father lay on his belly alongside Commander Yu; the Fang brothers were on his other side. The cannon had been set up on the dike, aimed at the stone bridge, its barrel stuffed with cotton rags, a fuse sticking out behind. Fang Seven had placed a bundle of sorghum tinder next to him, some of which was already smoldering. A gourd filled with gunpowder and a tin of iron pellets lay beside Fang Six.

Wang Wenyi was to Commander Yu's left, curled up, holding his long-barreled fowling piece in his hands. His wounded ear was stuck to the white bandage covering it.

The sun was stake-high, its white core girded by a pink halo. The flowing water glittered. A flock of wild ducks flew over from the sorghum field, circled three times, then dived down to a grassy sandbar. A few landed on the surface of the river and began floating downstream, their bodies settling heavily in the water, their heads turning and darting constantly. Father was feeling warm and tingly. His clothes, dampened by the dew, were now dry. He pressed himself to the ground, but felt a pain in his chest, as from a sharp stone. When he rose up to see what it was, his head and upper torso were exposed above the dike. "Get down," Commander Yu ordered. Reluctantly, he did as he was told. Fang Six began to snore. Commander Yu picked up a dirt clod and tossed it in his face. Fang Six woke up bleary-eyed and yawned so heroically that two fine tears appeared in the corners of his eyes.

"Are the Japs here?" he asked loudly.

"Fuck you!" Commander Yu snarled. "No sleeping."

The riverbanks were absolutely still; the broad highway lay lifeless in its bed of sorghum. The stone bridge spanning the river was strikingly beautiful. A boundless expanse of sorghum greeted the reddening sun, which rose ever higher, grew ever brighter. Wild ducks floated in the shallow water by the banks, noisily searching for food with their flat bills. Father studied their beautiful feathers and alert, intelligent eyes. Aiming his heavy Browning pistol at one of their smooth backs, he was about to pull the trigger when Commander Yu forced his hand down. "What the hell do you think you're doing, you little turtle egg?"

Father was getting fidgety. The highway lay there like death itself. The sorghum had turned deep scarlet.

"That bastard Leng wants to play games with me!" Commander Yu spat out hatefully. The southern bank lay in silence; not a trace of the Leng detachment. Father knew it was Leng who had learned that the convoy would be passing this spot, and that he'd brought Commander Yu into the ambush only because he doubted his own ability to go it alone.

Father was tense for a while, but gradually he relaxed, and his attention wandered back to the wild ducks. He thought about duck-hunting with Uncle Arhat, who had a fowling piece with a deep-red stock and a leather strap; it was now in the hands of Wang Wenyi. Tears welled up in his eyes, but not enough to spill out. Just like that day the year before. Under the warm rays of the sun, he felt a chill spread through his body.

Uncle Arhat and the two mules had been taken away by the Japs, and Grandma had washed her bloody face in the wine vat until it reeked of alcohol and was beet-red. Her eyes were puffy; the front of her pale-blue cotton jacket was soaked in wine and blood. She stood stock-still beside the vat, staring down at her reflection. Father recalled how she had fallen to her knees and kowtowed three times to the vat, then stood up, scooped some wine with both hands, and drank it. The rosiness of her face was concentrated in her cheeks; all the color had drained from her forehead and chin.

"Kneel down!" she ordered Father. "Kowtow."

He fell to his knees and kowtowed.

"Take a drink!"

He scooped up a handful of wine and drank it.

Trickles of blood, like threads, sank to the bottom of the vat, on the surface of which a tiny white cloud floated alongside the somber faces of Grandma and Father. Piercing rays emanated from Grandma's eyes; Father looked away, his heart pounding wildly. He reached out to scoop up some more wine, and as it dripped through his fingers it shattered one large face and one small one amid the blue sky and white cloud. He drank a mouthful, which left the sticky taste of blood on his tongue. The blood sank to the base of the vat, where it congealed into a turbid clot the size of a fist. Father and Grandma stared at it long and hard; then she pulled the lid over it and rolled the millstone back, straining to place it on top of the lid.

"Don't touch it!" she said.

Looking at the accumulation of mud and gray-green sowbugs squirming in the indentation of the millstone, he nodded, clearly disturbed by the sight.

That night he lay on his kang listening to Grandma pace the yard. The patter of her footsteps and the rustling sorghum in the fields formed Father's confused dreams, in which he heard the brays of our two handsome black mules.

Father awoke once, at dawn, and ran naked into the yard to pee; there he saw Grandma staring transfixed into the sky. He called out, "Mom," but his shout fell on deaf ears. When he'd finished peeing, he took her by the hand and led her inside. She followed meekly. They'd barely stepped inside when they heard waves of commotion from the southeast, followed by the crack of rifle fire, like the pop of a tautly stretched piece of silk pierced by a sharp knife.

Shortly after he and Grandma heard the gunfire, they were herded over to the dike, along with a number of villagers—elderly, young, sick, and disabled—by Japanese soldiers. The polished white flagstones, boulders, and coarse yellow gravel on the dike looked like a line of grave mounds. Last year's early-summer sorghum stood spellbound beyond the dike, somber and melancholy. The outline of the highway shining through the trampled sorghum stretched due north. The stone bridge hadn't been erected then, and the little wooden span stood utterly exhausted and horribly scarred by the passage of tens of thousands of tramping feet and the iron shoes of horses and mules. The smell of green shoots released by the crushed and broken sorghum, steeped in the night mist, rose pungent in the morning air. Sorghum everywhere was crying bitterly.

Father, Grandma, and the other villagers—assembled on the western edge of the highway, south of the river, atop the shattered remnants of sorghum plants—faced a mammoth enclosure that looked like an animal pen. A crowd of shabby laborers huddled beyond it. Two puppet soldiers herded the laborers over near Father and the others to form a second cluster. The two groups faced a square where animals were tethered, a spot that would later make people pale with fright. They stood impassively for some time before a thin-faced, white-gloved Japanese officer with red insignia on his shoulders and a long sword at his hip emerged from the tent, leading a guard dog, whose red tongue lolled from the side of its mouth. Behind the dog, two puppet soldiers carried the rigid corpse of a Japanese soldier. Two Japanese soldiers brought up the rear, escorting two puppet soldiers who were dragging a beaten and bloody Uncle Arhat. Father huddled close to Grandma; she wrapped her arms around him.

Fifty or so white birds, wings flapping noisily, sliced through the blue sky above the Black Water River, then turned and headed east, toward the golden sun. Father could see the draft animals, with scraggly hair and filthy faces, and our two black mules, which lay on the ground. One was dead, the hoe still stuck in its head. The blood-soaked tail of the other mule swept the ground; the skin over its belly twitched noisily; its nostrils whistled as they opened and closed. How Father loved those two black mules.

He remembers Grandma sitting proudly on the mule's back, Father in her lap, the three of them flying down the narrow dirt path through the sorghum field, the mule rocking back and forth as it gallops along, giving Father and Grandma the ride of their lives. Spindly legs conquer the dust of the road as Father shouts excitedly. An occasional peasant amid the sorghum, hoe in hand, gazes at the powdery, fair face of the distillery owner, his heart filled with envy and loathing.

Now one of the mules was lying dead on the ground, its mouth open, a row of long white teeth chewing the earth. The other sat suffering more than its dead comrade. "Mom," Father said to Grandma, "our mules." She covered his mouth with her hand.

The body of the Japanese soldier was placed before the officer, who continued to hold the dog's leash. The two puppet soldiers dragged the battered Uncle Arhat over to a wooden rack. Father didn't recognize him right away; he seemed just a strange, bloody creature in human form. As he was dragged up to the rack, his head turned to the left, then to the right, the crusty scab on his scalp looking like the shiny mud on the riverbank, baked by the sun until it wrinkles and begins to crack. His useless feet traced patterns in the dirt. The crowd slowly recoiled. Father felt Grandma's hands grip his shoulders tightly. The people seemed to shrink in size, their faces clay-colored or black. Crows and sparrows suddenly silenced, the people could hear the panting of the guard dog. The officer holding its leash farted loudly. Before the puppet soldiers dragged the strange creature over to the rack, they dropped it to the ground, an inert slab of meat.

"Uncle Arhat!" Father cried out in alarm.

Grandma covered his mouth again.

Uncle Arhat began to writhe, arching his buttocks as he rose to his knees, propped himself on his hands, and raised his arms. His face was so puffy the skin shone; his eyes were slits through which thin greenish rays emerged. Father was sure Uncle Arhat could see him.

His heart was pounding against the wall of his chest—thump thump thump—and he didn't know if it was from fear or anger. He wanted to scream, but Grandma's hand was clasped too tightly over his mouth.

The officer holding the leash shouted something to the crowd, and a crew-cut Chinese interpreted it for them. Father didn't hear everything the interpreter said. Grandma's hand was clasped so tightly over his mouth that he was having trouble breathing and his ears were ringing.

Two Chinese in black uniforms stripped Uncle Arhat naked and tied him to the rack. The Jap officer waved his arm, and two more black-clad men dragged and pushed Sun Five, the most accomplished hog-butcher in our village—or anywhere in Northeast Gaomi Township, for that matter—out of the enclosure. He was a short, bald man with a huge paunch, a red face, and tiny, close-set eyes buried alongside the bridge of his nose. He held a butcher knife in his left hand and a pail of water in his right as he shuffled up to Uncle Arhat.

The interpreter spoke: "The commander says to skin him. If you don't do a good job of it, he'll have his dog tear your heart out."

Sun Five mumbled an acknowledgment, his eyes blinking furiously. Holding the knife in his mouth, he picked up the pail and poured water over Uncle Arhat's scalp. Uncle Arhat's head jerked upward when the cold water hit him. Bloody water coursed down his face and neck, forming filthy puddles at his feet. One of the overseers brought another pail of water from the river. Sun Five soaked a rag in it and wiped Uncle Arhat's face clean. When he was finished, his buttocks twitched briefly. "Elder brother . . ."

"Brother," Uncle Arhat said, "finish me off quickly. I won't forget your kindness down in the Yellow Springs."

The Japanese officer roared something.

"Get on with it!" the interpreter said.

Sun Five's face darkened as he reached up and held Uncle Arhat's ear between his fingers. "Elder brother," he said, "there's nothing I can do. . . ."

Father saw Sun Five's knife cut the skin above the ear with a sawing motion. Uncle Arhat screeched in agony as sprays of yellow piss shot out from between his legs. Father's knees were knocking. A Japanese soldier walked up to Sun Five with a white ceramic platter, into which Sun put Uncle Arhat's large, fleshy ear. He cut off the other ear and laid it on the platter alongside the first one. Father watched the ears twitch, making thumping sounds.

The soldier paraded slowly in front of the laborers and villagers, holding the platter out for them to see. Father looked at the ears, pale and beautiful.

The soldier then carried the ears up to the Japanese officer, who nodded to him. He laid the platter alongside the body of his dead comrade; after a moment of silence, he picked it up and put it on the ground under the dog's nose.

The dog's tongue slithered back into its mouth as it sniffed the ears with its pointy, wet, black nose; but it shook its head, with its tongue lolling again, and sat down.

"Hey," the interpreter yelled at Sun Five. "Keep going."

Sun Five was walking around in circles, mumbling to himself. Father looked at his sweaty, greasy face, and watched his eyelids blink like the bobbing head of a chicken.

A mere trickle of blood oozed from the holes where Uncle Arhat's ears had been. Without them his head had become a neat, unmarred oval.

The Jap officer roared again.

"Hurry up, get on with it!" the interpreter ordered.

Sun Five bent over and sliced off Uncle Arhat's genitals with a single stroke, then put them into the platter held by the Japanese soldier, who carried it at eye level as he paraded like a marionette in front of the crowd. Father felt Grandma's icy fingers dig into his shoulders.

The Japanese soldier put the platter under the dog's nose. It nibbled, then spat the stuff out.

Uncle Arhat was screaming in agony, his bony frame twitching violently on the rack.

Sun Five threw down his butcher knife, fell to his knees, and wailed bitterly.

The Japanese officer let go of the leash, and the guard dog bounded forward, burying its claws in Sun Five's shoulders and baring its fangs in his face. He threw himself on the ground and covered his face with his hands.

The Japanese officer whistled, and the guard dog bounded back to him, dragging the leash behind it.

"Skin him, and be quick about it!" the interpreter demanded.

Sun Five struggled to his feet, picked up his butcher knife, and staggered up to Uncle Arhat.

Everyone's head jerked upward as a torrent of abuse erupted from Uncle Arhat's mouth.

Sun Five spoke to him: "Elder brother . . . elder brother . . . try to bear it a little longer. . . ."

Uncle Arhat spat a gob of bloody phlegm into Sun's face.

"Start skinning," shouted the interpreter. "Fuck your ancestors! Skin him, I said!"

Sun Five started at the point on Uncle Arhat's scalp where the scab had formed, zipping the knife blade down, once, twice . . . one meticulous cut after another. Uncle Arhat's scalp fell away, revealing two greenish-purple eyes and several misshapen chunks of flesh. . . .

Father told me once that, even after Uncle Arhat's face had been peeled away, shouts and gurgles continued to emerge from his shapeless mouth, while endless rivulets of bright-red blood dripped from his pasty scalp. Sun Five no longer seemed human as his flawless knifework produced a perfect pelt. After Uncle Arhat had been turned into a mass of meaty pulp, his innards churned and roiled, attracting swarms of dancing green flies. The women were on their knees, wailing piteously. That night a heavy rain fell, washing the tethering square clean of every drop of blood, and of Uncle Arhat's corpse and the skin that had covered it. Word that his corpse had disappeared spread through the village, from one person to ten, to a hundred, from this generation to the next, until it became a beautiful legend.

"If he thinks he can get away with playing games with me, I'll rip his head off and use it for a pisspot!"

The sun seemed to shrink as it rose in the sky, sending down white-hot rays; a flock of wild ducks flew through the rapidly dissipating mist atop the sorghum field, then another flock. Detachment Leader Leng's troops still hadn't shown up, and only an occasional wild hare disturbed the peace of the highway. A while later, a wily red fox darted across the highway. "Hey!" Commander Yu shouted after cursing Detachment Leader Leng. "Everybody up. It looks like we've been tricked by that son of a bitch Pocky Leng."

That was just what the troops, tired of lying there, had been waiting to hear. They were on their way up before the sound of Commander Yu's command had died out. Some sat on the dike to enjoy a smoke; others stood to take a long-postponed piss.

Father jumped up onto the dike, the head of the skinned Uncle Arhat floating in front of his eyes. Wild ducks startled into flight by the sudden emergence of men on the dike began landing in small clusters on a nearby sandbar, where they waddled back and forth, their emerald and yellow feathers glistening among the water weeds.

Mute walked up to Commander Yu, knife in one hand, his old Hanyang rifle in the other. Looking dejected, with lifeless eyes, he pointed to the sun in the southeastern sky and to the deserted highway. Finally, he pointed to his belly, grunted, and signaled in the direction of the village. Commander Yu thought for a moment, then called to the men on the western edge of the highway, "Come over here, all of you!"

The troops crossed the highway and formed up on the dike.

"Brothers," Commander Yu said, "if Pocky Leng's playing games with us, I'll lop his damned head off! The sun isn't directly overhead yet, so we'll wait a little longer. If the convoy hasn't come by noon, we'll go to Tan Family Hollow and settle accounts with Leng. For now, go into the sorghum field and get some rest. I'll send Douguan for food. Douguan!"

Father looked up at Commander Yu.

"Go tell your mom to have the women make some fistcakes, and tell her I want lunch here by noon. Say I want her to bring it herself."

Father nodded, hitched up his trousers, stuck the Browning pistol into his belt, and ran down the dike. After heading north down the highway for a short distance, he cut across the sorghum field, heading northwest, weaving in and out among the plants. In the sea of sorghum he bumped into some long mule bones. He kicked one, dislodging a couple of short-tailed, furry field voles that had been feasting on marrow. They looked up fearlessly, then burrowed back into the bone. The sight reminded Father of the family's two black mules, reminded him of how, long after the highway had been completed, the pungent smell of death hung over the village every time a southeastern wind rose.

A year earlier, the bloated carcasses of dozens of mules had been found floating in the Black Water River, caught in the reeds and grass in the shallow water by the banks; their distended bellies, baked by the sun, split and popped, released their splendid innards, like gorgeous blooming flowers, as slowly spreading pools of dark-green liquid were caught up in the flow of water.

5

ON HER SIXTEENTH BIRTHDAY, my grandma was betrothed by her father to Shan Bianlang, the son of Shan Tingxiu, one of Northeast Gaomi Township's richest men. As distillery owners, the Shans used cheap sorghum to produce a strong, high-quality white wine that was famous throughout the area. Northeast Gaomi Township is largely swampy land that is flooded by autumn rains; but since the tall sorghum stalks resist waterlogging, it was planted everywhere and invariably produced a bumper crop. By using cheap grain to make wine, the Shan family made a very good living, and marrying my grandma off to them was a real feather in Great-Granddad's cap. Many local families had dreamed of marrying into the Shan family, despite rumors that Shan Bianlang had leprosy. His father was a wizened little man who sported a scrawny queue on the back of his head, and even though his cupboards overflowed with gold and silver, he wore tattered, dirty clothes, often using a length of rope as a belt.

Grandma's marriage into the Shan family was the will of heaven, implemented on a day when she and some of her playmates, with their tiny bound feet and long pigtails, were playing beside a set of swings. It was Qingming, the day set aside to attend ancestral graves; peach trees were in full red bloom, willows were green, a fine rain was falling, and the girls' faces looked like peach blossoms. It was a day of freedom for them. That year Grandma was five feet four inches tall and weighed about 130 pounds. She was wearing a cotton print jacket over green satin trousers, with scarlet bands of silk tied around her ankles. Since it was drizzling, she had put on a pair of embroidered slippers soaked a dozen times in tong oil, which made a squishing sound when she walked. Her long shiny braids shone, and a heavy silver necklace hung around her neck—Great-Granddad was a silversmith. Great-Grandma, the daughter of a landlord who had fallen on hard times, knew the importance of bound feet to a girl, and had begun binding her daughter's feet when she was six years old, tightening the bindings every day.

A yard in length, the cloth bindings were wound around all but the big toes until the bones cracked and the toes turned under. The pain was excruciating. My mother also had bound feet, and just seeing them saddened me so much that I felt compelled to shout: "Down with feudalism! Long live liberated feet!" The results of Grandma's suffering were two three-inch golden lotuses, and by the age of sixteen she had grown into a well-developed beauty. When she walked, swinging her arms freely, her body swayed like a willow in the wind.

Shan Tingxiu, the groom's father, was walking around Great-Granddad's village, dung basket in hand, when he spotted Grandma among the other local flowers. Three months later, a bridal sedan chair would come to carry her away.

After Shan Tingxiu had spotted Grandma, a stream of people came to congratulate Great-Granddad and Great-Grandma. Grandma pondered what it would be like to mount to the jingle of gold and dismount to the tinkle of silver, but what she truly longed for was a good husband, handsome and well educated, a man who would treat her gently. As a young maiden, she had embroidered a wedding trousseau and several exquisite pictures for the man who would someday become my granddad. Eager to marry, she heard innuendos from her girlfriends that the Shan boy was afflicted with leprosy, and her dreams began to evaporate. Yet, when she shared her anxieties with her parents, Great-Granddad hemmed and hawed, while Great-Grandma scolded the girlfriends, accusing them of sour grapes.

Later on, Great-Granddad told her that the well-educated Shan boy had the fair complexion of a young scholar from staying home all the time. Grandma was confused, not knowing if this was true or not. After all, she thought, her own parents wouldn't lie to her. Maybe her girlfriends had made it all up. Once again she looked forward to her wedding day.

Grandma longed to lose her anxieties and loneliness in the arms of a strong and noble young man. Finally, to her relief, her wedding day arrived, and as she was placed inside the sedan chair, carried by four bearers, the horns and woodwinds fore and aft struck up a melancholy tune that brought tears to her eyes. Off they went, floating along as though riding the clouds or sailing through a mist.

Grandma was lightheaded and dizzy inside the stuffy sedan chair, her view blocked by a red curtain that gave off a pungent mildewy odor. She reached out to lift it a crack—Great-Granddad had told her not to remove her red veil. A heavy bracelet of twisted silver slid down to her wrist, and as she looked at the coiled-snake design her thoughts grew chaotic and disoriented. A warm wind rustled the emerald-green stalks of sorghum lining the narrow dirt path. Doves cooed in the fields. The delicate powder of petals floated above silvery new ears of waving sorghum. The curtain, embroidered on the inside with a dragon and a phoenix, had faded after years of use, and there was a large stain in the middle.

Summer was giving way to autumn, and the sunlight outside the sedan chair was brilliant. The bouncing movements of the bearers rocked the chair slowly from side to side; the leather lining of their poles groaned and creaked, the curtain fluttered gently, letting in an occasional ray of sunlight and, from time to time, a whisper of cool air. Grandma was sweating profusely and her heart was racing as she listened to the rhythmic footsteps and heavy breathing of the bearers. The inside of her skull felt cold one minute, as though filled with shiny pebbles, and hot the next, as though filled with coarse peppers.

Shortly after leaving the village, the lazy musicians stopped playing, while the bearers quickened their pace. The aroma of sorghum burrowed into her heart. Full-voiced strange and rare birds sang to her from the fields. A picture of what she imagined to be the bridegroom slowly took shape from the threads of sunlight filtering into the darkness of the sedan chair. Painful needle pricks jabbed her heart.

"Old Man in heaven, protect me!" Her silent prayer made her delicate lips tremble. A light down adorned her upper lip, and her fair skin was damp. Every soft word she uttered was swallowed up by the rough walls of the carriage and the heavy curtain before her. She ripped the tart-smelling veil away from her face and laid it on her knees. She was following local wedding customs, which dictated that a bride wear three layers of new clothes, top and bottom, no matter how hot the day. The inside of the sedan chair was badly worn and terribly dirty; like a coffin, it had already embraced countless other brides, now long dead. The walls were festooned with yellow silk so filthy it oozed grease, and of the five flies caught inside, three buzzed above her head while the other two rested on the curtain before her, rubbing their bright eyes with black sticklike legs. Succumbing to the oppressiveness in the carriage, Grandma eased one of her bamboo-shoot toes under the curtain and lifted it a crack to sneak a look outside.

She could make out the shapes of the bearers' statuesque legs poking out from under loose black satin trousers and their big, fleshy feet encased in straw sandals. They raised clouds of dust as they tramped along. Impatiently trying to conjure up an image of their firm, muscular chests, Grandma raised the toe of her shoe and leaned forward. She could see the polished purple scholar-tree poles and the bearers' broad shoulders beneath them. Barriers of sorghum stalks lining the path stood erect and solid in unbroken rows, tightly packed, together sizing one another up with the yet unopened clay-green eyes of grain ears, one indistinguishable from the next, as far as she could see, like a vast river. The path was so narrow in places it was barely passable, causing the wormy, sappy leaves to brush noisily against the sedan chair.

The men's bodies emitted the sour smell of sweat. Infatuated by the masculine odor, Grandma breathed in deeply—this ancestor of mine must have been nearly bursting with passion. As the bearers carried their load down the path, their feet left a series of V imprints known as "tramples" in the dirt, for which satisfied clients usually rewarded them, and which fortified the bearers' pride of profession. It was unseemly to "trample" with an uneven cadence or to grip the poles, and the best bearers kept their hands on their hips the whole time, rocking the sedan chair in perfect rhythm with the musicians' haunting tunes, which reminded everyone within earshot of the hidden suffering in whatever pleasures lay ahead.

When the sedan chair reached the plains, the bearers began to get a little sloppy, both to make up time and to torment their passenger. Some brides were bounced around so violently they vomited from motion sickness, soiling their clothing and slippers; the retching sounds from inside the carriage pleased the bearers as though they were giving vent to their own miseries. The sacrifices these strong young men made to carry their cargo into bridal chambers must have embittered them, which was why it seemed so natural to torment the brides.

One of the four men bearing Grandma's sedan chair that day would eventually become my granddad—it was Commander Yu Zhan'ao. At the time he was a beefy twenty-year-old, a pallbearer and sedan bearer at the peak of his trade. The young men of his generation were as sturdy as Northeast Gaomi sorghum, which is more than can be said about us weaklings who succeeded them. It was a custom back then for sedan bearers to tease the bride while trundling her along: like distillery workers, who drink the wine they make, since it is their due, these men torment all who ride in their sedan chairs—even the wife of the Lord of Heaven if she should be a passenger.

Sorghum leaves scraped the sedan chair mercilessly when, all of a sudden, the deadening monotony of the trip was broken by the plaintive sounds of weeping—remarkably like the musicians' tunes—coming from deep in the field. As Grandma listened to the music, trying to picture the instruments in the musicians' hands, she raised the curtain with her foot until she could see the sweat-soaked waist of one of the bearers. Her gaze was caught by her own red embroidered slippers, with their tapered slimness and cheerless beauty, ringed by halos of incoming sunlight until they looked like lotus blossoms, or, even more, like tiny goldfish that had settled to the bottom of a bowl. Two teardrops as transparently pink as immature grains of sorghum wetted Grandma's eyelashes and slipped down her cheeks to the corners of her mouth.

As she was gripped by sadness, the image of a learned and refined husband, handsome in his high-topped hat and wide sash, like a player on the stage, blurred and finally vanished, replaced by the horrifying picture of Shan Bianlang's face, his leprous mouth covered with rotting tumors. Her heart turned to ice. Were these tapered golden lotuses, a face as fresh as peaches and apricots, gentility of a thousand kinds, and ten thousand varieties of elegance all reserved for the pleasure of a leper? Better to die and be done with it.

The disconsolate weeping in the sorghum field was dotted with words, like knots in a piece of wood: A blue sky *yo*—a sapphire sky *yo*—a painted sky *yo*—a mighty cudgel *yo*—dear elder brother *yo*—

death has claimed you—you have brought down little sister's sky *yo*—.

I must tell you that the weeping of women from Northeast Gaomi Township makes beautiful music. During 1912, the first year of the Republic, professional mourners known as "wailers" came from Qufu, the home of Confucius, to study local weeping techniques. Meeting up with a woman lamenting the death of her husband seemed to Grandma to be a stroke of bad luck on her wedding day, and she grew even more dejected.

Just then one of the bearers spoke up: "You there, little bride in the chair, say something! The long journey has bored us to tears."

Grandma quickly snatched up her red veil and covered her face, gently drawing her foot back from beneath the curtain and returning the carriage to darkness.

"Sing us a song while we bear you along!"

The musicians, as though snapping out of a trance, struck up their instruments. A trumpet blared from behind the chair:

"Too-tah—too-tah—"

"Poo-pah—poo-pah—" One of the bearers up front imitated the trumpet sound, evoking coarse, raucous laughter all around.

Grandma was drenched with sweat. Back home, as she was being lifted into the sedan chair, Great-Grandma had exhorted her not to get drawn into any banter with the bearers. Sedan bearers and musicians are low-class rowdies capable of anything, no matter how depraved.

They began rocking the chair so violently that poor Grandma couldn't keep her seat without holding on tight.

"No answer? Okay, rock! If we can't shake any words loose, we can at least shake the piss out of her!"

The sedan chair was like a dinghy tossed about by the waves, and Grandma held on to the wooden seat for dear life. The two eggs she'd eaten for breakfast churned in her stomach; the flies buzzed around her ears; her throat tightened, as the taste of eggs surged up into her mouth. She bit her lip. Don't throw up, don't let yourself throw up! she commanded herself. You mustn't let yourself throw up, Fenglian. They say throwing up in the bridal chair means a lifetime of bad luck. . . .

The bearers' banter turned coarse. One of them reviled my great-granddad for being a money-grabber, another said something about a pretty flower stuck into a pile of cowshit, a third called Shan Bianlang a scruffy leper who oozed pus and excreted yellow fluids. He said the stench of rotten flesh drifted beyond the Shan compound, which swarmed with horseflies. . . .

"Little bride, if you let Shan Bianlang touch you, your skin will rot away!"

As the horns and woodwinds blared and tooted, the taste of eggs grew stronger, forcing Grandma to bite down hard on her lip. But to no avail. She opened her mouth and spewed a stream of filth, soiling the curtain, toward which the five flies dashed as though shot from a gun.

"Puke-ah, puke-ah. Keep rocking!" one of the bearers roared. "Keep rocking. Sooner or later she'll have to say something."

"Elder brothers . . . spare me . . ." Grandma pleaded desperately between agonizing retches. Then she burst into tears. She felt humiliated; she could sense the perils of her future, knowing she'd spend the rest of her life drowning in a sea of bitterness. Oh, Father, oh, Mother. I have been destroyed by a miserly father and a heartless mother!

Grandma's piteous wails made the sorghum quake. The bearers stopped rocking the chair and calmed the raging sea. The musicians lowered the instruments from their rousing lips, so that only Grandma's sobs could be heard, alone with the mournful strains of a single woodwind, whose weeping sounds were more enchanting than any woman's. Grandma stopped crying at the sound of the woodwind, as though commanded from on high. Her face, suddenly old and desiccated, was pearled with tears. She heard the sound of death in the gentle melancholy of the tune, and smelled its breath; she could see the angel of death, with lips as scarlet as sorghum and a smiling face the color of golden corn.

The bearers fell silent and their footsteps grew heavy. The sacrificial choking sounds from inside the chair and the woodwind accompaniment had made them restless and uneasy, had set their souls adrift. No longer did it seem like a wedding procession as they negotiated the dirt road; it was more like a funeral procession. My grandfather, the bearer directly in front of Grandma's foot, felt a strange premonition blazing inside him and illuminating the path his life would take. The sounds of Grandma's weeping had awakened seeds of affection that had lain dormant deep in his heart.

It was time to rest, so the bearers lowered the sedan chair to the ground. Grandma, having cried herself into a daze, didn't realize that one of her tiny feet was peeking out from beneath the curtain; the sight of that incomparably delicate, lovely thing nearly drove the souls out of the bearers' bodies. Yu Zhan'ao walked up, leaned over, and gently—very gently—held Grandma's foot in his hand, as though it were a fledgling whose feathers weren't yet dry, then eased it back inside the carriage. She was so moved by the gentleness of the deed she could barely keep from throwing back the curtain to see what sort of man this bearer was, with his large, warm, youthful hand.

I've always believed that marriages are made in heaven and that people fated to be together are connected by an invisible thread. The act of grasping Grandma's foot triggered a powerful drive in Yu Zhan'ao to forge a new life for himself, and constituted the turning point in his life—and the turning point in hers as well.

The sedan chair set out again as a trumpet blast rent the air, then drifted off into obscurity. The wind had risen—a northeaster—and clouds were gathering in the sky, blotting out the sun and throwing the carriage into darkness. Grandma could hear the *shh-shh* of rustling sorghum, one wave close upon another, carrying the sound off into the distance. Thunder rumbled off to the northeast. The bearers quickened their pace. She wondered how much farther it was to the Shan household; like a trussed lamb being led to slaughter, she grew calmer with each step. At home she had hidden a pair of scissors in her bodice, perhaps to use on Shan Bianlang, perhaps to use on herself.

The holdup of Grandma's sedan chair by a highwayman at Toad Hollow occupies an important place in the saga of my family. Toad Hollow is a large marshy stretch in the vast flatland where the soil is especially fertile, the water especially plentiful, and the sorghum especially dense. A blood-red bolt of lightning streaked across the northeastern sky, and screaming fragments of apricot-yellow sunlight tore through the dense clouds above the dirt road, when Grandma's sedan chair reached that point. The panting bearers were drenched with sweat as they entered Toad Hollow, over which the air hung heavily.

Sorghum plants lining the road shone like ebony, dense and impenetrable; weeds and wildflowers grew in such profusion they seemed to block the road. Everywhere you looked, narrow stems of cornflowers were bosomed by clumps of rank weeds, their purple, blue, pink, and white flowers waving proudly. From deep in the sorghum came the melancholy croaks of toads, the dreary chirps of grasshoppers, and the plaintive howls of foxes. Grandma, still seated in the carriage, felt a sudden breath of cold air that raised tiny goosebumps on her skin. She didn't know what was happening, even when she heard the shout up ahead:

"Nobody passes without paying a toll!"

Grandma gasped. What was she feeling? Sadness? Joy? My God, she thought, it's a man who eats fistcakes!

Northeast Gaomi Township was aswarm with bandits who operated in the sorghum fields like fish in water, forming gangs to rob, pillage, and kidnap, yet balancing their evil deeds with charitable ones. If they were hungry, they snatched two people, keeping one and sending the other into the village to demand flatbreads with eggs and green onions rolled inside. Since they stuffed the rolled flatbreads into their mouths with both fists, they were called "fistcakes."

"Nobody passes without paying a toll!" the man bellowed. The bearers stopped in their tracks and stared dumbstruck at the highwayman of medium height who stood in the road, his legs akimbo. He had smeared his face black and was wearing a conical rain hat woven of sorghum stalks and a broad-shouldered rain cape open in front to reveal a black buttoned jacket and a wide leather belt, in which a protruding object was tucked, bundled in red satin. His hand rested on it.

The thought flashed through Grandma's mind that there was nothing to be afraid of: if death couldn't frighten her, nothing could. She raised the curtain to get a glimpse of the man who ate fistcakes.

"Hand over the toll, or I'll pop you all!" He patted the red bundle.

The musicians reached into their belts, took out the strings of copper coins Great-Granddad had given them, and tossed these at the man's feet. The bearers lowered the sedan chair to the ground, took out their copper coins, and did the same.

As he dragged the strings of coins into a pile with his foot, his eyes were fixed on Grandma.

"Get behind the sedan chair, all of you. I'll pop if you don't!" He thumped the object tucked into his belt.

The bearers moved slowly behind the sedan chair. Yu Zhan'ao, bringing up the rear, spun around and glared. A change came over the highwayman's face, and he gripped the object at his belt tightly. "Eyes straight ahead if you want to keep breathing!"

With his hand resting on his belt, he shuffled up to the sedan chair, reached out, and pinched Grandma's foot. A smile creased her face, and the man pulled his hand away as though it had been scalded.

"Climb down and come with me!" he ordered her.

Grandma sat without moving, the smile frozen on her face.

"Climb down, I said!"

She rose from the seat, stepped grandly onto the pole, and alit in a tuft of cornflowers. Her gaze traveled from the man to the bearers and musicians.

"Into the sorghum field!" the highwayman said, his hand still resting on the red-bundled object at his belt.

Grandma stood confidently; lightning crackled in the clouds overhead and shattered her radiant smile into a million shifting shards. The highwayman began pushing her into the sorghum field, his hand never leaving the object at his belt. She stared at Yu Zhan'ao with a feverish look in her eyes.

Yu Zhan'ao approached the highwayman, his thin lips curled resolutely, up at one end and down at the other.

"Hold it right there!" the highwayman commanded feebly. "I'll shoot if you take another step!"

Yu Zhan'ao walked calmly up to the man, who began backing up. Green flames seemed to shoot from his eyes, and crystalline beads of sweat scurried down his terrified face. When Yu Zhan'ao had drawn to within three paces of him, a shameful sound burst from his mouth, and he turned and ran. Yu Zhan'ao was on his tail in a flash, kicking him expertly in the rear. He sailed through the air over the cornflowers, thrashing his arms and legs like an innocent babe, until he landed in the sorghum field.

"Spare me, gentlemen! I've got an eighty-year-old mother at home, and this is the only way I can make a living." The highwayman skillfully pleaded his case to Yu Zhan'ao, who grabbed him by the scruff of the neck, dragged him back to the sedan chair, threw him roughly to the ground, and kicked him in his noisy mouth. The man shrieked in pain; blood trickled from his nose.

Yu Zhan'ao reached down, took the thing from the man's belt, and shook off the red cloth covering, to reveal the gnarled knot of a tree. The men all gasped in amazement.

The bandit crawled to his knees, knocking his head on the ground and pleading for his life. "Every highwayman says he's got an eighty-year-old mother at home," Yu Zhan'ao said as he stepped aside and glanced at his comrades, like the leader of a pack sizing up the other dogs.

With a flurry of shouts, the bearers and musicians fell upon the highwayman, fists and feet flying. The initial onslaught was met by screams and shrill cries, which soon died out. Grandma stood beside the road listening to the dull cacophony of fists and feet on flesh; she glanced at Yu Zhan'ao, then looked up at the lightning-streaked sky, the radiant, golden, noble smile still frozen on her face.

One of the musicians raised his trumpet and brought it down hard on the highwayman's skull, burying the curved edge so deeply he had to strain to free it. The highwayman's stomach gurgled and his body, racked by spasms, grew deathly still; he lay spread-eagled on the ground, a mixture of white and yellow liquid seeping slowly out of the fissure in his skull.

"Is he dead?" asked the musician, who was examining the bent mouth of his trumpet.

"He's gone, the poor bastard. He didn't put up much of a fight!"

The gloomy faces of the bearers and musicians revealed their anxieties.

Yu Zhan'ao looked wordlessly first at the dead, then at the living. With a handful of leaves from a sorghum stalk, he cleaned up Grandma's mess in the carriage, then held up the tree knot, wrapped it in the piece of red cloth, and tossed the bundle as far as he could; the gnarled knot broke free in flight and separated from the piece of cloth, which fluttered to the ground in the field like a big red butterfly.

Yu Zhan'ao lifted Grandma into the sedan chair. "It's starting to rain," he said, "so let's get going."

Grandma ripped the curtain from the front of the carriage and stuffed it behind the seat. As she breathed the free air she studied Yu Zhan'ao's broad shoulders and narrow waist. He was so near she could have touched the pale, taut skin of his shaved head with her toe.

The winds were picking up, bending the sorghum stalks in ever deeper waves, those on the roadside stretching out to bow their respects to Grandma. The bearers streaked down the road, yet the sedan chair was as steady as a skiff skimming across whitecaps. Frogs and toads croaked in loud welcome to the oncoming summer rainstorm. The low curtain of heaven stared darkly at the silvery faces of sorghum, over which streaks of blood-red lightning crackled, releasing ear-splitting explosions of thunder. With growing excitement, Grandma stared fearlessly at the green waves raised by the black winds.

The first truculent raindrops made the plants shudder. The rain beat a loud tattoo on the sedan chair and fell on Grandma's embroidered slippers; it fell on Yu Zhan'ao's head, then slanted in on Grandma's face.

The bearers ran like scared jackrabbits, but couldn't escape the prenoon deluge. Sorghum crumpled under the wild rain. Toads took refuge under the stalks, their white pouches popping in and out noisily; foxes hid in their darkened dens to watch tiny drops of water splashing down from the sorghum plants. The rainwater washed Yu Zhan'ao's head so clean and shiny it looked to Grandma like a new moon. Her clothes, too, were soaked. She could have covered herself with the curtain, but she didn't; she didn't want to, for the open front of the sedan chair afforded her a glimpse of the outside world in all its turbulence and beauty.

6

FATHER PARTED THE SORGHUM and threaded his way northwest, toward our village, as fast as his legs would carry him. Badgers with humanlike feet scattered clumsily across the ditches, but he ignored them. Once he was on the road, and didn't have to worry about getting tangled up in the sorghum plants, he ran like the wind, his red cotton waistband sagging like a crescent moon under the weight of his Browning. Although the pistol banged painfully against his hip, the growing numbness made him feel like a real man—powerful, even invincible. He could see the village in the distance. The gloomy, faded gingko tree at the entrance, which had stood for nearly a century, waited in somber greeting. As he ran, he took the pistol from his waistband and aimed at birds gliding gracefully in the sky above him.

The street was deserted, except for somebody's lame, blind donkey, which was tethered to a crumbling wall; it stood motionless, its head drooping low. A solitary crow with wet dark-blue feathers was perched on a stone-roller. The villagers had gathered in the distillery compound, which had been paved with red gravel in the days when sorghum was purchased and stacked there, back when Grandma ambled unsteadily on her tiny feet, a white horsetail whisk in her hand and the glow of dawn in her cheeks, as she watched the drunken hands buy sorghum. Now the people faced southeast, awaiting the sound of gunfire. Children my father's age were uncharacteristically well behaved, no matter how they itched to act up.

Father and Sun Five, who had skinned and butchered Uncle Arhat the year before, ran into the square from different directions. Sun Five hadn't been the same since the skinning. Arms and legs thrashing, eyes staring straight ahead, cheeks twitching, a stream of gibberish pouring from his foaming mouth, he had fallen to his knees and shouted, "Elder brother elder brother elder brother, Commander made me do it, couldn't help myself. . . . You exist in heaven, where you ride a white horse on a carved saddle, wear fine clothes, carry a golden whip. . . ." When the villagers saw him like this, their loathing abated. A few months after he went mad, his behavior turned truly bizarre: He would begin shouting, and the corners of his eyes and mouth would turn up as snot and slobber dripped unchecked. No one could make any sense of his gibberish, and the villagers called it heavenly retribution.

Father ran up breathlessly, Browning in hand, his head covered with white sorghum powder and red dust. The ragged Sun Five, his belly a mass of wrinkles, stumbled into the square, his left leg rigid, his right leg rubbery. Everyone ignored him, for they were all too busy watching the impressive figure of my father.

Grandma walked up to him. Although still in her early thirties at the time, she wore her hair in a bun, neat bangs covering her shiny forehead like a beaded curtain. Her eyes were as moist as autumn rains; people blamed that on the wine fumes. More than fifteen years of romantic, soul-stirring adventures had turned her from a virginal teenager into a bold young woman.

"What's wrong?" she asked.

Still trying to catch his breath, Father stuck his Browning into his waistband.

"Didn't the Japs come?"

"We won't show that son of a bitch Detachment Leader Leng any mercy!" Father exclaimed.

"What happened?"

"Make some fistcakes."

"We didn't hear any fighting."

"Make some fistcakes," Father repeated. "And put in plenty of eggs and onions."

"Didn't the Japs come?" Grandma persisted.

"Commander Yu said to make some fistcakes, and he wants *you* to deliver them!"

"Fellow villagers," she said, "go home and make fistcakes."

Father turned to go, but Grandma stopped him. "Tell me what happened with the Leng detachment, Douguan."

He wrenched free of her grip and snarled, "They never showed up. Commander Yu isn't going to let them get away with it!" He ran off, leaving Grandma sighing as she watched the slight silhouette of his back. Sun Five was standing at a tilt in the spacious compound, staring stiffly at Grandma and gesticulating wildly, a stream of slobber running down his chin.

Ignoring Sun Five, Grandma walked up to a long-faced girl leaning against the wall, who smiled weakly, then fell to her knees, wrapped her arms tightly around Grandma's waist, and began to cry hysterically. "Lingzi," Grandma consoled her, touching her face, "be a good girl. Don't be afraid."

The prettiest girl in the village, Lingzi was seventeen at the time. When Commander Yu was recruiting troops, he assembled fifty or so men, one of whom was a gaunt young man with a pale face and long black hair, dressed in black except for a pair of white shoes. Lingzi was rumored to be in love with him. He spoke with a beautiful Beijing dialect, and never smiled; his brow was forever creased in a frown, with three vertical furrows above his nose. Everyone called him Adjutant Ren. Lingzi felt that beneath Adjutant Ren's cold, hard exterior raged a fire, and it put her on edge.

Yu Zhan'ao's troops drilled each morning on the square where we bought our sorghum. As soon as Liu Sishan, Commander Yu's bugler, sounded reveille, Lingzi dashed out of the house and ran to the parade ground to lie on the wall and await the arrival of Adjutant Ren, his wide leather belt and Browning pistol.

Adjutant Ren strode up to the troops, his chest thrown out proudly, and called them to attention. Two columns of soldiers clicked their heels snappily.

Adjutant Ren commanded, "Atten-hut! Legs straight, stomachs in, chests out, eyes forward, like panthers about to pounce.

"What the hell kind of way is that to stand?" He kicked Wang Wenyi. "Your legs are spread like a mule taking a piss. I'd beat some discipline into you if I could."

Lingzi liked seeing Adjutant Ren beat up on people and liked the way he chewed them out. His autocratic demeanor thoroughly intoxicated her. His favorite leisure activity was strolling around the parade ground with his hands clasped behind his back. Lingzi would hide behind the wall and drink in the sight.

"What's your name?" Adjutant Ren asked.

"Lingzi."

"Who were you watching from back there?"

"You."

"Do you know how to read?"

"No."

"Want to join the army?"

"No."

"I see."

Regretting her response, Lingzi told my father that the next time Adjutant Ren asked her if she wanted to join the army she'd say yes. But he never asked her again.

Lingzi and my father were sprawled atop the wall watching Adjutant Ren teach the men revolutionary songs. Father was so short at the time that he had to stand on a pile of rocks to see what was happening on the other side of the wall, while Lingzi rested her pretty chin on the wall and stared at Adjutant Ren, drenched in morning sunlight, as he taught them a song: "The sorghum is red, the sorghum is red, the Japs are coming, the Japs are coming. The nation is lost, our families scattered. Rise up, countrymen, take up arms to drive out the Japs and protect your homes. . . ."

The men, with tin ears and stiff tongues, never did learn how to sing it right, but the kids on the other side of the wall soon had it down pat. My father never forgot this song as long as he lived.

Lingzi screwed up her courage one day and went to find Adjutant Ren, but accidentally stumbled into the room of the quartermaster, Big Tooth Yu, a hard-drinking, insatiably lecherous forty-year-old uncle of Commander Yu. He was pretty drunk that day, and when Lingzi burst into his room, it was like a moth drawn to a fire, or a lamb entering a tiger's den.

Adjutant Ren ordered two soldiers to tie up the man who had deflowered the girl Lingzi. At the time, Commander Yu was staying at our house, and when Adjutant Ren came to make his report, he was asleep on Grandma's kang. She had already washed up and brushed her hair, and was about to fry some willowfish to go with the wine when the fuming Adjutant Ren burst into the room, frightening the wits out of her.

"Where's the commander?" Adjutant Ren asked her.

"He's on the kang, asleep."

"Wake him up."

Grandma woke Commander Yu, who walked out of the bedroom, stretched, yawned, and asked, "What is it?"

"Commander, if a Japanese raped my sister, should he be shot?"

"Of course!" Commander Yu replied.

"If a Chinese raped my sister, should he be shot?"

"Of course!"

"That's just what I wanted to hear," Adjutant Ren said. "Big Tooth Yu deflowered the local girl Cao Lingzi, and I've ordered the men to tie him up."

"Are you sure he did it?"

"When will he be shot, Commander?"

Commander Yu sucked in his breath. "Since when is sleeping with a woman a serious offense?"

"Commander, no one's above the law, not even a prince."

"And what do you think the punishment should be?" Commander Yu asked somberly.

"A firing squad!" Adjutant Ren replied without hesitation.

Commander Yu sucked in his breath again and began to pace impatiently, anger building up inside him. Finally, he smiled and said, "Adjutant Ren, what do you say we give him fifty lashes in front of the men and compensate Lingzi's family with twenty silver dollars?"

"Because he's your uncle?" Adjutant Ren asked caustically.

"Eighty lashes, then, and force him to marry Lingzi. I'll even call her Auntie!"

Adjutant Ren undid his belt and tossed it, along with the Browning pistol, to Commander Yu. Holding his hands in a salute in front of him, he said, "This will make it easier for both of us." He turned and walked out into the yard.

Commander Yu, pistol in hand, stared at Adjutant Ren's retreating back and growled through clenched teeth, "Go on, get the fuck out of here! No damned schoolboy is going to tell me what to do! In the ten years I ate fistcakes, nobody was that insolent to me."

"Zhan'ao," Grandma said, "you can't let Adjutant Ren go. Soldiers are easy to recruit, but generals are worth their weight in gold."

"Women don't understand these things!" Commander Yu said in frustration.

"I always thought you were tough, not spineless!"

Commander Yu aimed the pistol at her. "Have you lived long enough?" he snarled.

She tore open her shirt, exposing two tender mounds of flesh, and challenged him: "Go ahead, shoot!"

With a shout of "Mom!" Father rushed in and buried his head between her breasts.

As he looked at Father's neat, round head and Grandma's beautiful face, a torrent of memories flooded Granddad's mind. With a sigh, he lowered the pistol. "Button up," he said as he walked outside. Riding crop in hand, he untied his sleek brown colt and rode bareback to the parade ground.

When the troops relaxing on the wall saw Commander Yu ride up, they jumped to attention and held their breath.

Big Tooth Yu, his arms bound behind him, was tied to a tree.

Commander Yu dismounted and walked up to him. "Did you really do it?"

"Zhan'ao," he said, "untie me. I'll leave."

The soldiers stared wide-eyed at Commander Yu.

"Uncle," he said, "I'm going to have you shot."

"You bastard!" Big Tooth Yu bellowed. "You'd shoot your own uncle? Have you forgotten what I did for you? After your father died, I took care of you and your mother. If not for me, you'd have been dog food long ago!"

Commander Yu smacked him across the face with his riding crop. "You no-good bastard!" he railed before falling to his knees and saying, "Uncle, I, Yu Zhan'ao, will never forget your kindness in bringing me up. I will wear mourning clothes after your death and will memorialize you and tend your grave on all the holidays."

With that he jumped to his feet, mounted his horse, whipped it on the flank, and galloped off in the direction Adjutant Ren had taken. The horse's hooves shook the earth.

Father was there when they shot Big Tooth Yu. Mute and two other soldiers dragged him to the western edge of the village, choosing as the execution ground a spot beside a crescent-shaped inlet in a stream of black, stagnant, insect-laden water. A solitary willow tree, its leaves yellowed and dying, stood on the bank. The stillness of the bend was broken only by hopping toads; alongside a pile of damp hair clippings lay a single tattered woman's slipper.

They dragged Big Tooth Yu up to the edge of the inlet and stood him there, then looked at Mute, who unslung his rifle and cocked it; a bullet snapped into the chamber.

Big Tooth Yu turned to face Mute and smiled. To Father's eyes, it was a kindly, heartfelt smile, like the miserable dying rays of a setting sun.

"Untie me, Mute. I shouldn't die all trussed up!"

Mute thought for a moment before walking up, rifle in hand,

taking his knife from his waistband, and deftly cutting the ropes. Big Tooth Yu massaged his arms, then made a quarter-turn and shouted, "Shoot, Mute. Aim for my temple. Don't make me suffer!"

To Father's mind, a man at the point of death suddenly commands the respect of all other men. Big Tooth Yu was, after all, the seed of Northeast Gaomi Township. He had committed a grave offense that even death would not expiate, yet, as he prepared to die, he displayed the airs of a true hero; Father was so moved at that moment that he felt like leaping in the air.

Big Tooth Yu gazed down at the stagnant water, where green lotus leaves and a sole white blossom floated; his gaze then took in the shimmering stalks of sorghum on the opposite bank. In a loud voice he broke into song: "The sorghum is red, the sorghum is red, the Japs are coming, the Japs are coming. The nation is lost, our families scattered. . . ."

Mute raised his rifle, then lowered it, raised it and lowered it.

"Mute," the soldiers pleaded, "talk to Commander Yu. Let him go!"

Gripping his rifle tightly, Mute listened to Big Tooth Yu butcher the song.

Big Tooth Yu turned back, his eyes wide with anger, and screamed, "Go ahead and shoot! You're not going to make me do it myself, are you?"

Raising his rifle one last time, Mute took aim at Big Tooth Yu's tilelike forehead and pulled the trigger.

Father saw Big Tooth Yu's forehead explode into fragments even before the dull crack of rifle fire reached his ears. Mute stood with bowed head, the echo of the shot still hanging in the air, wisps of white smoke rising from the muzzle of his rifle. Big Tooth Yu's body froze for a second before plummeting into the water below like a felled tree.

Mute walked off, dragging his rifle behind him, followed by the two soldiers.

Father and a bunch of other kids crept timidly over to the inlet, where they could look down at Big Tooth Yu, whose body lay face up in the mud. All that was left of his face was the perfectly formed mouth. The fluids of his brain had oozed into his ears from the shattered scalp, and one of his eyeballs hung from the socket like a huge grape on his cheek. The white lotus blossom, its stem broken and trailing several white threads, lay next to his hand. Father could smell its perfume.

Now that it was over, Adjutant Ren brought up a cypress coffin with a thick layer of varnish and a yellow satin lining, into which he placed the neatly dressed body; following a proper funeral ceremony, Big Tooth Yu was buried beneath the little willow tree. Adjutant Ren wore his dapper black uniform to the funeral and had his hair slicked down neatly. A strip of red silk was wrapped around his left arm. Commander Yu, in hempen mourning clothes, wailed loudly, and as the procession left the village, he smashed a brand-new ceramic bowl against a brick.

Grandma made a set of white mourning clothes for Father—she wore sackcloth. Father, fresh willow switch in hand as he walked behind Commander Yu and Grandma, witnessed the smashing of the ceramic bowl against the brick, and was reminded of Big Tooth Yu's splintered forehead. He had a vague inkling that the two events were somehow linked. The collision of one event with another always produces a third inevitability.

Father looked on dispassionately, without shedding a tear, as the procession formed a ring around the willow tree, and sixteen robust young men slowly lowered the coffin into the yawning grave with eight thick ropes. Commander Yu scooped up a handful of dirt and flung it down on the glossy coffin lid. The thud resounded in everyone's heart. The men began shoveling dirt into the grave, drawing angry rumbles from the coffin as it slowly disappeared into the black soil, which rose higher and higher, until it filled the grave, then formed a mound like a steamed bun. Commander Yu fired three shots into the air above the willow tree, the bullets tearing through the crown of the tree, one after another, to shear off yellow leaves like fine eyebrows, which fluttered in the air. Three shiny casings leaped into the putrid water of the inlet, and were immediately retrieved by a boy who jumped down, his feet squishing in the soft green mud. Adjutant Ren took out his Browning and pulled off three shots, which shrieked like roosters as they sped above the sorghum. Commander Yu and Adjutant Ren faced each other, smoking guns in their hands. Adjutant Ren nodded. "He did himself proud!" He stuck his pistol into his belt and strode into the village.

Father watched Commander Yu slowly raise his weapon and aim it at Adjutant Ren's retreating back. The funeral party was stunned, but no one made a sound. Adjutant Ren, unaware of what was happening, strode confidently into the village, the bright yellow gear-wheel in the sky shining in his face. Father saw the pistol jerk once, but the explosion was so weak and so distant he wasn't sure he heard it. He watched the bullet's low trajectory as it parted Adjutant Ren's shiny black hair before moving on. Without so much as turning his head or breaking stride, Adjutant Ren continued on into the village.

The sound of whistling drifted toward Father's ears. It was the familiar sound of "The sorghum is red, the sorghum is red!" Hot tears filled his eyes. The receding figure of Adjutant Ren grew larger and larger. Commander Yu fired another shot; this time it was so loud it rocked the earth and startled the heavens. Father saw the bullet's flight and heard the explosion at the same time. The bullet struck a sorghum plant, severing its head, which was shattered by a second bullet as it settled slowly to the ground. Father was vaguely aware that Adjutant Ren bent over and plucked the yellow blossom from a bitterweed at the roadside, then held it up to his nose and savored its fragrance for a long time.

Father told me that Adjutant Ren was a rarity, a true hero; unfortunately, heroes are fated to die young. Three months after he had walked so proudly away from the heroic gathering, his Browning pistol went off while he was cleaning it and killed him. The bullet entered his right eye and exited through his right ear, leaving half of his face covered with a metallic blue powder. A mere three or four drops of blood seeped out of his right ear, and by the time the people who heard the shot had rushed over, he was lying dead on the ground.

Wordlessly, Commander Yu picked up Adjutant Ren's Browning pistol.

7

GRANDMA, CARRYING BASKETS OF FISTCAKES on the pole over her shoulder, and Wang Wenyi's wife, carrying two pails of mung-bean soup, rushed toward the bridge across the Black Water River. Though they had planned at first to head southeast through the sorghum field, they found the going too hard. "Let's take the road, Sister-in-Law," Grandma suggested. "The long way round is fastest."

They were like high-flying birds making good headway through the open sky. Grandma had put on a scarlet jacket and oiled her hair until it glistened like ebony. Wang's wife, a vigorous but diminutive woman, was nimble on her feet. Back when Commander Yu was recruiting troops, she had brought Wenyi over to the house and asked Grandma to speak to Commander Yu to sign him up as a guerrilla. Grandma had promised she would, and Commander Yu had taken him on for her sake.

"Are you afraid of dying?" Commander Yu had asked him.

"Yes."

"When he says yes he means no, Commander," Wang's wife had explained. "Japanese planes bombed our three sons into pulp."

Wang Wenyi was not cut out to be a soldier. His reactions were slow, and he couldn't tell his right from his left. During marching drills on the parade ground, he was hit by Adjutant Ren more times than you could count. His wife had an idea: he would carry a sorghum stem in his right hand, so when he heard a right-turn command he'd turn in that direction. Since he had no weapon, Grandma gave him our fowling piece.

When the women reached the bank of the twisting Black Water River they headed south, without stopping to enjoy the chrysanthemums on the bank or the dense thickets of blood-red sorghum beyond it. Wang Wenyi's wife had lived a life of suffering, Grandma one of privilege. Grandma was drenched with sweat, Wang Wenyi's wife was as dry as a bone.

Father had since returned to the bridgehead, where he reported to Commander Yu that the fistcakes would be there soon. Commander Yu patted him on the head for a job well done. Most of the soldiers lay around the sorghum field, soaking up the sun. Growing fidgety with impatience, Father strolled over to the field west of the road to see what Mute and his troops were up to. Mute was still honing his knife, so Father stopped in front of him, his hand resting on the

Browning at his belt, a victor's smile on his face. Mute looked up and grinned broadly.

Father presumed that the four linked rakes blocking the road, their teeth pointing skyward, must have reached the limits of their patience. The stone bridge spanning the river looked like an invalid just beginning his recovery. Father walked up to the dike and sat down, looking first east, then west, then to the river flowing beneath him, and finally to some wild ducks. The river was beautiful, owing to its profusion of living plants and tiny whitecaps, each filled with mystery. He spotted piles of white bones resting in thickets of reeds, and remembered our two big black mules.

In the spring, throngs of rabbits run wild in the fields. Grandma rides her mule, rifle in hand, as she hunts rabbits, with Father sitting behind her, his arms wrapped around her waist. Frightened by the mule, the rabbits fall easy prey to Grandma's shots. She invariably returns home with a string of rabbits around the mule's neck. A steel pellet once lodged between two of her back teeth when she was eating wild rabbit, and no amount of prying could dislodge it.

Father watched a column of dark red ants transport mud pebbles across the dike. When he laid a dirt clod in their way, they strained to climb over it instead of skirting it. He picked it up and heaved it into the river, where it broke the surface without a sound. Now that the sun was overhead, a fishy smell drifted over on the hot air. Bright glimmers of light flashed everywhere and made the area sizzle. It seemed to Father that the space between heaven and earth was filled with the red dust of sorghum and the fragrance of sorghum wine. He stretched out on the dike, face up, and in that moment his heart leaped into his throat; later on he realized that patience is always rewarded, and that the consequences of his waiting were perfectly common, ordinary, casual, and natural. For he had spotted four strange dark-green, beetlelike objects crawling noiselessly toward him on the highway that cut through the sorghum fields.

"Trucks," he muttered ambiguously. He was ignored.

"Jap trucks!" He scrambled to his feet, panic-stricken, and stared at the trucks streaking toward him like meteors, trailing long dark tails and preceded by crackling, swaying incandescent rays of light.

"Here come the trucks!" His words were a sword that decapitated the men with a single stroke. A dull silence settled over the sorghum field.

"Men," Commander Yu roared joyfully, "they're here after all. Get ready. And don't fire until I give the order."

On the west side of the road Mute jumped to his feet and slapped himself on the hip. Dozens of guerrillas crouched on the slope, weapons ready. They could hear the roar of the engines. Father lay at Commander Yu's side, gripping the heavy Browning so tightly that his wrist was soon hot and tingly, his palm sticky with sweat. The fleshy place between his thumb and forefinger twitched once, and was soon racked with spasms. In amazement, he watched the almond-sized spot jump rhythmically, like a chick trying to break out of its egg. He wanted to stop it, but was squeezing so tightly his arm began to tremble. Commander Yu laid his hand on Father's back, and the twitch stopped. He switched the Browning to his left hand, but the muscles of his right hand were so cramped it seemed forever before he could straighten his fingers.

The fast-approaching trucks were getting larger and larger, the eyes in front, as large as horse hooves, sweeping the area with their white rays. Their revving engines sounded like the wind before a downpour. Having never actually *seen* a truck before, Father assumed that these strange creatures survived on grass or some sort of fodder, and that they drank water or blood. They moved faster than our two strong, spindly-legged mules; the moon-shaped tires spun so fast they sent clouds of yellow dust soaring into the air. As they neared the stone bridge, the lead truck slowed down, allowing the clouds of dust to catch up and settle over the hood, obscuring the twenty or more khaki-clad men in the bed, shiny steel pots on their heads. Father subsequently learned that these pots were called "helmets." (In 1958, during the backyard-furnace campaign of the Great Leap Forward, when our wok was confiscated, my elder brother swiped a helmet from a pile of metal and brought it home to use as a cookpot. Father watched in fascination as the helmet changed color in the smoke and fire.)

The two trucks in the middle were stacked with small mountains of white sacks; the one bringing up the rear, like the one in front, was loaded with twenty or more Japanese soldiers.

They had nearly reached the dike, and their tires, spinning more slowly now, appeared swollen and awkward. The square nose of the lead truck reminded Father of the head of an enormous locust. As the yellow dust began to settle, loud farts created a dark blue mist at the rear.

Father scrunched his head down as a chill the likes of which he'd never known worked its way up from his feet to his belly. He shifted his buttocks back and forth to keep from wetting his pants. "Don't move, you little shit!" Commander Yu complained sternly.

Feeling as though his bladder were about to burst, Father got permission to crawl down and pee.

Once he had retreated into the sorghum field he released a mighty stream the color of red sorghum, which stung the head of his pecker as it gushed forth. Enormously relieved when he had finished, he glanced casually at the guerrillas' faces, whose expressions made them appear as malevolent and scary as temple icons. Wang Wenyi's tongue poked out between his lips; his staring eyeballs seemed frozen, like a lizard's.

The trucks, huge beasts on the prowl, held their breath as they crept forward. Something aromatic struck Father's nostrils. Just then Grandma, in her sweat-stained red silk jacket, and the panting wife of Wang Wenyi appeared on the dike of the meandering Black Water River.

Grandma with her baskets of fistcakes and Wang Wenyi's wife with her pails of mung-bean soup gazed at the miserable stone bridge across the Black Water River, feeling very much at ease. Grandma turned to Wang's wife and said with relief, "We made it, Sister-in-Law." Ever since her marriage, Grandma had lived a life of ease and comfort, and the carrying pole, with its heavy load of fistcakes, dug deeply into her delicate shoulder, leaving a dark-purple bruise that would accompany her as she departed this world and traveled to the kingdom of heaven. The bruise would be the glorious symbol of a heroic figure from the war of resistance.

Father was the first to see her. While the others were following the slow progress of the trucks with unblinking eyes, some secret force told him to look to the west, where he spotted her floating toward them like a gorgeous red butterfly. "Mom—"

His shout was like a command: a hail of bullets tore through the air from three machine guns mounted on the Japanese trucks. The sound was dull and muted, like the gloomy barking of dogs on a rainy night. Father watched as two shells opened holes in the breast of Grandma's jacket. She cried out in ecstasy, then crumpled to the ground, her carrying pole falling across her back. One of the baskets of fistcakes rolled down the southern slope of the dike, the other down the northern slope. Snow-white cakes, green onions, and diced eggs were scattered in the grass on both sides of the dike.

After Grandma fell, a mixture of red and yellow fluid from the boxy skull of Wang Wenyi's wife sprayed the area all the way to the sorghum stalks beside the dike. Father watched the diminutive woman stagger backward as the bullet hit her, then topple down the southern slope of the dike and roll into the water. The contents of one pail of mung-bean soup spilled onto the ground, followed by the second, like the blood of heroes. The first pail clanked down the dike into the Black Water River, then bobbed to the surface. It floated down past Mute, banged one or two times into a stanchion, then was picked up by the current and carried past Commander Yu, past my father, past Wang Wenyi, past Fang Six and Fang Seven.

"Mom—" Father screamed as though his guts were being ripped out as he leaped to the top of the dike. Commander Yu tried to grab him, but was too late. "Come back here!" he bellowed. Father didn't hear the command, he didn't hear anything. His skinny little frame flew along the narrow ridge of the dike, shimmering in the sun's rays. He threw down his Browning pistol, which landed amid the torn leaves of a golden bitterweed. He ran like the wind, his arms thrust out in front like wings, as he ran toward Grandma. The dike was still, but dust swirled noisily; the glimmering water stopped flowing. The sorghum beyond the dike remained dignified and solemn. Father was still running along the dike: Father was a giant, Father was magnificent, Father was gorgeous. He screamed at the top of his lungs: "Mom—Mom—Mom—" A single word drenched with human blood and tears, with deep familial love, with the loftiest of causes. When he reached the end of the eastern dike, he jumped over the rake barrier and scrambled up the western bank. Beneath the dike, the stony face of Mute sped by.

Father threw himself down on Grandma and called out "Mom!" one more time. She lay face down on the ground, pressed against the wild grass. The aroma of sorghum wine seeped from two exit wounds in her back. Father gripped her shoulders and rolled her over. There were no wounds on her face, which looked the same as always. Not a hair was out of place; bangs neatly covered her forehead; her brows drooped slightly. Her eyes were half open; the lips on her pale face showed up bright red. Father grasped her warm hand and called "Mom!" yet another time. She opened her eyes wide as a smile of supreme innocence spread across her face. She reached out to him.

The idling engines of the Jap trucks, which had stopped at the bridgehead, revved intermittently.

A tall figure appeared briefly on the dike to drag Father and Grandma down off the top. It was Mute, to his everlasting credit. Before Father had a chance to get his bearings, another gale of bullets truncated and smashed countless stalks of sorghum.

The four trucks closed up ranks just beyond the bridge, then stopped. Eight machine guns mounted on the first and last trucks were spraying so many bullets they formed hard ribbons of crisscrossing light that spread like broken fans, sometimes to the east of the road, sometimes to the west. Sorghum stalks wailed in concert, their shattered, severed limbs drooping low or arching high into the air. Bullets raised puffs of yellow dust on the dike and produced a tattoo of muffled thuds.

The soldiers on the outer slopes flattened themselves against the wild grass and black dirt, keeping perfectly still. The machine guns strafed the area for about three minutes, then stopped as abruptly as they had begun. The ground around the trucks was littered with the golden flashes of spent casings.

"Hold your fire," Commander Yu ordered softly.

The Japs were silent. Thin wisps of gunsmoke floated above the river, carried eastward by gentle air currents.

Father told me that in that moment of absolute quiet Wang Wenyi stumbled up onto the dike, where he stood stock-still, fowling piece in hand, wide-eyed and open-mouthed, the picture of great suffering. "Mother of my children!" he shrieked. Before he could take another step, dozens of machine-gun shells ripped a nearly transparent crescent moon in his belly. Gut-stained bullets tore wetly through the air above Commander Yu's head.

Wang Wenyi toppled off the dike and rolled into the water directly opposite the body of his wife. His heart was still beating, and there wasn't a mark on his head or face; a sense of perfect understanding flooded his mind.

Father once told me that Wang Wenyi's wife had fed her three sons so well they grew up chubby, lively, and flourishing. One day they went out to tend the sorghum, leaving their sons behind to play in the yard. A Japanese biplane streaked through the air above their house, making a strange growling sound as it laid a single egg, a direct hit on Wang Wenyi's yard, blowing all three children to bits that flew up to the eaves, were draped on the branches of trees, stained the wall. . . . On the day Commander Yu raised the flag of resistance against the Japanese, Wang Wenyi was brought over by his wife. . . .

Gnashing his teeth with rage, Commander Yu glared down at Wang Wenyi, half of whose head lay submerged in the river. "Don't any of you move!" he snarled in a low voice.

8

SCATTERED SORGHUM DANCES on Grandma's face, one grain landing between her slightly parted lips to rest on flawless white teeth. As he gazes at her lips, which are gradually losing their color, Father sobs "Mom," and his tears fall on her breast. She opens her eyes amid the pearly drops of sorghum. Rainbows of color, as though reflected off the pearls, are embedded in her eyes. "Son," she says, "your dad . . ."

"My dad, he's fighting."

"He's your real dad . . ." Grandma says. Father nods.

She struggles to sit up, but the movement of her body pumps streams of blood out of the two holes.

"Mom, I'll go get him," Father says.

She waves her hand and sits up abruptly. "Douguan . . . my son . . . help your mom up. . . . Let's go home, go home. . . ."

Father falls to his knees, drapes her arms around his neck, then stands up with difficulty, lifting her off the ground. Fresh blood quickly soaks his neck and assails his nose with the aroma of sorghum wine. His legs tremble under the weight of her body; he staggers into the sorghum field as bullets whizz overhead. He parts the densely packed plants, stumbling forward, his sweat and his tears merging with Grandma's fresh blood to turn his face into a demented mask. Grandma is getting heavier as the passing sorghum leaves lacerate him mercilessly. He falls, she falls on top of him. He strains to crawl out from under her, and after he lays her out on her back, she looks up, breathes a long sigh, and smiles weakly. Unfathomable mystery is embedded in that smile, an iron that burns a horseshoe brand into his memory.

Grandma lies on the ground, the warmth of her breast slowly dissipating. She is dimly aware that her son is undoing her jacket, that he is covering the wound over her breast with his hand, then the wound beneath her breast. Her blood stains his hand red, then green; her unsullied breast is stained green by her own blood, then red. Bullets have pierced her noble breast, exposing the pink honeycomb beneath it, and Father is in agony as he looks down at it. He cannot staunch the flow of blood, and as he watches it flow he can see her face pale. Her body grows so light it might float up into the air.

Grandma looks contentedly at Father's exquisite face. She and Commander Yu had joined to create him in the shadows of the sorghum field; lively images of the irretrievable past streak past her eyes like racehorses.

It was raining as she sat in the bridal sedan chair, like a boat on the ocean, and was carried into Shan Tingxiu's compound. The street was flooded with water, peppered by a layer of sorghum seeds. At the front door she was met by a wizened old man with a tiny queue in the shape of a kidney bean. The rain had stopped, but an occasional drop splashed onto the watery ground. Although the musicians had announced her arrival with their instruments, no one had emerged to watch the show; Grandma knew that was a bad sign. Two men came out to help her perform her obeisances, one in his fifties, the other in his forties. The fifty-year-old was none other than Uncle Arhat Liu, the other was one of the distillery hands.

The musicians and bearers stood in the puddles like drenched chickens, somberly watching the two dried-up men lead my soft-limbed, rosy-cheeked grandma into the dark wedding-chamber. The men exuded a pungent aroma of wine, as if they had been soaked in the vats.

Grandma was taken up to a kang in the worship hall and told to sit on it. Since no one came up to remove her red veil, she took it off herself. A man with a facial tic sat curled up on a stool next to her. The bottom part of his flat, elongated face was red and festering. He stood up and stuck a clawlike hand out toward Grandma, who screamed in horror and reached into her bodice for the scissors; she glared intently at the man, who recoiled and curled up on the stool again. Grandma didn't set down her scissors once that night, nor did the man climb down from his stool.

Early the next morning, before the man woke up, Grandma slipped down off the kang, burst through the front door, and opened the gate; just as she was about to flee the premises, a hand reached out and grabbed her. The old man with the kidney-bean queue had her by the wrist and was looking at her with hate-filled eyes.

Shan Tingxiu coughed dryly once or twice as his expression softened. "Child," he said, "now that you're married, you're like my own daughter. Bianlang doesn't have what everybody says. Don't listen to their talk. We've got a good business, and Bianlang's a good boy. Now that you're here, the home is your responsibility." Shan Tingxiu held out to her a ring of bronze keys, but she didn't take them from him.

Grandma sat up all the next night, scissors in hand.

On the morning of the third day, my maternal great-granddad led a donkey up to the house to take Grandma home; it was a Northeast Gaomi Township custom for a bride to return to her parents' home three days after her wedding. Great-Granddad spent the morning drinking with Shan Tingxiu, then set out for home shortly after noon.

Grandma sat sidesaddle on the donkey, swaying from side to side as the animal left the village. Even though it hadn't rained for three days, the road was still wet, and steam rose from the sorghum in the fields, the green stalks shrouded in swirling whiteness, as though in the presence of immortals. Great-Granddad's silver coins clinked and jingled in the saddlebags. He was so drunk he could barely walk, and his eyes were glassy. The donkey proceeded slowly, its long neck bobbing up and down, its tiny hooves leaving muddy imprints. Grandma had only ridden a short distance when she began to get lightheaded; her eyes were red and puffy, her hair mussed, and the sorghum in the fields, a full joint taller than it had been three days earlier, mocked her as she passed.

"Dad," Grandma called out, "I don't want to go back there anymore. I'll kill myself before I go back there again. . . ."

"Daughter," Great-Granddad replied, "you have no idea how lucky you are. Your father-in-law said he's going to give me a big black mule. I'm going to sell this runty little thing. . . ."

The donkey nibbled some mud-splattered grass that lined the road.

"Dad," Grandma sobbed, "he's got leprosy. . . ."

"Your father-in-law is going to give me a mule. . . ."

Great-Granddad, drunk as a lord, kept vomiting into the weeds by the side of the road. The filth and bile set Grandma's stomach churning, and she felt nothing but loathing for him.

As the donkey walked into Toad Hollow, they were met by an overpowering stench that caused its ears to droop. Grandma spotted the highwayman's bloated corpse, which was covered by a layer of emerald-colored flies. The donkey skirted the corpse, sending the flies swarming angrily into the air to form a green cloud. Great-Granddad followed the donkey, his body seemingly wider than the road itself: one moment he was stumbling into the sorghum to the left of the road, the next moment he was trampling on weeds to the right. And when he reached the corpse, he gasped "Oh!" several times, and said through quaking lips, "Poor beggar . . . you poor beggar . . . you sleeping there? . . ." Grandma never forgot the highwayman's pumpkin face. In that instant when the flies swarmed into the air she was struck by the remarkable contrast between the graceful elegance of his dead face and the mean, cowardly expression he'd worn in life.

The distance between them lengthened, one li at a time, with the sun's rays slanting down, the sky high and clear; the donkey quickly outpaced Great-Granddad. Since it knew the way home, it carried Grandma at a carefree saunter. Up ahead was a bend in the road, and as the donkey negotiated the turn, Grandma tipped backward, leaving the security of the animal's back. A muscular arm swept her off and carried her into the sorghum field.

Grandma fought halfheartedly. She really didn't feel like struggling. The three days she had just gotten through were nightmarish. Certain individuals become great leaders in an instant; Grandma unlocked the mysteries of life in three days. She even wrapped her arms around his neck to make it easier for him to carry her. Sorghum leaves rustled. Great-Granddad's hoarse voice drifted over on the wind: "Daughter, where the hell are you?"

The long, sorrowful blast of a bugle near the bridge is immediately followed by the staccato rhythm of machine-gun fire. Grandma's blood continues to flow in concert with her breathing. "Mom," Father pleads, "don't let your blood run out. You'll die when it's all gone." He scoops up a handful of black dirt and smears it over her wound; blood quickly seeps out from under it. He scoops up another handful. Grandma smiles in gratitude, her eyes fixed on the azure sky, deep beyond imagining, and fixed on the warm, forgiving, motherly, nurturing sorghum around her. A glossy green path, bordered by tiny white flowers, appears in her mind:

Grandma rode the donkey down this path, leisurely and carefree, while from deep amid the sorghum the stalwart young man raised his voice in a serenade that skimmed the top of the field. She was drawn to the serenade, her feet barely touching the tips of the sorghum plants, as though riding a green cloud. . . .

The man placed Grandma on the ground, where she lay as limp as a ribbon of dough, her eyes narrowed like those of a lamb. He ripped away the black mask, revealing his face to her. It's him! A silent prayer to heaven. A powerful feeling of pure joy rocked her, filling her eyes with hot tears.

Yu Zhan'ao removed his rain cape and tramped out a clearing in the sorghum, then spread his cape over the sorghum corpses. He lifted Grandma onto the cape. Her soul fluttered as she gazed at his bare torso. A light mist rose from the tips of the sorghum, and all around she could hear the sounds of growth. No wind, no waving motion, just the white-hot rays of moist sunlight crisscrossing through the open cracks between plants. The passion in Grandma's heart, built up over sixteen years, suddenly erupted. She squirmed and twisted on the cape.

Yu Zhan'ao, getting smaller and smaller, fell loudly to his knees at her side. She was trembling from head to toe; a redolent yellow ball of fire crackled and sizzled before her eyes. Yu Zhan'ao roughly tore open her jacket, exposing the small white mounds of chilled, tense flesh to the sunlight. Answering his force, she cried out in a muted, hoarse voice, "My God . . . ," and swooned.

Grandma and Granddad exchanged their love surrounded by the vitality of the sorghum field: two unbridled souls, refusing to knuckle under to worldly conventions, were fused together more closely than their ecstatic bodies. They plowed the clouds and scattered rain in the field, adding a patina of lustrous red to the rich and varied history of Northeast Gaomi Township. My father was conceived with the essence of heaven and earth, the crystallization of suffering and wild joy.

The braying donkey threaded its way into the sorghum field, and Grandma returned from the hazy kingdom of heaven to the cruel world of man. She sat up in a state of utter stupefaction, her face bathed in tears. "He really does have leprosy," she said. As Granddad knelt down, a sword appeared in his hand, as if by magic. He slipped it out of its scabbard; the two-foot blade was curved, like a leaf of chive. With a single swish, it sliced through two stalks of sorghum, the top halves thudding to the ground, leaving bubbles of dark-green liquid on the neat, slanted wounds.

"Come back in three days, no matter what!" Granddad said.

Grandma looked at him uncomprehendingly. He dressed while she tidied herself up, then put his sword away—where, she didn't know. Granddad took her back to the roadside and vanished.

Three days later, the little donkey carried Grandma back, and when she entered the village she learned that the Shans, father and son, had been murdered and tossed into the inlet at the western edge of the village.

Grandma lies there soaking up the crisp warmth of the sorghum field. She is as light as a house swallow gracefully skimming the tips of the plants. The fleeting images begin slowing down: Shan Bianlang, Shan Tingxiu, Great-Granddad, Great-Grandma, Uncle Arhat . . . so many hostile, grateful, savage, sincere faces appear and disappear. She is writing the final page of her thirty-year history. Everything in her past is like a procession of sweet, fragrant fruit falling rapidly to the ground. As for her future, she can only dimly see a few holes of light, which are quickly extinguished. She is holding on to the fleeting present with all her might.

Grandma feels Father's little paws stroking her. He calls out "Mom!" timidly. All her hate and her love evaporate. She longs to raise her arm and stroke Father's face, but it won't do her bidding. Rising into the air, she sees a multicolored ray of light streaming from above, and hears heaven's solemn music, played by horns and woodwinds, large and small.

Grandma is exhausted: the handle of the present, the handle of the world of men, is slipping from her grasp. Is this death? Will I never again see this sky, this earth, this sorghum, this son, the lover who has led his troops into battle? The gunfire is so far away, beyond a thick curtain of mist. Douguan! Douguan! Come help your mom. Pull your mom back. Your mom doesn't want to die. My heaven . . . you gave me a lover, you gave me a son, you gave me riches, you gave me thirty years of life as robust as red sorghum. Heaven, since you gave me all that, don't take it back now. Forgive me, let me go! Have I sinned? Would it have been right to share my pillow with a leper and produce a misshapen, putrid monster to contaminate this beautiful world? What is chastity then? What is the correct path? What is goodness? What is evil? You never told me, so I had to decide on my own. I loved happiness, I loved strength, I loved beauty; it was my body, and I used it as I thought fitting. Sin doesn't frighten me, nor does punishment. I'm not afraid of your eighteen levels of hell. I did what I had to do, I managed as I thought proper. I fear nothing. But I don't want to die, I want to live. I want to see more of this world. . . .

Grandma's sincerity moves the heavens. Fresh drops of a crystalline moisture ooze from her dry eyes, which emit a strange light. Once again she sees Father's golden face and two eyes that are so like Granddad's. Her lips quiver, she calls Douguan's name. "Mom," Father shouts excitedly, "you're going to be okay! You're not going to die. I've stopped the bleeding, it's stopped! I'll go get Dad, I'll tell him to come. Mom, you can't die, you have to wait for Dad!"

Father runs off, his retreating steps turning into a gentle monologue, then into the music from heaven that Grandma had heard a moment earlier. It is the music of the universe, and it emanates from the red sorghum. She gazes at the sorghum, and through the dimness of her vision the stalks turn crafty and surpassingly beautiful, grotesque, and bizarre. They begin to moan, to writhe, to shout, to entwine her; they are demonic one minute, intimate the next, and in her eyes they coil like snakes. But then they suddenly stretch out like spikes, and it is beyond her power to describe their brilliance. They are red and green, they are black and white, they are blue and green; they are laughing heartily, they are crying pitifully. Their tears are raindrops beating against the desolate sandbar of her heart.

The blue sky shines through the spaces between the sorghum stalks. It is so high, yet so low. Grandma feels as though heaven and earth, man, and the sorghum are intertwined, huddled beneath a gigantic canopy. White clouds dragging earthly shadows behind them brush leisurely against her face. A flock of white doves swoops down and perches on the stalks' tips, where their cooing wakes Grandma, who quickly distinguishes their shapes. The doves' red eyes, the size of sorghum seeds, are fixed on her. She smiles with genuine affection, and they return her smile. My darlings! she cries silently. I don't want to leave you! The doves peck at the sorghum grains, their chests slowly expanding, their feathers fanning out like petals in the wind and rain.

A large flock of doves had once nested in the eaves of our home. In the fall, Grandma placed a large basin of clear water in the yard, and when the doves returned from the fields they perched neatly on the rim of the basin to spit the sorghum seeds from their crops into water in which their reflections shimmered. Then they swaggered around the yard. Doves! Driven from their nests by the storms of war, they grieve over Grandma's imminent death.

Grandma's eyes glaze over once again, as the doves take flight, soaring through the vast blue sky, filling it with the rhythmic flapping of their wings. She floats upward to join them, spreading her newly sprouted wings to glide weightlessly in the air above the black soil and sorghum stalks. She gazes longingly at the ruins of her village, at the meandering river, at the crisscrossing roads and paths, at the bullet holes in the sky, and at the doomed creatures beneath her. For the last time she smells the aroma of sorghum wine and the pungent odor of hot blood. A scene she never witnessed suddenly takes shape in her mind: caught in a hail of gunfire, hundreds of her fellow villagers, their clothes in rags, lie in the sorghum field, arms and legs writhing in a macabre dance. . . .

The final thread linking her to mankind is about to part; all her melancholy and suffering, her anxieties and dejection settle onto the field below, striking the sorghum like hailstones and continuing down to the black soil to take root and give birth to bitter fruit for generations to come.

Grandma has completed her liberation. She flies off with the doves. Her shrinking thoughts, which might fit into a human fist, embrace only joy, contentment, warmth, comfort, and harmony. She is at peace. With genuine devotion she exclaims:

"Heaven! My heaven . . ."

9

WHILE THE MACHINE GUNS CONTINUED to strafe the area, the trucks' wheels began to creep up onto the stone bridge. Flying bullets kept Granddad and his troops pinned down. A few men stuck their heads above the dike, only to pay for their recklessness with their lives. Granddad's chest swelled with rage. All the trucks were now on the bridge, raising the machine-gun-fire trajectory. "Men," he shouted, "attack!" He pulled off three quick shots, downing two Japanese soldiers, whose bodies fell across the cab, their dark blood staining the hood. With the echo of his shots still in the air, a cacophonous burst of fire erupted from behind the dikes lining the road. Seven or eight more Japanese soldiers were cut down; two of them fell off the truck, arms and legs churning desperately as they burrowed into the black water on either side of the bridge. The Fang brothers' cannon roared, spewing a torrent of flame from its muzzle. Steel pellets and balls tore into the second truck in line, with its load of sacks, sending plumes of smoke skyward. White rice streamed from countless holes.

Father crawled on his belly from the sorghum field back to the dike, anxious to talk to Granddad, who was urgently reloading his pistol. The lead Jap truck revved its engine to get across the bridge, but the front wheels ran over the rake barrier; loud hissing sighs escaped from the punctured tires. The truck rumbled grotesquely as it dragged the linked rakes along, and to Father it looked like an enormous twisting snake that had swallowed a hedgehog it was trying to dislodge. The Japs on the lead truck jumped to the ground. "Old Liu," Granddad shouted, "sound the bugle!" The sound of Bugler Liu's horn chilled the air. "Charge!" Granddad commanded, leading the charge and firing without aiming, cutting down one Japanese soldier after another.

The troops on the west side of the road joined the attack, engaging the Japs in hand-to-hand combat. Granddad watched as Mute leaped up onto the bed of the lead truck. The two remaining Japs on the truck lunged with their bayonets. He warded off one with his knife, then neatly separated the soldier from his helmeted head, which sailed through the air, trailing a long howl before landing heavily on the ground, the thud driving the remnants of the scream out of its mouth. Father, amazed by the sharpness of the knife, stared at the stunned expression on the Jap's face. The cheeks were still quivering, the nostrils still twitching, as though it were about to sneeze.

Mute dispatched the other Jap, and when the man's headless torso fell against the truck's railing, the skin on his neck shrank inward around pulsating gushes of blood. The Japs in the rear truck lowered the barrel of their machine gun and fired a hail of bullets, mowing down Granddad's soldiers like so many saplings, which toppled onto the Jap corpses. Mute sat down hard on the cab, blood seeping from a cluster of chest holes.

Father and Granddad threw themselves to the ground and crawled back to the sorghum field. When they cautiously peeked over the top of the dike, they saw the rear truck chugging in reverse. "Fang Six," Granddad shouted, "the cannon! Nail that son of a bitch!" The Fang brothers turned their loaded cannon in the direction of the dike, but as Fang Six bent over to light the fuse he was hit in the belly. Green intestines slithered out of the hole. "Shit!" he blurted as he grabbed his belly with both hands and rolled into the sorghum field. The trucks would soon be off the bridge. "Fire that cannon!" Granddad screamed. Fang Seven picked up the smoldering tinder and touched it to the fuse with a shaky hand. It wouldn't light, it simply wouldn't light! Granddad rushed up, grabbed the tinder out of his hand, and blew on it. It flared up. He touched it to the fuse. It sizzled, smoked momentarily, then went out with a puff of white smoke. The cannon sat silently, as though dozing. Father just knew it wouldn't fire.

The Jap truck had already reached the bridgehead, and the second and third trucks had started moving backward to join it. In the river below, several Jap corpses floated eastward, seeping blood that attracted frenzied schools of white eels. After a moment of silence, the cannon belched thunderously, and its iron body leaped high above the dike as a wide swath of fire immolated one of the rice trucks.

The Japs aboard the first truck jumped down onto the dike and set up their machine gun. They opened fire. A bullet slammed into Fang Seven's face, shattering his nose and splattering Father with blood.

Two Japs in the cab of the blazing truck opened their doors and jumped out, straight into the river. The middle truck, unable to move either way, growled strangely, its wheels spinning. The rice rain continued to fall.

The Jap machine gun abruptly stopped firing, leaving only carbines to pop off an occasional shot. A dozen or so Japs ran at a crouch past the burning truck, heading north with their weapons. Granddad ordered his men to fire, but few responded. The dike was dotted top and bottom with the bodies of soldiers; wounded men were moaning and wailing in the sorghum field. Granddad fired, sending Japs flying off the bridge. Rifle fire from the western side of the road cut down more of them. Their comrades turned tail and ran. A bullet whizzing over from the southern bank of the river struck Granddad below the right shoulder; as his arm jerked, the pistol fell from his hand to hang by its strap from his neck. He backed into the sorghum field. "Douguan," he cried out, "help me." Ripping the sleeve of his shirt, he told Father to take a strip of white cloth from his waistband to bind the wound. That was when Father said, "Dad, Mom's asking for you."

"Good boy!" Granddad said. "Come help Dad kill every last one of those sons of bitches!" He reached into his belt, removed the abandoned Browning pistol, and handed it to Father, just as Bugler Liu came crawling up the dike dragging a wounded leg. "Shall I blow the bugle, Commander?"

"Blow it!" Granddad said.

Kneeling on his good leg, Bugler Liu raised the horn to his lips and sounded it to the heavens; scarlet notes emerged.

"Charge!"

Granddad's command was met by shouts from the west side of the road. Holding his pistol in his left hand, he jumped to his feet; bullets whizzed past his cheeks. He hit the ground and rolled back into the sorghum field. A scream of agony rose from the west side of the road, and Father knew that another comrade had been hit.

Bugler Liu sounded his horn once more; the scarlet blast struck the sorghum tips and set them shaking.

Granddad grabbed Father's hand. "Follow me, son."

Smoke billowed from the trucks on the bridge. Gripping Father's hand tightly, Granddad darted across the road to the west side; their progress was followed by a hail of bullets. Two soldiers with soot-streaked faces witnessed their approach. "Commander," they cried through cracked lips, "we're done for!"

Granddad sat down dejectedly in the sorghum field, and a long time passed before he raised his head again. The Japs held their fire. The crackling of burning trucks was answered by periodic blasts from Bugler Liu's horn.

His fear now gone, Father slipped off and moved west, carefully raising his head to peep through some dead weeds. He watched a Japanese soldier emerge from under the still-unburned canopy of the second truck, open the door, and drag out a skinny old Jap in white gloves and black leather riding boots, a sword on his hip. Hugging the side of the truck, they slipped off the bridge by shinnying down a stanchion. Father raised his Browning, but his hand shook like a leaf, and the old Jap's ass kept hopping up and down in his sights. He clenched his teeth, closed his eyes, and fired. The Browning roared: the bullet went straight into the water, turning a white eel belly up. The Jap officer dived into the water. "Dad," Father yelled, "an officer!"

Another explosion went off behind his head, and the old Jap's skull splintered, releasing a pool of blood on the surface of the water. The second soldier scrambled frantically to the far side of the stanchion.

Granddad pushed Father to the ground as another hail of Jap bullets swept over them and thudded crazily into the field. "Good boy," Granddad said. "You're my son, all right!"

What Father and Granddad didn't know was that the old Jap they'd just killed was none other than the famous general Nakaoka Jiko.

Bugler Liu's horn didn't let up. The sun, baked red and green by the flames from the trucks, seemed to shrivel.

"Dad," Father said, "Mom's asking for you. She wants to see you."

"Is she still alive?"

"Yes."

Father took Granddad by the hand and led him deep into the sorghum field, where Grandma lay, her face stamped with shadows of sorghum stalks and the noble smile she had prepared for Granddad; her face was fairer than ever. Her eyes were open.

For the first time in his life, Father noticed two trickles of tears slipping down Granddad's hardened face. Granddad fell to his knees beside Grandma's body and closed her eyes with his good hand.

In 1976, when my granddad died, Father closed his unseeing eyes with his left hand, from which two fingers were missing. Granddad had returned from the desolate Japanese mountains of Hokkaido scarcely able to speak, spitting out each word as though it were a heavy stone. The village held a grand welcoming ceremony in honor of his return, attended by the county head. I was barely two at the time, but I recall seeing eight tables beneath the gingko tree at the head of the village set with jugs of wine and dozens of white ceramic bowls. The county head picked up a jug and filled one of the bowls, which he handed to Granddad with both hands. "Here's to you, our aging hero," he said. "You've brought glory to our county!" Granddad clumsily stood up, and his ashen eyeballs fluttered as he said, "Woo—woo—gun—gun." I watched him raise the bowl to his lips. His wrinkled neck twitched, and his Adam's apple slid up and down as he drank. Most of the wine ran down his chin and onto his chest instead of sliding down his throat.

I recall our walks in the field; he held my hand and I led a little black dog with my other hand. His favorite spot was the bridgehead over the Black Water River, where he would stand supporting himself on one of the stone pillars for most of the morning or most of the afternoon, staring at the bullet holes on the bridge stones. When the sorghum was tall, he would take me into the field to a spot not far from the bridge. I suspected that was where Grandma had risen to heaven—an ordinary piece of black earth stained by her blood. That was before they tore down our old home.

One day Granddad picked up a hoe and began digging beneath a catalpa tree. He picked up some cicada larvae and handed them to me. I tossed them to the dog, who chewed them up without swallowing them. "What are you digging for, Dad?" asked my mother, who was anxious to go to the dining hall. He looked up at her with a gaze that seemed to belong to another world. She walked off, and he returned to his digging. When he'd dug a pretty deep hole, he cut through a dozen or so roots of varying thicknesses and removed a flagstone, then took a misshapen tin box out of an old, dark brick kiln. It crumbled when it fell to the ground, revealing a long, rusty metal object taller than me, which was showing through the rotting cloth wrapping. I asked what it was. "Woo—woo—gun—gun," he said.

Granddad laid the rifle on the ground to soak up the sun, then sat down in front of it, his eyes open one minute and closed the next, over and over and over. Finally, he got to his feet, picked up an ax, and began chopping up the rifle. When it was no more than a pile of twisted metal, he took the pieces and scattered them wildly around the yard.

"Dad, is Mom dead?" Father asked.

Granddad nodded.

"Dad!" Father shrieked.

Granddad stroked Father's head, then drew a small sword from his hip and chopped down enough sorghum to cover Grandma's body.

A blast of gunfire erupted on the southern dike, followed by sanguinary shouts and the sound of exploding grenades. Granddad dragged Father over to the bridgehead.

At least a hundred soldiers in gray uniforms burst from the field south of the bridge, driving a dozen or so Jap soldiers onto the dike, where they were cut down by bullets or run through with bayonets. Father saw Detachment Leader Leng, a holstered revolver hanging from his wide leather belt, surrounded by several burly bodyguards. His troops were flanking the burning trucks and heading west. The sight drew a strange laugh from Granddad, who planted his feet at the bridgehead, pistol in hand, and just stood there.

Detachment Leader Leng swaggered up. "You fought a good fight, Commander Yu!"

"You son of a bitch!" Granddad spat out.

"We almost made it in time, good brother!"

"You son of a bitch!"

"You'd be done for if we hadn't arrived!"

"You son of a bitch!"

Granddad aimed his pistol at Detachment Leader Leng, who flashed a signal with his eyes. Two ferocious bodyguards quickly forced Granddad's arm down. Father raised his Browning and fired into the ass of the man holding Granddad's arm.

The other guard sent Father reeling with a kick, then stepped on his wrist, bent down, and picked up the Browning.

The bodyguards tied up Granddad and Father.

"Pocky Leng, open your dog eyes and take a look at my men!"

The dikes on both sides of the road were strewn with the bodies of dead and wounded soldiers. Bugler Liu was still sounding his horn intermittently, but blood now flowed from the corners of his mouth and from his nose.

Detachment Leader Leng removed his cap and bowed toward the sorghum field east of the road. Then he bowed to the west.

"Release Commander Yu and his son!" he ordered.

The bodyguards let them go. Blood was seeping through the fingers of the man who was holding his hand over his wounded ass.

Detachment Leader Leng took the pistols from the bodyguards and returned them to Granddad and Father. His troops were rushing across the bridge, past the trucks and the Jap bodies, gathering up machine guns, carbines, bullets, cartridge clips, bayonets, scabbards, leather belts and boots, wallets, and razors. Some jumped into the river, where they captured the Jap hiding behind the stanchion and raised up the old Jap's body.

"This one's a general, Detachment Leader!" one of Leng's officers shouted.

Detachment Leader Leng excitedly looked over the railing. "Strip off his uniform and pick up everything that was on him." He turned back and said, "We'll meet again, Commander Yu!"

The bodyguards fell in around him as he headed to the southern edge of the bridge.

"Stop right there, Leng!" Granddad bellowed.

Detachment Leader Leng turned and said, "Commander Yu, you're not planning on doing anything foolish, are you?"

"You won't get away with this!" Granddad snarled.

"Tiger Wang, leave Commander Yu a machine gun."

A soldier walked up and laid a machine gun at Granddad's feet.

"You can have the trucks and the rice they're carrying."

Detachment Leader Leng's troops crossed the bridge, formed up ranks on the dike, and marched east.

The trucks were nothing but charred frames by the time the sun was setting; the stench from the melted tires was nearly suffocating. The bridge was blocked by the two undamaged trucks at either end. The river was filled with water as black as blood; the fields were covered with sorghum as red as blood.

Father picked up a nearly whole fistcake from the dike and handed it to Granddad. "Here, Dad, eat this. Mom made it."

"You eat it!" Granddad said.

Father stuffed it into Granddad's hand. "I'll get another one," he said.

Father picked up another fistcake and savagely bit off a chunk.

CHAPTER
TWO

Sorghum Wine

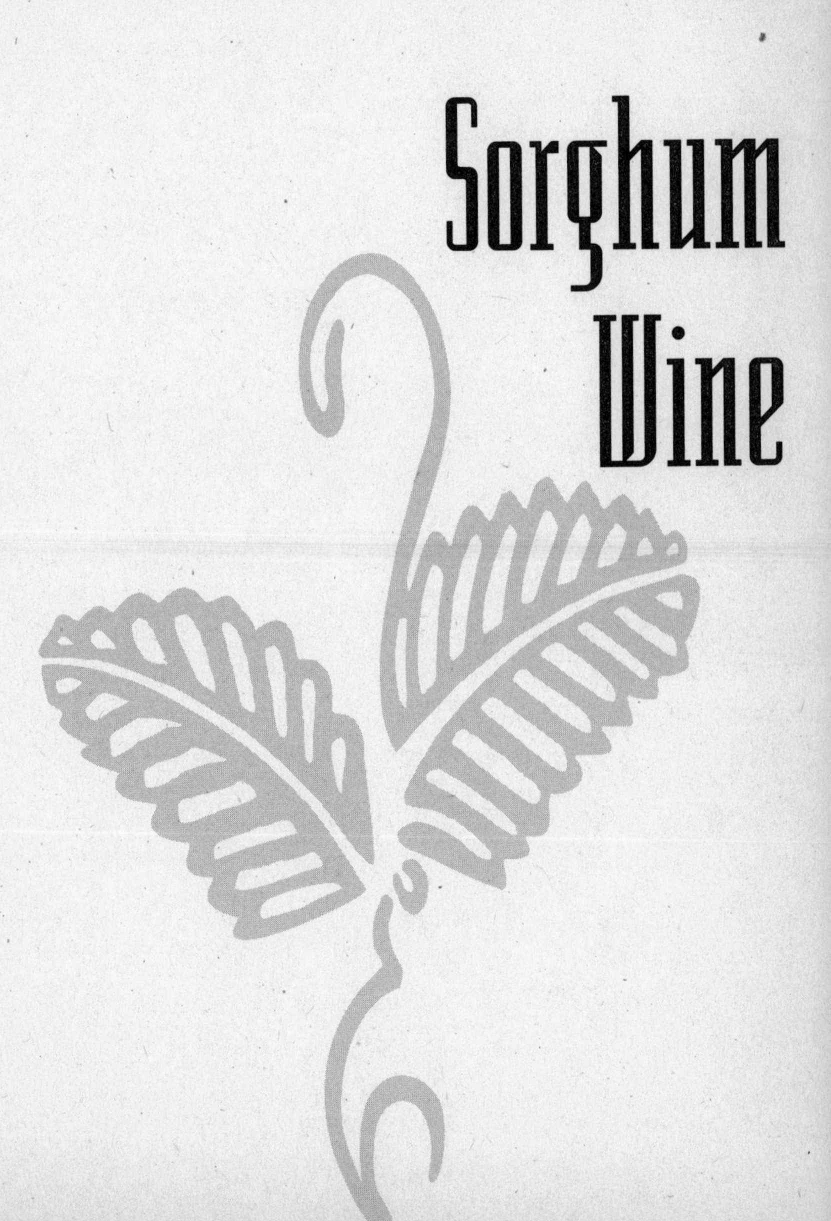

1

WHAT TURNS THE SORGHUM of Northeast Gaomi Township into a sweet, aromatic wine that leaves the taste of honey in your mouth and produces no hangover? Mother told me once, making sure I understood that I was not to give away this family secret, for, if I did, not only would our family's reputation suffer, but if our descendants ever decided to set up another distillery they'd have lost their unique advantage. Without exception, the craftsmen from our neck of the woods live by a simple rule: they would rather pass on their skills to their sons' wives than to their daughters. This established practice carries the same weight as the law in certain countries.

Mother said that the distillery was already a going concern under the operation of the Shan family. The wine they made wasn't bad, but it wasn't nearly as aromatic and rich as the wine that would come later, and it lacked the honeyed aftertaste. The incident that resulted in the unique flavor of our wine occurred after Granddad murdered the Shans, and Grandma, following a brief period of discomposure, pulled herself together to display her natural entrepreneurial skills.

Like so many important discoveries that spring from chance origins or a prankster's whim, the unique qualities of our wine were created when Granddad pissed in one of the wine casks. How could a man's piss turn a common cask of wine into a wine of unique distinction? you ask. Well, this takes us into the realm of science, and you won't hear any nonsense on the subject from me. Let those interested in the chemistry of brewing toss the matter around.

Later on, in order to improve upon the process, Grandma and Uncle Arhat hit upon the idea of substituting the alkali from old chamber pots for fresh piss—it was simpler, more efficient, and more controlled. This secret was shared only by Grandma, Granddad, and Uncle Arhat. I understand that the blending was done late at night, when everyone else was asleep. Grandma would light a candle in the yard, burn a wad of three hundred bank notes, then pour the liquid into the wine casks from a thin-necked gourd. She did it grandly, with an air of sublime mystery, in case there were prying eyes, for the astonished peeping Toms would assume that she was communing with spirits to seek divine assistance for the business. From then on, our wine prevailed over all our competitors', nearly cornering the market.

2

AFTER THE WEDDING, Grandma returned to her parents' home to spend three days before heading back to her in-laws'. She had no appetite during those three days, her mind distracted. Great-Grandma cooked all her favorite foods and tried to coax her into eating, but she refused everything and moped around the house like the walking dead. Even then her appearance didn't suffer: her skin remained milky, her cheeks rosy; her bright eyes, set in dark sockets, looked like small moons glowing through the mist. "You little urchin," Great-Grandma grumbled, "do you think you're an immortal or a Buddha who doesn't need to eat or drink? You'll be the death of your own mother!" She looked at Grandma, who sat as composed as the Guanyin bodhisattva, two tiny white tears slipping out of the corners of her eyes.

Great-Granddad awoke from his drunken stupor on the second day of Grandma's return, and immediately recalled Shan Tingxiu's promise to give him a big black mule. His ears rang with the rhythmic clippety-clop of the mule's hooves as it flew down the road. Such a mule: fetching black eyes like tiny lanterns, hooves like little goblets. "You old ass," Great-Grandma said anxiously, "your daughter won't eat. What are we going to do?"

Great-Granddad glanced out of the corner of his drunken eyes and said, "She's spoiled, spoiled rotten! Who does she think she is?"

He walked up to Grandma and said angrily, "What are you up to, you little tramp? People destined to marry are connected by a thread, no matter how far apart. Man and wife, for better or for worse. Marry a chicken and share the cop, marry a dog and share the kennel. Your dad's no high-ranking noble, and you're no gold branch or jade leaf. It was your good fortune to find a rich man like this, and your dad's good fortune, too. The first thing your father-in-law did was promise me a nice black mule. That's breeding. . . ."

Grandma sat motionless, her eyes closed. Her damp eyelashes might have been covered with a layer of honey, each thick, full lash sticking to the others and curling like a swallowtail. Great-Granddad glared at her, his anger rising. "Don't you act deaf and dumb with me. You can waste away if you want to, but you'll be the Shan family's ghost, because there's no place in the Dai family graveyard for you!"

Grandma just laughed.

Great-Granddad slapped her.

With a pop, the rosiness in Grandma's cheeks vanished, leaving a pallor behind. But the color gradually returned, and her face became the red morning sun. Her eyes shining, she clenched her teeth and sneered. Glaring hatefully at her dad, she said: "I'm just afraid . . . if you . . . then you can forget about seeing a single hair of that mule!"

Lowering her head, she picked up her chopsticks and gobbled down the still-steaming food in front of her, like a whirlwind scooping up snow. When she was finished, she threw the bowl high into the air, where it tumbled and spun, sailed over the beam, and picked up two cobwebs before falling to the floor; it bounced around in a half-circle before settling upside down. She picked up another bowl and heaved it; this one hit the wall and fell to the floor in two pieces. Great-Granddad was so shocked his mouth fell open, his sideburns quivered, and he was speechless. "Daughter," Great-Grandma exclaimed, "you finally ate something!"

After throwing the bowls, Grandma broke down and cried. It was an agreeable, emotional, moist sound, which the room couldn't hold, so it spilled outside and spread to the fields, to merge with the rustling of the pollinated late-summer sorghum. A million thoughts ran through her mind; over and over she relived what had happened from the time she had been placed in the bridal sedan chair until she had returned on the donkey's back to her parents' home. Every scene from those three days, every sound, every smell entered her mind . . . the horns and woodwinds . . . little tunes, big sounds . . . all that music turned the green sorghum red. It pounded a curtain of rain out of the clear sky: two cracks of thunder, a flash of lightning, rain falling like dense flax . . . turning her confused heart to flax, dense rain pouring in at an angle, then straight up, then straight down. . . .

Grandma thought back to the highwayman at Toad Hollow, and to the valiant actions of the young sedan bearer. He was their leader, the main dog of the pack. He couldn't be more than twenty-four—not a wrinkle on his rugged face. She recalled how close his face had been for a while, and how his lips, hard as mussel shells, had covered hers. Her blood had frozen for an instant, before gushing forth to dilate every blood vessel in her body. Her feet had cramped, her abdominal muscles had jerked madly. Their call to revolt had been aided by the vibrant sorghum—the powder on the stalks, so fine it was barely visible, spreading in the air above her and the sedan bearer. . . .

Grandma hoped that by concentrating on the youthful passion of that moment she could hold on to it, but it kept slipping away, here one moment, then gone. And yet the leper's face, like a long-buried rotten grape, kept reappearing, along with the ten hooked claws that were his fingers. Then there was the old man, with his tiny queue and the ring of brass keys at his belt. Grandma sat quietly, but even though she was dozens of li away from the spot, the rich taste of sorghum wine and the sour taste of sorghum mash seemed to roll around on her tongue. She recalled how the two male "serving girls" reeked like drunken geese fished out of a wine vat, the smell of alcohol seeping from every pore in their bodies. . . . He had cut a swath through the sorghum, leaving the blade of his razor-sharp sword wet with little horseshoes of inky green, sticky residue from the decapitated plants, their lifeblood. She remembered what he had said: "Come back in three days, no matter what!" Daggers of light had shot from his long, slitted eyes.

Grandma had a premonition that her life was about to change in extraordinary ways.

In some significant aspects, heroes are born, not made. Heroic qualities flow through a person's veins like an undercurrent, ready to be translated into action. During her first sixteen years, Grandma's days had been devoted to embroidery, needlework, paper cutouts, foot binding, the endless glossing of her hair, and all other manner of domestic things in the company of neighbor girls. What, then, was the source of her ability and courage to deal with the events she encountered in her adult years? How was she able to temper herself to the point where even in the face of danger she could conquer her fears and force herself to act heroically? I'm not sure I know.

Grandma wept for a long time without feeling much true grief; as she cried, she relived the joys and pleasures of her past, even the suffering and sorrow. The sounds of crying seemed to be a distant musical accompaniment to the beautiful and hideous images appearing and reappearing in her mind. Finally, she mused that human existence is as brief as the life of autumn grass, so what was there to fear from taking chances with your life?

"Time to leave, Little Nine," Great-Granddad said, calling her by her childhood name.

Leave! Leave! Leave!

Grandma asked for a basin of water to wash her face. Then she applied some powder and rouge. As she looked in the mirror, she loosened her hairnet, releasing long, flowing hair that quickly covered her back with its satiny sheen, all the way down to the curve of her legs. When she pulled it across her shoulder with her left hand, it spilled over her breast, where she combed it out with a pear-wood comb. Grandma had uncommonly thick, shiny, black hair that lightened a bit at the tips. Once it was combed out smooth, she twisted it into large ebony blossoms, which she secured with four silver combs. Then she trimmed her bangs so that they fell just short of her eyebrows. After rewrapping her feet, she put on a pair of white cotton stockings, tied her trouser cuffs tightly, and slipped on a pair of embroidered slippers that accentuated her bound feet.

It was Grandma's tiny feet that had caught the attention of Shan Tingxiu, and it was her tiny feet that had aroused the passions of the sedan bearer Yu Zhan'ao. She was very proud of them. Even a pock-faced witch is assured of marriage if she has tiny bound feet, but no one wants a girl with large unbound feet, even if she has the face of an immortal. Grandma, with her bound feet *and* lovely face, was one of the true beauties of her time. Throughout our long history, the delicate, pointed tips of women's feet have been viewed as genital organs, in a way, from which men have derived a sort of aesthetic pleasure that sets their sexual juices flowing.

Now that she was ready, Grandma left the house, clicking her feet. A blanket had been thrown over the back of the family's little donkey, in whose glistening eyes Grandma noticed a spark of human understanding. She swung her leg over the donkey's back and straddled it, unlike most women. Great-Grandma had tried to get her to ride sidesaddle, but Grandma dug in her heels and the donkey started off down the road, its rider sitting proudly on its back, head up and eyes straight ahead.

Once she was on her way, Grandma didn't look back, and although Great-Granddad was holding the reins at first, when they were out of the village she took them from him and guided the donkey herself, leaving him to trot along behind her.

Another thunderstorm had struck during the three days. Grandma noticed a section of sorghum the size of a millstone where the leaves were singed and shriveled, a spot of emaciated whiteness amid the surrounding green. Assuming that lightning was the culprit, she was reminded of the previous year, when lightning had struck and killed her friend Beauty, a girl of seventeen, literally frying her hair and burning her clothes to cinders. A design had been scorched into her back, which some people said was the script of heavenly tadpoles.

Rumors spread that greed had killed Beauty, who had caused the death of an abandoned baby. The details were lurid. On her way to market one day, she heard a bawling baby by the roadside. When she unwrapped the swaddling clothes she found a pink, newborn baby boy and a note that said: "Father was eighteen, mother seventeen, the moon was directly overhead, the three stars were in the western sky, when our son, Road Joy, was born. Father had already married Second Sister Zhang, a girl with unbound feet from West Village. Mother will marry Scar Eye from East Village. It breaks our hearts to abandon our newborn son. Snot runs down his father's chin, tears stream down his mother's cheeks, but we stifle our sobs so no one will hear us. Road Joy, Road Joy, our joy on the road, whoever finds you will be your parents. We have wrapped you in a yard of silk, and have left twenty silver dollars. We beg a kindhearted passerby to store up karma by saving our son's precious life."

People said that Beauty took the silk and the silver dollars, but abandoned the infant in the sorghum field, for which heaven punished her by sending down a bolt of lightning. Grandma refused to believe the rumors about her best friend, but as she pondered the tragic mysteries of life her heart was gripped by desolation and melancholy.

The rain-soaked road was still wet and pitted by pelting raindrops; soft mud, with a light oily sheen, filled the holes. Once again the donkey left its hoofprints in the mud. Katydids hid in the grass and on the sorghum leaves, vibrating their long silken beards and sawing their transparent wings to produce a cheerless sound. The long summer was about to end, and the somber smell of autumn was in the air. Swarms of locusts, sensing the change of season, dragged their seed-filled bellies out of the sorghum fields onto the road, where they bored their hindquarters into the hard surface to lay their eggs.

Great-Granddad snapped off a sorghum stalk and smacked the rump of the weary donkey, which tucked its tail between its legs and shot forward a few paces before resuming its unhurried pace. Great-Granddad must have been feeling very pleased with himself as he walked behind the donkey, for he began singing snatches of popular local opera, making up the words as he went along: "Wu Dalang drank poison, how bad he felt. . . . His seven lengths of intestines and the eight lobes of his lungs lurched and trembled. . . . The ugly man took a beautiful wife, bringing calamity to his door. . . . Ah—ye—ye . . . Big Wu's belly is killing him . . . waiting for Second Brother to complete his mission . . . to return home and avenge his murder. . . ."

Grandma's heart thumped wildly as she listened to Great-Granddad's crazy song. The image of that scowling young man, sword in hand, appeared in a flash. Who was he? What was he up to? It dawned on her that, even though they didn't know each other, their lives were already as close as fish and water. Their sole encounter had been lightning quick and was over in a flash, like a dream, yet not like a dream. She had been shaken to the depths of her soul, overcome by spirits. Resign yourself to your fate, she thought as she heaved a long sigh.

Grandma let the donkey proceed freely as she listened to her dad's fractured rendition of the Wu Dalang song. A breath of wind and a puff of fire, and there they were, in Toad Hollow. The donkey kept its nostrils closed tight as it pawed the ground, refusing to go any farther, even when Great-Granddad smacked it on the rump with his sorghum switch. "Get moving, you bastard! Get going, you rotten donkey bastard!" The switch sang out against the donkey's rump, but instead of moving forward, it backed up.

An awful stench assailed Grandma's nostrils. Quickly dismounting and covering her nose with her sleeve, she tugged on the reins to get the donkey moving. It looked up at her, its mouth open, tears filling its eyes. "Donkey," she said, "grit your teeth and walk past it. There's no mountain that can't be scaled and no river that can't be forded." Moved by her words, it raised its head and brayed, then galloped forward, dragging her along so fast her feet barely touched the ground and her clothes fluttered in the wind like red clouds tumbling in the sky. She glanced at the sham highwayman's corpse as they passed. A scene of filth and corruption greeted her eyes: a million fat maggots had gorged themselves until only a few pieces of rotting flesh covered his bones.

Grandma climbed back onto the donkey after they'd managed to drag one another past Toad Hollow. Gradually she became aware of the smell of sorghum wine floating on the northeast wind. She whipped up her courage, but as she drew nearer to the climactic scene of the drama her sense of fear and foreboding was as strong as ever. Steam rose from the ground under the blazing sun, but shivers ran down her spine. The village where the Shans lived was still far away, and Grandma, surrounded by the thick aroma of sorghum wine, felt as if the marrow in her spine had frozen solid. A man in the field to her right began to sing in a loud, full voice:

Little sister, boldly you move on
Your jaw set like a steel trap
Bones as hard as cast bronze

From high atop the embroidery tower
You toss down the embroidered ball
Striking me on the head
Now join me in a toast with dark-red sorghum wine.

"Hey there, opera singer, come out! That's terrible singing! Just awful!" Great-Granddad shouted toward the sorghum field.

3

FATHER FINISHED HIS FISTCAKE as he stood on the withered grass, turned blood-red by the setting sun. Then he walked gingerly up to the edge of the water. There on the stone bridge across the Black Water River the lead truck, its tires flattened by the barrier of linked rakes, crouched in front of the other three. Its railings and fenders were stained by splotches of gore. The upper half of a Japanese soldier was draped over one of the railings, his steel helmet hanging upturned by a strap from his neck. Dark blood dripped into it from the tip of his nose. The water sobbed as it flowed down the riverbed. The heavy, dull rays of sunlight were pulverized by tiny ripples on its surface. Autumn insects hidden in the damp mud beneath the water plants set up a mournful chirping. Sorghum in the fields sizzled as it matured. The fires were nearly out in the third and fourth trucks; their blackened hulks crackled and split, adding to the discordant symphony.

Father's attention was riveted by the sight and sound of blood dripping from the Japanese soldier's nose into the steel helmet, each drop splashing crisply and sending out rings of concentric circles in the deepening pool. Father had barely passed his fifteenth birthday. The sun had nearly set on this ninth day of the eighth lunar month of the year 1939, and the dying embers of its rays cast a red pall over the world below. Father's face, turned unusually gaunt by the fierce daylong battle, was covered by a layer of purplish mud. He squatted down upriver from the corpse of Wang Wenyi's wife and scooped up some water in his hands; the sticky water oozed through the cracks between his fingers and dripped noiselessly to the ground. Sharp pains racked his cracked, swollen lips, and the brackish taste of blood seeped between his teeth and slid down his throat, moistening the parched membranes. He experienced a satisfying pain, and even though the taste of blood made his stomach churn, he scooped up handful after handful of water, drinking it down until it soaked up the dry, cracked fistcake in his stomach. He stood up straight and took a deep breath of relief.

Night was definitely about to fall; the ridge of the sky's dome was tinged with the final sliver of red. The scorched smell from the burned-out hulks of the trucks had faded. A loud bang made Father jump. He looked up, just in time to see exploded bits of truck tires settling slowly into the river like black butterflies, and countless kernels of Japanese rice—some black, some white—soaring upward, then raining down on the still surface of the river. As he spun around, his eyes settled on the tiny figure of Wang Wenyi's wife lying at the edge of the river, the blood from her wounds staining the water around her. He scrambled to the top of the dike and yelled: "Dad!"

Granddad was standing on the dike, the flesh on his face wasted away by the day's battle, the bones jutting out beneath his dark, weathered skin. In the dying sunlight Father noticed that Granddad's short-cropped hair was turning white. With fear in his aching heart, Father nudged him timidly.

"Dad," he said, "Dad! What's wrong with you?"

Tears were running down Granddad's face. He was sobbing. The Japanese machine gun that Detachment Leader Leng had so magnanimously left behind sat at his feet like a crouching wolf, its muzzle gaping.

"Say something, Dad. Eat that fistcake, then drink some water. You'll die if you don't eat or drink."

Granddad's head drooped until it rested on his chest. He seemed to lack the strength to support its weight. He knelt at the top of the dike, holding his head in his hands and sobbing. After a moment or two, he looked up and cried out: "Douguan, my son! Is it all over for us?"

Father stared wide-eyed and fearfully at Granddad. The glare in his diamondlike pupils embodied the heroic, unrestrained spirit of Grandma, a flicker of hope that shone and lit up Granddad's heart.

"Dad," Father said, "don't give up. I'll work hard on my shooting, like when you shot fish at the inlet to perfect your seven-plum-blossom skill. Then we'll go settle accounts with that rotten son of a bitch Pocky Leng!"

Granddad sprang to his feet and bellowed three times—half wail, half crazed laughter. A line of dark-purple blood trickled out of the corner of his mouth.

"That's it, son, that's the way to talk!"

He picked up one of Grandma's fistcakes from the dark earth, bit off a chunk, and swallowed it. Cake crumbs and flecks of bubbly blood stuck to his stained teeth. Father heard Granddad's painful cries as the dry cake stuck in his throat and saw the rough edges make their way down his neck.

"Dad," Father said, "go drink some water to soak up the cake in your belly."

Granddad stumbled along the dike to the river's edge, where he knelt among the water plants and lapped up the water like a draft animal. When he'd had his fill, he drew his hands back and buried his head in the river, holding it under the water for about half the time it takes to smoke a pipeful of tobacco. Father started getting nervous as he gazed at his dad, frozen like a bronze frog at the river's edge. Finally, Granddad jerked his dripping head out of the water and gasped for breath. Then he walked back up the dike to stand in front of Father, whose eyes were glued to the cascading drops of water. Granddad shook his head, sending forty-nine drops, large and small, flying like so many pearls.

"Douguan," he said, "come with Dad. Let's go see the men."

Granddad staggered down the road, weaving in and out of the sorghum field on the western edge, Father right on his heels. They stepped on broken, twisted stalks of sorghum and spent cartridges that gave off a faint yellow glint. Frequently they bent down to look at the bodies of their fallen comrades, who lay amid the sorghum, deathly grimaces frozen on their faces. Granddad and Father shook them in hopes of finding one who was alive; but they were dead, all of them. Father's and Granddad's hands were covered with sticky blood. Father looked down at two soldiers on the westernmost edge of the field: one lay with the muzzle of his shotgun in his mouth, the back of his neck a gory mess, like a rotten wasps' nest; the other lay across a bayonet buried in his chest. When Granddad turned them over, Father saw that their legs had been broken and their bellies slit open. Granddad sighed as he withdrew the shotgun from the one soldier's mouth and pulled the bayonet from the other's chest.

Father followed Granddad across the road, into the sorghum field to the east, which had also been swept by machine-gun fire. They turned over the bodies of more soldiers lying strewn across the ground. Bugler Liu was on his knees, bugle in hand, as though he were blowing it. "Bugler Liu!" Granddad called out excitedly. No response. Father ran up and nudged him. "Uncle Liu!" he shouted, as the bugle dropped to the ground. When Father looked more closely, he discovered that the bugler's face was already as hard as a rock.

In the lightly scarred section of field some few dozen paces from the dike, Granddad and Father came upon Fang Seven, whose guts had spilled out of his belly, and another soldier, named Consumptive Four, who, after taking a bullet in the leg, had fainted from blood loss. Holding his bloodstained hand above the man's mouth, Granddad detected a faint sign of dry, hot breath from his nostrils. Fang Seven had stuffed his own intestines back into his abdomen and covered the gaping wound with sorghum leaves. He was still conscious. When he spotted Granddad and Father, his lips twitched and he said haltingly, "Commander . . . done for . . . When you see my old lady . . . give some money. . . . Don't let her remarry. . . . My brother . . . no sons . . . If she leaves . . . Fang family line ended. . . ." Father knew that Fang Seven had a year-old son, and that there was so much milk in his mother's gourdlike breasts that he was growing up fair and plump.

"I'll carry you back, little brother," Granddad said.

He bent over and pulled Fang Seven onto his back. As Fang screeched in pain, Father saw the leaves fall away and his white, speckled intestines slither out of his belly, releasing a breath of foul hot air. Granddad laid him back down on the ground. "Elder brother," Fang pleaded, "put me out of my misery. . . . Don't torture me. . . . Shoot me, please. . . ."

Granddad squatted down and held Fang Seven's hand. "Little brother, I can carry you over to see Zhang Xinyi, Dr. Zhang. He'll patch you up."

"Elder brother . . . do it now. . . . Don't make me suffer. . . . Past saving . . ."

Granddad squinted into the murky, late-afternoon August sky, in which a dozen or so stars shone brightly, and let out a long howl before turning to Father. "Are there bullets in your gun, Douguan?"

"Yes."

Father handed his pistol to Granddad, who released the safety, took another look into the darkening sky, and spun the cylinder. "Rest easy, brother. As long as Yu Zhan'ao has food to eat, your wife and child will never go hungry."

Fang Seven nodded and closed his eyes.

Granddad raised the revolver as though he were lifting a huge boulder. The pressures of the moment made him quake.

Fang Seven's eyes snapped open. "Elder brother . . ."

Granddad spun his face away, and a burst of flame leaped out of the muzzle, lighting up Fang Seven's greenish scalp. The kneeling man shot forward and fell on top of his own exposed guts. Father found it hard to believe that a man's belly could hold such a pile of intestines.

"Consumptive Four, you'd better be on your way, too. Then you can get an early start on your next life and come back to seek revenge on those Jap bastards!" He pumped the last cartridge into the heart of the dying Consumptive Four.

Though killing had become a way of life for Granddad, he dropped his arm to his side and let it hang there like a dead snake; the pistol fell to the ground.

Father bent over and picked it up, stuck it into his belt, and tugged on Granddad, who stood as though drunk or paralyzed. "Let's go home, Dad, let's go home. . . ."

"Home? Go home? Yes, go home! Go home . . ."

Father pulled him up onto the dike and began walking awkwardly toward the west. The cold rays of the half-moon on that August 9 evening filled the sky, falling lightly on the backs of Granddad and Father and illuminating the heavy Black Water River, which was like the great but clumsy Chinese race. White eels, thrown into a frenzy by the bloody water, writhed and sparkled on the surface. The blue chill of the water merged with the red warmth of the sorghum bordering the dikes to form an airy, transparent mist that reminded Father of the heavy, spongy fog that had accompanied them as they set out for battle that morning. Only one day, but it seemed like ten years. Yet it also seemed like the blink of an eye.

Father thought back to how his mother had walked him to the edge of the fog-enshrouded village. The scene seemed so far away, though it was right there in front of his eyes. He recalled how difficult the march through the sorghum field had been, how Wang Wenyi had been wounded in the ear by a stray bullet, how the fifty or so soldiers had approached the bridge looking like the droppings of a goat. Then there was Mute's razor-sharp saber knife, the sinister eyes, the Jap head sailing through the air, the shriveled ass of the old Jap officer . . . Mother soaring to the top of the dike as though on the wings of a phoenix . . . the fistcakes . . . fistcakes rolling on the ground . . . stalks of sorghum falling all around . . . red sorghum crumpling like fallen heroes. . . .

Granddad hoisted Father, who was asleep on his feet, onto his back and wrapped his arms—one healthy, the other injured—around Father's legs. The pistol in Father's belt banged against Granddad's back, sending sharp pains straight to his heart. It had belonged to the dark, skinny, handsome, and well-educated Adjutant Ren. Granddad was thinking about how this pistol had ended the lives of Adjutant Ren, Fang Seven, and Consumptive Four. He wanted nothing more than to heave the execrable thing into the Black Water River. But it was only a thought. Bending over, he shifted his sleeping son higher up on his back, partly to relieve the excruciating pain in his heart.

All that kept Granddad moving was a powerful drive to push on and continue the bitter struggle against wave after murky wave of obdurate air. In his dazed state he heard a loud clamor rushing toward him like a tidal wave. When he raised his head he spotted a long fiery dragon wriggling its way along the top of the dike. His eyes froze, as the image slipped in and out of focus.

When it was blurred he could see the dragon's fangs and claws as it rode the clouds and sailed through the mist, the vigorous motions making its golden scales jangle; wind howled, clouds hissed, lightning flashed, thunder rumbled, the sounds merging to form a masculine wind that swept across a huddled feminine world.

When it was clear he could see it was ninety-nine torches hoisted above the heads of hundreds of people hastening toward him. The dancing flames lit up the sorghum on both banks of the river. Granddad lifted Father down off his back and shook him hard.

"Douguan," he shouted in his ear, "Douguan! Wake up! Wake up! The villagers are coming for us, they're coming. . . ."

Father heard the hoarseness in Granddad's voice and saw two remarkable tears leap out of his eyes.

4

GRANDDAD WAS ONLY TWENTY-FOUR when he murdered Shan Tingxiu and his son. Even though by then he and Grandma had already done the phoenix dance in the sorghum field, and even though, in the solemn course of suffering and joy, she had conceived my father, whose life was a mixture of achievements and sin (in the final analysis, he gained distinction among his generation of citizens of Northeast Gaomi Township), she had nonetheless been legally married into the Shan family. So she and Granddad were adulterers, their relationship marked by measures of spontaneity, chance, and uncertainty. And since Father wasn't born while they were together, accuracy demands that I refer to Granddad as Yu Zhan'ao in writing about this period.

When, in agony and desperation, Grandma told Yu Zhan'ao that her legal husband, Shan Bianlang, was a leper, he decapitated two sorghum plants with his short sword. Urging her not to worry, he told her to return three days hence. She was too overwhelmed by the tide of passionate love to concern herself with the implications of his comment. But murderous thoughts had already entered his mind. He watched her thread her way out of the sorghum field and, through the spaces between stalks, saw her summon her shrewd little donkey and nudge Great-Granddad with her foot, waking the mud-caked heap from his drunken stupor. He heard Great-Granddad, whose tongue had grown thick in his mouth, say: "Daughter . . . you . . . what took you so long to take a piss? . . . Your father-in-law . . . going to give me a big black mule . . ."

Ignoring his mumbling, she swung her leg over the donkey's back and turned her face, brushed by the winds of spring, toward the sorghum field south of the road. She knew that the young sedan bearer was watching her. Struggling to wrench free of this unknown passion, she had a dim vision of a new and unfamiliar broad road stretching out ahead of her, covered with sorghum seeds as red as rubies, the ditches on either side filled with crystal-clear sorghum wine. As she moved down the road, her imagination colored the genuine article until she could not distinguish between reality and illusion.

Yu Zhan'ao followed her with his eyes until she rounded a bend. Feeling suddenly weary, he pushed his way through the sorghum and returned to the sacred altar, where he collapsed like a toppled wall and fell into a sound sleep. Later, as the red sun was disappearing in the west, his eyes snapped open, and the first things he saw were sorghum leaves, stems, and ears of grain that formed a thick blanket of purplish red above him. He draped his rain cape over his shoulders and walked out of the field as a rapid breeze on the road caused the sorghum to rustle noisily. He wrapped the cape tightly around him to ward off the chill, and as his hand brushed against his belly he realized how hungry he was. He dimly recalled the three shacks at the head of the village where he had carried the woman in the sedan chair three days ago, and the tattered tavern flag snapping and fluttering in the raging winds of the rainstorm. So hungry he could neither sit still nor stand straight, he strode toward the tavern. Since he had been hiring out for the Northeast Gaomi Township Wedding and Funeral Service Company for less than two years, the people around here wouldn't recognize him. He'd get something to eat and drink, find a way to do what he'd come to do, then slip into the sorghum fields, like a fish in the ocean, and swim far away.

At this point in his ruminations, he headed west, where bilious red clouds turned the setting sun into a blooming peony with a luminous, fearfully bright golden border. After walking west for a while, he turned north, heading straight for the village where Grandma's nominal husband lived. The fields were still and deserted. During those years, any farmer who had food at home left his field before nightfall, turning the sorghum fields into a haven for bandits.

Village chimneys were smoking by the time he arrived, and a handsome young man was walking down the street with two crocks of fresh well water over his shoulder, the shifting water splashing over the sides. Yu Zhan'ao darted into the doorway beneath the tattered tavern flag. No inner walls separated the shacks, and a bar made of adobe bricks divided the room in two, the inner half of which was furnished with a brick kang, a stove, and a large vat. Two rickety tables with scarred tops and a few scattered narrow benches constituted the furnishings in the outer half of the room. A glazed wine crock rested on the bar, its ladle hanging from the rim. A fat old man was sprawled on the kang. Yu Zhan'ao recognized him as the Korean dog-butcher they called Gook. He had seen Gook once at the market in Ma Hamlet. The man could slaughter a dog in less than a minute, and the hundreds of dogs that lived in Ma Hamlet growled viciously when they saw him, their fur standing straight up, though they kept their distance.

"Barkeep, a bowl of wine!" Yu Zhan'ao called out as he sat on one of the benches.

The fat old man didn't stir, his rolling eyes the only movement on the kang.

"Barkeep!" Yu Zhan'ao shouted.

The fat old man pulled back the white dog pelt covering him and climbed down off the kang. Yu Zhan'ao noticed three more pelts hanging on the wall: one green, one blue, and one spotted.

The fat old man took a dark-red bowl out of an opening in the bar and ladled wine into it.

"What do you have to go with the wine?" Yu Zhan'ao asked.

"Dog head!" the fat old man snarled.

"I want dog meat!"

"Dog head's all I've got!"

"Okay, then."

The old man removed the lid from the pot, in which a whole dog was cooking.

"Forget the head," Yu Zhan'ao demanded. "I want some of that meat."

Ignoring him, the old man picked up his cleaver and hacked at the dog's neck, spattering the scalding soup about. Once he'd severed the head, he stuck a metal skewer into it and held it out over the bar.

"I said I want dog meat!" Yu Zhan'ao snapped, his ire rising.

The old man threw the dog head down on the bar and said angrily, "That's what I've got. Take it or leave it!"

"Who do you think you're talking to?"

"Just sit there like a good little boy!" the old man warned. "What makes you think you can eat dog meat? I'm saving that for Spotted Neck."

Spotted Neck was a famous bandit chief in Northeast Gaomi Township. Just hearing the name was enough to intimidate Yu Zhan'ao, for Spotted Neck was reputed to be a crack shot. His trademark of firing three shots in a circular motion had earned him the nickname Three-Nod Phoenix. People who knew guns could tell just by listening that Spotted Neck was nearby. Reluctantly Yu Zhan'ao held his tongue and, with the bowl of wine in one hand, reached out and picked up the dog head, then took a spiteful bite out of the animal's snout. It was delicious, and he was ravenously hungry, so he dug in, eating quickly until the head and the wine were gone. With a final gaze at the bony skull, he stood up and belched.

"One silver dollar," the fat old man said.

"I've only got seven coppers," Yu Zhan'ao said, tossing the coins down on the table.

"I said one silver dollar!"

"And I said I've only got seven coppers!"

"Do you really expect to eat without paying, boy?"

"I've got seven copper coins and that's it." Yu Zhan'ao stood up to leave, but the fat old man ran around the bar and grabbed him. As they were struggling, a tall, beefy man walked into the bar.

"Hey, Gook, how come you haven't lit your lantern?"

"This guy thinks he can eat without paying!"

"Cut out his tongue!" the man said darkly. "And light the lantern!"

The fat old man let go of Yu Zhan'ao and walked behind the bar, where he stoked the fire and lit a bean-oil lamp. The glimmering light illuminated the stranger's dark face. Yu Zhan'ao noticed that he was dressed in black satin from head to toe: a jacket with a row of cloth buttons down the front, a pair of wide-legged trousers tied at the ankles with black cotton straps, and black, double-buckled cloth shoes. His long, thick neck had a white spot on it the size of a fist. This, Yu Zhan'ao thought to himself, must be Spotted Neck.

Spotted Neck sized up Yu Zhan'ao, then stuck out his left hand and rested three fingers on his forehead. Yu Zhan'ao looked at him curiously.

Spotted Neck shook his head disapprovingly. "Not a bandit?"

"I'm a sedan bearer for the service company."

"So you make your living with a pole," Spotted Neck said derisively. "Interested in eating fistcakes with me?"

"No," Yu Zhan'ao replied.

"Then get the hell out of here. You're still young, so I'll let you keep your tongue for kissing women! Go on, and watch what you say."

Yu Zhan'ao backed out of the tavern, not sure whether he was angry or scared. He had grudging respect for the way Spotted Neck carried himself, but not to the exclusion of loathing.

Born into poverty, Yu Zhan'ao had lost his father when he was just a boy. So he and his mother had eked out a living by tending three mou—less than half an acre—of miserable land. His uncle, Big Tooth Yu, who dealt in mules and horses, had occasionally helped mother and son financially, but not all that often.

Then, when he was thirteen, his mother began an affair with the abbot at Tianqi Monastery. The well-to-do monk often brought rice and noodles over, and every time he came, Yu Zhan'ao's mother sent the boy outside. Flames of anger raged inside him as sounds of revelry emerged from behind the closed door, and he could barely keep from torching the house. By the time he was sixteen, his mother was seeing the monk so frequently that the village was buzzing. A friend of his, Little Cheng the blacksmith, made him a short sword, with which he murdered the monk one drizzly spring night beside Pear Blossom Creek, named for the trees that lined it. They were in bloom on that wet night, blanketing the area with their delicate fragrance.

Granddad fled the village after the incident, taking odd jobs and finally getting hooked on gambling. Over time his skills improved, until the copper coins that passed through his hands stained his fingers green. Then, when Nine Dreams Cao, whose favorite pastime was nabbing gamblers, became magistrate of Gaomi County, he was arrested for gambling in a graveyard, given two hundred lashes with a shoe sole, forced to wear a pair of pants with one red leg and one black one, and sentenced to sweeping the streets of the county town for two months. When he'd completed his sentence he wandered into Northeast Gaomi Township, where he hired out to the service company. Upon learning that, after the death of the monk, his mother had hanged herself from the door frame, he went back one night to take a last look around. Some time later, the incident with my grandma occurred.

After walking outside, Yu Zhan'ao went into the sorghum field. He could see the dim lantern light in the tavern as he waited, following the progress of the new moon across the sky lit up with bright stars. Cool dew dripped from the sorghum stalks; cold air rose from the ground beneath him. Late that night he heard the tavern door creak open, flooding the night with lantern light. A fat figure hopped into the halo of light, looked around, then went back inside. Yu Zhan'ao could tell it was the dog butcher. After the man had gone back inside, the bandit Spotted Neck darted out the door and was quickly swallowed up by shadows. The fat old man closed the door and blew out the lantern, leaving the tattered flag above his tavern to flutter in the starlight as though calling to lost spirits.

As the bandit walked down the road, Yu Zhan'ao held his breath and didn't move a muscle. Spotted Neck chose a place right in front of him to take a piss; the foul odor hit Yu Zhan'ao full in the face. With his hand on his sword, he was thinking it would be so easy to put an end to this famous bandit chief. His muscles tensed. But then he had second thoughts. He had no grudge against Spotted Neck, who was a thorn in the side of County Magistrate Nine Dreams Cao, the man who had given Yu Zhan'ao two hundred lashes with a shoe sole. That was reason enough to spare Spotted Neck. But he was pleased to think: I could have killed the famous bandit chief Spotted Neck if I'd wanted to.

Spotted Neck never learned of this brush with death, nor did he imagine that within two years he would die stark-naked in the Black Water River at the hands of this same young fellow. After relieving himself, he hitched up his pants and walked off.

Yu Zhan'ao jumped to his feet and walked into the sleeping village, stepping lightly so as not to awaken the dogs. When he reached the Shans' gate, he held his breath as he familiarized himself with his surroundings. The Shan family lived in a row of twenty buildings, divided into two compounds by an interior wall and surrounded by an outer wall with two gates. The distillery was in the eastern compound, while the family lived in the western compound, in which there were three side rooms on the far edge. There were also three side rooms on the edge of the eastern compound, which served as bunkhouses for the distillery workers. In addition, a tent in the eastern compound accommodated a large millstone and the two big black mules that turned it. Finally, there were three connecting rooms at the southern edge of the eastern compound with a single door facing south. That was where the wine was sold.

Yu Zhan'ao couldn't see over the wall, so he quickly scaled it, making scraping noises that woke the dogs on the other side, who began to bark loudly. After retreating about half the distance an arrow flies, he hunkered down in the square where the Shans dried their sorghum. He needed a plan. The pleasant aroma from a pile of sorghum husks and another of leaves caught his attention. Kneeling down beside the dry husks, he took out his stone and flint, and lit them. But no sooner had they ignited than he had another idea, and he smothered the flames with his hands. He walked over to the pile of leaves, some twenty paces distant, and set fire to it. Less compact than the husks, they would burn more quickly and be easier to extinguish. On that windless night, the Milky Way stretched across the sky, surrounded by thousands of twinkling stars; flames quickly leaped into the air, lighting up the village as though it were daytime.

"Fire!" he yelled at the top of his lungs. "Fire—" Then he hid among the shadows of the western wall around the family compound. Tongues of flame licked the heavens, crackling loudly and setting the village dogs to barking. The distillery workers in the eastern compound, startled out of their sleep, began to shout. The gate banged open, and a dozen or so half-naked men came rushing out. The western gate also opened, and the wizened old man with the pitiful little queue stumbled out, screaming and wailing. Two big yellow dogs flew past him toward the raging fire and raised a howl.

"Fire . . . put it out. . . ." The old man was nearly in tears. The distillery hands rushed back into the compound, snatched up buckets on poles, and ran to the well. The old man also ran back inside, picked up a black tile crock, and ran toward the well.

After shedding his straw rain cape, Yu Zhan'ao crept along the base of the wall and entered the western compound, flattening up against the Shans' screen wall to watch the men scurry back and forth. One of them dumped a bucketful of water on the fire, the stream of liquid looking like a piece of white silk in the glare of the flames, in whose heat it curled and twisted. They poured bucketful after bucketful of water onto the fire, high arching waterfalls one minute and puffs of cotton the next, forming a scene of exquisite beauty.

A prudent voice of reason called out, "Let it burn, Master. It'll soon burn itself out."

"Put it out. . . . Put it out. . . ." He was in tears now. "Hurry up and put it out. . . . That's enough mule fodder for a whole winter. . . ."

With no time to waste on the scene outside, Yu Zhan'ao slipped into the house, where he was met by an overwhelming dampness. His hair stood on end. A mildewy voice emerged from inside the room to the west:

"Dad . . . what's burning?"

Having entered the house after staring at the flames, Yu Zhan'ao was forced to wait until his eyes had adjusted to the darkness. When the voice repeated the question, he headed toward it. The room was lit up by the glare through the paper window, making it easy for him to see the long, flat face on the pillow. He reached out and held down the head, which cried out in alarm, "Who . . . who are you?" Two claws dug into the back of Yu Zhan'ao's hand as he drew his sword and buried it in the pale skin of the long, thin neck. A breath of cool air escaped onto his wrist, followed by hot, sticky blood that gloved his hand. He felt like throwing up. Fearfully, he took his hand away. The wrinkled, flat head was convulsing on the pillow, golden blood spurting from the neck. He tried wiping his hand on the bedding, but the harder he wiped, the stickier it got, and the stronger his feelings of nausea grew. Grasping the slimy sword in his hand, he turned and ran into the outer room; there he scooped a handful of straw out of the stove to clean off his hand and his sword, which glinted in the light and seemed to come alive.

Every single day, he had engaged in secret swordplay with the weapon given to him by Little Cheng the blacksmith, and each time he heard the pillow talk emerging from his mother's room he sheathed and unsheathed it over and over. Villagers began taunting him by calling him Junior Monk, to which he reacted with a blood-curdling glare. The sword now lay beneath his pillow, keeping him awake at night with high-pitched shrieks. He knew the time had come.

The full moon was hidden behind dense leaden clouds that night, and as the villagers were falling asleep, a light rain began to fall, the scattered drops slowly soaking the ground and filling the hollows with silvery water. The monk opened the door and walked in under a yellow oilcloth umbrella. From the vantage point of his room, he watched the monk fold his umbrella and saw his shiny bald pate as he unhurriedly scraped the mud from the soles of his shoes on the threshold.

He heard his mother ask, "What are you doing here at this time of night?"

"I had to say a seventh-day funeral mass for the mother of 'Man-Biter' in West Village."

"I mean why so late? I didn't think you'd come."

"Why not?"

"It's raining."

"If it had been raining daggers, I'd have come with a pot over my head."

"Get in here, and be quick about it."

"Does your belly still hurt?" the monk asked softly as he entered her room.

"Not so bad, ahhh . . ."

"What's wrong?"

"The boy's dad has been dead nearly ten years, and look what I've become. I don't know if I'm up or I'm down."

"Be up. I'll chant a sutra for you."

He didn't close his eyes that night, as he listened to the shrieks of the sword beneath his pillow, to the patter of the rain outside, to the even breathing of the sleeping monk, and to his mother as she talked in her sleep. He sat up in alarm when he heard the strange laugh of an owl in a nearby tree. After dressing, he picked up the sword and stood with his ear cocked in the doorway of the room where his mother and the monk slept. His heart was a white wasteland, desolate and empty. Gently he opened the door and walked out into the yard, where he looked up into the sky: the leaden clouds were lighter than before and a glimmer of early-dawn light was visible. A gentle rain was still falling, slow and unhurried, silently moistening the earth and splattering weakly as it landed in puddles. He followed the winding road to Tianqi Monastery, which ran about three li and crossed a tiny brook on black stepping-stones.

During daylight hours the brook was so clear you could count the tiny fish and shrimp on the sandy bottom. But now it was gray and hazy under a thin mist, and the sound of splashing rainwater made him sorrowful and anxious. The stones were wet and slippery; the glimmering water was rising. He was mesmerized by the sight of ripples as the water struck the stones beneath his feet. The smooth sandy edge of the brook was lined by flower-laden pear trees. After fording the brook, he turned into the pear grove, where the sandy ground was firm yet slightly springy. The white pear blossoms poking through the mist were dazzling, but their redolence was snuffed out by the chilled air.

He located his father's grave in the depths of the pear grove, covered with weeds that hid a dozen or more treacherous holes burrowed into the ground by mice. Although he tried hard to recall his father's face, all he could conjure up was the faint image of a tall, skinny man with sallow skin and a light, wispy mustache.

After returning to the edge of the brook, he hid behind one of the trees and stared blankly at white ripples where the water struck the black stepping-stones. The sky, beginning to suffuse with light, had grown paler, the clouds parted to reveal the outline of the little road.

The monk walked quickly up the road under the yellow oilcloth umbrella that obscured his head. There were tiny water stains on his green cassock. Raising the hem with one hand and holding his umbrella high with the other, he crossed the brook, his rotund figure twisting as he stepped from stone to stone. Now that his pale, puffy face was visible, Yu Zhan'ao gripped the sword and listened to its high-pitched shriek. His wrist ached and began to turn numb; his fingers started to twitch. After fording the brook, the monk let go of the hem of his cassock and stomped his feet, splashing his sleeve with mud, which he flicked off with his fingernail.

This fair-skinned monk, who prided himself on always looking tidy and fresh, exuded a pleasant soapy odor, which Yu Zhan'ao could smell as he watched him fold his umbrella and shake off the water before slipping it under his arm. The twelve round burns on his pale scalp sparkled. Yu Zhan'ao recalled seeing his mother caress that scalp with both hands, as though she were stroking a Buddhist treasure, while he laid his head in her lap like a contented infant. By now the monk was so close he could hear his labored breathing. He was barely able to grip the sword handle, which was as slippery as a loach. He was drenched with sweat, his eyes were blurring, and he was getting light-headed. He was afraid he might faint.

As the monk passed by, he spat a gob of sticky phlegm, which landed on a twig and hung there sickeningly, giving rise to all sorts of nauseating thoughts in Yu Zhan'ao's mind. He inched closer, his head throbbing painfully. His temples felt like mallets pounding on a taut drum inside his head. The sword seemed to enter the monk's rib cage on its own. The monk stumbled a few steps before grabbing the trunk of a pear tree to steady himself, and turned to look at his assailant. There was pain in the monk's pitiful eyes, and a keen sense of regret in his heart. He said nothing as he slid slowly down the tree trunk to the ground.

When Yu Zhan'ao pulled the sword out of the monk's rib cage, a flow of lovely warm blood was released, soft and slippery, like the wing feathers of a bird. . . . The buildup of water on the pear tree finally gave way and splashed down on the sandy ground, bringing dozens of petals with it. A small whirlwind rose up deep in the pear grove, and he later recalled smelling the delicate fragrance of pear blossoms. . . .

He felt no remorse, though, over murdering Shan Bianlang, only disgust. The flames gradually died down, but the sky was still brightly lit. A ghostly shadow rustled at the base of the wall; the village was engulfed by a swelling tide of barking. Metal rims of water buckets clattered loudly; water sizzled and sputtered as it hit the roaring flames.

Six days earlier: The downpour had soaked the sedan bearers until they looked like drenched chickens, and the only dry spot on the young bride was her back. He stood with the other bearers and musicians in mud puddles, watching two slovenly old men lead the bride into the house. Not a single person in the large village came out to watch the excitement, and the bridegroom was nowhere in sight. A rusty odor seeped through the open door, and the sedan bearers knew without being told that the bridegroom, who wouldn't show his face, was indeed a leper. Seeing that there were no witnesses to the excitement, the musicians settled for a bland little tune.

A wizened old man came outside with a little basket of copper coins and croaked, "Here's your reward! Come and get it!" as he scattered a handful of coins on the ground. The bearers and musicians watched the coins splash in the puddles, but none made a move to pick them up. The old man bent over and picked up the coins, one at a time. That was when the idea of burying a knife in the old man's scrawny neck formed in Granddad's mind.

Now flames were lighting up that same compound and the couplets pasted up alongside the gate. Since he wasn't completely illiterate, he read them, and when he had finished, flames of indignation drove every trace of coolness out of his heart. He used some folk wisdom to absolve himself: charity for the sake of karma doesn't mean you'll die in bed; murder and arson are a sure path to the good life. Besides, he'd given the young woman his word, and had already murdered the man's son; by sparing the father, he'd only be subjecting him to the grief of seeing his son's corpse. There was no turning back. Now that he'd knocked over the gourd and spilled all the oil, he'd create a new life for the young woman. "Old Man Shan," he mumbled under his breath, "this day next year will be your first anniversary!"

The fire was dying out, returning the compound to darkness and the stars to the sky, although a few cinders remained in the pile of leaves. When water was dumped on the hot spots, white steam and glowing cinders rose dozens of feet into the air. The men stood, buckets in hand, casting large shadows on the ground.

"Don't be sad, Master. Financial losses, lucky bosses," said the voice of reason.

"Heaven has no eyes. . . . Heaven has no eyes . . ." Shan Tingxiu mumbled.

"Let the men go inside and get some rest, Master. They have to be up for work early in the morning."

"Heaven has no eyes. . . . Heaven has no eyes. . . ."

The men staggered into the eastern compound. Yu Zhan'ao hid behind the screen wall as the clatter of buckets on carrying poles moved past him, followed by silence. Shan Tingxiu stood in the gateway mumbling, but finally began to lose interest and carried his tile crock back into the compound, the two family dogs leading the way. Clearly exhausted, when they spotted Yu Zhan'ao they merely barked once or twice and headed for their pen, where they plopped down and didn't make another sound.

Yu Zhan'ao could hear the big mule in the eastern compound grind its teeth and paw the ground. The three stars had moved to the western sky, so it was after midnight. He braced himself, gripped his sword, and waited until Shan Tingxiu was a mere three or four paces from the door, then rushed him with such force that he buried the sword in his chest, past the hilt. The old man flew backward, his arms spread out, as if he were taking off into the air before falling on his back. His tile crock crashed to the ground and blossomed like a flower. The dogs barked listlessly a few more times and took no more notice. Yu Zhan'ao withdrew his sword, rubbed both sides of the blade on the old man's clothes, and turned to leave. But he stopped himself.

After dragging Shan Bianlang's body out into the yard, he removed some rope from a carrying pole at the base of the wall, tied the two frail corpses together at the waist, then hoisted them up and carried them out to the street. They hung limply over his shoulder, their dragging feet making pale designs in the dirt, the blood seeping from their wounds leaving red patterns on the ground. Yu Zhan'ao carried the bodies over to the western inlet, whose glassy surface reflected half the stars in the sky. A few sleepy white water lilies floated gracefully like sprites in a fairy tale. Thirteen years later, when Mute shot Yu Zhan'ao's uncle, Big Tooth Yu, there was hardly any water at this spot in the river, but these lilies were still there. Yu Zhan'ao dumped the bodies into the water with a loud splash. They sank quickly to the bottom, and when the ripples died, the sky once again owned the surface.

Yu Zhan'ao rinsed his hands, his face, and his sword in the river, but no matter how long he washed, he couldn't remove the smells of blood and mildew. He then headed down the road, forgetting all about retrieving his rain cape from the Shan compound. When he'd traveled about half a li, he turned into the stand of sorghum, and immediately stumbled and fell. Suddenly realizing how tired he was, he rolled over on his back, oblivious to the dampness, and gazed at the stars until he fell asleep.

5

FIVE MONKEYS SHAN, knowing there was something fishy about the fire that night, seriously considered getting up and helping to fight it, thus carrying out his responsibilities as village chief. But Little White Lamb, the voluptuous opium peddler, wrapped her arms around him and wouldn't let go. Two bandit gangs had once fought over this girl, with her fair skin and moist, captivating, suggestive eyes—what is called "fighting over the nest" in bandit parlance. She was a living sign that the war being waged by Gaomi County Magistrate Nine Dreams Cao was far from won.

In 1923, Nine Dreams Cao had been serving the Northern Warlord Government as magistrate for nearly three years, and his "three torches" were blazing. For him the earthly scourges were banditry, opium, and gambling, and the only way to put the world in order was to annihilate bandits, stamp out opium, and outlaw gambling. His favorite punishment was a beating with the sole of a shoe; hence his nickname, Shoe Sole Cao the Second. A complex individual for whom the words "good" and "bad" are woefully inadequate, he was involved in many important ways with my family, so it is appropriate to include him in this narrative as a link to what follows.

In two years of draconian decrees, Nine Dreams Cao had achieved considerable results in his rampage against the three scourges. But Northeast Gaomi Township was a long way from the county seat, and behind the scenes gambling, opium, and bandits flourished as never before.

Five Monkeys Shan slept till dawn with Little White Lamb in his arms. She awoke first. After lighting the bean-oil lamp, she stuck a silver pin into an opium pellet and thrust it into the flames. Once it caught fire, she stuffed it into a silver pipe and handed it to Five Monkeys Shan, who curled up in bed and inhaled for a minute or so. A tiny white dot glowed on the pellet. After holding his breath for two minutes, he exhaled streams of thin blue smoke through his mouth and nostrils, just as one of the Shan family's hired hands banged frantically on the door and reported: "Village Chief! Terrible news! Murder!"

Five Monkeys Shan accompanied the hired hand into the Shan compound, with several other men on his heels. Then he followed the trail of blood to the inlet at the western edge of the village. The crowd behind him swelled.

"The bodies must be at the bottom of the river," he said.

No one made a sound.

"Who'll go down and drag them up?"

The men exchanged glances, but said nothing.

The emerald-green water was smooth as glass. Water lilies floated placidly on the surface, with scattered dewdrops sticking to the leaves nearest the water, as moist and round as pearls.

"One silver dollar. Now who'll go?"

Still no sound.

An acrid stench rose from the inlet, and an unimaginably foul red glare emerged from a puddle of purplish blood in the reeds at the water's edge. The sun rose above the field, white at the top and green at the bottom, sizzling like a chunk of partially fired steel. A line of black clouds above the horizon of sorghum tips stretched far off into the distance, so level you'd think your eyes were playing tricks on you. The inlet sparkled like a river of gold, broken only by the water lilies, which seemed otherworldly.

"Who'll go down for a silver dollar?" Five Monkeys Shan asked in a booming voice.

The ninety-two-year-old woman from our village told me, "No man would have dared go into an inlet filled with the blood of a leper, not even for his own mother! If he did, he'd come out infected. If two went in, they'd both come out infected. Not for any amount of money . . . All that evil was caused by your grandma and your granddad!" I wasn't happy with the old hag for placing the blame on Granddad and Grandma, but as I looked at her clay-pot head I just smiled weakly.

"Nobody's willing to go down? Not a fucking one of you? Then we'll just let father and son cool off in the water! Old Liu, Arhat Liu, since you're the foreman, go into town and report this to Shoe Sole Cao the Second."

In preparation for the trip, Uncle Arhat Liu wolfed down some food, followed it with half a gourdful of wine, then led out one of the black mules, tied a burlap bag over its back, and mounted it. He headed west, toward the county town.

Uncle Arhat wore a somber expression that morning, from either anger or resentment. He was the first to suspect that something terrible had befallen his master and the master's son following the suspicious fire. Up at the first light of dawn, he was surprised to note that the western compound gate was wide open. He spotted blood on the ground as soon as he walked into the yard, and more of it inside the house. Even in his confused state he knew that the fire and blood-letting were linked.

Since he and all the other hands knew that the young master had leprosy, they did not enter the western compound unless it was absolutely necessary, and then only after spraying mouthfuls of wine over their bodies. Uncle Arhat believed that sorghum wine was an effective disinfectant for all kinds of dangerous germs. When Shan Bianlang's bride entered the compound three days earlier, no villagers were willing to assist, so naturally he and an old distillery hand were left to help her out of the sedan chair. As he held her arm and walked her into the house, he glanced at her out of the corner of his eye, seeing her delicate bound feet and her plump wrist, as big around as a lotus root, and he couldn't stifle a sigh. In the midst of his shock over the murder of Old Man Shan and his son days later, the image of Grandma's tiny feet and full wrist appeared and reappeared in his mind. He didn't know if the sight of all that blood made him sad or happy.

Uncle Arhat whipped the big black mule, wishing it could sprout wings and fly him to town. He knew there would be more excitement to come, since the flowery, jadelike little bride would be returning from her parents' home tomorrow morning on her donkey. Who would be the beneficiary of the Shan family's vast holdings? Things like that were best left to Nine Dreams Cao to decide. After having overseen Gaomi County for three years, Cao had earned the sobriquet "Upright Magistrate." People talked about how he dispatched cases with the wisdom of the gods, the vigor of thunder, and the speed of wind; about how he was just and honorable, never favoring his own kin over others; and about how he meted out death sentences without batting an eye. Uncle Arhat smacked the mule's rump harder.

The mule flew west toward the county town, pounding the ground with its rear hooves when its front legs were curled up, then stretching out its front legs and curling its rear legs. The movement produced a rhythm of hoofbeats that belied the seemingly chaotic motion. Dust flew like blossoming flowers in the glinting light of the horseshoes. The sun was still in the southeastern corner of the sky when Uncle Arhat reached the Jiao-Ping–Jinan rail line. The mule balked at crossing the tracks, so Uncle Arhat jumped down and tried to pull it across. But since he was no match for the animal's strength, he sat down on the ground, gasping for breath and trying to figure out what to do next. The sunlight hurt his eyes. He stood up, wrapped his jacket around the mule's eyes, and led it in a circle a few times before crossing the tracks.

Two black-uniformed policemen guarded the town's northern gate, each armed with a Hanyang rifle. Since it was market day in Gaomi County, a stream of pushcarts, peddlers with carrying poles, and people on mules and on foot passed through the town gate. Ignoring the traffic, the policemen busied themselves leering at pretty girls passing in front of them.

Uncle Arhat led his mule onto the main street of town, paved with green cobblestones that clattered loudly under the mule's shod hooves. To the south, the huge market square was jammed with people from every trade and occupation, haggling over prices, shouting and carrying on, buying and selling everything under the sun.

In no mood to get caught up in the excitement, Uncle Arhat led the mule up to the gate of the government compound, which looked like a dilapidated monastery, its tile roofs covered with yellow weeds and green grass. The red paint on the gate was peeling badly. An armed sentry stood to the left, while to the right a bare-chested man supported himself with both hands on a staff resting in a smelly honeypot.

Uncle Arhat bowed to the sentry. "Sir," he said, "I need to report to County Magistrate Cao."

"Magistrate Cao took Master Yan to market," the sentry replied.

"When will he be back?"

"How should I know? Go look for him at the market square if you're in such a hurry."

Uncle Arhat bowed again. "Thank you, sir."

Seeing that Uncle Arhat was about to walk away, the bare-chested man sprang into action, churning his staff up and down in the honeypot and shouting, "Come look, come look, everybody, come look. My name is Wang Haoshan. I cheated people with a phony contract, and the county magistrate sentenced me to stir up a honeypot. . . ."

Uncle Arhat and the mule entered the crowded market square, where people were selling baked buns, flatcakes, and sandals. There were scribes, fortune-tellers, beggars using every imaginable ploy, peddlers of aphrodisiacs, trained monkeys, gong-banging hawkers of malt sugar, knickknack vendors, storytellers with tales of romance and intrigue, dealers in leeks, cucumbers, and garlic, sellers of barber razors and pipe bowls, noodle sellers, rat-poison merchants, honeyed-peach sellers, child vendors—yes, even a "child market," where children with straw markers on their collars could be bought or sold. The black mule kept rearing its head, making the steel bit in its mouth sing out. The sun was directly overhead, blazing down on Uncle Arhat, drenching his purple jacket with his own sweat.

Uncle Arhat spotted the official he was looking for at the chicken market.

Magistrate Cao had a ruddy face, bulging eyes, a square mouth, and a thin mustache. He was decked out in a dark-green tunic and a brown wool formal hat. He carried a walking stick.

Caught up in resolving a dispute, he had drawn quite a crowd. Instead of forcing his way to the front, Uncle Arhat led the mule out of the crowd, which blocked his view of what was going on, then mounted up, giving himself the best seat in the house.

A little runt of a man was standing beside the tall Magistrate Cao, and Uncle Arhat assumed it must be the Master Yan to whom the sentry had referred. Two men and a woman stood cowering before Magistrate Cao, their faces bathed in sweat. The woman's cheeks were made even wetter by her tears. A fat hen lay on the ground at her feet.

"Worthy magistrate, your honor," she sobbed, "my mother-in-law can't stop menstruating, and we have no money for medicine. That's why we're selling this laying hen. . . . He says the hen is his. . . ."

"The hen *is* mine. If the magistrate doesn't believe me, ask my neighbor here."

Magistrate Cao pointed to a man in a skullcap. "Can you verify that?"

"Worthy magistrate, I am Wu the Third's neighbor, and this hen of his wanders into my yard every day to steal my chickens' food. My wife's always complaining about it."

The woman screwed up her face, without saying a word, and burst out crying.

Magistrate Cao removed his hat, spun it around on his middle finger, then put it back on.

"What did you feed your chicken this morning?" he asked Wu the Third, who rolled his eyes and replied, "Cereal mash mixed with bran husks."

"He's telling the truth, he is," the man in the skullcap confirmed. "I saw his wife mixing it when I went over to borrow his ax this morning."

Magistrate Cao turned to the crying woman. "Don't cry, countrywoman. Tell me what you fed your chicken this morning."

"Sorghum," she said between sobs.

"Little Yan," Magistrate Cao said, "kill the chicken!"

With lightning speed, Yan slit the hen's crop and squeezed out a gooey mess of sorghum seeds.

With a menacing laugh Magistrate Cao said, "You're a real scoundrel, Wu the Third. Now, since you caused the death of this hen, you can pay for it. Three silver dollars!"

Wu the Third, shaking like a leaf, reached into his pocket and pulled out two silver dollars and twenty copper coins. "Magistrate, your honor," he said fearfully, "this is all I have."

"You're getting off light!" Magistrate Cao said, handing the money to the woman.

"Magistrate, your honor," the woman said, "a hen isn't worth all that much. I only want what's coming to me."

Magistrate Cao raised his hands to his forehead, uttered an exclamation, and said, "You're truly a decent, upright woman. Nine Dreams Cao salutes you!" Bringing his legs together, he removed his hat and bowed low.

The poor woman was so flustered she could only gaze at Nine Dreams Cao through tear-filled eyes. Once she'd regained her senses, she fell to her knees and said over and over, "His honor, the upright magistrate! His honor, the upright magistrate!"

Magistrate Cao placed his walking stick under her arm. "Up, get up."

The countrywoman got to her feet.

"I can tell you are a filial daughter by the way you came to market in shabby clothes and poor health to sell a hen for the sake of your mother-in-law. Nothing impresses the magistrate like filial piety. Take the money and look after your mother-in-law. Take the chicken as well. Clean it and make a nice soup for her."

Money in one hand, chicken in the other, the woman walked away, murmuring her gratitude.

Meanwhile, the deceitful Wu the Third and the neighbor who had served as his witness stood under the blazing sun trembling with fright.

"Wu the Third, you scoundrel," Nine Dreams Cao commanded, "drop your pants."

Wu was too bashful to do as he was told.

"You tried to cheat that good woman in broad daylight," Magistrate Cao rebuked him. "It's pretty late for modesty, isn't it? Do you know what shame is selling for these days? Drop 'em!"

Wu the Third dropped his pants.

Nine Dreams Cao took off one of his shoes and handed it to Little Yan. "Two hundred lashes. All cheeks. Ass and face!"

Holding Magistrate Cao's thick-soled shoe in his hand, Little Yan kicked Wu the Third to the ground, took aim at his exposed backside, and started in, fifty on each side, until Wu was screaming for his parents and begging for mercy, his buttocks swelling up in plain sight of everyone. Then it was his face's turn, again fifty on each side; that stopped his screams.

Magistrate Cao placed the tip of his walking stick on Wu the Third's forehead and said, "Will you try something like that again, you old scoundrel?"

Wu the Third, whose cheeks were so puffy he could barely open his mouth, responded by pounding his head on the ground as though he were crushing garlic.

"As for you," Nine Dreams Cao said, pointing to the man who'd served as witness, "an ass-kisser who'd make up a story like that is the scum of the earth. I'm not going to give you a taste of the bottom of my shoe, because your ass would only soil it. Since you prefer something sweet, I'll let you lick the ass of your rich buddy. Little Yan, go buy a pot of honey."

Little Yan moved toward the crowd, which parted to let him pass. The false witness fell to his knees and banged his head so hard on the ground that his skullcap fell off.

"Get up! Get up! Get up!" Nine Dreams Cao commanded. "I'm not going to have you beaten or punished. I'm going to treat you to some honey, so what are you pleading for?"

When Little Yan returned with the honey, Nine Dreams Cao pointed to Wu the Third. "Spread it on his ass!"

Little Yan rolled Wu over on his belly, picked up a stick, and spread the potful of honey over his swollen buttocks.

"Start licking," Nine Dreams Cao ordered the false witness. "You like kissing ass, don't you? Okay, start licking!"

The false witness kept kowtowing loudly. "Magistrate, your honor," he pleaded, "Magistrate, your honor, I promise I'll never again . . ."

"Get the shoe ready, Little Yan," Nine Dreams Cao said. "And really put some arm into it this time."

"Don't hit me," the false witness screamed, "don't hit me! I'll lick it."

He crawled up to Wu the Third, stuck out his tongue, and began lapping up the sticky, transparent threads of honey.

The looks on the hot, sweaty faces of the observers can hardly be described.

Sometimes fast, sometimes slowly, the false witness licked on, stopping only to throw up, which turned Wu the Third's buttocks into a mottled mess. Seeing that he'd accomplished his purpose, Nine Dreams Cao roared, "That's enough, you scum!"

The man stopped licking, pulled his jacket up over his head, and lay on the ground, refusing to get up.

As Nine Dreams Cao and Little Yan turned to leave, Uncle Arhat jumped off his mule and shouted, "Upright Magistrate! I come to file a grievance—"

6

JUST AS GRANDMA was about to climb off her donkey, the village chief, Five Monkeys Shan, stopped her: "Young mistress, don't get down. The county magistrate wants to see you."

Grandma was taken to the inlet at the western edge of the village in the custody of two armed soldiers. Great-Granddad had such severe leg cramps he couldn't walk, and it took the nudge of a rifle in his back to get him moving; he fell in behind the donkey, his knees knocking.

Grandma noticed a black colt tied to the willow tree at the inlet. It was beautifully liveried, its forehead decorated with a red silk tassel. A few yards away, a man sat behind a table with a tea service. At the time, Grandma didn't know that he was the illustrious Magistrate Cao. Another man stood next to the table, the magistrate's capable enforcer, Master Yan, or Yan Luogu. Rounded-up villagers stood in front of the table, crowded together as though huddling to keep warm. A squad of twenty soldiers fanned out behind them.

Uncle Arhat stood behind another table, soaked to the skin.

The bodies of Shan Tingxiu and his son were laid out beneath the willow, not far from the tethered colt. Already beginning to stink, they oozed a foul yellow liquid. Above the bodies, a flock of crows hopped around on the branches, making the canopy of foliage come alive.

This was Uncle Arhat's chance to get, finally, a clear look at Grandma's full, round face. Her almond-shaped eyes were large, her long neck was like alabaster, her lush hair was rolled up into a bun at the back of her head. Her donkey stopped in front of the table, Grandma sitting tall and straight on its back, the picture of grace. As he watched Magistrate Cao's dark, solemn eyes sweep across my grandma's face and breast, a thought flashed into Uncle Arhat's mind: The old master and his son came to grief because of this woman. She must have taken a lover, who had set the fire to "lure the tiger out of the mountain," then had killed father and son to clear the way for himself. When the radishes have been picked, the field is bare. Now she could carry on however she pleased. . . .

But when he looked at Grandma, Uncle Arhat was immediately besieged with doubts. No matter how a murderer tries to mask it, the look of evil always shows through. This woman sitting on her donkey . . . like a beautiful statue carved from wax, gently swinging her dainty, pointed feet, her expression a mixture of solemnity, tranquillity, and grief—unlike a bodhisattva, yet surpassing a bodhisattva. Great-Granddad stood alongside the donkey in stark contrast: his age against her youth, his decrepitude against her freshness, all serving to accentuate her radiance.

"Have that woman come forward to answer some questions," Magistrate Cao ordered.

Grandma didn't stir. Village Chief Five Monkeys Shan shuffled up and shouted angrily, "Climb down from there! His honor the county magistrate has ordered you to dismount!"

Magistrate Cao raised his hand to call off Five Monkeys Shan, then rose and said genially, "You there, woman, dismount. I want to ask you some questions."

Great-Granddad lifted Grandma down off the mule.

"What is your name?" Magistrate Cao asked her.

Grandma stood stiffly, her eyelids slightly lowered, and said nothing.

Great-Granddad answered for her in a quaking voice, "Your honor, the unworthy girl's name is Dai Fenglian. We call her Little Nine. She was born on the ninth day of the sixth month—"

"Shut up!" Magistrate Cao barked.

"Who said you could talk?" Five Monkeys Shan castigated Great-Granddad.

"Damned fools!" Magistrate Cao banged his fist on the table, causing Five Monkeys Shan and Great-Granddad to shrink in terror. As a benevolent expression reappeared on the magistrate's face, he pointed to the bodies beneath the willow tree and asked, "You there, woman, do you know those two men?"

Grandma glanced out of the corner of her eye, and her face paled. She shook her head in silence.

"They are your husband and your father-in-law. They have been murdered!" Magistrate Cao shouted.

Grandma reeled before collapsing to the ground. The crowd surged forward to help her up, and in the confusion her silver combs were knocked loose, releasing clouds of black hair like a liquid cataract. Grandma, her face the color of gold, sobbed for a moment, then laughed hysterically, a trickle of blood seeping from her lower lip.

Magistrate Cao banged the table again. "Listen, everyone, to my verdict. When the woman Dai, a gentle willow bent by the wind, magnanimous and upright, neither humble nor haughty, heard that her husband had been murdered, she was stricken with overpowering grief, spitting a mouthful of blood. How could a good woman like that be an adulteress who plotted the death of her own husband? Village Chief Five Monkeys Shan, I can see by your sickly pallor that you are an opium smoker and a gambler. How can you, as village chief, defy the laws of the county? That is unforgivable, not to mention your tactics to defile someone's good name, which adds to your list of crimes. I am not fooled in my judgments. No disciples of evil and disorder can evade the eyes of the law. It must have been you who murdered Shan Tingxiu and his son, so you could get your hands on the Shan family fortune and the lovely woman Dai. You schemed to manipulate the local government and deceive me, like someone wielding an ax at the door of master carpenter Lu Ban, or waving his sword at the door of the swordsman Lord Guan, or reciting the *Three Character Classic* at the door of the wise Confucius, or whispering the 'Rhapsody on the Nature of Medicine' in the ear of the physician Li Shizhen. Arrest him!"

Soldiers rushed up and tied Five Monkeys Shan's hands behind his back. "I'm not guilty, I'm innocent. Your honor, Magistrate . . ." he shrieked.

"Seal his mouth with the sole of your shoe!"

Little Yan drew out of his waistband a large shoe made just for this purpose and smacked Five Monkeys Shan across the mouth three times.

"It was you who murdered them, wasn't it?"

"I'm innocent I'm innocent I'm innocent . . ."

"If you didn't do it, who did?"

"It was . . . oh my, I don't know, I don't know. . . ."

"A few minutes ago you had it all figured out, and now you say you don't know. Use the shoe sole again!"

Little Yan smacked Five Monkeys Shan across the mouth a dozen times, splitting his lips, from which frothy blood began to ooze. "I'll tell," he muttered tearfully, "I'll tell. . . ."

"Who's the murderer?"

"It . . . it . . . was a bandit, it was Spotted Neck!"

"He did it on your orders, didn't he?"

"No! It was it was it was . . . Oh, Master, please don't hit me. . . ."

"Listen to me, everybody," Nine Dreams Cao said. "Since assuming office as head of the county, I have worked hard to stamp out opium, outlaw gambling, and annihilate bandits, and I have had notable success with the first two. Only bandits remain a serious problem, running rampant in Northeast Gaomi Township. The county government has called upon all law-abiding citizens to report incidents and expose offenders in order to bring peace to the land.

"Since the woman Dai was legally wed into the Shan family, she may assume its possessions and wealth. Anyone attempting to take advantage of this poor widow, or scheming to deprive her of what is legally hers, will be charged with banditry and disposed of accordingly!"

Grandma took three paces forward and knelt before Magistrate Cao, raising her lovely face and calling out:

"Father! My true father!"

"I am not your father," Magistrate Cao corrected her. "Your father is there, holding the donkey."

She crawled forward and wrapped her arms around Magistrate Cao's legs. "Father, my true father, now that you're the county magistrate, don't you know your own daughter? Ten years ago you fled the famine with your little girl and sold her. You may not know me, but I know you. . . ."

"My goodness! What kind of talk is that? It's a bunch of nonsense!"

"Father, how's my mother? Little Brother must be about thirteen now. Is he in school? Father, you sold me for two pecks of red sorghum, but I held your hand and wouldn't let go. You said, 'Little Nine, when Father has turned things around he'll come back for you.' But now that you're the county magistrate you say you don't know me. . . ."

"The woman is mad, she has mistaken me for someone else!"

"I'm not mistaken! I'm not! Father! My true father!" She held tightly to Magistrate Cao's legs and rocked back and forth, glistening tears streaming down her face, the sun glinting off her jadelike teeth.

Magistrate Cao lifted Grandma up and said, "I can be your foster-father!"

She tried to fall to her knees again, but was supported under the arms by Magistrate Cao. She squeezed his hand and said with childish innocence, "Father, when will you take me to see Mother?"

"Soon, very soon! Now, let go, let go of me. . . ."

Grandma let go of his hand.

Magistrate Cao took out a handkerchief to wipe his sweaty brow.

Everyone stared at the two of them.

Nine Dreams Cao removed his hat and twirled it on his finger as he stammered to the onlookers, "Fellow villagers—I have always advocated—stamp out opium—outlaw gambling—annihilate bandits—"

He had barely finished when—*pow! pow! pow!*—three shots rang out, and three bullets flew over from the sorghum field by the inlet, releasing three puffs of smoke when they hit the brown hat perched atop his middle finger. It sailed into the air, as though in the grip of a demon, and landed in the dirt, still twirling.

The gunshots were met by gasps and whistles from the crowd. "It's Spotted Neck!" someone shouted.

"Three-Nod Phoenix!"

"Quiet down! Quiet down!" Magistrate Cao shouted from his refuge under the table.

The people, crying for their parents, scattered like wild animals.

Little Yan quickly untied the black colt from the willow tree, dragged Magistrate Cao out from under the table, helped him onto the horse, and swatted it on the rump. The colt, its mane standing straight up, its tail bristling, ran like the wind with the county magistrate in the saddle, while the soldiers fired a few random shots toward the sorghum field before making themselves scarce.

The banks of the inlet grew strangely quiet.

Grandma rested her hand somberly on the donkey's head and stared toward the sorghum field. Great-Granddad had thrown himself under the donkey and covered his ears with his hands. Steam rose from the clothes of Uncle Arhat, who hadn't moved.

The water in the inlet was smooth as ever; the floating white lilies had spread open, their petals like ivory. The village chief, Five Monkeys Shan, whose face was bruised and swollen by the shoe sole, shrieked: "Spare me, Spotted Neck! Spare me!"

His shrieks were answered by three more rapid gunshots, and Grandma saw the bullets strike his head. Three tufts of hair stood straight up as he fell over, kissing the ground with his open mouth, a mottled liquid oozing from the upturned back of his head.

Grandma's expression didn't change; she gazed at the sorghum field as though awaiting something. A breeze swept across the inlet, raising ripples on the surface, setting the lilies in motion, and bending the rays of light on the water. Half of the gathered crows had flown down to the bodies of Shan Tingxiu and his son; the other half remained perched on the willow branches, raising a clamor. Their tail feathers fanned out in the breeze, revealing glimpses of the dark-green skin around their rectums.

A tall, husky man emerged from the sorghum field and walked along the bank of the inlet. He wore a rain cape that came down to his knees and a conical hat woven out of sorghum stalks. The strap was made of emerald glass beads. A black silk bandana was tied around his neck. He walked to the body of Five Monkeys Shan and looked down at it. Then he walked over to Magistrate Cao's hat, picked it up, and twirled it on the barrel of his pistol before heaving it in the air. It sailed into the inlet.

The man looked straight at my grandma, who returned his gaze.

"Were you bedded by Shan Bianlang?" he asked.

"Yes," Grandma said.

"Shit!" He turned and walked back into the sorghum field.

Uncle Arhat was utterly confused by what he'd seen, and couldn't have told you which way was up.

The bodies of the old master and his son were now completely covered by crows, some of which were pecking at the eyes with their hard black beaks.

Uncle Arhat was trying to make sense of everything that had happened since he'd lodged his complaint at the Gaomi market the day before.

Magistrate Cao had led him into the county-government building, where he lit candles and listened to his account as they gnawed on green radishes. Early the next morning, Uncle Arhat guided the magistrate to Northeast Gaomi Township, followed by Little Yan and a couple of dozen soldiers. They reached the village at about ten o'clock. After a quick surveillance, the county magistrate summoned Village Chief Five Monkeys Shan, and ordered him to round up the villagers and drag the corpses from the water.

The surface of the inlet shone like chrome, and the depth of the water seemed unfathomable. The county magistrate ordered Five Monkeys Shan to dive for the bodies, but he shrank back, complaining that he didn't know how to swim. Uncle Arhat summoned up his courage. "County Magistrate, they were my masters, so bringing them out should be my job." He told one of the other hands to fetch a bottle of wine, which he rubbed over his body before diving in. The water was as deep as a staff, so he took a long breath and sank to the bottom, his feet touching the spongy warm mud. He searched around blindly with his hands, but found nothing. So he rose to the surface, took another deep breath, and dived again. It was cooler down there. When he opened his eyes, all he could see was a layer of yellow. His ears were buzzing. A large blurry object swam up to him, and when he reached out to it a sharp pain shot through his finger, like a wasp sting. He screamed, and swallowed a mouthful of brackish water. Flailing his arms and legs for all they were worth, he swam to the surface; on the bank, he gasped for breath.

"Find something?" the magistrate asked.

"Nnn-no . . ." His face was ashen. "In the river . . . something strange . . ."

As he gazed down into the inlet, Magistrate Cao took off his hat, twirled it on his finger, then turned and ordered two soldiers, "Hand grenades!"

Little Yan herded the villagers a good twenty paces away.

Magistrate Cao walked over to the table and sat down.

The soldiers flattened out on the riverbank, and each took a muskmelon hand grenade out of his belt. They pulled the pins, banged the grenades against their rifles, and flung them into the inlet, where they hit the water with a splash, raising concentric circles on the surface. The soldiers pressed their faces against the ground. Silence—not even a bird chirped. A long time passed, but nothing happened in the river. By then the concentric circles had reached the shore; the water was as smooth as a bronze mirror, and just as mysterious.

Magistrate Cao gnashed his teeth and ordered, "One more time!"

The soldiers heaved two more grenades, which sputtered as they sailed through the air, leaving a trail of white smoke; when they hit the water, two muffled explosions rose from the bottom, sending plumes of water a dozen feet into the air.

Magistrate Cao rushed up to the bank, followed by the villagers. The water continued roiling for a long time. Then a trail of bubbles rose to the surface and popped, revealing at least a dozen big-mouthed, green-backed carp that bellied-up to the surface. As the ripples smoothed out, a foul stench settled over the water, which was bathed in sunlight. The light illuminated the villagers, and Magistrate Cao's face began to glow.

Suddenly two trails of pink bubbles gurgled up in the middle of the inlet and burst, as the people on the bank held their breath. A layer of golden husks covered the surface of the river under the blazing sun, nearly blinding the onlookers. Two black objects rose slowly beneath the trail of bubbles, and then the surface was broken by two pairs of buttocks; the bodies rolled over, exposing the distended bellies of Shan Tingxiu and his son. Their faces remained just below the surface, as though held back by shyness.

The magistrate ordered a distillery worker to run back and fetch a long hooked pole, with which Uncle Arhat snagged the legs of Shan Tingxiu and his son—producing a sickening sound that made everyone's gums crawl, as though they had all bitten into sour apricots—then slowly dragged the bodies toward the bank.

The little donkey raised its head toward the heavens and brayed.

"Now what, young mistress?" Uncle Arhat asked.

Grandma thought for a moment. "Have someone buy a couple of cheap coffins in town so we can bury them as soon as possible. And pick out a gravesite. When you're finished, come to the western compound. I want to talk to you."

"Yes, ma'am," he replied respectfully.

Uncle Arhat, together with the dozen or so hired hands, laid the elder and younger masters in their coffins and buried them in the sorghum field. They worked feverishly, in silence. By the time they'd buried the dead, the sun was in the western sky, and crows were circling above the gravesite, their wings painted purple by rays of sunlight. Uncle Arhat said to the men, "Go back and wait for me. Don't say anything. Watch my eyes for a signal."

He went to the western compound to receive instructions from Grandma, who was sitting cross-legged on the blanket she'd taken from the donkey's back. Great-Granddad was feeding straw to the animal.

"Everything has been taken care of, young mistress," Uncle Arhat said. "These are Elder Master's keys."

"Keep them for now," she said. "Tell me, is there someplace in the village where you can buy stuffed buns?"

"Yes."

"Buy two basketfuls, and give them to the men. Tell them to come here when they're done. And bring me twenty buns."

Uncle Arhat brought the twenty buns wrapped in fresh lotus

leaves. Grandma took them and said, "Now go back to the eastern compound and have the men eat as quickly as possible."

Uncle Arhat murmured his acknowledgment as he backed away.

Grandma then placed the twenty buns in front of Great-Granddad and said, "You can eat these on the road."

"Little Nine," he protested, "you're my very own daughter!"

"Go on," she demanded, "I've heard enough!"

"But I'm your dad!" he rebuked her angrily.

"You're no father of mine, and I forbid you ever to enter my door again!"

"I *am* your father!"

"Magistrate Cao is my father. Weren't you listening?"

"Not so fast. You can't just throw one father away because you found yourself a new one. Don't think having you was easy on your mother and me!"

Grandma flung the buns in his face. They hit like exploding grenades.

Great-Granddad cursed and ranted as he led the donkey out the gate: "You misbegotten ingrate! What makes you think you can turn your back on your own family? I'm going to report you to the county authorities for being disloyal and unfilial! I'll tell them you're in league with bandits. I'll tell them you schemed to have your husband killed. . . ."

As Great-Granddad's shouts and curses grew more distant and fainter, Uncle Arhat led the hired hands into the compound.

Grandma touched up her hair and smoothed out her clothes, then announced in a stately manner: "Men, you have worked hard! I'm young, and have no experience in managing affairs, so I'll need to rely on everyone's help to get by. Uncle Arhat, you have served the family loyally for over a decade, and from now on you'll be in charge of all distillery affairs. Now that the elder and younger master have left us, we need to clean the table and start a new banquet. We will have the backing of my foster-dad at the county level, and will do nothing to offend our greenwood friends. If we treat the villagers and our customers fairly and courteously, there's no reason why we can't stay in business. I want you to burn everything the elder and younger masters used. Anything that can't be burned will be buried. Tonight you'll need to get plenty of rest. Well, what do you think, Uncle Arhat?"

"We will carry out the young mistress's orders," he responded.

"If any of you wants to leave, I won't stand in your way. Anyone who finds it difficult to work for a woman should look for employment elsewhere."

The men exchanged glances. "We'll do our best for the young mistress," they said.

"Then that's all for now."

The men retired to the bunkhouse in the eastern compound, buzzing about all that had happened. "Turn in," Uncle Arhat said to them. "Get some sleep. We have to be up early tomorrow."

In the middle of the night, when Uncle Arhat got up to feed the mules, he heard Grandma sobbing in the western compound.

Bright and early the next morning, he went out to look around. The gate to the western compound was closed, and there was no sound from inside. He stood on a stool and looked over the gate. Grandma was seated on the ground next to the wall, with only the comforter beneath her; she was fast asleep.

Over the next three days, the Shan family compound was turned upside down. Uncle Arhat and the hired hands, their bodies sprayed with wine, removed the elder and younger masters' possessions—bedding, clothing, straw mats, eating utensils, sewing items, anything and everything—piled it in the middle of the yard, doused it with wine, and set it on fire. Then they dug a deep hole, into which they threw anything that didn't burn.

When the house had been cleared out, Uncle Arhat carried a bowl of wine to Grandma. A string of bronze keys lay at the bottom. "Young mistress," he said, "the keys have been disinfected in wine three times."

"Uncle," Grandma replied, "you should be in charge of the keys. My possessions are your possessions."

Her comment so terrified him he couldn't speak.

"This is no time to decline my offer. Go buy some fabric and whatever else I'll need to furnish the house. Have someone make bedding and mosquito nets. Don't worry about the cost. And have the men disinfect the house, including the walls, with wine."

"How much wine should they use?"

"As much as they need."

So the men sprayed wine until heaven and earth were soaked. Grandma stood in the intoxicating air with a smile on her lips.

The disinfecting process used up nine whole vats of wine. Once the spraying was completed, Grandma told the men to soak new cloth in the wine and scrub everything three or four times. That done, they whitewashed the walls, painted the doors and windows, and spread fresh straw and new mats over the kangs, until they had created a new world, top to bottom.

When their work was finished, she gave them each three silver dollars.

Ten days later, the odor of wine had faded and the whitewash made the place smell fresh. Feeling lighthearted, Grandma went to the village store, where she bought a pair of scissors, some red paper, needles and thread, and other domestic utensils. After returning home, she climbed onto the kang beside the window with its brand-new white paper covering and began making paper cutouts for window decorations. She had always produced paper cutouts and embroidery that were so much nicer than anything the neighbor girls could manage—delicate and fine, simple and vigorous, in a style that was all her own.

As she picked up the scissors and cut a perfect square out of the red paper, a sense of unease struck her like a bolt of lightning. Although she was seated on the kang, her heart had flown out the window and was soaring above the red sorghum like a dove on the wing. . . . Since childhood she had lived a cloistered life, cut off from the outside world. As she neared maturity, she had obeyed the orders of her parents, and been rushed to the home of her husband. In the two weeks that followed, everything had been turned topsy-turvy: water plants swirling in the wind, duckweeds bathing in the rain, lotus leaves scattered on the pond, a pair of frolicking red mandarin ducks. During those two weeks, her heart had been dipped in honey, immersed in ice, scalded in boiling water, steeped in sorghum wine.

Grandma was hoping for something, without knowing what it was. She picked up the scissors again, but what to cut? Her fantasies and dreams were shattered by one chaotic image after another, and as her thoughts grew more confused, the mournful yet lovely song of the katydids drifted up from the early-autumn wildwoods and sorghum fields. A bold and novel idea leaped into her mind: a katydid has freed itself from its gilded cage, where it perches to rub its wings and sing.

After cutting out the uncaged katydid, Grandma fashioned a plum-blossom deer. The deer, its head high and chest thrown out, has a plum tree growing from its back as it wanders in search of a happy life, free of care and worries, devoid of constraints.

Only Grandma would have had the audacity to place a plum tree on the back of a deer. Whenever I see one of Grandma's cutouts, my admiration for her surges anew. If she could have become a writer, she would have put many of her literary peers to shame. She was endowed with the golden lips and jade teeth of genius. She said a katydid perched on top of its cage, and that's what it did; she said a plum tree grew from the back of a deer, and that's where it grew.

Grandma, compared with you, I am like a shriveled insect that has gone hungry for three long years.

As she was cutting the paper, the main gate suddenly creaked open, and a strangely familiar voice called out in the yard: "Mistress, are you hiring?"

The scissors dropped from Grandma's hand onto the kang.

7

THE FIRST THING FATHER SAW after Granddad shook him awake was a long, coiling dragon coming straight for them as though on wings. Bold howls rose from beneath upraised torches. Father wondered how this wriggling line of torches could have so deeply moved a man like Granddad, who could kill without batting an eye. He was weeping openly. "Douguan," he mumbled between sobs, "my son . . . our fellow villagers are coming. . . ."

Several hundred villagers—men and women, boys and girls—crowded round. Those not holding torches were armed with hoes, rakes, and clubs. Father's best friends squeezed up to the front, holding torches made of sorghum stalks that were tipped with cotton wadding dipped in bean oil.

"Commander Yu, you won the battle!"

"Commander Yu, we have slaughtered cattle, pigs, and sheep for a feast for you and your men."

Granddad fell to his knees in front of the solemn, sacred torches, which lit up the meandering river and the vast, mighty sorghum. "Fellow villagers," he said in a trembling voice, "I, Yu Zhan'ao, should be condemned for all time for being duped by Pocky Leng's treachery. . . . My men . . . all lost in the fight!"

The torches closed in around him; smoke rose in the air, flames flickered uneasily, and drops of burning oil sizzled as they fell to the ground like red thread. Red cinders in a floral pattern covered the dike. A fox in the sorghum field howled. Fish, attracted by the light, schooled just below the surface. The people were speechless. Amid the crackling of flames, a thunderous sound came rolling toward them from some distant spot in the field.

An old man, his face dark, his beard white, one eye much larger than the other, handed his torch to the man beside him, bent down, and slipped his arms under my granddad's. "Get up, Commander Yu, get up, get up."

"Get up, Commander Yu," the villagers echoed, "get up, get up."

Granddad rose slowly to his feet, as the heat from the old man's hands warmed the muscles of his arms. "Fellow villagers," he said, "let's take a look around."

The torchbearers fell in behind Granddad and Father, the flames lighting up the blurry riverbed and the sorghum fields all the way up to the battleground near the bridge. The burned-out trucks cast eerie shadows. Corpses strewn across the battlefield gave off an overpowering stench of blood, which merged with the smell of scorched metal, of the sorghum that served as a vast backdrop, and of the river, so far from its source.

Women began to wail as drops of burning oil fell from the torches onto the people's hands and feet. The men's faces looked like steel fresh from the furnace. The white stone bridge had turned scarlet.

The old man with the dark face and white beard shouted, "What are you crying for? This was a great victory! There are four hundred million of us Chinese. If we take on the Japs, one on one, how do you think their little country will fare? If one hundred million of us fought them to the death, they'd be wiped out, but there'd still be three hundred million of us. That makes us the victors, doesn't it? Commander Yu, this was a crushing victory!"

"Old uncle, you're just saying that to make me feel good."

"No, Commander Yu, it really was a great victory. Give the order; tell us what to do. China may have nothing else, but it's got plenty of people."

Granddad straightened up. "You people, gather up the bodies of our fallen comrades!"

The villagers spread out and gathered up the bodies from the sorghum fields on both sides of the highway, then laid them out on the dike on the western edge of the bridge, heads facing south, feet north. Pulling Father along behind him, Granddad walked down the column of bodies, counting them. Wang Wenyi, Wang's wife, Fang Six, Fang Seven, Bugler Liu, Consumptive Four . . . one face after another. Tears ran down Granddad's deeply lined face like rivers of molten steel in the light of the torches.

"What about Mute?" Granddad asked. "Douguan, did you see Uncle Mute?"

The image of Mute's razor-sharp saber knife slicing off the Jap's head, and of the head sailing, screaming, through the air, flashed into Father's mind. "On the truck," he said.

The torches encircled one of the trucks. Three men climbed onto it as Granddad ran up. They lifted Mute's body over the railing and onto Granddad's back. One man held Mute's head, another his legs, and they staggered up the dike with their load, to lay it on the easternmost edge of the grisly column. Mute, bent at the waist, was still gripping his blood-spattered saber knife. His lifeless eyes were staring, his mouth open, as though frozen in a scream.

Granddad knelt and pressed down on Mute's knees and chest; Father heard the dead man's spine groan and crack as his body straightened out. Granddad tried to wrench the sword free, but the death grip thwarted his attempts. He brought the arm down so that the sword lay alongside Mute's leg. One of the women knelt and rubbed Mute's eyes. "Brother," she said, "close your eyes, close them now Commander Yu will avenge your death. . . ."

"Dad, Mom's still in the field. . . ." Father began to weep.

With a wave of his hand, Granddad said, "You go. . . . Take some people with you and carry her back. . . ."

Father darted into the sorghum field, followed by several villagers with torches, whose burning oil brushed the dense stalks. The aggrieved dry leaves crackled and burned when they were splattered, and as the fires spread, the stalks bowed their heavy heads and wept hoarsely.

Father parted the sorghum to reveal the body of Grandma, lying on her back and facing the remote, inimitable sky above Northeast Gaomi Township, filled with the spirits of countless stars. Even in death her face was as lovely as jade, her parted lips revealing a line of clean teeth inlaid with pearls of sorghum seeds, placed there by the emerald beaks of white doves.

"Carry her back," Granddad said.

A group of young women lifted her up. With torches casting a wide net of light along the route, the sorghum field turned into a fairyland, and each member of the procession was surrounded by an eerie halo of light.

One woman carried Grandma's body onto the dike and laid it at the westernmost end of the corpses.

The old man with the white beard asked, "Commander Yu, where will we find enough coffins for them all?"

Granddad thought for a moment. "We won't carry them back," he said finally, "and we don't need coffins. For now, we'll bury them in the sorghum field. Once I've rallied our forces, I'll come back and give them a proper sendoff."

The old man sent a group back to weave additional torches, since they would be burying the dead through the night. "While you're at it," Granddad added, "bring some draft animals, so we can tow that truck back with us, and chop down enough sorghum stalks to cover the bodies and line the bottoms of the graves before filling them in with dirt."

Grandma was the last to be interred. Once again her body was enshrouded in sorghum. As Father watched the final stalk hide her face, his heart cried out in pain, never to be whole again throughout his long life. Granddad tossed in the first spadeful of dirt. The loose clods of black earth thudded against the layer of sorghum like an exploding grenade shattering the surrounding stillness with its lethal shrapnel. Father's heart wept blood.

Grandma's grave mound was the fifty-first in the field. "Fellow villagers," the old man said, "on your knees!"

The village elders fell to their knees before the line of graves, the fields around them vibrating with the sound of weeping. The torches were beginning to die out. Just then a star fell from the southern sky, its brilliance not fading from view until it had passed below the tips of sorghum.

It was nearly dawn when the old torches were replaced by new ones. A milky gleam gradually penetrated the fog over the river. The dozen or so draft animals grazed noisily on the sorghum stalks and chewed the fallen ears of grain.

Granddad ordered the people to remove the linked rakes from the road and push the first truck across the highway and into the ditch on the eastern shoulder. When it was done, he picked up a shotgun, aimed at the gas tank, and fired, filling it with holes through which the gasoline spurted out. Then, taking a torch, he stepped back, aimed carefully, and flung it. A towering white flame shot into the air, igniting the frame and quickly turning the truck into a pile of twisted metal.

The villagers put their shoulders to the undamaged truck loaded with rice, pushing it across the bridge and onto the highway, then tipped the burned-out hulk of the third truck into the river. The gas tank of the fourth truck, which had retreated to the road south of the bridge, was also blasted by the shotgun and set afire, sending more flames shooting up into the heavens. All that remained on the bridge were piles of cinders. Flames rose into the sky to the north and south of the river, punctuated by the occasional crack of an exploding shell. The Jap corpses, burned to an oily crisp, added the stench of roasted flesh to the acrid smell in the air. The people's throats itched, their stomachs churned.

"What'll we do with their bodies, Commander Yu?" the old man asked.

"If we bury them, they'll stink up our soil! If we burn them, they'll foul our air! Dump them into the river and let them float back home."

Thirty or more corpses were dragged up onto the bridge, including the old Jap, who had been stripped of his general's uniform by the Leng Detachment soldiers.

"You women look away," Granddad announced.

He took out his short sword, split open the crotches of the Jap soldiers' pants, and sliced off their genitalia. Then he ordered a couple of the coarser men to stuff the things into the mouths of their owners. Finally, working in pairs, the men picked up the Japanese soldiers—basically decent men, perhaps, maybe handsome at one time, virtually all in the prime of their youth—and, *one two three,* heaved them over the side: "Jap dogs," they shouted, "go back home!" The Japanese soldiers flew through the air, carrying the family jewels in their mouths, and landed in the river with a splash, a whole school of them caught up in the eastward flow.

The faint rays of dawn found the villagers too exhausted to move. The fires along the banks were dying out beneath the still-dark sky. Granddad told the villagers to hitch the animals up to the front bumper of the undamaged rice truck.

The animals strained, the ropes were yanked taut, and the axles groaned as the truck crawled forward like a clumsy beetle. The front wheels kept veering from side to side, so Granddad halted the animals, opened the door, and slid into the cab to try his hand at steering. The ropes snapped taut as the animals strained forward again, and Granddad wrestled with the steering wheel until he began to get the hang of it. Now that the truck was heading straight, the terrified villagers fell in behind it. Keeping one hand on the steering wheel, Granddad felt around the dashboard with the other. He snapped on a switch, sending two rays of light shooting out the front.

"It opened its eyes!" someone shouted from behind him.

The headlights lit up the road ahead as well as the hairs on the animals' backs. Feeling very good about things, Granddad pushed and turned and twisted and pulled every button and switch and lever and knob he could find. A shrill noise rang out, and the horn began to blare. So you haven't lost your voice! Granddad was thinking. Deciding to have a little fun, he turned the ignition switch; a rumbling emerged from its belly as the truck shot forward crazily, knocking down mules and oxen, and bumping horses and donkeys out of the way, scaring

Granddad so badly he was drenched with sweat, front and back. Having climbed onto the tiger's back, he didn't know how to get down.

The dumbstruck villagers watched the truck knock the animals down and drag them along. It traveled a few dozen yards before careening into a ditch west of the road and coming to a shuddering halt, the raised wheels on one side spinning like windmills. Granddad smashed the glass and climbed out, his hands and face smeared with blood.

He stood looking at the demonic creature, a grim smile on his face.

After the villagers had unloaded the rice from the back of the remaining truck, Granddad blasted holes in the gas tank and once again ignited the gasoline with a torch. The flames licked the heavens.

8

FOURTEEN YEARS EARLIER, Yu Zhan'ao, a bedroll over his back, and dressed in clean, freshly starched white pants and jacket, stood in the yard of our home and shouted: "Mistress, are you hiring?"

With a hundred thoughts running through her mind, Grandma's natural instincts deserted her. Her scissors dropped to the kang, and she fell backward onto the brand-new purple comforter.

His nostrils filled with the odor of fresh whitewash and a delicate feminine fragrance, Yu Zhan'ao's courage mounted. He barged into the room.

"Mistress, are you hiring?"

Grandma lay face up and blurry-eyed on the comforter.

Yu Zhan'ao threw down his bedroll and slowly approached the kang. At that moment his heart was like a warm pond in which toads frolicked while swifts skimmed the surface. When his dark chin was only about the thickness of a piece of paper from Grandma's face, she slapped him on his dark, shiny scalp, then sat up quickly, picked up her scissors, and screamed, "Who are you? What do you think you're doing? How dare you barge into a strange woman's room!"

Startled, he backed up and said, "You . . . you really don't know me?"

"How dare you talk like that! I lived a cloistered life at home until my wedding day, less than two weeks ago. How would I know you?"

"Okay, if that's the way you want it," he said with a smile. "I hear you're shorthanded at the distillery, and I need work to put food in my belly!"

"All right, as long as you don't mind hard work. What's your name? How old are you?"

"My name's Yu Zhan'ao. I'm twenty-four."

"Take your bedroll outside," she said.

Yu Zhan'ao obediently walked outside and waited under a blazing sun. Traces of burned leaves remained in the yard, and he relived the memory of what had happened there recently. He waited for about half an hour, growing more restless by the minute, and was barely able to keep from rushing inside and settling accounts with that woman.

After murdering Shan Tingxiu and his son, he had not run away, but had hidden in the field near the inlet to watch the excitement. Even now he sighed in wonder over Grandma's amazing performance. She might be young, but she had teeth in her belly and could scheme with the best of them. A woman to be reckoned with, certainly no economy lantern. Maybe she was treating him like this today just in case there were prying eyes and ears. He waited a bit longer, but still she didn't come out. The yard was silent except for a calling magpie perched on the ridge of the roof. In the grip of anger, he was rushing toward the house, prepared to make a scene, when he heard Grandma's voice through the window: "Report to the eastern compound."

Realizing his mistake in not following the proper etiquette, Yu Zhan'ao let go of his anger and walked over to the eastern compound, where he saw rows of wine vats, piles of sorghum, and a crew of hired hands working inside the steamy distillery. He strode into the tent and asked a worker standing on a high stool feeding sorghum into a bucket above the millstone, "Hey, who's in charge here?"

The man looked at him out of the corner of his eye. When he had fed all the sorghum into the bucket, he jumped down off the stool and backed away from the millstone, holding a sieve in one hand and the stool in the other. Then he gave a shout, and the mule, wearing a black blindfold, began turning the millstone. Its hooves had worn a groove in the ground around the stone. A dull grinding sound emerged as crushed grain poured like raindrops from the space between the stones into a wooden pan below. "The foreman's in the shop," the man said, pursing his lips and pointing with his chin to the buildings west of the main gate.

With his bedroll in his hand, Yu Zhan'ao entered through the back door and spotted the familiar figure of an old man sitting behind the counter working his abacus, occasionally taking a sip from a small, dark-green decanter beside it.

"Foreman," Yu Zhan'ao announced, "are you hiring?"

Uncle Arhat looked up at Yu Zhan'ao and reflected for a moment. "Are you looking for permanent or temporary work?"

"Whatever you need. I'm interested in working for as long as I can."

"If you want to work for a week or so, I can do the hiring. But if you're interested in a permanent job, the mistress has to approve."

"Then you'd better go ask her."

Yu Zhan'ao walked up and sat on one of the stools as Uncle Arhat lowered the counter bar and walked out the rear door. But he turned and came back in, picked up a crudely made bowl, half-filled it with wine, and set it on the counter. "Your mouth must be dry. Have some wine."

Yu Zhan'ao's thoughts were on the woman's remarkable schemes as he drank. "The mistress wants to see you," Uncle Arhat said when he returned. They went over to the western compound. "Wait here," Uncle Arhat said.

Grandma walked outside with poise and grace. After grilling Yu Zhan'ao for a while, she waved her hand and said, "Take him over there. We'll try him for a month. His wages start tomorrow."

So Yu Zhan'ao became a hired hand in the family distillery. With his strength and clever hands, he was an ideal worker, and Uncle Arhat sang his praises to Grandma. At the end of the first month, he summoned him and said, "The mistress likes the way you work, so we'll keep you on." He handed him a cloth bundle. "She wants you to have these."

He undid the bundle. Inside was a pair of new cloth shoes. "Foreman," he said, "please tell the mistress that Yu Zhan'ao thanks her for the gift."

"You can go," said Uncle Arhat. "I expect you to work hard."

"I will," Yu Zhan'ao promised.

Another two weeks passed, and Yu Zhan'ao was finding it harder and harder to control himself. The mistress came to the eastern compound every day to look around, but directed her questions only to Uncle Arhat, paying hardly any attention to the sweaty hired hands. That did not sit well with Yu Zhan'ao.

Back when the distillery was run by Shan Tingxiu and his son, the workers' meals were prepared and sent over by café owners in the village. But after Grandma took charge, she hired a middle-aged woman whom everyone called "the woman Liu," and a teenaged girl named Passion. They lived in the western compound, where they were responsible for all the cooking. Then Grandma increased the number of dogs in the compound from two to five. Now that the western compound was home to three women and five dogs, it became a lively little world of its own. At night the slightest disturbance set off the dogs, and any intruder not bitten to death would surely have the wits frightened out of him.

By the time Yu Zhan'ao had been working the distillery cooker for eight weeks, it was the ninth lunar month, and the sorghum in the fields was good and ripe. Grandma told Uncle Arhat to hire some temporary laborers to clean the yard and open-air bins in preparation for the harvest. They were clear, sunny days with a deep sky. Grandma, dressed in white silk and wearing red satin slippers, carried a willow switch around the yard, with her running dogs on her heels, drawing strange looks from the villagers, although none dared so much as fart in her presence. Yu Zhan'ao approached her several times, but she stayed aloof and wouldn't bestow a word on him.

One night Yu Zhan'ao drank a little more than usual, and wound up getting slightly drunk. He tossed and turned on the communal kang, but couldn't fall asleep, as moonlight streamed in through the window in the eastern wall. Two hired hands sat beneath a bean-oil lantern mending their clothes.

Then Old Du took out his stringed instrument and began playing sad tunes, striking resonant chords in the hearts of the listeners. Something was bound to happen. One of the men mending his clothes was so moved by Old Du's melancholy tunes that his throat began to itch.

"It's no fun being alone," he sang hoarsely, "no fun at all. Tattered clothes never get sewn. . . ."

"Why not get the mistress to sew them for you?"

"The mistress? I wonder who will feast on that tender swan."

"The old master and his son thought it would be them, and they wound up dead."

"I hear she had an affair with Spotted Neck while she was still living at home."

"Are you saying Spotted Neck murdered them?"

"Not so loud. 'Words spoken on the road are heard by snakes in the grass!' "

Yu Zhan'ao lay on the kang sneering.

"What're you smirking for, Little Yu?" one of them asked.

Emboldened by the wine, he blurted out, "I murdered them!"

"You're drunk!"

"Drunk? I tell you, I murdered them!" He sat up, reached into the bag hanging on the wall, and pulled out his short sword. When he slid it out of the scabbard, it caught the moon's rays and shone like a silverfish. "I'll tell you guys," he said with a thick tongue, "our mistress . . . I slept with her. . . . Sorghum fields . . . Came at night and set a fire . . . stabbed one . . . stabbed the other. . . ."

One of his listeners quietly blew out the lantern, throwing the room into a murky darkness in which the moonlit sword shone even more brightly.

"Go to sleep go to sleep go to sleep! We have to be up early tomorrow to make wine!"

Yu Zhan'ao was still mumbling. "You . . . damn you . . . pretend you don't know me after you hitch up your pants . . . work me like an ox or a horse. . . . Don't think you can get away with it. . . . Tonight I'm going to . . . *butcher* you. . . ." He climbed off the kang, sword in hand, and staggered outside. The other men lay in the dark, staring wide-eyed at the moon glinting off the weapon in his hand, not daring to utter a sound.

Yu Zhan'ao walked into the moonlit yard and looked at the glazed wine vats glistening in the light like jewels. A southern breeze swept over from the fields, carrying the bittersweet aroma of ripe sorghum and making him shiver. The sound of a woman's giggle drifted over from the western compound. As he slipped into the tent to move the bench outside, he was met by the pawing sounds of the black mule tethered behind the feed trough. Ignoring the animal, he carried the bench over to the wall. When he stepped on it and straightened up, the top of the wall reached his chest. A light behind the window illuminated the paper cutout. The mistress was playing games with the girl Passion on the kang. "Aren't you a couple of naughty little monkeys?" he heard the woman Liu say. "It's bedtime; now, go to sleep!" Then she added, "Passion, look in the pot and see if the dough has begun to rise."

Holding the sword in his mouth, Yu Zhan'ao climbed up onto the wall. The five dogs rushed over, looked up, and began to bark, frightening him so badly he lost his balance and tumbled into the western compound. If Grandma hadn't rushed out to see what was going on, the dogs probably would have torn him to pieces, even if there had been two of him.

After calling off the dogs, Grandma shouted for Passion to bring out the lantern.

The woman Liu, rolling pin in hand, came running out on big feet that had once been bound and screamed, "A thief! Grab him!"

Passion followed, lantern in hand, the light falling on the battered face of Yu Zhan'ao. "So it's you!" Grandma said coldly.

She picked up the sword and tucked it into her sleeve. "Passion, go fetch Uncle Arhat."

No sooner had Passion opened the gate than Uncle Arhat entered the compound. "What's going on, Mistress?"

"This hired hand of yours is drunk," she said.

"Yes, he is," Uncle Arhat confirmed.

"Passion," Grandma said, "bring me my willow switch."

Passion fetched Grandma's white willow switch. "This'll sober you up," Grandma said as she twirled the switch in the air and brought it down hard on Yu Zhan'ao's buttocks.

Stung by the pain, he experienced a sense of numbing ecstasy, and when it reached his throat it set his teeth moving and emerged as a stream of gibberish: "Mistress Mistress Mistress . . ."

Grandma whipped him until her arm was about to fall off, then lowered the switch and stood there panting from exhaustion.

"Take him away," she said.

Uncle Arhat stepped up to pull Yu Zhan'ao to his feet, but he refused to get up. "Mistress," he shouted, "a few more lashes . . . just give me a few more. . . ."

Grandma whipped him twice on the neck with all her might, and he rolled around on the ground like a little boy, kicking the air with his legs. Uncle Arhat called for a couple of hired hands to carry him back to the bunkhouse, where they flung him down on the kang; he rolled around like a squirming dragonfly, a stream of filth and abuse gushing from his mouth. Uncle Arhat picked up a decanter, told the men to pin his arms and legs, and poured wine down his throat. As soon as the men let go, his head lolled to the side and he grew silent. "You drowned him!" one of them exclaimed fearfully, bringing the lantern up. Yu Zhan'ao's face was contorted out of shape, and he sneezed violently, extinguishing the lantern.

He didn't wake up until the sun was high in the sky. He walked into the distillery as though stepping on cotton; the men watched him curiously. Recalling the beating he'd received the night before, he rubbed his neck and his buttocks, but felt no pain. Thirsty, he picked up a ladle, scooped some wine from the flow, tipped back his head, and drank it down.

Old Du the fiddler said, "Little Yu, your mistress gave you quite a beating last night. I'll bet you won't be climbing *that* wall again."

Up till then the gloomy young man had instilled a measure of fear in the others, but that had evaporated when they heard his pitiful screams, and now they outdid one another teasing him mercilessly. Without a word in reply, he grabbed one of them, raised his fist, and buried it in the man's face. A quick exchange of glances, and the others rushed up, threw him to the ground, and began raining blows on him with fists and feet. When they'd had their fill, they took off his belt, stuck his head into the crotch of his pants, tied his hands behind his back, and threw him to the ground.

Like a stranded tiger or a beached dragon, Yu Zhan'ao struggled to get free, rolling around on the ground like a ball for as long as it takes to smoke a couple of pipefuls. Finally, having seen enough, old Du went up, untied Granddad's hands, and freed his head from his pants. Yu Zhan'ao's face was pallid as a sheet of gold paper as he lay on the pile of firewood like a dying snake. It took him a long time to catch his breath. Meanwhile, the others held on to their tools, just in case he took it into his head to get even. But he just staggered over to one of the vats, ladled out some wine, and began gulping it down. When he was finished, he climbed back up onto the pile of firewood and fell fast asleep.

From then on, Yu Zhan'ao got roaring drunk every day, then climbed up onto the pile of firewood and lay there, his moist blue eyes half closed, a mixed smile on his lips: the left side foolish, the right side crafty, or vice versa. For the first few days, the men watched him with interest; after a while, they began to grumble. Uncle Arhat tried to get him to do some work, but Yu Zhan'ao just looked at him out of the corner of his eye and said, "Who the hell do you think you are? I'm the master here. That kid in her belly is mine."

By then my father had grown in Grandma's belly to about the size of a little ball, and in the mornings the sound of her retching in the yard drifted over to the western compound. The experienced old-timers talked about nothing else. When the woman Liu brought over their food, they asked her, "Old Woman Liu, is the mistress with child?"

She glared at them. "Watch out, or someone might cut out your tongue!"

"Looks like Shan Bianlang knew what he was doing after all!"

"Maybe it's the old master's."

"No wild guessing! Do you really think a spirited girl like that would let one of the Shan men touch her? I'll bet it was Spotted Neck."

Yu Zhan'ao jumped up from the pile of firewood and gestured gleefully. "It was me!" he shouted. "Ha ha, it was me!"

They had a good laugh over that, and cursed him roundly.

On more than one occasion, Uncle Arhat urged Grandma to dismiss Yu Zhan'ao, but she invariably replied, "Let him rant and rave if he wants to. I'll fix his wagon sooner or later."

One day she walked into the compound, her thickening waist obvious to all, to speak with Uncle Arhat.

Avoiding her eyes, he said softly, "Mistress, it's time to break out the scales and buy the sorghum."

"Is everything ready? The compound and the grain bins?"

"Everything's ready."

"When did you do it in the past?"

"Just about now."

"Let's wait a while longer this year."

"We might lose out. There are at least ten other distilleries."

"The harvest has been so good this year there's more than they can handle. Put up a notice that we're not ready yet. We'll buy when the others have had their fill. By then we can name our own price, and the grain will have had more time to dry out."

"You're probably right."

"Anything else we need to talk about?"

"Not really, except for that hired hand. He gets so drunk every day he can hardly move. Let's pay him off and get rid of him."

Grandma thought for a moment. "Take me to the distillery so I can see for myself."

Uncle Arhat led the way to the distillery, where the workers were just then pouring fermented mash into the distiller. The firewood beneath the cooker crackled and the water roiled, sending clouds of steam into the distiller, a three-foot-high wooden vessel with tightly woven bamboo strips at the base, which fit over the cooker. Four men with wooden spades ladled the sorghum mash, a green-spotted, sweet-smelling fermented mixture, from the vat into the steaming distiller. Since the steam had nowhere else to go, it filtered up through the cracks in the base, and the alert men dumped the mash wherever the steam was coming through, to keep the heat from dissipating.

When they saw Grandma approaching, they threw themselves into their work. From his firewood perch, Yu Zhan'ao, who looked like a dirty-faced, ragged beggar, stared at Grandma with a cold glint in his eyes.

"I came to see how sorghum is converted into wine," Grandma said.

Uncle Arhat moved a stool over for her.

The men, favored by her presence, worked as never before. The stoker kept the fires blazing under the cookpots. The water bubbled, sending sizzling steam snaking its way up through the distiller to merge with the panting sounds of the workers. When they had filled the distiller with mash, they covered it with a tight-fitting honeycombed lid to let the mixture cook until wisps of steam began to ooze from the tiny openings in the lid. They quickly brought over a double-plate pewter object with a concave center. Uncle Arhat told Grandma it was the distiller. She walked over to get a closer look, then returned to the stool without a word.

The men placed the pewter distiller over the wooden one to block out the steam. The only sounds came from the roaring fires beneath the cookpot. The wooden distiller was white one minute and orange the next, as a delicate, sweet aroma, sort of like wine but not quite, seeped through the wooden vessel.

"Add cool water," Uncle Arhat said.

The men climbed up onto a bench and began pouring cool water into the concave center of the pewter distiller. One of them stirred the water rapidly with what looked like an oar, and after about half the time it takes a joss stick to burn down, Grandma's nostrils were filled with the smell of wine.

"Get ready to catch the wine," Uncle Arhat ordered.

Two men ran up with wine crocks woven of wax reeds and covered with ten layers of paper, then sealed with many coats of varnish. They placed the crocks under distiller spouts that looked like duck beaks.

Grandma stood up and stared at the spouts as the stoker shoved pieces of pine-oil-soaked firewood into the stoves, which crackled loudly and spat out clouds of white smoke that lit up the men's greasy, sweaty chests.

"Change the water!" Uncle Arhat shouted.

Two men rushed into the yard and came running back with four buckets of cool well water. The man on the stool pulled a lever, releasing the heated water from the top of the distiller. Then he poured in the fresh water and continued stirring.

Grandma was stirred by the solemn, sacred labor. Just then she felt my father move inside her belly, and looked over at Yu Zhan'ao, who was lying on the pile of firewood staring at her with a sinister glint in his eyes, the only cold spots in the steamy distilling tent. The stirring in her heart cooled off. She averted her eyes and calmly watched the two men with the crocks, who were waiting for the wine to flow.

The aroma grew heavier as wisps of steam escaped through the seams of the wooden distiller. Grandma watched the spouts brighten, the glow freezing for a moment, then slowly beginning to stir as clear, bright drops of liquid rolled down into the wine crocks like tears.

"Change the water!" Uncle Arhat yelled. "Stoke the fire!"

Hot water poured from the open faucets as more cool water was dumped in, maintaining a steady temperature on the lid, causing the steam between the layers to cool and form a liquid, which gushed out through the spouts.

The first wine out was warm, transparent, and steamy. Uncle Arhat picked up a clean ladle, half-filled it, and handed it to Grandma. "Here, Mistress, taste it."

The rich aroma made her tongue itch. Father stirred in her belly again. He was thirsty for the wine. First she sniffed it and touched it to her tongue, then took a sip to savor its bouquet. It was amazingly aromatic and slightly pungent. She took a mouthful and swished it around with her tongue. Her cheeks softened as though they were being rubbed gently with silky cotton. Her throat went slack, and the mouthful of warm wine slid down. Her pores snapped open, then closed, as a feeling of incredible joy suffused her body. She swigged three mouthfuls in rapid succession, her belly feeling as though it were being massaged by a greedy hand. Finally, she tipped back her head and drained the ladle. By then her face was flushed and her eyes sparkled; she had never looked so beautiful, so irresistible. The men gaped with astonishment, neglecting their work.

"Mistress, you sure know how to drink!" they complimented her.

"It's the first drink I've ever had," she replied modestly.

"If that's how you handle the first one, with a little practice you could finish off a whole crock."

By now the wine was gushing from the spouts—one crock, then another, each of which was stacked alongside the pile of firewood. Suddenly Yu Zhan'ao climbed down off the pile, undid his pants, and pissed into one of the brimming crocks. The shocked men numbly watched the steam of clear liquid splash into the wine crock and send sprays over the sides. When he'd finished, he smirked and staggered up to Grandma, whose cheeks were flushed. She didn't move as he wrapped his arms around her and planted a kiss on her face. She paled, stumbled, and sat down hard on the stool.

"That child in your belly," he demanded angrily. "Is it mine or isn't it?"

Grandma was crying. "If you say so . . ."

Yu Zhan'ao's eyes blazed and his muscles grew taut, as if he were a workhorse standing up after rolling in the dirt. He stripped down to his shorts. "Now watch me clean the distiller!"

Cleaning the distiller is the hardest job of all. Once the wine has stopped flowing through the spouts, the pewter distiller is removed; then the honeycombed wooden lid is lifted from the wooden distiller, which is filled with sorghum mash, dark yellow and scalding hot. Yu Zhan'ao climbed onto a bench, wielding a short-handled wooden spade, and scooped the mash out into the frame. His movements were so slight he seemed to be using only his forearms. The heat turned his skin scarlet, and sweat ran down his back like a river, smelling strongly of wine.

My granddad Yu Zhan'ao worked with such consummate skill that Uncle Arhat and the other men looked on in awe. Talents hidden for months were now on display. When he'd finished, he drank some wine, then said to Uncle Arhat, "Foreman, that's not all I can do. Now look. When the wine comes down the spouts, the steam dissipates. If you put another, smaller distiller over the spouts, you'd have nothing but the best wine."

Uncle Arhat shook his head. "I doubt that," he said.

"If not," Granddad said, "you can chop off my head!"

Uncle Arhat glanced at Grandma, who sniffled once or twice. "That's not my business. I don't care. Let him do what he wants."

She returned to the western compound, sobbing.

From that day on, Granddad and Grandma shared their love like mandarin ducks or Chinese phoenixes. Uncle Arhat and the hired hands were so tormented by their naked, demonic exhibition of desire that their intelligence failed them, and even though they had a bellyful of misgivings, in time, one after another, they became my granddad's loyal followers.

Granddad's skills revolutionized the operation, giving Northeast Gaomi Township its first top-line distilled wine. As for the crock into which he had pissed, since the men dared not dispose of it on their own, they just moved it over to a corner and left it there. Late one overcast afternoon, as a strong southeast wind carried the aroma of sorghum wine across the compound, the men were suddenly aware of an unusually rich and mellow fragrance. Uncle Arhat, whose sense of smell was keenest, sought out the source, and was astonished to discover that it came from the piss-enhanced crock in the corner. Without a word to anyone, he lit the bean-oil lantern, turned up the wick, and settled down to study the phenomenon.

First he scooped out a dipperful of the wine, then let it drip slowly back into the crock and watched it form a soft green liquid curtain that was transformed into a multipetaled flower, like a chrysanthemum, when it hit the surface. The unique fragrance was more volatile than ever. He scooped up a tiny bit of the wine, tasting it first with the tip of his tongue, then taking a decisive swig. After rinsing his mouth with cool water, he drank some ordinary sorghum wine from one of the other crocks. He flung down the dipper, rushed out, burst through the western compound gate, and ran across the yard, shouting, "Mistress, joyful news!"

9

AFTER BEING SENT AWAY by Grandma with a bundle of hot buns, Great-Granddad led his donkey home, cursing all the way. As soon as he arrived, he blurted out to Great-Grandma how my grandma had acknowledged Magistrate Cao as her foster-dad and had disowned her real father. Enraged by the news, Great-Grandma added her fulminations to his, and the two of them looked like old toads fighting over a cicada. After a while, she said, "Forget your anger, old man. As they say, 'Strong winds eventually cease, unhappy families return to peace.' Go see her in a couple of days. She's inherited so much wealth that we could live on what slips through her fingers."

"All right," he agreed. "I'll go see the misbegotten ingrate in a couple of weeks."

Two weeks later, he rode up on his donkey, only to find the main gate shut tight. Grandma ignored his shouts. After he'd yelled himself hoarse, he turned and rode away.

Granddad was already working in the distillery by the time Great-Granddad next returned, and Grandma's five dogs constituted an impregnable line of defense. His pounding at the gate was met by a chorus of barks, and when, at last, the woman Liu opened the gate, he was immediately surrounded by dogs, content to bark for the moment. Poor Great-Granddad quaked in fright.

"Who are you looking for?" the woman Liu asked him.

"And who are you?" Great-Granddad fired back indignantly. "I've come to see my daughter!"

"Just who is your daughter?"

"The woman who runs this place."

"Wait here. I'll go tell her."

"Tell her her real father's here!"

The woman Liu returned with a silver dollar in her hand. "You there, old man, the mistress says she has no father, but she's willing to give you a silver dollar to buy some buns for your trip."

"Misbegotten ingrate!" Great-Granddad railed. "Get your ass out here! Who the hell do you think you are, disowning your own father as soon as you're rolling in money!"

The woman Liu flung the silver dollar to the ground. "Go on, you pigheaded old man," she said. "If you make the mistress mad, you'll get more than you bargained for."

"I'm her father!" he insisted. "She murdered her father-in-law. Is her own father going to be next?"

"Go on," the woman Liu urged him, "get going. If you don't, I'll have to sic the dogs on you!"

She gave a signal to the dogs, and they crowded up closer. The green dog nipped the leg of the donkey, which brayed, jerked the reins free, and galloped away. Great-Granddad bent over, picked up the silver dollar, and stumbled after the donkey, with the barking dogs on his heels all the way to the edge of the village.

The third time Great-Granddad came to see Grandma, he demanded one of the big black mules, insisting that her father-in-law had promised him one before he was murdered, and that his death did not invalidate the promise. He threatened to take his complaint to the county government if Grandma reneged on the promise.

"You're nothing to me," she said. "I don't know you. And if you keep harassing me, I'll report you to the authorities."

Great-Granddad found someone to write out a complaint for him, then rode his donkey into town to see Magistrate Cao and bring formal charges against Grandma.

Following the shock of having his hat shot full of holes by Spotted Neck, Magistrate Cao had returned home and promptly fallen ill. So, when he read the complaint, which was linked to the homicides at Northeast Gaomi Township, sweat dripped from his armpits.

"Old man," he said, "you've charged your daughter with having an illicit affair with a bandit. Where's your proof?"

"Your honor, County Magistrate," Great-Granddad replied, "the bandit in question is sharing my daughter's kang at this very minute. He's none other than Spotted Neck, the man who shot your hat full of holes."

"Old man, you know, don't you, that if what you're saying is true your daughter's life is in danger."

"Magistrate, honor compels me to forsake family loyalty . . . but for . . . my daughter's property . . ."

"Why, you money-grubbing old son of a bitch!" the magistrate bellowed. "You'd sacrifice your own daughter to get your hands on that little property she has! No wonder she disowned you. You're no 'father' in my book. Give him fifty lashes with a shoe sole and send him on his way!"

Poor Great-Granddad—not only was his complaint rejected, but the fifty lashes left his buttocks in such sad shape he couldn't even sit on his donkey, and had to lead it behind him as he staggered home. Shortly after leaving town, he heard hoofbeats behind him, and when he turned to look, he recognized the county magistrate's black colt. Fearing for his life, he fell to his knees.

The rider was Magistrate Cao's right-hand man, Master Yan. "Old man," he hailed him, "get up, get up. The magistrate said that, since he's your daughter's foster-dad, there's a certain kinship between the two of you. The whipping was intended as a lesson for you. He wants you to take these ten silver dollars home to open a small business and forget about ill-gotten wealth."

Great-Granddad accepted the silver dollars and kowtowed gratefully, not rising to his feet until the black colt had crossed the railroad tracks.

Magistrate Cao had been sitting alone in the main hall of the government office thinking for half an hour when Little Yan returned from delivering the money. The magistrate led him into a small room and closed the door. "I'm convinced that the man sharing the woman Dai's kang is Spotted Neck," he said, "the most notorious bandit in Northeast Gaomi Township. Nabbing him will be like cutting down the tree and watching the Northeast Gaomi Township monkeys scatter. The reason I had you beat the old man today was to keep the news from leaking out."

"You have great foresight," Little Yan said.

"I was duped by the woman Dai that day."

"Even the wisest man occasionally falls prey."

"Take twenty soldiers on fast horses to Northeast Gaomi Township and capture the bandit leader."

"The woman, too?"

"No," the magistrate cautioned him, "no, no, under no circumstances. If you took her into custody, it would be a great loss of face for you-know-who Cao, wouldn't it? Besides, my judgment that day was intended to help her. What a tragedy for such a lovely young thing to be married to a leper. No wonder she took a lover. No, just nab Spotted Neck, and let her off the hook, so she can have a chance to live a good life."

"A high wall surrounds the Shan compound," Little Yan said, "and a pack of mean dogs guards the inside. We won't catch Spotted Neck flatfooted. If we try to break down the gate or scale the wall in the middle of the night, he'll pick us off like clay pigeons, won't he?"

"You're too simple-minded," Magistrate Cao said. "I've got a wonderful plan."

Late that night, Little Yan and twenty soldiers rode out of the city, according to the magistrate's plan, heading for Northeast Gaomi Township. Since it was late autumn—the tenth lunar month—the sorghum in the fields had already been harvested and lay in large piles. The riders reached the western edge of the village just before daybreak, when crystalline dew covered the dark weeds and the chilly autumn air cut like a knife. They dismounted and waited for orders from Little Yan, who told them to tether their horses behind a pile of sorghum and leave two soldiers to watch them. Then they changed clothes and prepared for action.

The sun rose red in the sky, the black earth was covered by a blanket of white, and a fine layer of dew settled on the men's eyelashes and brows and the downy hairs on the muzzles of the horses. Little Yan looked at his pocket watch. "Let's go!" he said.

With eighteen soldiers behind him, he cautiously entered the village. They were armed with carbines, loaded and ready. Two took up positions at the village entrance, two more at the head of the lane. Another lane, two more soldiers in hiding, and so on. By the time they reached the compound gate, their number was reduced to Little Yan and six soldiers disguised as peasants, one carrying a pole with two empty wine crocks over his shoulder.

When the woman Liu opened the gate, Little Yan signaled the soldier with the wine crocks, who squeezed past her into the compound. "What do you think you're doing?" she said angrily.

"I came to see the owner," the soldier said. "I bought two crocks of wine a couple of days ago, and ten people died from drinking it. What kind of poison did you put in it?"

While he was stating his case, Little Yan and the other soldiers slipped into the compound and hid quietly by a corner of the wall. The watchdogs surrounded the man with the wine crocks and barked frantically.

Grandma walked out, sleepy-eyed, buttoning up her clothes. "Go to the shop if you have business here," she said testily.

"There's poison in your wine," the soldier said. "Ten people died from drinking it. I demand to see the owner."

"What kind of nonsense is that?" Grandma shot back. "We sell wine all over this area, and we've never had any problems. How could members of *your* family alone die from drinking it?"

As the dispute raged between Grandma and the tall soldier, surrounded by the five dogs, Little Yan signaled his troops, who streaked into the house on his heels. The soldier outside threw down his wine crocks, pulled a pistol from his belt, and aimed it at Grandma.

Granddad was getting dressed when he was pushed down onto the kang by Little Yan and his men, who tied his hands behind his back and dragged him out into the yard.

The dogs rushed up to save him, and the soldiers opened fire. Fur flew, blood was everywhere.

The woman Liu soiled her pants as she slumped to the ground.

"Gentlemen," Grandma protested, "we've done nothing to harm you, and have no grudge against you. If it's money or food you want, just say so. There's no need to use your weapons."

"Shut up!" Little Yan shouted. "Take him away!"

Then she recognized Yan. "Don't you work for my foster-dad?" she asked urgently.

"This has nothing to do with you," he said. "Just get on with your life!"

Uncle Arhat ran out of the shop when he heard gunfire in the western compound. But the instant his head popped through the gate, a bullet whizzed past his ear, and he quickly pulled back. There wasn't a soul on the quiet street, though all the dogs in the village were howling. Little Yan and his men dragged Granddad out of the compound and down the street. The two soldiers left behind had already brought the horses up, and when the men hiding at the village entrance and the heads of the lanes saw that everything had gone smoothly, they left their positions and mounted up. Granddad was tied face down across the back of a horse with a purple mane. On Little Yan's command, they galloped out of the village on the road to the county town.

When they arrived at the government compound, the soldiers dragged Granddad off the horse. Magistrate Cao walked up to him, stroking his mustache and grinning from ear to ear. "So, Spotted Neck, you shot three holes in the magistrate's hat. Well, the magistrate is going to repay you with three hundred lashes with the sole of a shoe."

Bruised, shaken, and dazed by the jarring trip, Granddad could do nothing but vomit as they dragged him off the horse.

"Commence the beating!" Little Yan ordered.

The soldiers walked up and kicked Granddad to the ground, raised extra-large shoes nailed to long sticks, and began beating him for all they were worth. At first he gritted his teeth, but he was soon shouting for his parents.

"Spotted Neck," Nine Dreams Cao said, "now you see what you're up against with Shoe Sole Cao the Second!"

The beating had cleared Granddad's head. "You've got the wrong man!" he screamed. "I'm not Spotted Neck. . . ."

"So you think you can lie your way out of it! Three hundred more lashes!" Magistrate Cao shouted angrily.

The soldiers kicked Granddad to the ground again and pelted him again with the shoe soles. By now his buttocks were numb. He looked up and screamed, "Nine Dreams Cao, everybody calls you Cao the Upright Magistrate, but you're nothing but a muddled dogshit official! Spotted Neck has a big spot on his neck. Look at my neck; do you see anything there?"

The startled Nine Dreams Cao waved his hand, and the soldiers backed off. Two others lifted Granddad up so Magistrate Cao could examine his neck.

"How do you know Spotted Neck has a big spot on his neck?" Magistrate Cao asked him.

"I've seen him."

"If you know Spotted Neck, then you must be a bandit, too. I haven't got the wrong man!"

"Thousands of people in Northeast Gaomi Township know Spotted Neck. Does that make them all bandits?"

"You were sleeping on a widow's kang in the middle of the night, so, even if you're not a bandit, you're still a scoundrel. I haven't got the wrong man!"

"Your foster-daughter was willing."

"She was willing?"

"Yes."

"Who are you?"

"One of her hired hands."

"Aiyaya! Little Yan, lock him up."

Grandma and Uncle Arhat rode up to the government-compound gate on their two big black mules just then. Uncle Arhat stood outside the gate holding the reins while Grandma ran into the yard, wailing and screaming. A sentry barred her way with his rifle. She spat in his face. "This is the county magistrate's foster-daughter," Uncle Arhat explained. No sentry would stop her now. She barged into the main hall . . .

That afternoon, the county magistrate sent Granddad back to the village in a curtained sedan chair.

He spent the next two months convalescing on Grandma's kang.

Grandma rode into the county town to deliver a heavy bundle to her foster-mother as a gift.

10

THE TWENTY-THIRD DAY of the twelfth month in the year 1923; the Kitchen God is sent to heaven to make his report. A member of Spotted Neck's gang had kidnapped my grandma that morning. The ransom demand was received in the afternoon: the distillery was to pay one thousand silver dollars for the hostage's safe return. If they failed to do so, they could retrieve her body from the Temple of the Earth God at the eastern edge of Li Village.

By rummaging through chests and cupboards, Granddad scraped together two thousand silver dollars, which he stuffed into a flour sack and told Uncle Arhat to deliver on one of the mules.

"Didn't they only ask for one thousand?"

"Just do as I say."

Uncle Arhat left on the mule.

Uncle Arhat returned with my grandma before nightfall, escorted by two mounted bandits with rifles slung over their backs.

When they spotted Granddad they said, "Proprietor, our leader says you can sleep with the gate open from now on!"

Granddad told Uncle Arhat to fetch a crock of the piss-enhanced wine for the bandits to take back with them. "See what your leader thinks of this wine," he said. Then he escorted the bandits to the edge of the village.

When he returned home, he closed the gate, the front door, and the bedroom door behind him. He and Grandma lay on the kang in each other's arms. "Spotted Neck didn't take advantage of you, did he?"

Grandma shook her head, but tears rolled down her cheeks.

"What's wrong? Did he rape you?"

She buried her head in his chest. "He . . . he felt my breast. . . ."

Granddad stood up angrily. "The baby, is he all right?"

Grandma nodded.

In the spring of 1924, Granddad rode his mule on a secret trip to Qingdao, where he bought two pistols and five thousand cartridges. One of the repeaters was German-made, called a "waist-drum," the other a Spanish "goosehead."

After returning with the pistols, he locked himself up in his room for three days, breaking the weapons down and putting them back together over and over and over. With the coming of spring, the ice in the river melted, and fish that had spent a suffocating winter at the bottom swam sleepily to the surface to bask in the sun. Granddad took the pistols and a basketful of cartridges down to the river, where he spent the entire spring picking off fish. When there were no more large ones, he went after little ones. If he had an audience, he shot wildly, hitting nothing; but if he was alone, each round smashed a fish's head. Summer arrived, and the sorghum grew.

It poured rain on the seventh night of the seventh month, complete with thunder and lightning. Grandma handed Father, who was nearly four months old, to Passion and followed Granddad into the shop in the eastern compound, where they closed the doors and windows and had Uncle Arhat light the lamp. Grandma laid out seven copper coins on the counter in the shape of a plum blossom. Granddad swaggered back and forth beyond the counter, then spun around, drew his pistols, and began firing—*pow pow, pow pow, pow pow pow*—seven rapid shots. The coins flew up against the wall; three bullets fell to the floor, the other four were stuck in the wall.

Grandma and Granddad walked up to the counter, where they held up the lantern and saw there wasn't a mark on the surface.

He had perfected his "seven-plum-blossom skill."

Granddad rode the black mule up to the wine shop on the eastern edge of the village. Cobwebs dotted the frame of the door, which he pushed open and walked inside. A strong smell of putrefaction made his head reel. Covering his nose with his sleeve, he looked around. The fat old man was sitting beneath the beam, a noose around his neck. His eyes were open; his black tongue was sticking out through parted lips.

Granddad spat twice to clear out his mouth and led the mule to the edge of the village, where he stood thoughtfully for a long time, while the mule pawed the ground and swished its hairless tail to drive away swarms of black flies as big as beans. Finally, he mounted the mule, which stretched out its neck and began heading home; but Granddad jerked back the icy metal bit in its mouth and smacked it on the rump, turning down the path by the sorghum field.

The little wooden bridge over the Black Water River was still intact at the time, and whitecaps from the swollen river splashed up onto the bridge planks. The roar of the river frightened the mule, which balked at the bridgehead and refused to cross, even when Granddad showed it his fists. So he rose up in the saddle and sat down hard, forcing the mule to trot out into the middle of the bridge, its back sagging. He reined it to a halt. A shallow layer of clear water washed across the planks, and a red-tailed carp as thick as a man's arm leaped out of the water west of the bridge, describing a rainbow in the air before splashing into the water on the eastern side.

Granddad watched the westward flow of water as it washed the mule's hooves clean. The mule lowered its lips to touch the spray above the churning water, which splashed its long, narrow face. It closed its nostrils and bared its white, even teeth.

Green-tipped sorghum on the southern bank waved in the wind as Granddad rode eastward along the riverbank. When the sun was directly overhead, he dismounted and led the animal into the sorghum field. The black, rain-soaked earth was like a gooey paste that swallowed up the mule's hooves and covered Granddad's feet. The mule struggled to keep its heavy body moving forward. White puffs of air and green, powdery froth shot from the animal's nostrils. The pungent, vinegary smell of sweat and the putrid stench of black mud made Granddad feel like sneezing. He and his mule parted the dense, tender green sorghum to clear a lane through the field; but the stalks righted themselves slowly, leaving no sign that anyone had passed by. Water seeped from the ground where they had walked, quickly filling the indentations.

Granddad's legs and the mule's belly were splattered with mud. The sound of their movement was harsh and grating in the stifling air of the field, where the sorghum grew unchecked. Before long, Granddad was breathing hard; his throat was parched, his tongue sticky and foul-tasting. Having no more perspiration to sweat, his pores oozed a sticky liquid like pine oil, which stung his skin. The sharp sorghum leaves cut his bare neck.

The angered mule kept shaking his head, wanting desperately to leap into the air and gallop along the tips of the sorghum, or, like our other black mule, to be at the trough feeding wearily on a mixture of sorghum leaves and scorched grain.

Granddad walked confidently and steadfastly down a furrow, his plan well thought out. The mule, whose eyes were watering from brushing up against sorghum leaves, kept looking at its master, sometimes sadly, sometimes angrily, as it was led through the field. Fresh footprints appeared on the ground in front of them, and Granddad detected traces of the smell he had been anticipating. The mule shortened the distance between them, still snorting, still weaving its bulky body among the sorghum stalks. Granddad coughed, more loudly than necessary, and a wave of intoxicating fragrance wafted toward him from up ahead. He knew, his sixth sense told him, that he was a mere step or two from the spot that had obsessed him for so long.

Granddad followed the trail without having to look at the footprints. He sang out to break the stillness: ". . . One horse far away from the state of Xiliang . . ."

He sensed footsteps behind him, but kept walking, as though blissfully ignorant. Suddenly a hard object poked him in the ribs. He raised his hands compliantly. Hands reached into his shirt and removed his pistols. A strip of black cloth was wrapped around his eyes.

"I want to see your chief," he said.

A bandit wrapped his arms around Granddad, picked him up off the ground, and spun him around for a minute or two, then let him fall hard onto the spongy black ground. His forehead and hands covered with mud, he climbed to his feet by grabbing on to a stalk of sorghum; his ears were ringing and he saw a flash of green, then a flash of black. He could hear the heaving breathing of the man beside him. The bandit broke off a stalk of sorghum and thrust one end into Granddad's hand. "Let's go!" he said.

Granddad heard the footsteps of the bandit behind him and a sucking sound as the mule pulled its hooves out of the gooey mud. When the bandit removed Granddad's blindfold, he covered his eyes with his hands, squeezed out a dozen or so tears, then let his hands drop. In front of him was a camp trampled out of the sorghum. A dozen men with rain capes over their shoulders stood in front of the two tents, where a man sat on a wooden stump; there was a big spot on his neck.

"Where's your leader?"

"Are you the proprietor of the distillery?" Spotted Neck asked him.

"Yes."

"What do you want here?"

"To pay my respects to an expert and learn from him."

Spotted Neck sneered. "Don't you go down to the river to shoot fish for target practice every day?"

"I can't get the knack of it."

Spotted Neck held up Granddad's pistols and looked down the barrels, then cocked them. "Fine weapons. What are you practicing with these for?"

"To use on Nine Dreams Cao."

"Isn't he your old lady's foster-dad?"

"He gave me three hundred and fifty lashes with the sole of his shoe! All because of you."

Spotted Neck laughed. "You murdered two men and took possession of their woman. You deserve to have your head lopped off."

"He gave me three hundred and fifty lashes!"

Spotted Neck raised his right hand and pulled off three quick shots—*pow pow pow*—then did the same with his left. Granddad sat down hard on the ground, buried his head in his arms, and screeched. The bandits roared with laughter.

"How could a scared rabbit like that murder anyone?" Spotted Neck wondered aloud.

"He saves his courage for sex," one of the bandits said.

"Go home and take care of business," Spotted Neck said. "Now that the Gook is dead, your home will be the contact point."

"I want to learn how to shoot so I can kill Nine Dreams Cao!" Granddad repeated.

"I hold the life of Nine Dreams Cao in the palm of my hand, and I can take it from him any time I want," Spotted Neck said.

"Does that mean I've wasted my time coming here?" Granddad asked unhappily.

Spotted Neck tossed Granddad's two pistols to him. He barely caught one; the other landed on the ground, its muzzle buried in the mud. He picked it up, shook off the mud, and wiped the barrel on his sleeve.

One of the bandits walked up to blindfold Granddad, but Spotted Neck waved him off. "No need for that," he said as he stood up. "Come on, let's take a bath in the river. We'll walk part of the way with the proprietor here."

One of the bandits led the mule. Granddad fell in behind the animal, followed by Spotted Neck and his gang of bandits. When they reached the riverbank, Spotted Neck looked at Granddad with a cold glint in his eyes. Granddad wiped the mud and sweat from his face. "I guess I was wrong to come," he said, "wrong to come. This heat's enough to kill a man."

He took off his muddy clothes, casually tossed the two pistols onto the pile of clothing, then ran down to the river and dived in, splashing around like a fritter in hot oil. His head bobbed up and down; his arms flailed like those of a man trying to pull up a clump of water grass.

"Doesn't he know how to swim?" one of the bandits asked.

Spotted Neck just snorted.

"He'll drown, chief!"

"Go in and drag him out!" Spotted Neck ordered.

Four bandits dived in and carried Granddad, who had swallowed a caskful of water, up to the bank, where he lay like a dead man.

"Bring his mule over," Spotted Neck said.

One of the men led the mule over.

"Lay him across the mule's back," Spotted Neck said.

The bandits lifted him up onto the mule's back, his bloated belly pressing down on the saddle.

"Make it run!" Spotted Neck said.

With one bandit leading the mule, another in back, and two more holding on to Granddad, the mule trotted down the riverbank; by the time it had traveled about the distance of two arrow shots, a murky column of water shot out of Granddad's mouth.

The bandits lifted Granddad off the mule and laid him out naked on the dike. He looked up at the tall, hulking Spotted Neck with eyes as dull as those of a dead fish.

Spotted Neck removed his rain cape and said with a friendly smile, "You just got a new lease on life, young man."

Granddad's ashen cheeks twitched painfully.

Spotted Neck and his men stripped and dived into the river. Excellent swimmers, they had a frolicking water fight, sending sprays of the Black Water River flying in all directions.

Slowly Granddad got to his feet and draped Spotted Neck's rain cape over his shoulders. After blowing his nose and clearing his throat, he flexed his arms and legs. His saddle was dripping wet, so he dried it off with Spotted Neck's clothes. The mule touchingly stretched its satiny, glistening neck toward Granddad. He patted it. "Be patient, Blackie, be patient."

Granddad picked up his pistols as the bandits swam toward the riverbank like a flock of ducks. He fired seven shots in perfect cadence. The brains and blood of seven bandits were splattered across the cruel, heartless waters of the Black Water River.

Granddad fired seven more shots.

By then Spotted Neck had crawled up onto the shore. The Black Water River had washed his skin as clean as a snowflake. Standing fearlessly in a clump of yellowing grass at the river's edge, he commented with considerable admiration, "Nice shooting!"

The blazing, golden sun lit up the drops of water rolling down his naked body.

"Spotty," Granddad asked him, "did you touch my woman?"

"What a rotten shame!"

"What got you into this business, anyway?"

"You won't die in bed," Spotted Neck replied.

"Aren't you going back in the water?"

Spotted Neck backed up until he was standing in the shallow water. "Shoot me here," he said, pointing to his heart. "The head is so messy!"

"All right," Granddad agreed.

The seven bullets Granddad fired surely turned Spotted Neck's heart into a honeycomb. He merely moaned once as he fell backward, his legs sticking out of the water like fins for a moment before he sank to the bottom like a fish.

The following morning, Granddad and Grandma rode their black mules over to the home of Great-Granddad, who was melting silver into longevity ingots. When they burst in on him, he knocked over the smelting kettle in alarm.

"I hear Nine Dreams Cao rewarded you with ten silver dollars," Granddad said.

"Spare me, worthy son-in-law. . . ." Great-Granddad fell to his knees.

Granddad took out ten silver dollars and stacked them on Great-Granddad's shiny scalp.

"Hold your head up straight, and don't move!" he demanded.

He moved back a few steps. *Pow pow.* Two silver dollars sailed into the air.

Two more shots sent two more silver dollars flying.

Before Granddad had fired ten shots, Great-Granddad lay in a blubbering heap on the floor.

Grandma took out a hundred silver dollars and tossed them on the floor, which shone like silver.

11

GRANDDAD AND FATHER returned to their razed home, where they retrieved fifty silver dollars from a hiding place in the wall. Then, dressed as beggars, they went to a small shop in town, near the railway station, where a red lantern hung. They bought five hundred bullets from a heavily made-up woman, then hid out for several days, until they found a way to sneak out through the town gate. They planned to settle accounts with Pocky Leng.

On the afternoon of the sixth day following the ambush and battle at the Black Water River bridge—the fifteenth day of the eighth lunar month in the year 1939—Granddad and Father drove a billy goat, nearly dead from the dung building up inside it, to the sorghum field at the western edge of the village. More than four hundred Japs and six hundred of their puppet soldiers had encircled our village like a steel hoop on a barrel. Granddad and Father hurriedly cut open the billy goat's stitched-shut rectum, and after relieving itself of pounds of dung, it dumped several hundred cartridges onto the ground. They quickly scooped them up, ignoring the stinking filth, and engaged the invaders in a solemn and stirring battle in the sorghum field.

Although they killed dozens of Japanese soldiers and dozens of puppet soldiers, they were still outnumbered. As night fell, the villagers tried to breach the encirclement at the southern edge of the village, where there was no gunfire, but were met by a withering hail of machine-gun fire. Hundreds of men and women were killed instantly in the sorghum field, and their mortally wounded comrades crushed countless stalks of red sorghum in their own death agonies.

The Japs torched the village before withdrawing. Flames shot up into the heavens, and kept burning, turning half the sky white. The moon that night was full and blood-red, but the war below turned it pale and weak, like a faded paper cutout hanging grimly in the sky.

"Where to now, Dad?"

No response.

CHAPTER THREE

Dog Ways

1

THE GLORIOUS HISTORY OF MAN is filled with legends of dogs and memories of dogs: despicable dogs, respectable dogs, fearful dogs, pitiful dogs. When Granddad and Father wavered at one of life's cross-roads, hundreds of dogs under the leadership of the three from our family—Blackie, Green, and Red—clawed out pale paths in the earth near the sorghum field south of our village, where the massacre of our people had occurred. By that time, our dogs were nearly fifteen years old, a time of youth for humans, but an advanced age for dogs, an age of confidence.

That massacre on the night of the Mid-Autumn Festival in 1939 decimated our village and turned hundreds of dogs into homeless strays. Drawn to the stench of human blood and gore, they were easy targets for Granddad and Father, who lay in wait at the bridgehead over the Black Water River. Granddad's pistol barked loudly as it emitted puffs of scalding smoke, its barrel turning dark red under the autumn moon, which was as white and cold as frost. Father's intense longing for Grandma during lulls in his pitched battle with the crazed, corpse-eating dogs makes me feel lost when I think of it, lost like a homeless stray.

In the aftermath of the slaughter of the townspeople, the sorghum field was covered by pristine moonlight, bleak, quiet, and still. Fires roared in the village, the tongues of flame frantically licking the low sky and snapping like flags in a strong wind. Only three hours earlier,

Japanese soldiers and their Chinese puppet troops had cut a swath through the village and torched the houses before leaving through the northern gate. Now Granddad's right arm, wounded a week before, was festering and oozing pus, hanging useless like a piece of dead meat. As Father helped him bandage the wound, Granddad threw his overheated pistol onto the moist black earth of the sorghum field, where it sizzled. Once his wound was tended, he sat down and listened to the snorts and whinnies of Japanese warhorses and the whirlwind of pounding hooves galloping out of the village to form up ranks. The sounds were swallowed up by the field, along with the brays of pack mules and the footsteps of exhausted soldiers.

Father stood beside the seated figure of Granddad, and strained to get a fix on the hoofbeats of the horses. Earlier that afternoon, the Japanese cavalry, tormented by Granddad's and Father's sniper fire, had abandoned their assault on the village's stubborn defenses to rake through the sorghum field. Father had nearly died of fright when a huge, fiery red beast bore down on him until all he could see was a hoof as big as a plate coming straight at his head, the arc of the horseshoe flashing like lightning. He screamed for his dad, then covered his head and hunkered down among the sorghum stalks. A muddle of foul-smelling sweat and urine splashed down as the horse passed over him, a stench he didn't think he'd ever be able to wash off.

He remembered Grandma, seven days earlier, as she lay face up, with sorghum seeds and grains scattered over her face. Her pearly-white teeth shone between blood-drained lips, ornamented by the diamondlike grains.

The charging horse turned with difficulty and headed back, stalks of sorghum struggling bitterly against its rump, some bending and breaking, others snapping back into place. They shivered in the autumn winds like victims of malaria. Father saw the flared nostrils and fleshy lips of the panting warhorse; bloody froth sprayed from between its gleaming white teeth and dripped from its greedy lower lip. Clouds of white dust from the agitated sorghum stung its watery eyes. Seated atop the sleek warhorse was an awesome young Japanese cavalryman whose head, encased in a little square cap, barely cleared the tops of the stalks around him. The ears of grain whipped, pushed, and pricked him mercilessly, even mocked him. He squinted his eyes with loathing and repugnance for the stalks that were raising welts on his handsome face. Father watched him attack the sorghum ears with his sword, lopping some off so cleanly they fell silently, their headless stumps deathly still, while others protested noisily as they hung by threads.

Father saw the Japanese cavalryman rear his horse up and begin another charge, his sword raised high. He picked up his useless Browning pistol, which earlier had both sinned against him and distinguished itself in battle, and hurled it at the oncoming horse, striking it squarely on the forehead with a dull thud. The animal raised its head as its front legs buckled; its lips kissed the black earth, and its neck twisted to the side so it could pillow its head on the ground. The rider, thrown from the saddle, must have broken his arm in the fall, because Father saw the sword drop from his hand and heard a loud crack. A fragment of bone ripped through the sleeve of his uniform, and the limp arm began to twitch as though it had a will of its own. What was at first a clean wound, showing nothing more than a gleaming white piece of bone, gruesome and deathlike, soon began to spurt fresh red blood, alternating between gushes and a slow ooze, droplets shining like so many strings of bright cherries. One of the cavalryman's legs was pinned beneath the horse's belly, the other was draped over its head, the two forming a large obtuse angle. Father never dreamed that a mighty warhorse and its rider could be brought down so easily.

Just then Granddad crept out from among the sorghum stalks and called out softly: "Douguan."

Father got uneasily to his feet and looked at Granddad.

The Japanese cavalry troops were making another whirlwind pass from deep in the sorghum field, filling the air with a mixture of sounds, from the dull thud of hooves on the spongy black earth to the crisp snapping of sorghum stalks.

Granddad wrapped his arms around Father and pressed him to the ground as the horses' broad chests and powerful hooves passed over them; groaning clods of dark earth flew in their wake, sorghum stalks swayed reluctantly behind them, and golden-red grains were scattered all over the ground, filling the deep prints of horseshoes in the soil.

The sorghum gradually stopped swaying in the wake of the cavalry charge, so Granddad stood up. Father didn't realize how forcefully

Granddad had pushed him to the ground until he noticed the deep imprints of his knees in the dark soil.

The Japanese cavalryman wasn't dead. Shocked into consciousness by excruciating pain, he rested his good arm on the ground and awkwardly shifted the leg resting on the horse's head back into a riding position. The slightest movement of the dislocated leg, which no longer seemed to belong to him, made him groan in agony. Father watched sweat drip from his forehead and run down his face through the grime of mud and gunpowder residue, exposing streaks of ghastly-pale skin. The horse hadn't died, either. Its neck was writhing like a python, its eyes fixed on the sky and sun of the unfamiliar Northeast Gaomi Township. Its rider rested for a minute before straining to free his other leg.

Granddad walked up and yanked the leg free, then lifted him up by the scruff of his neck; his legs were so rubbery the entire weight of his body was supported by Granddad's grip. As soon as Granddad let go, he crumpled to the ground like a clay doll dunked in water. Granddad picked up the glinting sword and swung it in two arcs—one down and one up—lopping off the heads of a couple of dozen sorghum stalks, whose dry stumps stood erect in the soil.

Then he stuck the point of the sword up under the man's handsome, straight, pale nose and said in a controlled voice, "Where's your arrogance now, you Jap bastard?"

The cavalryman's shiny black eyes were blinking a mile a minute as a stream of gibberish poured from his mouth. Father knew he was pleading for his life as he reached into his shirt pocket with his trembling good hand and pulled out a clear plastic wallet, which he handed to Granddad as he muttered: *"Jiligulu, minluwala . . ."*

Father walked up to get a closer look at the plastic wallet, which held a color photograph of a lovely young woman holding a pudgy infant in her milky-white arms. Peaceful smiles adorned their faces.

"Is this your wife?" Granddad asked him.

The man jabbered brokenly.

"Is this your son?" Granddad asked him.

Father stuck his head up so close he could see the woman's sweet smile and the disarmingly innocent look of her child.

"So you think this is all it takes to win me over, you bastard!"

Granddad tossed the wallet into the air, where it sailed like a butterfly in the sunlight before settling slowly, carrying the sun's rays back with it. He jerked the sword out from under the man's nose and swung it disdainfully at the falling object; the blade glinted coldly in the sunlight as the wallet twitched in the air and fell in two pieces at their feet.

Father was immersed in darkness as a cold shudder racked his body. Streaks of red and green flashed before his tightly shut eyes. Heartbroken, he couldn't bear to open his eyes and see what he knew were the dismembered figures of the lovely woman and her innocent baby.

The Japanese cavalryman dragged his pain-racked body over to Father, where he grabbed the two halves of the plastic wallet. Blood dripped from the tips of his yellow fingers. As he clumsily tried to fit the two halves of his wife and son together with his usable hand, his dry, chapped lips quivered, his teeth chattered, and broken fragments of words emerged: "*Aya . . . wa . . . tu . . . lu . . . he . . . cha . . . hai . . . min . . .*"

Two streaks of glistening tears carved a path down his gaunt, grimy cheeks. He held the photograph up to his lips and kissed it, a gurgling sound rising from his throat.

"You goddamn bastard, so you can cry, too? Since you know all about kissing your wife and child, why go around murdering ours? You think that if you squeeze out a few drops of stinking piss I won't kill you?" Granddad screamed as he raised the glinting blade of the Japanese sword over his head.

"Dad—" Father screamed, grabbing Granddad's arm with both hands. "Dad, don't kill him!"

Granddad's arm shook in Father's grasp. With teary, pity-filled eyes, Father pleaded with Granddad, whose heart had been hardened so much that killing had become commonplace.

As Granddad lowered his head, the wind carried a barrage of earthshaking thuds from Japanese mortars and the crackle of machine-gun fire raking the ranks of village defenders. From deep in the sorghum field they heard the shrill whinnies of Japanese horses and the heavy pounding of their hooves on the dark soil. Granddad shook his arm violently, tossing Father aside.

"You little shit, what the hell's gotten into you?" he lashed out.

"Who are those tears for? For your mother? For Uncle Arhat? For Uncle Mute and all the others? Or maybe it's for this no-good son of a bitch! Whose pistol brought him down? Wasn't he trying to trample you and slice you in two with his sword? Dry your tears, son, then kill him with his own sword!"

Father backed up, tears streaming down his face.

"Come here!"

"No—Dad—I can't—"

"Fucking coward!"

Granddad kicked Father, took a step backward, and raised the sword over his head.

Father saw a glinting arc of steel, then darkness. A liquid ripping sound blotted out the thuds of Japanese mortars, pounding Father's eardrums and tying his guts into knots. When his vision returned, the handsome young Japanese cavalryman lay on the ground sliced in half. The blade had entered his left shoulder and exited on the right, beneath his ribs. His multicolored innards writhed and quivered, emitting a steamy, powerful stench. Father felt his own intestines twist and leap into his chest. A torrent of green liquid erupted from his mouth. He turned and ran.

Although Father didn't have the nerve to look at the Japanese cavalryman's staring eyes beneath those long lashes, he couldn't escape the image of the body lying there sliced in two. With one stroke of the sword, Granddad seemed to have cut everything in two. Even himself. The grotesque illusion of a blood-soaked sword glinting in the sky suddenly flashed in front of Father's eyes, slicing people in two, as if cleaving melons: Granddad, Grandma, Uncle Arhat, the Japanese cavalryman and his wife and child, Uncle Mute, Big Liu, the Fang brothers, Consumptive Four, Adjutant Ren, everyone.

Granddad threw the sword to the ground and took off after Father, who was running blindly through the sorghum. More Japanese cavalry troops bore down on them; mortar shells shrieked through the sky above the sorghum field and exploded among the men stubbornly defending their village with shotguns and homemade cannons.

Granddad caught up with Father, grabbed him by the scruff of the neck, and shook him hard. "Douguan! Douguan! You little bastard!

Have you gone crazy? What do you want, to crawl into a hole somewhere and die?"

Father clawed at Granddad's powerful hands and shrieked, "Dad! Dad! Dad! Take me home. Take me home! I don't want to fight anymore. I don't want to fight! I saw Mom! I saw Master! I saw Uncle!"

Granddad slapped him hard across the mouth. Father's neck snapped to the side and went limp from the force of the blow. His head rolled against his chest; a bloody froth oozed from the corner of his mouth.

2

WHEN THE JAPANESE TROOPS WITHDREW, the full moon, thin as a paper cutout, rose in the sky above the tips of the sorghum stalks, which had undergone such suffering. Grain fell sporadically like glistening tears. A sweet odor grew heavy in the air; the dark soil of the southern edge of our village had been thoroughly soaked by human blood. Lights from fires in the village curled like foxtails, as occasional pops, like the crackling of dry wood, momentarily filled the air with a charred odor that merged with the stifling stench of blood.

The wound on Granddad's arm had turned worse, the scabs cracking and releasing a rotting, oozing mixture of dark blood and white pus. He told Father to squeeze the area around the wound. Fearfully, Father placed his icy fingers on the discolored skin around the suppurating wound and squeezed, forcing out a string of air bubbles that released the putrid smell of pickled vegetables. Granddad picked up a piece of yellow spirit currency that had been weighted down by a dirt clod at the head of a nearby gravesite and told Father to smear some of the salty white powder from the sorghum stalks on it. Then he removed the head of a cartridge with his teeth and poured the greenish gunpowder onto the paper, mixed it with the white sorghum powder, and took a pinch with his fingers to daub on the open wound.

"Dad," Father said, "shall I mix some soil into it?"

Granddad thought for a moment. "Sure, why not?"

Father bent down and picked up a clod of dark earth near the roots of a sorghum stalk, crumbled it in his fingers, and spread it on the paper. After Granddad mixed the three substances together and covered the wound with them, paper and all, Father wrapped a filthy strip of bandage cloth around it and tied it tight.

"Does that make it feel better, Dad?"

Granddad moved his arm back and forth. "Much better, Douguan. An elixir like this will work on any wound, no matter how serious."

"Dad, if we'd had something like that for Mother, she wouldn't have died, would she?"

"No, she wouldn't have. . . ." Granddad's face clouded.

"Dad, wouldn't it've been great if you'd told me about this before? Mother was bleeding so much I kept packing dirt on the wounds, but that only stopped it for a while. If I'd known to add some white sorghum powder and gunpowder, everything would have been fine. . . ."

All the while Father was rambling, Granddad was loading his pistol. Japanese mortar fire raised puffs of hot yellow smoke all up and down the village wall.

Since Father's Browning pistol lay under the belly of the fallen horse, during the final battle of the afternoon he used a Japanese rifle nearly as tall as he was; Granddad used his German automatic, firing it so rapidly it spent its youth and was ready for the trash heap. Although battle fires still lit up the sky above the village, an aura of peace and quiet had settled over the sorghum fields.

Father followed Granddad, dragging his rifle behind him as they circled the site of the massacre. The blood-soaked earth had the consistency of liquid clay under the weight of their footsteps; bodies of the dead merged with the wreckage of sorghum stalks. Moonlight danced on pools of blood, and hideous scenes of dismemberment swept away the final moments of Father's youth. Tortured moans emerged from the field of sorghum, and here and there among the bodies some movement appeared. Father was burning to ask Granddad to save those fellow villagers who were still alive, but when he saw the pale, expressionless look on his father's bronze face, the words stuck in his throat.

During the most critical moments, Father was always slightly more alert than Granddad, perhaps because he concentrated on surface phenomena; superficial thought seems ideally suited to guerrilla fighting.

At that moment, Granddad looked benumbed; his thoughts were riveted on a single point, which might have been a twisted face, or a shattered rifle, or a single spent bullet. He was blind to all other sights, deaf to all other sounds. This problem—or characteristic—of his would grow more pronounced over the coming decade. He returned to China from the mountains of Hokkaido with an unfathomable depth in his eyes, gazing at things as though he could will them to combust spontaneously.

Father never achieved this degree of philosophical depth. In 1957, after untold hardships, when he finally emerged from the burrow Mother had dug for him, his eyes had the same look as in his youth: lively, perplexed, capricious. He never did figure out the relationship between men and politics or society or war, even though he had been spun so violently on the wheel of battle. He was forever trying to squeeze the light of his nature through the chinks in his body armor.

Granddad and Father circled the site of the massacre a dozen times, until Father said tearfully, "Dad . . . I can't walk anymore. . . ."

Granddad's robot movements stopped; taking Father's hand, he backed up ten paces and sat down on a patch of solid, dry earth. The cheerless and lonely sorghum field was highlighted by the crackle of fires in the village. Weak golden flames danced fitfully beneath the silvery moonlight. After sitting there for a moment, Granddad fell backward like a capsized wall, and Father laid his head on Granddad's belly, where he fell into a hazy sleep. He could feel Granddad's feverish hand stroking his head, which sent his thoughts back nearly a dozen years, to when he was suckling at Grandma's breast.

He was four at the time, and growing tired of the yellowed nipple that was always thrust into his mouth. Having begun to hate its sour hardness, he gazed up into the look of rapture in Grandma's face with a murderous glint in his eyes and bit down as hard as he could. He felt the contraction in Grandma's breast as her body jerked backward. Trickles of a sweet liquid warmed the corners of his mouth, until Grandma gave him a swat on the bottom and pushed him away. He fell to the ground, his eyes on the drops of fresh red blood dripping from the tip of Grandma's pendulous breast. He whimpered, but his eyes were dry. Grandma, on the other hand, was crying bitterly, her shoulders heaving, her face bathed in tears. She lashed out at him, calling him a wolf cub, as mean as his wolf of a father.

Later on he learned that that was the year Granddad, who loved Grandma dearly, had fallen in love with the hired girl, Passion, who had grown into a bright-eyed young woman. At the moment, when Father bit Grandma, Granddad, who had grown tired of her jealousy, was living with Passion in a house he'd bought in a neighboring village. Everyone said that this second grandma of mine was no economy lantern, and that Grandma was afraid of her, but this is something I'll clear up later. Second Grandma eventually had a girl by Granddad. In 1938, Japanese soldiers murdered this young aunt of mine with a bayonet, then gang-raped Second Grandma—this, too, I'll clear up later.

Granddad and Father were exhausted. The wound throbbed in Granddad's arm, which seemed to be on fire. Father's feet had swollen until his cloth shoes nearly split their seams, and he fantasized about the exquisite pleasure of airing the rotting skin of his feet in the moonlight. But he didn't have the strength to sit up and take off his shoes. Instead, he rolled over and rested his head on Granddad's hard stomach so he could look up into the starry night and let the moon's rays light up his face. He could hear the murmuring flow of the Black Water River and see black clouds gather in the sky above him. He remembered Uncle Arhat's saying once that, when the Milky Way lay horizontally across the sky, autumn rains would fall. He had only really seen autumn water once in his life:

The sorghum was ready for harvest when the Black Water River rose and burst its banks, flooding both the fields and the village. The stalks strained to keep their heads above water; rats and snakes scurried and slithered up them to escape drowning. Father had gone with Uncle Arhat to the wall, which the villagers were reinforcing, and gazed uneasily at the yellow water rushing toward him. The villagers made rafts from kindling and paddled out to the fields to hack off the ears of grain, which were already sprouting new green buds. Bundles of soaked deep-red and emerald-green ears of sorghum weighted down the rafts so much it's a wonder they didn't sink. The dark, gaunt men, barefoot and bare-chested, wearing conical straw hats, stood with their legs akimbo on the rafts, poling with all their strength as they rocked from side to side.

The water in the village was knee-high, covering the legs of livestock, whose waste floated on the surface. In the dying rays of the autumn sun, the water shone like liquefied metal; tips of sorghum stalks too far away to be harvested formed a canopy of golden red just above the rippling surface, over which flocks of wild geese flew. Father could see a bright, broad body of water flowing slowly through the densest patch of red sorghum, in sharp contrast to the muddy, stagnant water around him; it was, he knew, the Black Water River. On one of the rafts lay a silver-bellied, green-backed grass carp, a long, thin sorghum stalk stuck through its gills. The farmer proudly held it up to show the people on the wall; it was nearly half as tall as he was. Blood oozed from its gills, and its mouth was open as it looked at my father with dull, sorrowful eyes.

Father was thinking about how Uncle Arhat had bought a fish from a farmer once, and how Grandma had scraped the scales from its belly, then made soup out of it; just thinking about that delicious soup gave him an appetite. He sat up. "Dad," he said, "aren't you hungry? I am. Can you find me something to eat? I'm starving. . . ."

Granddad sat up and fished around in his belt until he found a bullet, which he inserted into the cylinder; then he snapped it shut, sending the bullet into the chamber. He pulled the trigger, and there was a loud crack. "Douguan," he said, "let's go find your mother. . . ."

"No, Dad," Father replied in a high-pitched, frightened voice, "Mother's dead. But we're still alive, and I'm hungry. Let's get something to eat."

Father pulled Granddad to his feet. "Where?" Granddad mumbled. "Where can we go?" So Father led him by the hand into the sorghum field, where they walked in a crooked line, as though their objective was the moon, hanging high and icy in the sky.

A growl emerged from the field of corpses. Granddad and Father stopped in their tracks and turned to see a dozen pairs of green eyes, like will-o'-the-wisps, and several indigo shadows tumbling on the ground. Granddad took out his pistol and fired at two of the green eyes; there was a flash, and the howl of a dying dog accompanied the extinguishing of those eyes. Granddad fired seven shots in all, and several wounded dogs writhed in agony among the corpses. While he was emptying his pistol into the pack, the uninjured dogs fled into the sorghum field, out of range, where they howled furiously at the two humans.

The last couple of bullets from Granddad's pistol had traveled only thirty paces or so before thudding to the ground. Father watched them tumble in the moonlight, so slowly he could have reached out and caught them. And the once crisp crack of the pistol sounded more like the phlegmatic cough of a doddering old man. A tortured, sympathetic expression spread across Granddad's face as he looked down at the weapon in his hand.

"Out of bullets, Dad?"

The five hundred bullets they'd brought back from town in the goat's belly had been used up in a matter of hours. The pistol had aged overnight, and Granddad came to the painful realization that it was no longer capable of carrying out his wishes; time for them to part ways.

Holding the gun out in front of him, he carefully studied the muted reflection of the moonlight on the barrel, then loosened his grip and let the gun fall heavily to the ground.

The green-eyed dogs returned to the corpses, timidly at first. But their eyes quickly disappeared, and the moonlight was reflected off rolling waves of bluish fur; Granddad and Father could hear the sounds of dogs tearing human bodies with their fangs.

"Let's go into the village, Dad," Father said.

Granddad wavered for a moment, so Father tugged on him, and they fell into step.

By then most of the fires in the village had gone out, leaving red-hot cinders that gave off an acrid heat amid the crumbling walls and shattered buildings. Hot winds whirled above the village roads. The murky air was stifling. Roofs of houses, their supports burned out beneath them, had collapsed in mountains of smoke, dust, and cinders. Bodies were strewn atop the village wall and on the roads. A page in the history of our village had been turned. At one time the site had been a wasteland covered with brambles, underbrush, and reeds, a paradise for foxes and wild rabbits. Then a few huts appeared, and it became a haven for escaped murderers, drunks, gamblers, who built homes, cultivated the land, and turned it into a paradise for humans, forcing out the foxes and wild rabbits, who set up howls of protest on the eve of their departure. Now the village lay in ruins; man had created it, and man had destroyed it. It was now a sorrowful paradise, a monument to both grief and joy, built upon ruins. In 1960, when the dark cloud of famine settled over the Shandong Peninsula, even though I was only four years old I could dimly sense that Northeast Gaomi Township had never been anything but a pile of ruins, and that its people had never been able to rid their hearts of the shattered buildings, nor would they ever be able to.

That night, after the smoke and sparks from the other houses had died out, our buildings were still burning, sending skyward green-tinged tongues of flame and the intoxicating aroma of strong wine, released in an instant after all those years. Blue roof tiles, deformed by the intense heat, turned scarlet, then leaped into the air through a wall of flames that illuminated Granddad's hair, which had turned three-quarters gray in the space of a week. A roof came crashing down, momentarily blotting out the flames; which then roared out of the rubble, stronger than ever. The loud crash nearly crushed the breath out of Father and Granddad.

Our house, which had sheltered the father and son of the Shan family as they grew rich, then had sheltered Granddad after his murderous deed, then had sheltered Grandma, Granddad, Father, Uncle Arhat, and all the men who worked for them, a sanctuary for their kindnesses and their grievances, had now completed its historical mission. I hated that sanctuary: though it had sheltered decent emotions, it had also sheltered heinous crimes. Father, when you were hiding in the burrow we dug for you in the floor of my home back in 1957, you recalled those days of your past in the unrelenting darkness. On no fewer than 365 occasions, in your mind you saw the roof of your house crash down amid the flames, and wondered what was going through the mind of your father, my granddad. So my fantasies were chasing yours while yours were chasing Granddad's.

As he watched the roof collapse, Granddad became as angry as he'd been the day he abandoned Grandma and moved to another village to be with his new love, Passion. He had learned then that Grandma had shamelessly taken up with Black Eye, the leader of an organization called the Iron Society, and at the time he wasn't sure what filled his heart—loathing or love, pain or anger. When he later returned to Grandma's arms, his feelings for her were so confused he couldn't sort them out. In the beginning, his emotional warfare scarred only his own heart, and Grandma's scarred only her own. Finally, they hurt each other. Only when Grandma smiled up at him as she lay dead in the sorghum field did he realize the grievous punishment life had meted out to him. He loved my father as a magpie loves the last remaining egg in its nest. But by then it was too late, for fate, cold and calculating, had sentenced him to a cruel end that was waiting for him down the road.

"Dad, our house is gone. . . ." Father said.

Granddad rubbed Father's head as he stared at the ruins of his home, then took Father's hand and began stumbling aimlessly down the road under the waning light of the flames and the waxing light of the moon.

At the head of the village they heard an old man's voice: "Is that you, Number Three? Why didn't you bring the oxcart?"

The sound of that voice gave Granddad and Father such a warm feeling they forgot how tired they were and rushed over to see who it was.

A hunched-over elderly man rose to greet them, carefully sizing up Granddad with his ancient eyes, nearly touching his face. Granddad didn't like his watchful look and was repulsed by the greedy stench that came from his mouth.

"You're not my Number Three," the old man said unhappily, his head wobbling as he sat down on a pile of loot. There were trunks, cupboards, dining tables, farm tools, harnesses, ripped comforters, cooking pots, earthenware bowls. He was sitting on a small mountain of stuff and guarding it as a wolf guards its kill. Behind him, two calves, three goats, and a mule were tied to a willow tree.

"You old dog!" Granddad growled through clenched teeth. "Get the hell out of here!"

The old man rose up on his haunches and said amiably, "Ah, my brother, let's not be envious. I risked my life to drag this stuff out of the flames!"

"I'll fuck your living mother! Climb down from there!" Granddad lashed out angrily.

"You have no right to talk to me like that. I didn't do anything to you. You're the one who's asking for trouble. What gives you the right to curse me like that?" he complained.

"Curse you? I'll goddamn kill you! We're not in a desperate struggle with Japan just so you can go on a looting binge! You bastard, you old bastard! Douguan, where's your gun?"

"It's under the horse's belly," Father said.

Granddad jumped up onto the mountain of stuff and, with a single kick, sent the old man sprawling onto the ground. He rose to his knees and begged, "Spare me, Eighth Route Master, spare me!"

"I'm not with the Eighth Route Army," Granddad said, "or the Ninth Route. I'm Yu Zhan'ao the bandit!"

"Spare me, Commander Yu, spare me! What good would it do to let all this stuff burn? I'm not the only 'potato picker' from the village. Those thieves got all the good stuff. I'm too old and too slow, and all I could find was this junk."

Granddad picked up a wooden table and threw it at the old man's bald head. He screamed and held his bleeding scalp as he rolled in the dirt. Granddad reached down and picked him up by his collar. Looking straight into those tortured eyes, he said, "Our hero, the 'potato picker,' " then raised his fist and drove it with a loud crack into the old man's face, sending him crumpling to the ground, face up. Granddad walked up and kicked him in the face, hard.

3

MOTHER AND MY THREE-YEAR-OLD LITTLE UNCLE already had spent a day and a night hiding in the dry well. The morning before, she had gone to the working well with two earthenware jugs over her shoulder. No sooner had she bent over to see her face in the water than she heard the clang of a gong from the village wall and the shouts of the night watchman, Old Man Wu: "The Japs are here, they've surrounded the village!" She was so frightened she dropped the jugs and carrying pole into the well, spun on her heel, and ran home. But before she got there she met her parents, my maternal grandfather and grandmother; he was armed with a musket, his wife was carrying her son and a cloth-wrapped parcel.

Ever since the battle at the Black Water River, the villagers had been preparing for the calamity they expected to come any day. Only three or four families had gone into hiding; the others, though frightened, were reluctant to give up their broken-down homes, their wells—bitter and sweet—and their quilts, no matter how thin and tattered they might have been. During the week of the lull, Granddad had taken Father into the county town to buy bullets, driven by a desire to settle accounts with Pocky Leng. It never occurred to him that the Japanese bloodbath would inundate his own village.

On the evening of the fifteenth day of the eighth lunar month, Zhang Ruolu the Elder—he with one large eye and one small, he with the extraordinary bearing, he the intellectual who had studied in a private school, he who had played such a vital role in the burial of the martyred warriors—mobilized all able-bodied residents to reinforce the village wall and repair the gates, and appointed night watchmen to bang gongs and shout warnings at the first sighting of enemy troops. The villagers, male and female, young and old, took turns manning the wall. Mother told me that the voice of Ruolu the Elder was loud and crisp, almost metallic. "Fellow villagers," he said, "a people united in spirit can move Mount Tai. Only if we're united in spirit can we keep the Japs out of our village!"

As he was speaking, a shot rang out from the farmland beyond the village, and an elderly watchman's head exploded; he rocked back and forth, then tumbled off the wall, sending the villagers scurrying for cover. Ruolu the Elder, dressed in tight pants and shirt, stood in the middle of the road and shouted, "Fellow villagers, calm down! Mount the wall as we planned! Don't be afraid to die. Those who fear death will find it, those who don't will live on! Our lives are all that stand between the Japs and our village!"

Mother watched the men run to the wall and throw themselves down on their bellies. My maternal grandmother, whose knees were knocking, was frozen to the spot. "Beauty's dad," she shouted tearfully, "what about the children?" My maternal grandfather ran back to her, rifle in hand, and lashed out, "What are you wailing about? Now that it's come to this, it makes no difference whether we live or die!" She didn't dare utter a sound, but the tears kept flowing. He turned to look at the village wall, which hadn't yet come under fire, grabbed Mother with one hand and her mother with the other, and ran with them to the vegetable garden behind the house, where there was an old abandoned well, its rickety windlass still in place. He looked down into the well and said, "Since there's no water, we'll hide the children here for the time being. We can come back for them after we've driven the Japs off." Grandmother stood like a block of wood and bowed to his wishes.

Grandfather took the loose end of rope from the windlass and tied it around my mother's waist, just as a shriek split the sky above them and a howling black object crashed into the neighbor's pigsty. There was an ear-splitting explosion, and everything seemed to disintegrate as a column of smoke rose from the sty; pieces of shrapnel, patches of dung, and chunks of pig flew in all directions. A stumpy leg fell right in front of Mother, the white tendons all curled inward like river leeches. It was the first mortar explosion my fifteen-year-old mother had ever heard. The surviving pigs squealed frantically and came dashing out of the sty; Mother and my little uncle were crying hysterically.

"They're firing mortars!" Grandfather announced. "Beauty, you're fifteen now, so you'll have to take care of your brother down in the well. I'll come back for you after the Japs are gone." As another mortar shell exploded in the village, he cranked the windlass and lowered Mother into the well. When her feet touched the broken bricks and crumbling clay at the bottom, she looked up at the ray of light far above her, barely able to make out Grandfather's face. "Untie the rope," she heard him yell. After doing as she was told, she watched the rope rise jerkily up the well. She could hear her parents arguing, the exploding Jap mortar shells, and finally the sound of her mother crying. Grandfather's face reappeared in the ray of light. "Beauty," he shouted, "here comes your brother. Make sure you catch him."

Mother observed the wailing descent of my three-year-old uncle, his arms and legs flailing. The rotting piece of rope quivered in the air; the windlass protested with long-drawn-out creaks. Grandmother leaned into the well opening until nearly all the upper half of her body was in view; sobbing uncontrollably, she called out my uncle's name: "Harmony, my little Harmony . . ." Mother watched Grandmother's glistening tears fall like crystal beads to the bottom of the well. The rope played out as Little Uncle's feet touched the bottom, where he tearfully implored his mother, "Ma, pull me up, I don't, I don't want to be down here, I want to stay with you, Ma, Ma."

Grandmother reached out for the rope and strained to pull it back up. "Harmony, my darling baby, my precious son . . ."

Then Mother saw Grandfather grab Grandmother's hand, which had a death grip on the rope. Grandfather shoved her hard, and Mother saw her fall sideways. The rope snapped taut, and Little Uncle flew into Mother's arms.

"You fucking woman!" Grandfather screamed. "Do you want them up here so they can die with the rest of us? Get over to the wall, and be quick about it! No one'll get out alive if the Japs enter the village!"

"Beauty—Harmony—Beauty—Harmony—" But Grandmother's shouts seemed so far away. Another mortar shell exploded; dirt fell on them. They didn't hear Grandmother's voice anymore after the explosion. Above them only a single ray of light and the old windlass.

Little Uncle was still crying as Mother untied the rope from around his waist. "Good little Harmony," she said to comfort him. "Don't cry, baby brother. The Japs'll come if you keep crying. If they hear a kid crying they'll come with their red eyes and green fingernails. . . ."

That stopped him. He looked up at her with his tiny, round black eyes, and threw his pudgy little arms around her neck. More and more mortar explosions lit up the sky, joined now by machine-gun and rifle fire. *Pop pop pop,* a pause, then *pop pop pop.* Mother looked skyward, listening carefully for movement around the well. She heard the distant shouts of Ruolu the Elder and the screams of the villagers. The well was cold and damp. A chunk of the side fell off, exposing pale earth and the roots of a tree. The bricks were covered with a layer of dark-green moss. Little Uncle stirred in her arms and began to sob again. "Sis," he said, "I want my mama, I want to go back up. . . ."

"Harmony, good Little Brother . . . Mom went with Dad to fight the Japs. They'll come get us as soon as they've driven them off. . . ." Mother, who was trying to comfort her baby brother, started to sob, too. They hugged each other tightly as their sobs and tears merged.

Dawn was breaking, as Mother could tell from the pale light above her. Somehow they'd gotten through the long night. An eerie, frightening silence hung over the well. She looked up and saw a ray of red light illuminate the walls far above her. The sun was up. She listened carefully, but the village seemed as still as the well, although every once in a while she thought she heard what sounded like a peal of thunder rolling across the sky. She wondered if her parents would come to take them out of the well on this new day, back to the world of light and air, a world where there were no banded snakes or skinny toads. The events of the previous day seemed so far away that she felt as though she'd spent half her lifetime at the bottom of the well. Dad, she was thinking, Mom. If you don't come, Brother and I surely will die down here. She resented her parents for casting their own children into the well and simply vanishing, not caring whether they were dead or alive. The next time she saw them, she'd make a huge scene to release the bellyful of grievances she'd already stored up. How could she have known that, as she was being carried away by these hateful thoughts, her mother—my maternal grandmother—had been blown to pieces by a Japanese mortar shell, and her father—my maternal grandfather—had exposed himself to enemy gunfire on the wall, only to have half of his head blown away by a bullet that seemed to have eyes?

Mother prayed silently: Dad! Mom! Come back, hurry! I'm hungry, I'm thirsty, and Brother's sick. You'll kill your own children if you don't come fast!

She heard the faint sounds of a gong from the village wall, or maybe it was from someplace else, then a distant shout: "Is there anybody here—is there anybody left—the Japs are gone—Commander Yu's here—"

Mother picked Little Uncle up in her arms and got to her feet. "Here!" she shouted hoarsely. "Here we are—we're down in the well—save us, hurry—" She reached up and began to shake the rope hanging from the windlass, keeping at it for nearly an hour. Gradually her arms grew slack, and her brother fell to the ground with a weak groan. Then silence. She leaned against the wall and slid slowly down, until she was sitting on the cold broken bricks, drained and totally dejected.

Little Uncle climbed into her lap and said calmly, "Sis . . . I want my mama. . . ."

A powerful sadness overcame Mother as she wrapped her arms around Little Uncle. "Harmony," she said, "Mom and Dad don't want us anymore. You and I are going to die here in this well. . . ."

He was burning up with fever, and hugging him was like holding a charcoal brazier. "Sis, I'm thirsty. . . ."

Mother's gaze fell on a puddle of filthy green water in a corner of the well. A scrawny toad sat in the middle of the pool, its back covered with ugly bean-sized warts, the yellowish skin beneath its mouth popping in and out, its bulging eyes glaring at her. She shuddered, her skin crawled, and she squeezed her eyes shut. Her mouth was parched, too, but she'd rather have died of thirst than drink that nasty toad-water.

Since the previous morning, not a minute had passed when Mother wasn't in the grip of terror and panic: terror caused by the sounds of gunfire in and around the village, panic over her baby brother's struggle to survive. At fifteen, she was still a frail child, and it was a strain to have to carry her pudgy little brother all the time, especially when he was constantly squirming and making the pitiful sounds of a dying kitten. She spanked him once, and the little bastard responded by sinking his teeth into her.

Now that he was feverish, Little Uncle drifted in and out of consciousness and lay limp in the arms of my mother, who sat on a piece of broken brick until her buttocks were painfully sore, then totally numb. The gunfire, dense one minute and scattered the next, never completely stopped. Sunlight crept slowly over the western wall, then the eastern wall, as darkness spread inside. Mother knew she'd spent a whole day in the well, and that any time now her parents would be coming back. She stroked her baby brother's scalding face; his breath burned her fingers. She laid her hand over his rapidly beating heart and could hear a wheeze in his chest. At that moment it occurred to her that he might very well die, and she shuddered. But she forced the thought out of her mind. Any minute now, she thought, to keep her spirits up, any minute now. It's getting dark outside, and even the swallows have gone home to roost, which means that Mom and Dad will be here soon.

The light on the walls turned dark yellow, then deep red. A cricket hidden in one of the cracks began to chirp; mosquitoes warmed up their engines and took off into the air. Just then Mother heard the sound of a mortar barrage from someplace near the village wall, and what sounded like human and animal screams from the northern end of the village. This was followed by blasts from a machine gun in the southern end. When the gunfire ended, sounds of shouting men and galloping horses swept into the village like a tidal wave. Utter chaos. Pounding of hooves and tramping boots around the opening of the well. *Gulugulu*—loud Japanese voices. Little Uncle began to whimper, but Mother clapped her hand over his mouth and held her breath. His face twisted violently under her hand, and she could feel the thumping of her own heart.

As the sun's rays died out, Mother looked up at the red sky. Fires crackled all around, sending hot ashes over the opening of the well; mixed with the sound of licking flames were the cries of children, the screams of women, and the bleating of goats, or maybe it was the tearful lowing of cows. Even from the bottom of the well, she could smell the stench of burning.

She had no idea how long she'd shuddered over the fires raging above her, since she'd lost all sense of time, but she could tell from the tiny slice of darkening sky that the fires were dying out. At first she heard an occasional burst of gunfire and the sound of a roof collapsing. But after a while there was nothing but silence, plus a few dim stars that appeared in the circle of sky above.

Mother fell asleep, and awoke chilled. By now her eyes had grown accustomed to the darkness, and when she looked up at the pale-blue sky and the gentle rays of the morning sun reflected off the walls, she felt giddy. Her clothes were soggy from the dampness; the cold air touched her bones. She hugged her little brother tightly. Even though his fever seemed to have abated during the night, he was still much hotter than she. So Mother soaked up Little Uncle's warmth, while he was cooled by her; during their time together at the bottom of the well, they achieved true life-sustaining symbiosis. Mother, who did not know that her parents were dead, expected to see their faces and to hear their familiar voices at any time; had she known, she might not have survived those days and nights in the well.

When I look back upon my family's history, I find that the lives of all the key members have at some point been linked inextricably with some sort of dark, dank cave or hole, beginning with Mother. Granddad later outdid all the others, setting a record among civilized people of his generation for living in a cave. Finally, Father would produce an epilogue that, in political terms, would be anything but glorious, but when viewed from the human angle must be considered splendid. When the time came, he would wave his sole remaining arm toward the red clouds of dawn and come running on the wind to Mother, Elder Brother, Elder Sister, and me.

Mother was freezing on the outside but burning up inside. She hadn't eaten or drunk anything since the previous morning. A searing thirst had tormented her since the night before, when the village was engulfed in flames; then, in the middle of the night, an overwhelming hunger reached its peak. As dawn was about to break, her guts seemed to twist into knots, until all she could feel was the gnawing pain in her belly. But now the mere thought of food nauseated her; it was the thirst she found unbearable. Her lungs felt dry and chapped, each breath producing the rustling sound of withered sorghum leaves.

Once again Little Uncle said meekly through blistered lips, "Sis . . . I'm thirsty. . . ." Mother didn't have the heart to look into his small, wizened face, and there were no words to console him. The promises she'd made throughout the day and night had come to nothing. No sound, not even the bark of a dog, emerged from the village. That was when it occurred to her that her parents might be dead or might have been captured by the Japs. Her eyes stung, but she had no more tears to shed—the wretched state of her baby brother had forced her to grow up.

Momentarily forgetting her suffering, she laid him down on the brick floor and stood up to survey the walls around her. They were damp, of course, and the luxuriant appearance of moss briefly gave her new hope; but it offered no relief for their thirst, and it wasn't edible. She squatted down and picked up a brick, then another. They were very heavy, as though water was stored up inside them. A red centipede crawled out of the hollow where the bricks had been, and Mother jumped away, not daring to pick up any more. Nor did she dare sit down, for something horrible had occurred the morning before that made her realize she was now a woman.

Years later, Mother told my wife that her first menstrual period had come while she was down in that dark, dank well, and when my wife told me, the two of us felt enormous compassion for the fifteen-year-old girl who would later give birth to me.

Mother had no choice but to pin her final scrap of hope on that puddle of filthy water in which the toad was soaking, no matter how much its hideous features frightened or disgusted her. Nothing had changed from the day before: the toad hadn't moved, its somber eyes still glaring at her with hostility, its warty skin still making her skin crawl. Her newfound courage quickly evaporated. Poison darts emanating from the toad's eyes prickled her all over. She averted her eyes, but that didn't blot out the terrifying image of the toad.

Mother turned to look at her dying brother, and as she did so, her eye caught a tiny clump of milky-white mushrooms growing beneath two bricks. Her heart racing with excitement, she slid the bricks away and picked some of the mushrooms. Her innards twisted into knots as she gazed at the food in her hand. She shoved a mushroom into her mouth and swallowed it whole. It tasted so good that her hunger pangs returned in a flash. She put another in her mouth. Little Uncle moaned softly, but Mother consoled herself with the thought that she should try them first, in case they were toadstools. That's right, isn't it? Of course it is. She put one into Little Uncle's mouth, but his jaws didn't move; he just looked at her through tiny slits. "Harmony, eat it. I found it for you. Eat it." She held up another and waved it under his nose. His jaws twitched, as though he were chewing, so she fed him another one. But he coughed and spat them both out. By then his lips were so chapped they bled. He lay on the brick floor, close to death.

Mother swallowed a dozen or so little mushrooms, and her intestines, which had gone into hibernation, suddenly came to life, writhing painfully and making a huge racket. She was sweating more than she had at any time since being lowered into the well; it would be the last time. Sweat drenched her clothes; her armpits and the backs of her knees were wet and sticky. The chilled air seemed to penetrate the marrow of her bones, and she slumped unaware to the floor and lay beside her baby brother. At noon on her second day in the well, Mother fell into a swoon.

When she woke up, dusk was falling. She saw reddish-purple rays of light on the eastern wall as the sun sank in the west. The ancient windlass was bathed in the sunset, giving her the contradictory sensations of seeing remote antiquity and the approach of doomsday at the same time. The ringing in her ears, which hardly ever stopped, was now joined by the sound of footsteps out there, but she couldn't tell if it was real or an illusion. She no longer had the strength to cry out, and was so thirsty her chest seemed to be baking in a fire. Even the act of breathing brought excruciating pain. Little Uncle was already beyond suffering, beyond joy; he lay on the brick floor, a pile of withered yellow skin. When Mother looked down into his glazed eyes, everything turned dark in front of her: the black shroud of death was settling over the dry well.

The second night at the bottom of the well seemed to fly by; Mother passed it in a semiwakeful state. Several times she dreamed she'd sprouted wings and was circling ever upward toward the opening of the well. But the shaft seemed endless, and no matter how far she flew she never drew any closer to the opening. She tried flapping her wings faster, but the elongation of the shaft kept pace with her. Once during the night she awoke briefly to feel her brother's cold body beside her. Unable to bear the thought that he was dead, she tried to convince herself that she must be hot and feverish. A curved ray of moonlight fell on the puddle of greenish water, illuminating the toad like a precious gem bobbing in a sea of emeralds. At that moment Mother imagined that she and the sacred amphibian had reached an understanding: it would give up as much of its water as she needed, for which she would fling it out of the well, like a stone, if that was what it wanted. Tomorrow, she thought, if I hear footsteps tomorrow, I'll hurl pieces of brick out of the well, even if it's Japanese soldiers or Chinese puppet troops passing by. She needed to let people know there was somebody down there.

When dawn broke again, Mother had learned everything there was to know about the bottom of the well. Taking advantage of her early-morning energy level, she scraped off a layer of green moss and stuffed it into her mouth. It didn't taste bad, maybe a little pungent. The problem was her throat, which was so dry it wouldn't function properly, and the chewed moss came right back up when she tried to swallow it. Her gaze returned to the puddle of water and the toad, which maintained its venomous glare. Finding it more than she could bear, she turned her head and cried angry, fearful tears.

At around noon, she was certain she heard footsteps and human voices. Overjoyed, she rose unsteadily to her feet and shouted at the top of her lungs; but no sound emerged. Though she grabbed a piece of brick, she was able to lift it no higher than her waist before it slipped out of her hand and fell to the ground. Her last gasp. Hearing the footsteps and voices disappear in the distance, she sat crestfallen beside the body of her brother, and as she looked into his face she acknowledged the fact that he was dead. She laid her hand on his cold face, revulsion welling up in her chest. Death had separated them. The glare in his sightless eyes belonged to a different world.

She spent that night in a state of absolute terror, for she believed she had seen a snake as thick as the handle of a sickle. It was black with little yellow spots down the center of its back. Its head was flat, like a spatula, its neck ringed by a yellow band. The cold, gloomy atmosphere of the well originated in this snake's body. Several times she thought she could feel it wrapping itself around her, its flicking tongue aiming red darts at her and exhaling blasts of cold air.

Eventually, she did in fact spot the clumsy, slow-moving snake in a hole in the wall above the toad, only its hideous head sticking out. Covering her eyes with her hands, she backed up as far as she could. Gone were all thoughts of trying to drink the dirty water, now guarded by a venomous snake above and a toad below.

4

FATHER, Wang Guang (male, fifteen, short and skinny, dark face), Dezhi (male, fourteen, tall and skinny, yellow complexion, rheumy eyes), Guo Yang (male, over forty, crippled, walked on crutches), Blind Eye (real name and age unknown, never without his battered three-string zither), the woman Liu (over forty, big and tall, ulcerated legs)—the six survivors of the massacre—stared blankly at Granddad, all except Blind Eye, of course. They were standing on the village wall, the early-morning sun reflecting off their faces. Both sides of the wall were strewn with the bodies of courageous defenders and frenzied attackers. The muddy water of the ditch beyond the wall soaked the bloated corpses of several eviscerated Japanese warhorses. Everywhere there were shattered walls and ruined dikes, and white smoke curling into the sky. The sorghum fields beyond the village were trampled and destroyed. Incineration and blood were the pervasive smells of the morning; red and black the colors; grief and solemnity the moods.

Granddad's eyes were bloodshot, his hair seemed to have turned completely white, his back was hunched, and his large, swollen hands rested uneasily on his knees.

"Fellow villagers . . ." His voice was hoarse and gravelly. "I brought death and destruction down on the entire village. . . ."

They began to sob, and crystalline tears welled up even in Blind Eye's hollow sockets.

"What now, Commander Yu?" Guo Yang asked through blackened teeth as he got to his feet with the aid of crutches.

"Will the Japs be back, Commander Yu?" Wang Guang asked.

"Are you going to help us get away from here, Commander Yu?" the sobbing woman Liu asked.

"Get away?" Blind Eye said. "To where? The rest of you can run if you want to, but if I'm going to die it'll be right here."

He sat down, hugged his battered zither to his chest, and began to pluck it, his mouth twisting, his cheeks twitching, his head swaying.

"Fellow villagers, we can't run away," Granddad said. "Not after so many men have died. The Japs'll be back, so, while there's time, gather up the weapons and ammunition from the bodies. We'll take the Japs on until either the fish die or the net breaks!"

They fanned out in the field, stripping the bodies of weapons and ammunition, making trip after trip with their booty to the village side of the wall. Guo Yang, on his crutches, and the woman Liu, with her ulcerated legs, worked the nearby corpses, while Blind Eye sat beside the growing pile of weapons and ammunition, cocking his ear to pick up any sounds, like a good sentry.

At midmorning they assembled at the wall to watch Granddad take an inventory of the arsenal. Since the battle had lasted till dark, the Japs had been unable to make a final sweep of the battlefield, much to Granddad's advantage.

They had picked up seventeen Japanese "38" repeater rifles and thirty-four leather pouches, with a total of 1,007 copper-jacketed cartridges. There were twenty-four Chinese copies of the Czech "79" rifle and twenty-four bandoliers with 412 cartridges. They brought back fifty-seven Japanese petal-shaped muskmelon grenades and forty-three Chinese grenades with wooden handles. There was also a Japanese "tortoiseshell" pistol with thirty-nine cartridges, one Luger and seven bullets, nine Japanese sabers, and seven carbines with over two hundred rounds of ammo.

The inventory completed, Granddad asked Guo Yang for his pipe, which he lit and began puffing as he sat on the wall.

"Dad, can we form our own army?" Father asked.

Granddad looked at the pile of weapons and kept silent. When he'd finished his pipe he said, "It's time to choose, my sons, one weapon apiece."

He picked up the pistol in the tortoiseshell holster and fastened it around his waist. He also picked out a "38" repeater rifle with a fixed bayonet. Father grabbed the Luger. Wang Guang and Dezhi each chose a Japanese carbine.

"Give the Luger to Uncle Guo," Granddad said.

Stung by the order, Father grumbled.

"I want you to use a carbine," Granddad said. "A gun like that's no good in battle."

"I'll take a carbine, too," Guo Yang said. "Give the Luger to Blind Eye."

"Make us something to eat," Granddad said to the woman Liu. "The Japs'll be back soon."

Father picked up a "38" repeater rifle and noisily worked the bolt back and forth.

"Be careful," Granddad cautioned him. "It might go off."

"I know. Don't worry."

"They're coming, Commander," Blind Eye said softly. "I hear them."

"Get down," Granddad ordered. "Hurry!"

They crouched down among the white wax reeds on the inside slope of the wall, keeping their eyes riveted on the sorghum field beyond the ditch. All except Blind Eye, who was still sitting alongside the pile of weapons, rocking his head as he plucked his zither.

"You get down here, too!" Granddad ordered him.

Blind Eye's face twitched painfully and his lips quivered. The same tune emerged over and over from his battered zither, like raindrops in a tin bucket.

What appeared on the other side of the ditch was not human figures, but hundreds of dogs emerging from the sorghum field and rushing headlong toward the scattered corpses, hugging the ground. Fur of every imaginable color pulsated in the sunlight. Leading the pack were the three dogs from our family.

My father, always one to squirm, was getting impatient. He aimed at the pack of dogs and fired. The bullet whizzed over their heads and tore into the sorghum stalks.

Wang Guang and Dezhi, holding real rifles for the first time in their lives, aimed at the swaying sorghum and fired. Their bullets either tore aimlessly through the sky or smacked wildly into the ground.

"Hold your fire!" Granddad barked angrily. "This ammo isn't for you kids to play with!" He kicked Father's upturned rump.

The movement deep in the sorghum field gradually subsided, and a mighty shout rent the air: "Hold your fire—whose troops are you—"

"Your old ancestors' troops!" Granddad shouted back. "You damned yellow-skinned dogs!"

He aimed his "38" and fired a round in the direction of the shout.

"Comrades—we're the Jiao-Gao regiment—anti-Japanese troops!" the man in the sorghum field yelled. "Tell me, whose troops are you?"

"Damn them!" Granddad cursed. "All they know how to do is shout!"

The eighty soldiers of the Jiao-Gao regiment emerged from the sorghum field in a crouch. Their uniforms were in tatters, their faces sallow; they looked like wild animals terrified by the sight of guns. For the most part they were unarmed, except for a couple of wooden-handled grenades hanging at their belts. The squad up front carried old Hanyang rifles; a few of the others had muskets.

The previous afternoon, Father had seen this group of men hiding deep in the sorghum field and sniping at the Japs who were attacking the village.

The troops made their way up to the wall, where a tall fellow, apparently an officer, said, "Squad One up to the hill for sentry duty! The rest of you can take a break."

As the Jiao-Gao soldiers broke ranks and sat on the wall, a handsome young man stepped forward, took a piece of yellow paper from his knapsack, and began teaching the men a song: "The wind is howling"—he began—"The wind is the wind is the wind is the wind is howling"—the troops followed—"watch me, sing together—The horses are neighing—The Yellow River is roaring the Yellow River is roaring the Yellow River is roaring the Yellow River is roaring—In Henan and Hebei the sorghum is ripe the sorghum is ripe—The fighting spirit of anti-Japanese resistance heroes in the green curtain is high the fighting spirit of heroes in the green curtain is high—Raise your muskets and cannon your muskets and cannon wield your sabers and your spears your sabers and your spears defend your homes defend North China defend the country—"

Oh, how Father envied the youthful expressions on the weathered faces of the Jiao-Gao soldiers, and as he listened to them sing, his throat began to itch. All of a sudden he recalled the handsome young Adjutant Ren and the way he'd led the singing.

He, Wang Guang, and Dezhi picked up their rifles and walked up to enjoy the singing of the Jiao-Gao soldiers, who envied them their new Japanese "38" rifles and carbines.

The man in command of the Jiao-Gao regiment was named Jiang. He had such small feet they called him Little Foot Jiang. He walked up to Granddad, a boy of sixteen or seventeen at his side. He had a pistol stuck in his belt and was wearing a khaki cap with two black buttons. His teeth were pearly white. In heavily accented Beijing dialect, he said, "Commander Yu, you're a hero! We witnessed your battle with the Japs yesterday!"

He stuck out his hand, but Granddad just gave him a cold stare and snorted contemptuously.

The embarrassed Commander Jiang pulled back his hand, smiled, and continued: "I've been asked by the special committee of the Binhai area to talk to you. They're so impressed with your fervent nationalism and heroic spirit of self-sacrifice in this great war of national survival that they have ordered me to propose that we join forces in a coordinated move to resist the Japanese. . . ."

"Horseshit!" Granddad interrupted him. "I don't believe a word of it. Join forces, you say? Where were you when we fought the Jap armored troops? Where were you when they surrounded the village? My troops were wiped out, their blood forming a river across the land, and you come here talking about joining forces!"

He angrily kicked the yellow casing of a spent cartridge into the ditch. Blind Eye was still plucking his zither, the sound of raindrops in a tin bucket.

Jiang would not be put off, no matter how awkward Granddad's harangue made him feel. "Commander Yu, please don't disappoint us. And don't underestimate our strength."

"Let's open the skylight and let the sun shine in," Granddad said. "Just what do you have in mind?"

"We want you to join the Jiao-Gao regiment."

"In other words, take orders from you," Granddad sneered.

"You, sir, can be part of the regimental leadership."

"My title?"

"Deputy regiment commander!"

"Taking orders from you?"

"We all take orders from the Binhai-area special committee."

"*I* don't take orders from anybody!"

"Commander Yu, as the saying goes, 'A great man understands the times, a smart bird chooses the tree where it roosts, and a clever man chooses the leader he'll follow.' Don't pass up this chance!"

"Are you finished?"

Jiang laughed openly. "Commander Yu," he said, "you're no fool. Look at my troops. They're hot-blooded young men, but empty-handed for the most part. The weapons and ammo you've got here . . ."

"Don't even think it!"

"We just want to borrow some. We'll give them back as soon as you've formed your own army."

"Pah! Do you think Yu Zhan'ao's a three-year-old child?"

"Don't get me wrong, Commander Yu. Where the fate of the nation is concerned, all people share responsibility. In this war of resistance against Japan, you contribute what you can—men for some, weapons for others. It would be a national disgrace to let those weapons and all that ammo lie there unused."

"I've heard enough! Don't expect me to piss in your bottle. If you had any balls, you'd find your weapons in the hands of the Japanese!"

"We fought them yesterday!"

"And how many strings of firecrackers did you set off?" Granddad asked sarcastically.

"Not firecrackers—bullets and hand grenades. And we lost six of our comrades. We deserve at least half the weapons!"

"I lost all my men at the bridgehead over the Black Water River, for one ancient machine gun!"

"It was Pocky Leng's troops who took everything else!"

"And I suppose the eyes of Little Foot Jiang's troops don't light up just as bright when they see weapons? Well, this is one man you're not going to sucker!"

"I advise you to be careful, Commander Yu," Jiang warned Granddad. "My patience has limits."

"Are you threatening me?" Granddad asked stiffly, resting his hand on the butt of his pistol.

Commander Jiang's look of anger quickly gave way to a smile. "You've got me all wrong, Commander Yu. We'd never steal food from a friend's bowl. Just because we can't make a deal doesn't mean we're not on the same side."

He turned to his troops and said, "Clean up the battlefield. Bury our fellow villagers, and don't forget to pick up all the spent cartridge casings."

The troops fanned out across the battlefield to search for cartridge casings. While they were burying the bodies, a battle between crazed dogs and the surviving humans resulted in the dismemberment of many of the corpses.

"We're in a terrible fix, Commander Yu," Jiang said. "We have no weapons or ammunition, and five out of every ten casings we take back to the munitions plant for recasting come out as duds. We're caught between Pocky Leng, who squeezes us, and the puppet troops, who slaughter us, so you have to give us some of the weapons you've got here. Don't treat the Jiao-Gao regiment with contempt."

Granddad looked at the troops carrying the dead back and forth near the sorghum field and said, "You can have the sabers, and the '79' carbines, and the wooden-handled grenades."

Jiang grabbed Granddad's hand and exclaimed, "Commander Yu, you're a true friend. . . . We make our own wooden-handled grenades, so how about this: you keep the grenades and give us some '38' rifles instead."

"No," Granddad said tersely.

"Just five."

"No!"

"Three, then. How's that? Just three."

"I said no!"

"Okay, two. You can part with at least two, can't you?"

"Shit!" Granddad grumbled. "You're like a damned livestock auctioneer."

"Squad One, get over here to pick up the weapons."

"Not so fast," Granddad said. "Stand over there."

He personally handed out the twenty-four Czech "79" rifles and the canvas cartridge belts, then hesitated for a moment before tossing in a "38" repeater rifle.

"That's it," he said. "And we keep the sabers."

"Commander Yu," Jiang complained, "you agreed to give us two '38' rifles."

"If I hear another word from you," Granddad said testily, "you won't even get one!"

"Okay," Jiang said, throwing his hands up in front of him. "Don't get mad!"

The Jiao-Gao soldiers who were given weapons grinned from ear to ear. One or two members of the burial detail stumbled upon additional weapons, and they also picked up the automatic pistol Granddad had tossed away and Father's discarded Browning. Their pockets bulged with spent cartridge casings.

"Comrades," Jiang said, "hurry up and get those bodies buried. We have to withdraw before the Japs come back for their dead."

As the Jiao-Gao regiment was falling in beside the wall, a couple of dozen bicycles came flying down the road from the eastern tip of the village. Wheels glistened, spokes flashed. Commander Jiang barked out an order and the soldiers hit the ground, as the riders pedaled unsteadily up to Granddad.

It was Detachment Leader Leng's mobile platoon, a crack group of riders armed with pistols. Dressed in neat gray uniforms, with leggings and cloth shoes, they were quite a sight. Pocky Leng was known as a first-rate cyclist who could ride on a single railway track for a mile and a half. Commander Jiang shouted another order, and the Jiao-Gao troops emerged from their hiding places among the trees, quickly forming up ranks behind Granddad.

Detachment Leader Leng's soldiers dismounted and walked their bicycles the rest of the way along the top of the wall. Leng emerged from the crowd, surrounded by bodyguards.

The mere sight of Pocky Leng was enough to make Granddad reach for his pistol.

"Take it easy, Commander Yu," Jiang cautioned him, "take it easy."

The gloved Detachment Leader Leng, smiling broadly, came up and shook hands with Jiang without taking off his glove. Jiang smiled as he reached inside his pants and brought out a fat, light-brown louse, which he flipped into the ditch.

"Your esteemed unit is still in the thick of things, I see," Detachment Leader Leng said to him.

"We've been fighting since yesterday afternoon," Jiang said.

"Ending in a brilliant victory, I assume?"

"In cooperation with Commander Yu, we killed twenty-six Japanese and thirty-six puppet soldiers, plus four warhorses. Where were the crack guerrilla troops and fierce leaders of your esteemed unit yesterday?"

"We were harassing the town of Pingdu and forcing the Japs to retreat in panic. You could call that the classic 'Encircle the Wei to rescue the Zhao' ploy, wouldn't you say, Commander Jiang?"

"Fuck your old lady, Pocky Leng!" Granddad growled. "Feast your eyes on the Zhaos you rescued! All the villagers are right here."

He pointed to the blind and crippled men on the wall.

The pale marks on Pocky Leng's face reddened. "Yesterday afternoon my troops fought at Pingdu till they were bathed in blood, suffering enormous losses. My conscience is clear."

"Since you and your esteemed troops knew the enemy had surrounded the village, why didn't you come to the rescue?" Jiang asked. "Why pass up a fight in your own backyard, and travel a hundred li just to harass the town of Pingdu? These aren't motorcycles your esteemed troops are riding, you know. And even if you were so anxious for some action you had to go off to harass Pingdu, the enemy troops you routed should still be in retreat. But you, Commander, look fit and relaxed, not a speck of dirt on you. I wonder how you set about commanding this great battle."

Leng turned red all the way to the roots of his ears. "I'm not going to argue with you, Jiang! I know why you're here, and you know why I'm here."

"Detachment Leader Leng," Jiang said, "as I see it, you went about yesterday's battle at Pingdu all wrong. Now, if I'd been in command of your esteemed unit, instead of coming to break the encirclement of the village I'd have spread the men out in an ambush in the cemetery, using the gravestones as cover. Then I'd have set up the eight machine guns you captured after the ambush at the Black Water River and fired on the Japs when they came down the road. Since they and their horses would be exhausted after fighting all day, and low on ammo in unfamiliar surroundings in the dark, they'd be sitting ducks. They couldn't possibly get away. That way you'd have performed a great service for the people and made heroes of your soldiers. Your glory would have been added to that of the ambush at the Black Water River, and you'd have a brilliant reputation! What a shame, Detachment Leader Leng, that you missed your chance. Instead of making heroes of your soldiers and serving the people, here you are, trying to gain some little advantage from orphans and widows. Although I'm normally immune to shame, what you have done shames me!"

All the red-faced Leng could do was stammer: "Jiang . . . look down on me. . . . Wait till I fight a major battle, then you'll see. . . ."

"When that day comes, we'll stand shoulder to shoulder with you!"

"I don't need your help! I can fight my own battles!"

"You have my undying admiration!" Jiang said.

Detachment Leader Leng mounted his bicycle and was about to

ride off when Granddad stepped up and grabbed the front of his shirt. "When this war with Japan is over, Leng," he said with murder in his eyes, "you and I have some unfinished business!"

"You don't scare me!" Leng snarled.

Pushing down hard on his pedal, he rode off, followed by his two dozen troops, like a pack of dogs chasing a rabbit.

"Commander Yu," Jiang said, "the Jiao-Gao regiment will always be your devoted ally."

He thrust his hand out to Granddad, who reached out awkwardly and shook it. Tough though it was, Granddad could also feel its warmth.

5

THE TIME: forty-six years later. The place: the spot where Granddad, Father, and Mother had fought a heroic battle against a pack of dogs led by the three from our family—Blackie, Red, and Green. On one stormy night lightning split open a mass grave where Communists, Nationalists, commoners, Japanese, and puppet troops were buried—a site called All-Souls Grave—spreading rotting bones over a ten-yard area, where they were washed clean by the rain and turned a somber white. I was home on summer holiday at the time, and when I heard that All-Souls Grave had opened up I rushed over to see for myself, our blue-coated little dog following hard on my heels. It was still drizzling, and the dog darted in front of me, his paws splashing loudly in the muddy puddles. It wasn't long before we were in the midst of bones that had been sent flying with explosive force, and Blue ran up to sniff them, quickly shaking his head to show that they didn't interest him.

People stood fearfully around the exposed graveyard. I squeezed in among them until I could see the skeletons at the bottom of the pit, piles of bones exposed to the sun for the first time in all those years. I doubt that even the provincial party secretary could have told which of them belonged to Communists, which to Nationalists, which to Japanese soldiers, which to puppet soldiers, and which to civilians. The skulls all had the exact same shape, and all had been thrown into the same heap. The scattered raindrops beat a desolate rhythm on the white bones, forceful and fiendish. Skeletons lay on their backs, nearly submerged in the icy water, like fermenting sorghum wine that had been stored up for years.

The villagers picked up the bones that had been scattered around the area and tossed them back in. A momentary dizziness came over me, and when it passed I took another look, discovering the skulls of dozens of dogs mixed in with the human heads in the grave. The bottom of the pit was a shallow blur of white, a sort of code revealing that the history of dogs and the history of man are intertwined. I helped pick up the scattered bones, but put on a pair of white gloves just to be on the safe side. Noticing the hateful stares of the villagers, I quickly took them off and stuffed them into my pants pockets, then walked down the bone-strewn road all the way to the edge of the sorghum field, a good hundred yards away.

There in the short green grass, still dripping with water, lay the curved dome of a human skull. The flat, broad forehead showed that it hadn't belonged to any ordinary person. I picked it up with three fingers and had started running back with it when I spotted another muted gleam of white in the grass not far away. This one was a long, narrow skull with several sharp teeth still in its opened mouth; I knew it was one I didn't have to pick up, for it belonged to the same species as the little blue-coated friend tagging along behind me. Maybe it had been a wolf. All I knew for sure was that it had been blown over here by the explosive force, for the specks of dirt on its freshly cleaned surface proved it had lain in the mass grave for decades. I picked it up anyway. The villagers were tossing bones stolidly into the grave, some cracking and splitting when they hit. I tossed in the fragment of the human skull. But when it came to the large canine skull I hesitated. "Toss it in," an old man said; "the dogs back then were as good as humans." So I tossed it into the open pit. Once All-Souls Grave had been filled in, it looked just as it had before the lightning hit. In order to calm the frightened souls of the dead, Mother burned a stack of yellow spirit money at the head of the grave.

After helping fill in the pit, I stayed with her to look down at this resting place of a thousand bodies, and kowtowed three times.

"It's been forty-six years," Mother said. "I was fifteen then."

6

I WAS FIFTEEN THEN. When the Japanese surrounded the village, your maternal grandfather and grandmother lowered me and your young uncle into a dry well. We never saw them again. Later on I learned they were killed that very morning.

I don't know how many days I hunkered down inside that well. Your uncle died there, and his body began to stink. The toad and yellow-banded snake stared at me until I nearly died of fright. I was sure I'd die down in that well. But finally your father and your granddad came along. . . .

Granddad wrapped the fifteen "38" rifles in oil paper and tied them with rope, then carried them to the edge of the well. "Douguan, look around and make sure nobody can see us."

Granddad knew that Detachment Leader Leng and the Jiao-Gao soldiers still had their hearts set on these guns. The night before, when he and the others were asleep in a tent at the foot of the village wall, Blind Eye, who was keeping guard, heard something bump up against a wax tree on the downward slope. Then he detected the soft sound of footsteps coming toward the tent; he could tell there were two people, one brave, the other not so brave. He could hear them breathing. Raising his rifle, he shouted, "Halt right there!" The men threw themselves to the ground in panic and began crawling backward. Getting a fix on the direction, Blind Eye aimed and pulled the trigger. *Bang!* He heard the men roll down the slope and dart in among the stand of wax trees. He aimed and fired again. Someone yelled. Granddad and the others, awakened by the gunfire, ran up, weapons in hand, just in time to see two dark figures dart across the ditch and vanish into the sorghum field.

"There's nobody around, Dad," my father said.

"Remember this well," Granddad said.

"I will. It belongs to Beauty's family."

"If I die," Granddad said, "come get these guns and use them as a bartering chip to join up with the Jiao-Gao regiment. They're at least better than Detachment Leader Leng's troops."

"Let's not join up with anyone," Father said. "Let's recruit our own army. We still have a machine gun."

Granddad snorted with a wry smile. "It's not as easy as you think, son," he said. "I'm worn out."

After Father uncoiled the rope from the rickety windlass, Granddad tied it around the bundle of guns.

"Are you sure the well is dry?" Granddad asked.

"I'm sure. Wang Guang and I played hide-and-seek here once." Father bent over to peer into the well, where he saw the outlines of two bodies in the dark recesses.

"Dad, there's somebody down there!" he screamed.

They knelt on the step at the mouth of the well and strained to see who it was.

"It's Beauty!" Father said.

"Take a good look. Is she alive?"

"I think I can see her breathing—there's a snake coiled beside her—and her baby brother Harmony's there, too. . . ." Father's words echoed off the walls of the well.

"Are you afraid to go down there?"

"I'll go down, Dad. Beauty's my best friend!"

"Watch out for that snake."

"Snakes don't scare me."

Granddad untied the well rope from the bundle of guns and secured it around Father's waist, then lowered him slowly into the well, keeping the weight on the windlass.

"Be careful," Father heard Granddad say from the top of the well as his foot touched a protruding brick and he stepped down on the floor. The black snake with the colorful band raised its head menacingly and flicked out its forked tongue, hissing at Father. During his days of fishing and crabbing at the Black Water River, Father had learned how to deal with snakes, and he and Uncle Arhat had eaten one, baked in dry cow dung. Uncle Arhat told him that snake meat is a cure for leprosy; after eating it, they had both felt hot all over.

Now Father stood at the bottom of the well without moving, and, the instant the snake lowered its head, he reached down, grabbed it by the tail, and shook it with all his might until he heard its bones crack. Then he grabbed it just behind the head and twisted it hard. "Dad," he shouted, "stand clear!"

Granddad backed away from the mouth of the well as the half-dead snake came flying out. Granddad's skin crawled. "That little imp's got the nerves of a thief!"

Father helped Beauty sit up and shouted in her ear, "Beauty! Beauty! It's me, Douguan. I'm here to save you!"

Father tied the rope around Beauty's waist. Granddad carefully turned the windlass and hauled Mother out of the well. Then he brought up the body of my young uncle.

"Dad, send the guns down!" Father said.

"Stand clear."

The windlass creaked as the bundle of guns was lowered into the well. Then Father untied the rope and put it around his waist.

"Pull me up, Dad," he said.

"Is the rope secure?"

"Yes."

"Make sure it's tight. This is no time to be careless."

"It's good and tight, Dad."

"Did you tie a square knot?"

"What's wrong with you, Dad? It was me who tied the rope around Beauty, wasn't it?"

Father and Granddad looked down at Beauty as she lay on the ground. Her skin was stretched taut over her cheekbones, her eyes were sunken, her gums protruded, and her hair was a tangled mess. Her baby brother's fingernails had turned blue.

7

MOTHER'S HEALTH IMPROVED under the loving care of the lame woman Liu. She and Father had been good friends, but after her rescue from the well they were like brother and sister. Then Granddad came down with a serious case of typhoid fever, and at times he seemed on the brink of death. Once, as he lay there semiconscious, he hallucinated that he smelled the sweet fragrance of sorghum porridge, so Father and the others quickly picked some sorghum, and the woman Liu cooked it in front of Granddad until it was soft and pasty. After he ate a bowlful, the capillaries in his nose burst and released a torrent of thick, dark blood. His appetite returned then, and he was on the mend. By mid-October, he was able to hobble out into the garden to soak up the warm rays of the late-autumn sun.

I heard that at the time a clash between the troops of Pocky Leng and Little Foot Jiang occurred near Wang Gan Aqueduct, with heavy casualties on both sides. But Granddad was far too sick to worry about that—or anything else, for that matter.

Father and the others threw up a few temporary shelters in the village, then scavenged the junk piles for the odds and ends they would need to harvest enough sorghum to get them through the winter and the spring. Autumn rains had fallen steadily since the end of August, turning the dark earth into a sea of mud. Half of the rain-soaked stalks lay rotting on the ground, where the fallen seeds had taken root and were already beginning to germinate. Tender green stalks crowded their way through the spaces between the blue-gray and dark-red patches of decay, and the ears of sorghum swayed in the air or dragged along the ground like bushy, matted foxtails. Steel-gray rainclouds, heavy with water, scurried across the sky, and cold, hard raindrops thudded into the stalks. Flocks of crows struggled to stay aloft on wings weighted down with moisture. During those foggy days, sunlight was as precious as gold.

Father, who ruled the roost after Granddad fell ill, led Wang Guang, Dezhi, Guo Yang (whom we called Gimpy), Blind Eye, and Beauty over to the marshland, where they fought the corpse-eating dogs with rifles. The ensuing battles would turn Father into a marksman.

Every once in a while, Granddad asked him weakly, "What are you doing, son?"

With a murderous frown creasing his brow, Father would say, "We're killing the dogs, Dad!"

"Let it lie," Granddad would say.

"I can't," Father would reply. "We can't let them feed on people's bodies."

Nearly a thousand corpses had piled up in the marshland, all laid out by the Jiao-Gao soldiers, who lacked the time to give them a proper burial. The few spadefuls of dirt that had been tossed haphazardly over the corpses were washed away by the autumn rains. The bloated corpses produced an exceptional stench that brought crows and mad dogs scurrying over to rip open the abdomens, which intensified the reek of death.

When the dog pack was at full strength, there were probably six hundred in all, made up primarily of village dogs whose masters lay rotting in the marshland. The remainder, those that came and went in a frenzy, were dogs from neighboring villages that had homes to return to. They were led by our family's three dogs: Red, Green, and Blackie.

The hunters split up into three teams: Father and Mother, Wang Guang and Dezhi, Gimpy and Blind Eye. They dug trenches in the marshland and took up positions to watch the paths that had been scratched out by the dogs. Father cradled his rifle; Mother held her carbine. "Douguan, why can't I hit what I'm shooting at?" she asked.

"You're too eager. If you take careful aim and squeeze the trigger, you can't miss."

Father and Mother were watching the path in the southeast corner of the field, a two-foot-wide white scar in the earth. The troops emerging onto this path were led by our dog Red, whose thick coat shone after his rich diet of human corpses. His legs had grown firm and muscular from all the exercise, and the battles with humans had put a keen edge on his intelligence.

The fog-shrouded paths were quiet when the sun's red rays began to light up the sky. The canine forces had dwindled after a month of seesaw battles, so that the dogs lying among the corpses probably numbered a hundred, and a couple of hundred others had deserted. Their combined forces now, in the neighborhood of 230, tended to run in packs, and since Father and the others were becoming better marksmen all the time, the dogs always left behind at least a dozen corpses after each frenzied attack.

They were waiting for the dogs' first sortie of the day, like people anticipating the arrival of food on the table. Noticing the rustling of distant stalks of sorghum, Father said softly, "Get ready, here they come." Mother silently released the safety on her rifle and laid her cheek against the rain-soaked stock. The rustling movement flowed to the edge of the marshland like an ocean wave, and Father could hear the panting dogs. He knew that hundreds of greedy canine eyes were fixed on the broken and severed limbs in the marshland, that the dogs' red tongues were licking the putrid remnants caught in the corners of their mouths, and that their stomachs, filled with green bile, were growling.

As though on command, more than two hundred of them broke out of the sorghum field, barking madly. The fur on their necks stood straight up; bright coats glistened in the fog. Wang Guang and Gimpy opened fire as the dogs ripped the flesh from the corpses with single-minded ferocity. The wounded dogs yelped in pain, while those that had been spared continued to tear frantically at their prey.

Father took aim at the head of a clumsy black dog and pulled the trigger. The dog yelped as the bullet shattered its ear. Then Father saw the head of a spotted white dog explode and the animal crumple to the ground, a piece of dark intestine still in its mouth. It never made a sound. "Beauty, you hit it!" he shouted.

"Was it me?" she squealed excitedly to Father, who had lined Red up in his sights. Hugging the ground as he ran, he streaked from one patch of stalks to another. Father pulled the trigger and the bullet whizzed past Red, barely missing his back. He picked up a woman's bloated leg in his razor-sharp teeth and began to eat, each powerful bite making a loud crunch as the bone shattered. Mother fired; her bullet struck the dark earth in front of Red and spattered his face with mud. He shook his head violently, then picked up the pale leg and ran off. Wang Guang and Dezhi wounded several dogs, whose blood smeared the corpses and whose whimpers struck terror into the hunters' hearts.

When the pack retreated, the hunters closed up ranks so they could clean their weapons. Since they were running low on ammunition, Father reminded them to make every bullet count, emphasizing the importance of eliminating the leaders of the pack. "They're as slippery as loaches," Wang Guang said. "They always slink away before I can reload."

Dezhi blinked his rheumy eyes and said, "Douguan, how about a sneak attack?"

"What do you mean?"

"Well, they have to go somewhere to rest," Dezhi said, "and I'll bet it's near the Black Water River. After stuffing their bellies, they probably go there for the water."

"He's got a point," Gimpy agreed.

"Then let's go," Father said.

"Not so fast," Dezhi cautioned. "Let's go back and get some grenades. We'll blow 'em up."

Father, Mother, Wang Guang, and Dezhi split up to follow two separate paths made by the dogs in the muddy earth, which had turned springy from all the claws that had passed over it. The paths led straight to the Black Water River, where Father and Mother could hear the roar of water and the sounds of the dogs. The paths converged as they neared the riverbank to form a broad single path.

That's where Father and Mother met up with Wang Guang and Dezhi. And that's where they spotted more than two hundred dogs spread out over the weed-covered riverbank; most were crouching, although some were gnawing at shiny clods of black earth stuck between their toes. A few stood at the water's edge, raising their legs to piss into the river, while others were drinking. Now that their bellies were full, they circled the area, passing dark-brown canine farts. The weeds were nearly covered with reddish or white dogshit, and the odor of the turds and farts was different from any Father and the others had ever smelled. It was easy to spot the three leaders, even though they were spread out among the others.

"Shall we toss them now, Douguan?" Wang Guang asked.

"Get ready," Father said. "We'll lob them together."

They were each holding two petal-shaped muskmelon hand grenades. After pulling the pins, they banged the grenades together. "Now!" Father yelled, and eight arching missiles landed amid the dogs, who first watched with curiosity as the black oblong objects fell from the sky, then instinctively crouched down. Father marveled at the incredible intelligence of the three dogs from our family, who cunningly flattened out on the ground just before the eight superior Japanese grenades exploded, almost at the same instant, the frightful blast spraying dark shrapnel in all directions. A dozen or more dogs were blown to bits, at least twenty others gravely wounded. Dog blood and dog meat sailed into the air above the river and splattered on the surface like hailstones. White eels, blood eaters, swarmed to the spot, squealing as they fought over the dog meat and dog blood. The pitiful whimpering of the wounded dogs was terrifying. Those that had escaped injury scattered, some dashing wildly down the riverbank, others leaping into the Black Water River to swim frantically to the opposite bank.

Father wished he hadn't left his rifle behind, for some of the dogs, blinded by the blast, were running in circles on the riverbank, whimpering in panic, their faces covered with blood. It was a pitiful, exhilarating sight. Our three dogs swam across the river, followed by about thirty others, and clambered up onto the opposite bank with their tails between their legs, their wet fur stuck to their skin; they, too, were a sorry sight, but once they reached solid ground, they shook themselves violently, sending beads of water flying from their tails, their bellies, and their chins. Red glared hatefully at Father and barked, as though accusing him and his friends of violating a tacit agreement by invading their bivouac area and using new, cruelly undoglike weapons.

"Lob some across the river!" Father said.

They picked up more grenades and heaved them with all their might toward the opposite bank. When the dogs saw the black objects arching above the water, they raised an imploring howl, as though calling for their mothers and fathers, then leaped and rolled down the riverbank, making a quick dash to the sorghum field on the southern bank. Father and the others weren't strong enough to reach the bank with their grenades, which landed harmlessly in the river and sent up four columns of silvery water. The surface roiled for a moment, as a school of fat white eels floated belly up.

The dogs stayed away from the sight of the massacre for two days following the sneak attack, a time during which canine and human forces maintained strict vigilance as they made battle preparations.

Father and his friends, recognizing the enormous power of the grenades, held a strategy session to find ways of putting them to even better use. When Wang Guang returned from a reconnaissance mission to the riverbank, he brought news that all that remained were a few canine corpses, a blanket of fur and dogshit, and an overpowering stench. Not a single living dog—which meant they'd moved to another bivouac area.

According to Dezhi, since the leaders of the routed dog pack had been spared, it would only be a matter of time before they closed up ranks and returned to fight over the corpses. Their counterattack was bound to be particularly ferocious, since the survivors now had rich battle experience.

The final suggestion was made by Mother, who recommended arming the wooden-handled grenades and burying them along the paths. Her suggestion met with unanimous approval, so they split up into groups to bury forty-three of the grenades beneath the three paths. Of the fifty-seven muskmelon grenades they'd started with, twelve had been used during the attack on the Black Water River shoal, so there were forty-five left—fifteen for each group.

Cracks developed in the unity of the canine forces over the two days as a result of casualties and desertion, which depleted their number to 120 or so. The three original brigades were re-formed into a single unified force of crack troops. Since their bivouac area had been overrun by those four bastards with their strange, exploding dung-beetles, they were forced to move three li downriver to a spot on the southern bank just east of the stone bridge.

It was to be a morning of great significance. The dogs, itching for a fight, snarled and snapped at one another as they made their way to the new bivouac area, sneaking an occasional glance at their leaders, who were calmly sizing each other up. Once they reached a spot east of the bridge, they formed a circle on the shoal, sat back on their haunches, and howled at the overcast sky. Blackie and Green were twitching noticeably, causing the fur on their backs to ripple like ocean waves. Months of vagabond lives and feasting on rotting meat had awakened primal memories anesthetized over eons of domestication. A hatred of humans—those two-legged creatures that walked erect—seethed in their hearts, and eating human flesh held greater significance than just filling their growling bellies; more important was the vague sensation that they were exacting terrible revenge upon those rulers who had enslaved them and forced them into the demeaning existence of living off scraps. The only ones capable of translating these primitive impulses into high theory, however, were the three dogs from our family. That was why they enjoyed the support of the pack dogs, although that alone would have been insufficient; their size and strength, their quickness, and their willingness to martyr themselves by attacking with unparalleled ferocity all made them natural leaders. Now, though, they had begun to fight among themselves for sole dominion over the pack.

One of the battles occurred when a dog in Green's brigade, an impudent male with thick lips, bulging eyes, and a coat of bluish fur, took liberties with a pretty spotted-faced female who was one of Red's favorites. Infuriated, Red charged the motley male and knocked him into the river. After climbing out and shaking the water off his fur, Thick Lips launched into an angry tirade, which earned him the jeers of the other dogs.

Green barked loudly at Red to defend the honor of his brigade, but Red ignored him and knocked the motley cur back into the river. As he swam back to shore, his nostrils skimming the surface, he looked like a huge river rat. The spotted-faced female stood beside Red, wagging her tail.

Green barked contemptuously at Red, who returned the insult.

Blackie placed himself between his two companions of earlier days, like a peacemaker.

Now that the dog pack was reassembled at a new bivouac area, they busied themselves drinking water and licking their wounds as the ancient rays of the sun danced on the surface of the gently flowing Black Water River. A wild rabbit raised its head on the embankment; scared witless by what it saw, it quietly slipped away.

In the warm mid-autumn sun, an atmosphere of lethargy settled over the dog pack. The three leaders formed a seated triangle, eyes drooping as though reliving the past.

Red had led a peaceful life as a distillery watchdog. The two old yellows were still alive then, and even though there were occasional disputes among the five dogs, they were, for the most part, one big, happy family. He was the runt of the group, and once, when he developed a case of scabies, the other dogs drove him away. So he went straight to the eastern compound to roll around in the sorghum chaff, and his skin cleared up. But he returned more antisocial than when he'd left, and was disgusted by how Blackie and Green fawned over the strong and bullied the weak, and by their smarmy tail-wagging.

Red sensed that the violent upheaval of the pack was a power struggle, and since the conflicts had been shifted onto the three leaders, the other dogs grew relatively peaceful. But the mangy cur, who hadn't mended his ways despite repeated warnings, was now trying to stir up trouble among the other dogs in the pack.

The flash point was reached when an old bitch with a torn ear walked up to Blackie and put her wet, icy nose up against his, then turned and wagged her tail at him. Blackie got to his feet and began cavorting with his new paramour, while Red and Green looked on. Red quietly crouched down and glanced over at Green, who sprang instantly and pinned the amorous Blackie to the beach.

The dog pack stood as one to watch the fang-to-fang battle erupting in front of them.

Green, enjoying the element of surprise, quickly gained the advantage by burying his teeth in Blackie's neck and shaking him violently. The green fur on his neck stood straight up as a thunderous roar burst from his throat.

Blackie, whose head was spinning from the attack, jerked backward to free his neck from his attacker's jaws, losing a chunk of flesh the size of a man's palm. He stood up shakily, racked by spasms of pain and crazed with anger. He was seething over the perversely undoglike sneak attack by Green. Blackie barked furiously, lowered his head, and threw himself on Green, aiming straight for his chest, into which he sank his teeth, peeling away a huge flap of skin. Green immediately went for Blackie's wounded neck, but this time, not content with merely biting, he was actually devouring the torn flesh.

Red got slowly to his feet and looked icily at Green and Blackie. Blackie's neck was nearly broken. He raised his head, but it drooped back down. He raised it again, and again it drooped. Blood gushed from the wound. He was clearly finished. Green arrogantly bared his fangs and barked triumphantly. Then he turned, and was eyeball to eyeball with the long, cruelly mocking face of Red. Green shuddered. Without warning, Red pounced on Green, using his favorite trick to flip the wounded dog over on his back, and before Green could scramble to his feet, Red had buried his teeth in his chest and was pulling on the ripped flap of skin. With a powerful jerk of his head, he pried the skin loose, exposing the raw flesh beneath it. As Green struggled to his feet, the loose flap of skin hung down between his legs and brushed the ground. His whimper signaled the knowledge that it was all over for him. Red walked up and drove his shoulder into his barely standing victim, sending him tumbling to the ground, and before he could struggle to his feet, he was swarmed over by a dense pack of dogs, whose fangs quickly turned him into a bloody pulp.

Now that Red had defeated his most powerful opponent, his tail shot up as he roared at the battered and bloodied Blackie, who barked pitifully, his tail tucked between his legs. He looked up at Red with despairing eyes, silently begging for mercy. But the other dogs, eager to bring the battle to an end, rushed forward, forcing Blackie to make a suicidal leap into the river. His head bobbed into sight once or twice before he sank beneath the surface. A few gurgling bubbles rose from the depths.

The dogs formed a circle around Red, bared their teeth, and let forth celebratory howls at the bleached sun hanging in the sky on this rare clear day.

The sudden disappearance of the dog pack made Father and the others nervous and introduced chaos into their lives. A heavy autumn rain struck all living things with a monotonous sound. The hunters had lost the stimulus of battling the mad dogs and had turned into addicts in need of a fix: their noses ran, they yawned, they nodded off.

On the morning of the fourth day after the disappearance of the dog pack, Father and the others lazily took up their positions at the edge of the marshland, watching the swirling mist and smelling the stench of the land.

By then Gimpy had handed over his rifle and disappeared to a distant village to help his cousin run an eatery. Since Blind Eye could not function alone, he stayed back in the tent, company for my ailing granddad. That left only Father, Mother, Wang Guang, and Dezhi.

"Douguan," Mother said, "the dogs won't come back. They're scared of the grenades." She gazed wistfully at the three dog paths, shrouded in mystery, more eager than the others to have the dogs return. All her intelligence had telescoped into the forty-three wooden-handled grenades buried in the paths.

"Wang Guang," Father ordered, "make another reconnaissance!"

"I just made one yesterday. There was a fight east of the bridge.

Green's dead. They must have split up," Wang Guang complained. "I say, instead of wasting our time here, we should go join up with the Jiao-Gao forces."

"No," Father insisted, "they'll be back. They're not going to pass up a feast like this."

"There are corpses everywhere these days," Wang Guang argued. "Those dogs aren't stupid enough to come looking for a meal of exploding hand grenades."

"It's the number of corpses here," Father said. "They can't bear to leave them."

"If we're going to join up with anybody, let's make it Pocky Leng's troops. Those gray uniforms and leather belts are really impressive."

"Look over there!" Mother said.

They crouched and watched the dog path where Mother was pointing. The sorghum stalks, pelted by sheets of glistening raindrops, were trembling. Everywhere you looked there were tightly woven clumps of delicate yellow shoots and seedlings that had sprouted out of season. The air reeked with the odor of young seedlings, rotting sorghum, decaying corpses, and dogshit. The world facing Father and the others was filled with terror, filth, and evil.

"Here they come!" Father said, betraying his excitement.

The sorghum canopy rustled. The grenades hadn't gone off.

"Douguan," Mother said anxiously, "something's wrong!"

"Don't panic," he said, "they'll set them off any minute."

"Why not scatter them with our rifles?" Dezhi asked.

Too impatient to wait, Mother fired off a round, causing a momentary confusion in the sorghum field, which was immediately engulfed by exploding grenades. Severed sorghum stalks and dog limbs flew into the sky; the painful whimpers of wounded dogs hung in the air. More explosions sent shrapnel and debris whistling over the heads of Father and his friends.

Finally, a couple of dozen dogs emerged from the three paths, only to be met by gunfire that sent them scurrying back into the protection of the sorghum. More explosions.

Mother leaped into the air and clapped her hands.

She and her friends were unaware of the changes in the canine forces. The shrewd Red, now undisputed leader, had led his troops dozens of li away for a thorough reorganization, and this latest attack demonstrated a grasp of military strategy with which even humans, given all their intelligence, could have found no fault. His enemy consisted of a few strange yet canny youngsters, including one who seemed vaguely familiar. Not until he'd disposed of those little bastards would his pack be free to enjoy the feast set out in the marshland. So he sent a pointy-eared mongrel to lead half the dogs in a frontal charge from which there would be no retreat. Meanwhile, he led sixty others in a flanking maneuver to the rear of the marshland, from where they could launch a surprise attack and tear those little bastards, who had blood on their hands, to pieces. Just before setting out, Red, whose tail curled into the air, had brushed his cold nose up against the similarly cold noses of each of his troops, then had gnawed at the dried-mud clods stuck to his claws. The others had done the same.

He had completed his flanking maneuver, and had his eyes on those wildly gesturing little people, when he heard the explosions of the hand grenades. The sound struck terror in his heart and, as he immediately observed, threw his troops into a panic. The dogs were terrified, and he knew that if he shrank back now his army would be routed. So he bared his fangs and let loose a blood-curdling cry to the confused troops behind him. Then he turned and charged into Father's encampment, his troops on his tail, like a sleek, colorful, ground-hugging cloud.

"Dogs behind us!" Father shouted in alarm as he swung his rifle around and blew away one of the attackers without taking aim. The dog, a big brown beast, thudded to the ground, then was trampled as the rest of the animals charged.

Wang Guang and Dezhi were firing as fast as they could, but for every dog that fell, several moved up to take its place. The dogs' misanthropy had now climaxed; their teeth glinted and their eyes shone like ripe red cherries. Wang Guang threw down his weapon, turned, and ran into the marshland, where he was immediately surrounded by a dozen dogs. In an instant the little fellow simply vanished. The animals, used to feeding on human beings, had become true wild beasts, quick and skillful in their craft. They tore chunks out of Wang Guang and were soon gnawing on his brittle bones.

Father, Mother, and Dezhi stood back to back, so terrified they were shaking like leaves. Mother wet her pants. What began as a calm attack during which they picked off the dogs from a distance evaporated when Red's troups surrounded them. They kept firing, killing and wounding dogs until their ammunition was exhausted. Father's bayonet, which glinted menacingly in the sun, posed a serious threat to the dogs; but Mother's and Dezhi's carbines had no bayonets, so the circling dogs concentrated on them. Three backs were nearly fused together. They could feel one another shaking in fright. "Douguan," Mother murmured, "Douguan . . ."

"Don't be scared," Father demanded. "Scream as loud as you can. Try to get my dad to come to our rescue."

Seeing that Father was in charge, Red glared contemptuously at the bayonet out of the corner of his eye.

"Dad—help, save us!" Father screamed.

"Uncle—hurry!" Mother cried at the top of her lungs.

A few of the dogs tried to mount an assault but were beaten back. Mother rammed the barrel of her rifle into a charging dog's mouth, knocking out two of its teeth. Another one recklessly charged Father, whose bayonet sliced open its face. While his troops charged and fell back, Red crouched on the perimeter, his eyes riveted on Father.

The standoff continued for about as long as it takes to smoke a couple of pipefuls. Father's legs were getting rubbery, and he could barely lift his arms. He screamed again for Granddad to come save them. Mother was pressed so tightly to him that he felt as though his back were up against a wall.

"Douguan," whispered Dezhi, "I'll draw them away so you two can escape."

"No!" Father said emphatically.

"Here I go!"

He burst out of the encampment and ran like the wind toward the sorghum field, with dozens of dogs on his heels. They quickly caught him and began tearing him to shreds. But Father didn't dare watch Dezhi's agonies, for Red continued to stare at him without blinking.

Two Japanese grenades exploded in the sorghum field where Dezhi had fled. Bent by the concussion, the stalks emitted a sigh that made the skin on Father's cheeks crawl. First the sounds of broken canine bodies crashing to the ground, then the pitiful wails of dogs wounded in the blasts frightened the ones circling Father and Mother. They backed off, giving Mother the chance she needed to take out a muskmelon grenade and lob it into their midst. They watched the scary black object arch toward them, then let out a howl before scattering in panic. But the grenade fell harmlessly to the ground—she had forgotten to pull the pin. All the dogs fled, all except Red. When he saw Father turn to look at Mother, he sprang like lightning; the silvery rays of the sun struck this leader of dogs, his body forming a beautiful arc in the sky. Instinctively Father fell back, as Red's claws slashed across his face.

The initial assault had failed, although a piece of skin the size of Father's mouth had been ripped from his cheek, which was immediately covered with sticky blood. Red charged again, and this time Father raised his rifle to ward him off. Forcing the barrel of the rifle upward with his front paws, Red lowered his head to avoid the bayonet and lunged at Father's chest. Father spotted the clump of white fur on Red's belly and aimed a kick, just as Mother fell forward and knocked him flat on his back. Spotting his opportunity, Red fell on Father and shrewdly sank his teeth in his crotch at the very moment that Mother brought the butt of her rifle crashing down on his bony skull. Momentarily stunned, he backed up a few steps, then sprang forward in another attack. He was maybe three feet in the air when his head suddenly slumped forward as a shot rang out. One of his eyes was smashed. Father and Mother looked up to see a spindly, hunched-over, white-haired old man holding a scorched-looking wooden staff in his left hand and a smoking Japanese pistol in his right—it was Granddad.

He took a few faltering steps forward and cracked Red over the head with his staff. "Rebel bastard!" he cursed. Red's heart was still beating, his lungs were still heaving, his powerful hind legs were scratching two deep furrows in the black earth. His rich, beautiful red fur blazed like a million tongues of flame.

8

THE BITE HAD BEEN ABSORBED with less than full force, possibly because Father was wearing two pairs of pants, but the results were bad enough: The dog's teeth had ripped open one side of his scrotum, leaving an elliptical testicle the size of a quail's egg hanging by a thin, nearly transparent thread. When Granddad moved him, the little red thing dropped into the crotch of his pants. Granddad cupped it in the palm of his hand. It seemed to weigh a thousand pounds, the way he was bent over. His large, rough hand shook as though the thing were burning a hole in it. "Uncle," Mother asked him, "what's wrong with you?"

She was watching the muscles in his face twitch painfully, and noticed that his pale skin seemed covered with a yellow cast; despair filled his eyes.

"It's all over. . . . Everything ended in that instant. . . ." Granddad mumbled in a voice that quavered like an old, old man's.

He took out his pistol and shouted, "You've ruined me! Dog!"

He aimed the weapon at Red, who was still panting faintly, and pumped several shots into him.

Father struggled to his feet, rivulets of fresh, warm blood coursing down the inside of his thigh. He didn't seem to be in much pain. "Dad," he said, "we won."

"Uncle, hurry up and take care of Douguan's wound!" Mother said.

Father looked at the testicle cupped in Granddad's hand and asked with a note of astonishment, "Dad, is that mine? Is it?" A wave of nausea hit him. He fainted.

Granddad threw down his staff, tore off two clean sorghum leaves, and gently wrapped the thing up, then handed it to Mother. "Beauty," he said, "hold it carefully. I'm taking him to Dr. Zhang Xinyi." He bent over, picked Father up, and then hobbled off down the road. Dogs wounded by the exploding grenades in the marshland whimpered pitifully.

Dr. Zhang Xinyi, a man in his fifties, parted his hair right down the middle, something you seldom saw in the countryside. He wore a long, dark-blue gown, and had a pale face atop a frame so thin he seemed incapable of withstanding even the slightest breeze.

By the time Granddad had carried Father to the doctor, his back was bent almost double and his face had a ghostly pallor.

"Is that you, Commander Yu? You certainly look different," Dr. Zhang said.

"Name your price, Doctor."

Father had been laid out on the wooden-plank bed. "Is this your son, Commander?" Dr. Zhang asked him.

Granddad nodded.

"The one who killed the Japanese general at the Black Water River bridge?"

"I only have one son!"

"I'll do the best I can!" Dr. Zhang took some tweezers, a pair of scissors, a bottle of sorghum wine, and a vial of iodine out of his instrument bag, then bent over to examine the injury on Father's face.

"Take a look down there first, please, Doctor," Granddad said somberly. Then he turned to Mother and took the sorghum leaves in which the testicle was wrapped out of her hands. He placed it on the wooden cabinet beside the bed. The leaves spread open.

Dr. Zhang picked up the messy thing with his tweezers. His long, nicotine-stained fingers shook as he stammered, "Commander Yu . . . not that I'm unwilling to do my best, but your son's wound . . . My skills are not great, and I haven't the proper medication. . . . You must see someone more talented than I, Commander. . . ."

Granddad bent over and stuck his face right up into Dr. Zhang's, his rheumy eyes boring into the man. "Where can I find someone more talented?" he asked hoarsely. "Tell me, where can I go? Should I take him to the Japanese?"

"Commander," Zhang Xinyi defended himself, "that's not what your humble servant meant. . . . Your esteemed son is injured in a critical place, and the slightest slip could bring an end to your glorious line. . . ."

"I brought him here," Granddad said, "because I have faith in you. Do what you can."

"Since Commander Yu says so," Zhang Xinyi said, gritting his teeth, "I'll do it."

He soaked a cotton ball in the wine and cleaned the wound. The pain brought Father to. He tried to slide off the bed, but Granddad climbed up and held him down.

"Commander Yu," Zhang Xinyi said, "we'll have to strap him down."

"Douguan!" Granddad said. "You're my son, and I expect you to tough it out. Bite down hard!"

"But, Dad," Father groaned, "it hurts. . . ."

"Tough it out!" Granddad said sternly. "Think about Uncle Arhat!"

Father didn't dare argue. Sweat covered his forehead.

Zhang Xinyi took out a needle and sterilized it in the wine before threading it. Then he began stitching the torn scrotum closed.

"Sew that back inside!" Granddad said.

Zhang Xinyi looked at the testicle lying in the opened sorghum leaves on the wooden cabinet and said with embarrassment, "Commander Yu . . . it won't do any good. . . ."

"Is it your intention to bring the Yu line to an end?" Granddad asked glumly.

Large beads of sweat glistened on Dr. Zhang's gaunt face. "Commander Yu . . . think about it. . . . Connecting blood vessels were severed. If I put it back in, it would still be dead."

"Sew the blood vessels together."

"Commander Yu, nobody in the world can reconnect blood vessels. . . ."

"Then . . . is that the end of it?"

"That's hard to say, Commander Yu. He might still be all right. The other one's just fine. Maybe he'll be all right with just one. . . ."

"You think so?"

"It's possible."

"Damn it to hell!" Granddad swore sorrowfully. "Bad things always happen to me!"

After the wound down below had been taken care of, Father's face was attended to. Dr. Zhang's sweat-soaked clothing stuck to his back as he sat on a stool and panted breathlessly.

"How much, Dr. Zhang?"

"Don't worry about a fee, Commander Yu. As long as your esteemed son gets better, I consider myself lucky," he said weakly.

"Dr. Zhang, I, Yu Zhan'ao, am strapped at the moment. But someday I'll thank you properly."

He picked up Father and carried him out of Dr. Zhang's house.

Granddad looked down attentively at my father, who lay semiconscious in the shack, his face covered with gauze, with only his shifting eyes exposed. Dr. Zhang had dropped by once to change his dressings. "Commander Yu," he said, "there's no infection, and that's a good sign."

"Tell me," said Granddad, "didn't you say he'd be all right with just one?"

"Commander, we can't worry about that yet. Your esteemed son was bitten by a mad dog, and we're lucky he's still alive."

"He might as well be dead if that thing's useless." Observing the murderous look in Granddad's eyes, Dr. Zhang mumbled something obsequious and slinked away.

Granddad picked up his gun and walked over to the marshland to sort out his chaotic thoughts. Mournful signs of autumn were all around: the ground was covered with frost, and there were sharp, icy brambles on the soggy marshland floor. Granddad was sick and very weak, his son was hovering between life and death, the family was broken up, some gone and some dead, the people were suffering, Wang Guang and Dezhi were dead, Gimpy had gone far away, the ulcer on the woman Liu's leg was still oozing pus and blood, Blind Eye did nothing all day long but sit, the girl Beauty was too young to know anything, he was being pulled by the Jiao-Gao troops and squeezed by Pocky Leng's troops, the Japanese saw him as their mortal enemy. He climbed to the top of a rise in the marshland to gaze out over the scattered, broken remains of human bodies and sorghum stalks, utterly disheartened. What had he gotten from decades of fighting and vying over women? Only the desolate scene in front of him.

The autumn of 1939 was one of the most difficult periods in Granddad's life: his troops had been wiped out, his beloved wife had been killed, his son had been severely wounded, his home and the land around it had been torched, his body was racked with illness; war had destroyed nearly everything he owned. His eyes roamed over the corpses of men and dogs, a skein of threads getting more and more tangled wherever he looked, until it became a blur. Several times he drew his pistol, thinking of saying goodbye to this lousy, fucking world. But a powerful desire for revenge won out over cowardice. He hated the Japanese, he hated the troops of Pocky Leng and of Jiao-Gao.

On this very spot, the Jiao-Gao forces had taken over twenty rifles from him, then vanished without a trace. There was no sign that they'd engaged the Japanese; he had heard only that they'd clashed with the troops of Pocky Leng. And Granddad suspected that it was the Jiao-Gao forces who had stolen the fifteen rifles he and Father had hidden in the dry well.

The woman Liu, who still had a pretty face even in her forties, came to the edge of the marshland to find Granddad, trying to comfort him with affectionate gazes at his silver hair. She touched his arm with her large, rough hand and said, "You shouldn't be sitting here thinking like that. Let's go back. As the ancients said, 'Heaven never seals off all the exits.' You should concentrate on getting your health back by eating and drinking and breathing as much and as hard as you can. . . ."

Her words touched him. He looked up at her kind face and tears began to fill his eyes. "Sister-in-law," he moaned.

She stroked his bent back. "Just look," she said, "a man barely forty reduced to this by his suffering."

She supported him as they walked back together. He looked at her lame leg and asked with concern, "Is it any better?"

"The ulcer has healed, but it's thinner than the other one."

"It'll fill out later."

"I don't think Douguan's injury is as serious as it looks."

"What do you think, will he be all right with only one?"

"I think so. Single-stalk garlic is always the hottest."

"You really think so?"

"My younger brother-in-law was born with only one, and look how many kids he's got."

Late at night, Granddad rested his weary head in the warmth of the woman Liu's bosom as she stroked his bony frame with her large hands. "Can you do it again?" she whispered. "Do you still have the strength?

Don't despair. Doesn't it make you feel better to do it to me . . . ?"

Granddad smelled the slightly sour, slightly sweet odor of the woman Liu's breath and fell fast asleep.

Mother could not rid her mind of the picture of Dr. Zhang picking up that purplish, flattened ball with his tweezers. He had examined it carefully before tossing it into a dish filled with dirty cotton balls and pieces of skin and dead flesh. Yesterday it had been Douguan's jewel; today it lay in a dish of filthy debris. Mother, who was over fifteen and had begun to understand a thing or two, felt both bashful and frightened. While she was taking care of Father, she kept staring at his gauze-wrapped penis; her heart fluttered, her cheeks burned, she blushed deep red.

Then she learned that the woman Liu was sleeping with Granddad.

"Beauty," the woman Liu said to her, "you're fifteen now, and no longer a child. Try playing with Douguan's penis; if it gets hard, he's your man."

Mother was so embarrassed she nearly cried.

Father's stitches were removed.

Mother slipped into the shack where Father was sleeping and tiptoed up to his kang, her cheeks burning. She knelt beside him and carefully pulled down his pants. In the light streaming into the room she looked at his injured, grotesque penis. The head, wild and proud, had an air of defiance. Timidly she held it in her sweaty hand and felt it gradually get warmer and thicker. It began to throb, just like her heart. Father woke up and squinted at her. "Beauty, what are you doing?"

Mother shrieked in alarm, jumped to her feet, and ran out, bumping smack into Granddad in the doorway.

Granddad grabbed her by the shoulders and demanded, "What's wrong, Beauty?"

Mother burst out crying, wrenched free of Granddad's grip, and ran away.

Granddad rushed into the shack, then rushed out again like a man crazed and ran straight to the woman Liu. He grabbed her breasts and squeezed them tightly. "Single-stalk garlic is the hottest!" he said almost incoherently. "Single-stalk garlic *is* the hottest!"

Granddad fired three shots in the air, then brought his hands together in front of his chest and screamed: "Heaven has eyes!"

9

GRANDDAD TAPPED THE WALL with his knuckles. Sunlight streaming in through the window reflected off the Gaomi statuette on the highly polished kang table. The window was covered by paper that Grandma had cut into strange, ingenious designs. In five days everything in the place would be reduced to ashes in a terrible battle. It was the tenth day of the eighth lunar month, 1939. Granddad had just returned from the highway, his arm in a sling and reeking of gasoline. He and Father had buried the Japanese machine gun with the twisted barrel and were searching the house for the money Grandma had hidden.

When the wall produced a hollow sound, Granddad smashed a hole in it with the butt of his pistol, then reached in and pulled out a red cloth packet. He shook it. It jingled. He poured its contents out onto the kang—fifty silver dollars.

Pocketing the silver dollars, he said, "Let's go, son."

"Go where, Dad?"

"Into town to buy bullets. It's time to settle scores with Pocky Leng."

The sun had nearly set when they reached the northern outskirts of the city. Snaking darkly through the sorghum fields, a black locomotive chugged along the tracks of the Jiao-Ping and Jinan rail line, belching puffs of dark smoke above the sorghum tips. Sunlight reflecting off the tracks nearly blinded them. The loud shriek of the whistle terrified Father, who squeezed Granddad's hand.

Granddad led Father to a large grave mound, in front of which stood a white tombstone twice as tall as a man. The chiseled words had been rubbed so smooth they were barely discernible, and the area was surrounded by trees so thick it would have taken at least two people to wrap their arms around any one of them. The black canopy of leaves rustled even when there was no wind, and the grave itself was walled off, like a black island, by stalks of blood-red sorghum.

Granddad dug a little hole in front of the tombstone and tossed his pistol in. Father also threw his Browning in the hole.

After crossing the tracks, they looked up at the high gateway in the city wall, over which flew a Japanese flag, its rising sun and spokelike rays catching the red rays of the setting sun. Sentries stood on both sides of the gate, a Japanese to the left and a Chinese to the right. While the Chinese soldier questioned and searched locals entering town, his Japanese counterpart stood watching, his rifle ready.

Now that they'd crossed the tracks, Granddad hoisted Father up onto his back and whispered, "Pretend you've got a bellyache. Groan a little."

Father groaned. "Like that, Dad?"

"Put a little more feeling into it."

They fell into a line of people heading into the city. "What village are you from?" the Chinese soldier asked haughtily. "What's your business in town?"

"Fish Beach, north of town," Granddad answered meekly. "My son has cholera. I'm taking him to see Dr. Wu."

Father was so wrapped up in the conversation between Granddad and the sentry he forgot to groan. But he screamed in pain when Granddad pinched him hard on the thigh.

The sentry waved them past.

"You little bastard!" Granddad cursed angrily when they were safely out of earshot. "Why didn't you groan?"

"That pinch hurt, Dad, it hurt a lot!"

Granddad led Father down a narrow cinder-paved street toward the train station. The sun's rays were dying out; the air was foul. Father saw that two blockhouses had been built alongside the run-down train station. Two Japanese soldiers with leashed police dogs marched back and forth. Dozens of civilians squatted or stood beyond the railing waiting for a train, and a Chinese in a black uniform was positioned on the platform, red lantern in hand, as an eastbound train sounded its whistle. The ground shook, and the police dogs barked at the coming train. A little old woman hobbled back and forth in front of the waiting passengers, hawking cigarettes and melon seeds. The train chugged into the station and ground its wheels to a halt. There were, Father saw, more than twenty cars behind the locomotive—ten boxcars, followed by ten or more flatcars filled with cargo covered carelessly by green tarpaulins. Japs standing on the train called out to their comrades on the platform.

Father heard a sudden crack of gunfire from the sorghum field north of the tracks and saw a tall Jap soldier on one of the flatcars sway momentarily, then tumble headlong to the ground. The howl of a wolf sounded from one of the blockhouses, and the people, those disembarking and those waiting to board the train, scattered. The police dogs barked furiously; the machine guns on top of the blockhouses began spraying the area to the north. The train started up amid the confusion, belching puffs of black smoke and sending a shower of ashes onto the platform.

Granddad grabbed Father's hand and dragged him quickly down a dark lane. He pushed open a half-closed gate and walked into a tiny courtyard, where a small red paper lantern hung from the eave of the house. A woman stood in the doorway, her face so heavily powdered you couldn't tell her age. She was grinning broadly through painted lips; her teeth glistened. Black hair was piled up on her head, and she wore a silk flower behind her ear.

"My dear elder brother!" she called out with affected sweetness. "Now that you're a commander, you don't give a second thought to your little sister." She threw her arms around Granddad's neck like a little girl.

"Don't do that," he complained. "Not in front of my son. I can't waste time with you today! Are you still playing games with Fifth Brother?"

The woman stormed over to the gate and shut it, then took down the lantern and walked inside. "Fifth Brother was caught and beaten by the garrison command," she said with a pout.

"Isn't Song Shun of the garrison command his sworn brother?"

"Do you really think you can trust fair-weather friends like that? After what happened at Qingdao, I've been sitting on the razor's edge."

"Fifth Brother would never give you away. He proved that when he was grilled by Nine Dreams Cao."

"What are you doing here? They say you fought some Japanese armored troops."

"It was a fiasco! I'm going to murder that motherfucking Pocky Leng!"

"Don't mess with that slippery toad. He's too much for you."

Granddad took the silver dollars out of his pocket and tossed them down on the table. "I want five hundred red-jacketed bullets."

"Red-jacketed, blue-jacketed, I got rid of them all when Fifth Brother was arrested. I can't make bullets out of thin air."

"Don't give me that! Here's fifty dollars. Tell me, have I, Yu Zhan'ao, ever treated you wrong?"

"My dear elder brother," the woman said, "what kind of talk is that? Don't treat your little sister like a stranger."

"Then don't get me mad!" threatened Granddad.

"You'll never get out of town."

"That's my problem, not yours. I want five hundred large cartridges and fifty small ones."

The woman walked out into the yard to see if anyone was around, then returned to the house, opened a secret door in the wall, and took out a box of shells that shone like gold.

Granddad picked up a sack and stuffed the bullets inside, then tied it around his waist. "Let's go!" he said.

The woman stopped him. "How do you plan to get away?"

"By crawling across the tracks near the train station."

"No good," she said. "There are blockhouses there, with searchlights, dogs, and guards."

"We'll give it a try," Granddad said mockingly. "If it doesn't work, we'll be back."

Granddad and Father made their way down the dark lane toward the train station and hid alongside the wall of a blacksmith shop; from here they had a clear view of the brightly lit platform and the sentries standing on it. Granddad led Father to the western end of the station, where there was a freight yard. A barbed-wire fence ran from the station all the way to the city wall, and searchlights on top of the blockhouses swept the area, illuminating a dozen or more sets of tracks.

They crawled up next to the barbed-wire fence and tugged on it, hoping to open a hole big enough to crawl through. But it was too taut, and one of the barbs punctured the palm of Father's hand. He whimpered.

"What's wrong?" Granddad whispered.

"I cut my hand, Dad," Father whispered back.

"We can't get through. Let's go back!"

"If we had our guns . . ."

"We still couldn't make it."

"We could shoot out the lights!"

They retreated into the shadows, where Granddad picked up a brick and threw it toward the tracks. One of the sentries shrieked in alarm and fired. The searchlight spun around and swept the area as a machine gun opened fire, the sound so loud that Father nearly went deaf. Sparks flew from bullets ricocheting off the tracks.

The fifteenth day of the eighth lunar month, the Mid-Autumn Festival, is one of the biggest market days in Gaomi County. The people still had to go on living, even though it was wartime. Business was business. The roads were filled with people at eight o'clock in the morning, when a young man named Gao Rong manned his post at the northern gate to search and question those entering and leaving town. He knew the Japanese soldier was watching him with ill-concealed disgust.

An old man in his fifties and a teenage boy were driving a goat out of town. The old man's face was dark, his eyes steely; the boy's face was red and he was sweating, as from a case of nerves.

"Where are you going?"

"Leaving town. Going home," the old man replied.

"Not going to market?"

"Already been. Bought this half-dead goat. Cheap."

"When did you come into town?"

"Yesterday afternoon. We stayed with a relative. Bought the goat first thing this morning."

"Now where are you going?"

"Leaving town. Going home."

"Okay, you can pass!"

The goat's belly was so big it could barely walk. When Granddad whipped it with a broken-off sorghum stalk, it cried out in agony.

They stopped at the gravesite to retrieve their weapons.

"Shall we let the goat go, Dad?"

"No. Let's take it with us. We'll kill it when we get home, so we can celebrate the Mid-Autumn Festival."

They arrived at the village entrance at noon, near the tall black-earth wall that had been repaired not many years before. A hail of gunfire erupted from the heart of the village and beyond, and Granddad immediately knew that what they'd been dreading had finally happened. He was reminded of the premonition he'd had for the past several days, and was glad he'd decided to go into town that morning. They'd fought the odds and accomplished their task; that was all anyone could ask of them.

Granddad and Father hurriedly picked up the half-dead goat and carried it into the sorghum field, where Father cut the hemp they'd used to sew up its rectum. They'd stuffed 550 bullets up the goat's ass in that woman's house, until its belly drooped like a crescent moon. During the trip back, Father had been worried that the bullets would split the goat's belly or that the animal would somehow digest them.

As soon as the hemp was cut, the goat's rectum opened up like a plum flower, and pellets came pouring out. After relieving itself violently, the goat crumpled to the ground. "Oh no, Dad!" Father cried in alarm. "The bullets have turned into goat pellets."

Granddad grabbed the goat by its horns and jerked it to its feet, then bounced it up and down. Shiny bullets came spilling out. They scooped up the bullets, loaded their weapons, and stuffed the rest of the ammunition into their pockets. Not worrying whether the goat was dead or alive, they ran through the sorghum field straight for the village.

The Japs had surrounded the village, over which a pall of gunsmoke hung. The first thing Father and Granddad saw was eight mortar pieces hidden in the sorghum field, the tubes about half the height of a man and as thick as a fist. Twenty or more khaki-clad soldiers manned the mortars under the command of a skinny Jap waving a small flag. When he lowered his flag, the soldiers dropped their shells into the tubes, and the glistening objects were launched into the air in whistling arcs, to land inside the village wall. Eight puffs of smoke rose from the village, followed by eight dull thuds that quickly merged into a single loud explosion. Eight columns of smoke blossomed like dark, hazy flowers. The Japs fired another salvo.

Like a man wakened from a dream, Granddad picked up his rifle and fired it. The Japanese waving the flag crumpled to the ground. Father saw the bullet bury itself in the man's bony skull, which looked like a dry radish. His first thought was, The battle's on! Looking confused, he fired his weapon, but the bullet struck the base of a mortar with a loud metallic ping. The Japs manning the mortars picked up their rifles and began firing. Granddad grabbed Father and dragged him down among the sorghum stalks.

The Japanese and their Chinese lackeys launched an attack, running at a crouch into the sorghum field and firing indiscriminately.

Machine-gun fire erupted. Crows perched on the village wall were silent. When the puppet troops reached the wall, wooden-handled grenades sailed over toward them and exploded in their ranks, bringing down at least a dozen men. Granddad hadn't known about Ruolu the Elder's purchase of grenades from Detachment Leader Leng's munitions factory. Their comrades turned and ran. So did the Japanese. Dozens of men armed with hunting rifles and homemade cannons clambered up onto the wall, opened fire, then ducked back down, silent again. Later on, Granddad learned that similarly heated, bizarre battles had occurred at the northern, eastern, and western edges of the village.

The Japs fired another salvo of mortars, scoring direct hits on the iron gate. *Thump, thump,* the gate was shattered, leaving a gaping breach.

Granddad and Father opened fire again on the Japs manning the mortars. Granddad fired four shots, bringing down two Jap soldiers. Father fired only a single shot. Holding his Browning in both hands, he took careful aim at a Jap straddling a mortar and fired. The bullet struck the man in the buttocks. Terrified, he fell forward across the muzzle, his body muffling the sound of the explosion before being ripped apart. Father jumped for joy, just as something whizzed noisily past his head. The mortar tube had exploded, sending the bolt flying a good ten yards to land just beyond Father's head. It missed killing him by only a few inches.

Years later, Father was still talking about that glorious single shot.

As soon as the village gate was blown apart, a squad of Japanese cavalry stormed the village, sabers drawn. Father stared at the handsome, valiant warhorses with three parts terror and seven parts envy. The sorghum stalks snagged their legs and scratched their faces; it was hard going for the horses. Metal rakes and wooden plows, bricks and roof tiles, quite possibly even bowls of steaming sorghum porridge, rained down on them from the gatehouses, forcing the screaming riders to cover their heads, and so frightening their mounts that they reared up in protest and some turned back. Granddad and Father had odd grins on their faces as they watched the chaotic cavalry charge.

Granddad's and Father's diversion brought throngs of puppet soldiers down on their heads, and before long the cavalry joined the search-and-destroy mission. Time and again the cold glint of a Japanese saber came straight at Father, but it was always deflected by sorghum stalks. A bullet grazed Granddad's scalp. The dense sorghum was saving their lives. Like hunted rabbits, they crawled on the ground, and by midafternoon they'd made it all the way to the Black Water River.

After counting their remaining ammunition, they re-entered the sorghum field, and had walked a li or so when they heard shouts ahead: "Comrades"—"Charge"—"Forward"—"Down with the Jap imperialists."

The battle cries were followed by bugles and then the *rat-tat-tat* of what sounded like a couple of heavy machine guns.

Granddad and Father ran toward the source of the noise as fast as their legs would carry them. When they arrived at the spot, it was deserted; amid the sorghum stalks they found two steel oil drums in which strings of firecrackers were exploding.

"Only the Jiao-Gao regiment would pull a stunt like this," Granddad said, with his lip curled.

The Jap cavalry and puppet foot-soldiers sprayed the area with fire as they made a flanking movement. Granddad retreated, dragging Father with him. Several Jiao-Gao soldiers ran toward them at a crouch, grenades hanging from their belts. Father saw one of them kneel and fire toward a clump of sorghum stalks shaking violently under the charge of a stallion. The ragged gunfire sounded like an earthenware vat being smashed. The soldier tried to pull back the bolt of his rifle to eject the spent cartridge, but it was jammed. A warhorse bore down on him. Father watched the Japanese rider wave his glinting saber and cut through the air, barely missing the soldier's head. The man threw down his rifle and ran, but was soon overtaken by the galloping horse, and the saber came slicing down through his skull, soaking nearby sorghum leaves with his gore. Father saw nothing but inky darkness as he slumped to the ground.

When he awoke, he had been separated from Granddad by the Japanese cavalry charge. The sun bore down on the tips of the sorghum, casting dark shadows around him. Three furry fox kits darted in front of him, and he instinctively grabbed one of the bushy tails. An angry growl erupted from nearby stalks, as the mother fox leaped out of the cover, baring her fangs threateningly. He quickly released the kit.

Gunfire continued at the eastern, western, and northern edges of the village, as a deathly stillness enveloped the southern edge. Father called out softly, then began to shout at the top of his lungs. No reply from Granddad. A dark cloud of fear settled over his heart as he ran panic-stricken toward the sound of gunfire. Dimming rays of sunlight bathed the sorghum tassels, which suddenly seemed hostile. He started to cry.

Searching for Granddad, Father stumbled across the bodies of three Jiao-Gao soldiers, all hacked to death, their hideous faces frozen in the gloomy darkness. He then ran smack into a crowd of terrified villagers cowering amid the sorghum stalks.

"Have you seen my dad?"

"Is the village open, boy?"

He could tell by their accent that they were from Jiao County. He heard an old man instructing his son: "Yinzhu, remember what I told you. Don't pass up quilt covers, even if the cotton's all tattered. But look first for a cookpot, because ours is ruined."

The old man's rheumy eyes looked like gobs of snot stuck in the sockets. Having no time to waste on them, Father continued north. When he reached the edge of the village, he was confronted by a scene that had appeared in Grandma's dreams, and Granddad's dreams, and over and over in his own. People were pouring out through the village wall—men and women, young and old—like a raging torrent, heading for the sorghum fields to escape the heavy fighting on the eastern, northern, and western edges of the village.

Gunfire erupted in front of Father, who saw a hail of bullets rip into the sorghum field that dominated the front of the village. The villagers—men and women, young and old—were mowed down along with the sorghum stalks, every last one of them. The air was spattered with fresh blood, turning half the sky red. Father sat down hard on the ground, his mouth hanging slack. Blood everywhere, and everywhere its sweet stench.

The Japanese entered the village.

The sun, stained by human blood, set behind the mountain as the crimson full moon of mid-autumn rose above the sorghum.

My father heard Granddad's muted call:

"Douguan—!"

CHAPTER FOUR

Sorghum Funeral

1

IN THE CRUEL FOURTH LUNAR MONTH, frogs lay their transparent eggs in the Black Water River under radiant starlight. Then, in the sweltering heat of the sun, swarms of inky-black, squirming tadpoles emerge into the warmth of water that looks like freshly extracted bean oil to form inky-black schools that swim with the slowly flowing river. Dog-turd reeds grow in profusion on the banks; wild mustard flowers so red they seem purple bloom furiously amid the water grasses.

It was a good day for birds. Clay-colored larks covered with white dots soared in the high sky, filling the air with shrill cries. Glossy swallows skimmed the mirrorlike surface of the river. The dark, rich soil of Northeast Gaomi Township revolved ponderously beneath the birds' wings. Hot winds from the west rolled across the land, and murky dust clouds attacked the Jiao-Ping highway.

It was also a good day for Grandma. Granddad, who had joined the Iron Society, eventually replacing Black Eye as its leader, was about to fulfill his promise to give her a proper funeral, now that nearly two years had passed. News of the impending ceremony had spread a month earlier among the villages of Northeast Gaomi Township. The eighth day of the fourth lunar month had been chosen. By noon of the seventh day, donkey carts and ox carts began arriving, carrying common folk from far away, including wives and children. Hawkers and peddlers had a field day. On the streets and in the shade of trees at the head of the village, dumpling peddlers set up their earthen stoves, flatcake vendors heated their pots, and cold-bean-noodle stands with white canvas awnings were thrown up. Gray hair and ruddy cheeks, men, women, boys, and girls, seemed to fill every inch of space in our village.

By the spring of 1941, the Leng detachment and the Jiao-Gao regiment had worn each other down with their frequent clashes, and had been further harassed by the systematic kidnappings by Granddad's Iron Society and an annihilation campaign by the Japanese and their Chinese puppet troops. The Leng detachment apparently had fled to the Three Rivers Mountain region of Changyi to rest and build up their strength, while the Jiao-Gao regiment hid out in the Great Marshy Mountain region of Pingdu County to lick its wounds. The Iron Society, under the leadership of Granddad and his erstwhile romantic rival, had grown, in a little over a year, into a force of over two hundred rifles and fifty or more fine horses; but their movements were so secretive and so shrouded in religious superstition that the Japanese and their puppets seemed to take no notice of them.

In national terms, 1941 witnessed the cruelest stage of the war of resistance against Japan; the people of Northeast Gaomi Township, however, enjoyed a brief respite of peace and quiet. The survivors planted a new crop on top of last year's rotting sorghum. The seeds were barely in the ground when a light but adequate rain fell to soak the thirsty earth. Then the radiant sun took over, and, seemingly overnight, tender shoots covered the ground. Drops of fragrant dew were impaled on the tips of delicate red shoots. Grandma's funeral fell on a day of rest for the farmers.

On the evening of the seventh, the area around the village walls was packed with people, while dozens of wagons, their donkeys and oxen tethered to trees and axles, were lined up on the dusty street. The setting sun shone on the glossy spring hides of livestock and turned immature leaves blood-red, their shadows ancient coins stamped on the animals' backs.

As the sun fell behind the mountain, an herbal physician rode his mule into the village from the west. Clumps of bristly hairs emerged from the blackness of his nostrils; his scalp and forehead were covered by a tattered felt cap, out of place on this late-spring day, and a somber glare radiated from beneath his slanting eyebrows.

The physician and his scrawny mule swaggered past the marketplace, drawing curious stares. The melodious tinkle of a little brass bell in his hand produced an air of unfathomable mystery, and the people fell in behind him instinctively, kicking up a cloud of dust that settled on the foul-smelling back of the sweaty mule and on the physician's greasy face. His eyes blinked constantly, and he sneezed with a loud, tinny sound, as his mule released a string of farts. That broke the spell. The people laughed and drifted off to find a spot to set up camp for the night.

A new moon covered the village with hazy shadows. Cool breezes swept in from the fields, and the croaking of frogs in the Black Water River filled the air; more visitors arrived for the funeral, but there was no room in the village, so they slept in the fields.

The physician took a tour on his mule around the tent set up by Granddad's Iron Society. A towering, intimidating presence, it was the largest structure ever seen in our village. Grandma's bier rested in the center of the tent, through whose seams filtered the light of many candles. Two Iron Society soldiers with pistols in their belts stood guard at the entrance, their shiny heads shaved back from their foreheads, a sight that instilled fear in whoever saw them. All two hundred soldiers were quartered in satellite tents, while their fifty or more sturdy mounts were tethered to the crotches of willow trunks in front of a long feeding trough. The horses snorted, pawed the ground, and swished their tails to drive off hordes of horseflies. Grooms dumped dry mash into the trough, saturating the air under the trees with the redolence of parched sorghum.

The aroma caught the attention of the physician's scrawny mule, which strained toward the trough. Following his mount's pitiful gaze, he said, as much to himself as to his mule, "Hungry? Listen to me. Rivals and lovers are destined to meet. Men die over riches, birds perish over food. The young must not scoff at the old, for flowers don't bloom forever. One must know when to yield to others. No sign of weakness, it will work to one's later advantage. . . ."

The physician's crazy ramblings and furtive behavior caught the attention of two Iron Society soldiers, disguised as common folk, who fell in behind him as he led his animal toward the horses. They quickly blocked his way, one in front and one in back, pistols in hand.

Showing no sign of fear, he merely split the darkness with a sad, shrill laugh that made the soldiers' hands tremble. The one in front saw the physician's smoldering eyes, the one behind saw the back of his neck stiffen when he laughed. The heavy silence was broken by the whinnies of two horses fighting over food in the trough.

The central tent was lit up by twenty-four tall red candles that flickered uneasily, casting a fearful light on the objects inside. Grandma's scarlet bier was surrounded by snow pines and snow willows made of paper; beside it stood two papier-mâché figures—a boy in green on the left, a girl in red on the right—crafted by Baoen, the township's famous funeral artisan, from sorghum stalks and colored paper.

On Grandma's host tablet behind the coffin was an inscription:

For the Spirit of My Departed Mother, Surnamed Dai.
Offered by Her Filial Son, Yu Douguan.

A drab brown incense-holder in front held smoldering yellow joss sticks, whose fragrant smoke curled into the air, the ash suspended above the scarlet flames of the candles. Father had shaved the front of his scalp to show that he, too, was a member of the Iron Society. Granddad, also shaved, sat behind a table next to Black Eye, the society leader, watching the Jiao County funeral master instruct my father in the three prostrations, six bows, and nine kowtows. As the funeral master droned on with infinite patience, Father started getting fidgety, and went through the motions, cutting corners wherever he could.

"Douguan," Granddad said sternly, "stop clowning around! Do your filial duties, no matter how unpleasant they may be!"

The Iron Society, which spent an enormous sum of money on my grandma's funeral, financed its activities in Northeast Gaomi Township after the departure of the Leng detachment and the Jiao-Gao regiment by issuing its own currency, in denominations of one thousand and ten thousand yuan, printed on coarse straw paper. The designs were very simple (a strange humanoid astride a tiger), the printing haphazard at best (using printing blocks carved for holiday posters). At the time no fewer than four separate currencies circulated in Northeast Gaomi, their strength and fluctuating value determined by the power of the issuing authority. Currency backed by military force constituted the greatest exploitation of the people, and Granddad was able to finance Grandma's funeral by relying on this sort of concealed tyranny. The

Jiao-Gao regiment and the Leng detachment had been squeezed out, so Granddad's coarse currency was very strong in Northeast Gaomi Township for a while. But then the bottom dropped out, a few months after Grandma's funeral, and the tiger-mount currency wasn't worth the paper it was printed on.

The two Iron Society soldiers entered the funeral tent with the physician in tow; they blinked in the bright candlelight.

"What's this all about?" Granddad snarled, rising from his seat.

One of the soldiers went down on his knee and covered the shaved part of his head with both hands. "Deputy Commander, we've caught a spy!"

Black Eye, whose left eye was rimmed by dark moles, kicked the table leg and barked out an order: "Off with his head! Then rip out his heart and liver and cook them to go with the wine!"

"Not so fast!" Granddad countermanded. He turned to Black Eye. "Blackie, shouldn't we find out who he is before we kill him?"

"Who the fuck cares who he is!" Black Eye picked a clay teapot up off the table and threw it to the ground. Then he stood up, his pistol sticking out of his belt, and glared at the soldier who had made the report.

"Commander . . ." the soldier stammered fearfully.

"I'll fuck your living mother, Zhu Shun! 'Commander' means nothing to you, I see! You son of a bitch, get out of my sight. You're a fucking thorn in my eye!" The ranting Black Eye looked down at the teapot on the ground and gave it a swift kick, sending shards of clay flying; some of them landed in the grove of graceful snow willows beside the coffin and made them rustle.

A boy about Father's age bent over, picked up the pieces of the teapot, and tossed them outside the tent.

"Fulai," Granddad said to the boy, "put the commander to bed. He's drunk!"

Fulai stepped up and put his arms around Black Eye, who sent him reeling. "Drunk? Who's drunk? You ungrateful shit! I set up shop, and you eat free. A tiger kills its prey just so the bear can eat it! You little shit, you won't get away with throwing sand in my black eye! Just wait!"

"Blackie," Granddad said, "you don't want to lay your prestige on the line in front of the men." His lips curled into a grim smile, and cruel wrinkles appeared at the corners of his mouth.

Black Eye rested his hand on the Bakelite handle of his pistol. In a tired, strangely hoarse voice he said, "Get the fuck out of here! And take that little son of a bitch with you!"

"It's easy to invite the gods, hard to send them away," Granddad said.

Black Eye drew his pistol and waved it in front of Granddad, who held out his green ceramic cup, took a sip of wine, and swished it around in his mouth before leaning forward and spitting it in Black Eye's face. Then, with a flick of his wrist, he flung the cup at the muzzle of Black Eye's pistol; the cup shattered on impact, the pieces flying everywhere. Black Eye's hand twitched, and the muzzle of the pistol drooped.

"Put your gun away!" Granddad shouted in a steely voice. "I'm not finished with you yet, Blackie, so don't get smart with me!"

Black Eye's face was bathed in sweat. He grumbled, picked up his pistol, stuck it in his leather belt, and sat down.

The mule-riding physician, who had watched the episode with a disdainful smile, suddenly started laughing so hard he could barely stand, so hard that hot tears streamed down his cheeks. His behavior made everyone squirm uncomfortably.

"What's so funny?" Black Eye asked. "I'll fuck your mother! I asked you, what's so funny?"

The laughter stopped as abruptly as it had begun, and the physician said dryly, "Fuck away, if that's what you want. My mother's been dead and buried in the black earth for ten years, and she's all yours!"

Black Eye was speechless. The moles around his eye turned the color of fresh leaves. Leaping to his feet, he slapped the physician seven or eight times, sending trickles of blood out his nostrils and down the bristly black hairs. The physician licked his lips greedily, his shiny white teeth stained with blood.

"How'd you get here?" Granddad asked him.

"My mule!" the physician replied, stretching his neck as though he were swallowing a mouthful of blood. "What have you done with my mule?"

"I guarantee you he's a Japanese spy!" Black Eye said. "Bring me a whip. I'll teach the son of a bitch something!"

"My mule! Give me back my mule! I want my mule. . . ." There was panic in the physician's voice. He tried to run out of the tent, but was stopped by the guards. One of them punched him in the temple. His head slumped forward, as though his neck had snapped like a sorghum stalk. He crumpled to the ground.

"Search him!" Granddad ordered.

The Iron Society soldiers searched him thoroughly, but all they found was a couple of marbles, one bright green, the other bright red, each with a little cat's-eye bubble in the center. Granddad held them up to the candlelight to reflect the brilliant rays. They were beautiful. With a perplexed shake of his head, he set them on the table. Father reached out and snatched them away.

"Give one to Fulai," Granddad told him.

Reluctantly, Father held them out to Fulai, who was standing beside Black Eye. "Which one do you want?"

"The red one."

"No," Father said. "You can have the green one."

"I want the red one."

"The green one; take it or leave it." Fulai grudgingly took the green one out of Father's hand.

As the physician's neck gradually straightened, the ominous light in his eyes was as strong as ever. His bloodstained, wispy beard bristled.

"Talk! Are you a Japanese spy or not?" Granddad asked him.

Like a stubborn child, the physician picked up where he'd left off: "My mule, my mule! I won't say a word until you bring me my mule."

Granddad laughed mischievously, then said, "Bring it over. Let's see what he's trying to sell."

The scrawny mule was led to the tent, where the dazzling candlelight, the shiny coffin, and the dark, forbidding paper figures so frightened it that it balked at the entrance and refused to take another step. The physician covered its eyes with his hands and led the animal inside. Its skinny legs shook, and a *rat-tat-tat* of loud farts was released toward Grandma's bier.

The physician threw his arms around the mule's neck and patted its bony forehead. "Scared, fellow?" he asked tenderly. "Don't be. I'm telling you, don't be scared. Not even if they lop off your head and leave a scar as big as a bowl! Even if it's the size of a basin, in twenty years you'll come back as a real hero!"

"Okay, talk! Who sent you? What are you here for?" Granddad asked him.

"My dad's ghost sent me here to sell my potion." He took his saddlebags off the mule's back, removed a packet of patent medicine, and began to chant, "A dash of croton beans, two of bezoar, three of blister beetle, four of musk, seven onion whites, seven dates, seven grains of pepper, seven slices of ginger."

Everyone's mouth dropped in astonishment as they looked at the expression on the physician's face. The mule, having grown used to its surroundings, began pawing the ground casually with its pale, cracked hooves.

"What kind of potion?" Black Eye asked.

"Fast-action abortion medicine," the physician said with a cunning smile. "Even if you're made of bronze, iron, or steel, one packet of this medicine, taken in three portions, will drive the baby right out of you. Money-back guarantee."

"You goddamned immoral bastard!" Black Eye lashed out.

"There's more, there's more!" He reached into his saddlebags and held up another packet as he chanted, "A dog's penis has the emperor, a goat's penis has the minister. Some rice wine and crown-prince ginseng, the bark of eucommia, some chain fern and ursine seal, the tips of March bamboo shoots as a base."

"What's it good for?" Black Eye asked.

"Impotence. Whether you're as wispy as a silkworm's thread or as soft as fluffed cotton, one packet, taken in three portions, and you'll have a rod of steel that'll get you through the night. Money-back guarantee."

Black Eye rubbed his shiny forehead with his hand and smiled lewdly. "You're a goddamn wild man engaged in inhuman business!" he said, and asked to see the potion.

The physician handed Black Eye something that looked like a withered branch. He held it under his nose and sniffed it. "You call this a goddamn dog's penis?"

"The genuine article, the penis of a black dog!"

"Old Yu, take a look and tell me if this isn't the dried root of an ordinary tree." Black Eye handed it to Granddad, who held it up to a candle and examined it through squinting eyes.

The physician suddenly began to quake, and his bristly chin twitched noticeably. Father stopped playing with his marble, his heart racing as he watched the physician shrink in front of his eyes.

Suddenly the physician thrust his left hand into his saddlebags and caught everyone by surprise by spraying a packet of medicine in Granddad's face. Something in his left hand flashed—a green-tinted dagger. Everyone stood stupefied as the physician, agile as a black cat, stabbed at Granddad's throat. But Granddad had leaped to his feet and instinctively covered his neck with his arm, which took a long gash from the physician's dagger. Granddad kicked over the table, whipped out his pistol, and got off three quick shots. But since his eyes were stinging from the medicine powder, his shots went wild, one hitting the tent, another slamming into the heavily varnished coffin and ricocheting out the tent opening, the third shattering the mule's right foreleg. It brayed pitifully as a stream of white and red liquid spurted from its smashed kneecap. Tormented by pain, the mule crashed into the paper snow pines and snow willows, which rustled loudly as they crumpled and fell to the ground. The candles around the coffin were sent flying, their glowing wicks and hot wax quickly igniting the paper and straw and immersing Grandma's momentarily gloomy spirit table in a burst of radiance. The tinder-dry sides of the tent curled toward the tongues of flame, as Iron Society soldiers came to life and converged on the tent.

Amid the growing conflagration, the physician, whose skin shone like ancient bronze, rushed Granddad again with his dagger. Black Eye, the trace of a gloating smile on his lips, stood off to the side but didn't fire his pistol. Father whipped out his Luger, cocked it, and fired a single round, striking the physician squarely in his right shoulder. His arm sagged, and the dagger dropped harmlessly onto the table. Father cocked his pistol again and a fresh bullet entered the chamber. Granddad shouted, "Hold your fire!"

Bang, bang, bang. Black Eye's pistol barked three times, and the physician's head exploded like a hardboiled egg. Granddad glared at Black Eye.

Iron Society soldiers swarmed into the tent, where the fire was raging. The mule, shrouded in flames, writhed on the ground.

A mad dash for the opening.

"Put out the fire!" Black Eye screamed. "Hurry! Fifty million tiger-mount bills to whoever saves the coffin!"

The spring rains had only recently passed, and the pond at the head of the village was filled with water. Together the Iron Society soldiers and common folk who had come for the funeral pushed the red billowing cloud of the burning tent to the ground, and put out the fire.

Green smoke rose from the seared coffin. In the muted light of the dying flames, it seemed as sturdy as ever. The curled body of the mule lay beside it, the stench of its scorched hide filling the air.

2

THE DATE FOR GRANDMA'S FUNERAL wasn't changed in spite of the unforeseen events of the night before. The old Iron Society groom bandaged Granddad's injury as best he could, while Black Eye watched with a mocking look and recommended postponing the funeral. Granddad emphatically rejected the suggestion. He didn't sleep a wink that night; he sat on a bench without moving, his bloodshot eyes half open, his cold hand resting on the rough Bakelite handle of his pistol, as though he were glued to the spot.

Father lay on a grass mat and stared at Granddad until he drifted off into a troubled sleep. He woke before daybreak and cast a furtive glance at Granddad, intransigent in the flickering candlelight. His arm was stained with the dark dried blood that had oozed out from under the bandage. Not daring to say anything, Father closed his eyes again until the five funeral musicians hired for the event ran up against the envious local musicians, and their battle of horns disrupted everyone's sleep. Father's nose began to ache; scalding tears flowed from his eyes and ran into his ear. Here I am, he was thinking, nearly sixteen already. I wonder if these turbulent days will ever end. He looked at his father's bloody shoulder and waxen face, and a feeling of desolation that didn't suit his tender years entered his heart.

A lone village rooster announced the coming day, and a predawn breeze carried the acrid smell of spring into the tent, where it caused the candles to flicker. The voices of early risers were now discernible; warhorses tethered to nearby willows began pawing the ground and snorting; Father curled up comfortably, and thought of Beauty, who would one day be my mother, and the tall, robust woman Liu, who should rightfully be considered my third grandma. They had disappeared three months earlier, when Father and Granddad had gone for training with the Iron Society to a remote little outpost south of the railroad tracks; when they returned, their huts were empty and their loved ones gone. The sheds they'd thrown up in the winter of 1939 were covered with cobwebs.

As soon as the red morning sun had made its entrance, the village came to life. Food peddlers raised their voices to attract customers, as the steamy, tantalizing odors of buns in ovens, wontons in pots, and flatcakes in skillets began to waft through the air. A pockfaced peasant argued with a peddler of buns, who refused to accept North Sea currency; the peasant had none of the Iron Society's tiger-mount currency. By then twenty of the little buns had already found their way into the peasant's stomach. "That's all I've got," he said. "Take it or leave it." The crowd urged the peddler to accept the North Sea currency, whose value would be restored as soon as the Jiao-Gao regiment fought its way back. He did, and moved on, raising his voice: "Buns! Meat-filled buns! Fresh from the oven!"

The tent showed the effects of the raging fire of the night before. Iron Society soldiers had dragged the physician and his scrawny mule the fifty paces or so to the inlet, where the stench of their scorched bodies attracted scavenger birds. The area around Grandma's coffin had been swept clean of torn canvas, and the occasional unbroken wineglass lying in the cinders had been smashed by rakes. Grandma's coffin shone in the early-morning light, hideous and scary. The deep-scarlet surface, once so somber and mysterious, had been eaten away by flames, and the thick varnish had melted and split, leaving a maze of deep cracks. The coffin was so enormous that, as my father stood at its sweeping head, it seemed like the tallest thing in the world, and he had trouble breathing. He recalled how the coffin had been seized, and how its owner, an old man who must have been at least a hundred and still wore his white hair in a little queue, had refused to let go of the front edge:

"This is my home. . . . No one else can have it. . . . I was a licentiate in the Great Qing dynasty, even the county magistrate called me 'elder brother.' . . . You'll have to kill me first . . . you pack of brigands. . . ." His tears had given way to curses.

Granddad had stayed behind that day, sending a cavalry detachment under the command of his trusted lieutenant to confiscate the coffin. Father tagged along. He had heard that this particular coffin had been made in the first year of the Republic from four pieces of cypress, four and a half Chinese inches thick. It had been varnished yearly ever since, thirty coats already. The ancient owner rolled on the ground in front of the coffin, and it was impossible to tell if he was laughing or crying. Clearly he had lost his mind. The lieutenant tossed a bundle of Iron Society tiger-mount currency into his hands and said, "We pay for what we take, you old bastard!" The old man ripped open the bundle and began tearing at the bills with his few remaining teeth as he cursed: "You bunch of bandits, not even the emperor stole people's coffins. . . . You brigands . . ." "You old bastard offspring of a stinking donkey!" the cavalry-detachment commander shouted back. "Now, you listen to me. Everybody has a role in the war of resistance against Japan. Consider yourself lucky if they roll you up in sorghum leaves and dump you in the ground. How the hell do you rate a coffin like this? This coffin is for a hero of the resistance!" "What hero?" "The wife of Commander Yu, who is now in charge of the Iron Society, that's who." "Heaven and earth won't allow it, they won't allow it! No woman can sleep in my home. . . . I'll kill myself first. . . ." He ran toward the coffin and rammed his head straight into it, producing a hollow thud. Father saw the scrawny neck bury itself in his chest and the flattened head sink into the space between his bony shoulders. . . . Father could still see the tufts of white hair in the old man's nostrils and the wispy goatee on his chin, which jutted up like a gold ingot.

Granddad made a sling out of black cloth for his injured right arm; his gaunt face was deeply etched with exhaustion. The commander of the cavalry detachment walked over from the ring of horses and asked him something. Father heard him answer, "Five Troubles, you don't need to ask my permission. Go ahead!"

Granddad looked long and meaningfully into the eyes of Five Troubles, who nodded, turned, and walked back to the horses.

Just then Black Eye emerged from one of the other sheds and stood in front of Five Troubles to block his way. "What the hell are you up to?" he asked angrily.

"I'm posting sentries on horseback," Five Troubles said with a scowl.

"I didn't give the order!"

"No, you didn't."

Granddad walked up and said with a wry smile, "Blackie, are you sure you want to take me on?"

"Do whatever you want," Black Eye said. "I was only asking."

Granddad patted his broad, round shoulder with his good hand and said, "You've got a role in this funeral, too. We can settle our differences afterward."

Black Eye just shrugged the shoulder Granddad had patted and screamed angrily at the people milling around the village wall, "Don't stand so damned close! You women there, are you going to wear sackcloth head coverings or not?"

Five Troubles took a brass whistle out of his shirt and blew it three times. Fifty Iron Society soldiers scrambled out of tents near the willow grove and ran up to their tethered horses, which whinnied with excitement. The men were crack soldiers and carried light, excellent weapons: razor-sharp sabers in their hands and Japanese rifles slung over their backs. Five Troubles and four of his burliest men had Russian submachine guns. They mounted, closed ranks, and formed two tight columns. The horses trotted out of the village toward the bridge at the Black Water River. The hair fringing their hooves quivered in the morning breeze; silver light flashed from their glistening metal shoes. Five Troubles led on his powerful dappled colt. Father watched the horses gallop across the smooth black earth like a dark gathering cloud rolling off into the distance.

The funeral master, dressed in a Chinese robe and traditional overjacket, stood on a stool and shouted at the top of his lungs, "Drum-and-bugle corps—"

A drum-and-bugle corps in black uniforms with red caps squeezed through the crowd and ran over to the six-foot-high roadside bandstands, built of wood and reeds. They took their positions.

The funeral master raised his voice: "Ready—"

Horns and woodwinds took up sound and the excited people crushed forward, craning their necks to get a good look. Those in back pushed forward in waves, causing the rickety bandstands to creak and sway. The frightened musicians broke ranks, screaming like demons, and the oxen and donkeys tied to nearby trees raised a noisy complaint.

"What now, Blackie?" Granddad asked courteously.

Black Eye shouted, "Old Three, bring out the troops!"

Fifty or more Iron Society soldiers appeared at once. They prodded the crowd, by then out of control, with their rifles. It was impossible to calculate how many thousands of people had converged on the village to watch the funeral, but they simply overwhelmed the exhausted soldiers.

Black Eye whipped out his pistol and fired into the sky, then again, over the sea of black heads. When the soldiers also began firing wildly into the sky, the front ranks of the surging crowd scurried backward, while those in back kept pushing forward, leaving straight up as the only direction left for those caught in the middle; the crowd looked like a black inchworm in motion. Shrieking children were knocked to the ground. Musicians plunged off the swaying bandstands, their screams merging with those of the people being trampled to create the most piercing scream in a whirlpool of chaotic screams. At least a dozen old and infirm people were trampled to death in the stampede, and months later the rotting carcasses still drew flies.

The soldiers finally managed to quell the riot, and the hapless musicians returned to their bandstands. Realizing the danger, most of the people headed to the outskirts to line the road to Grandma's gravesite and wait for the procession to pass. Five Troubles ordered his troops to patrol the road.

The badly shaken funeral master stood on his tall stool and shouted, "Lesser canopy!"

Two Iron Society soldiers with white sashes around their waists carried up a small, sky-blue canopy, a yard tall, and rectangular, with a ridge down the middle and curled-up ends, like the heads of dragons. Inlaid pieces of glass the color of blood formed the crown.

"Host tablet, please!" the funeral master shouted.

Mother once told me that a host tablet is used for the ghost of the deceased. Later on, I learned that the host tablet actually indicates the social status of the deceased at the time of the funeral, and has nothing to do with ghosts; its common name is "spirit tablet." Leading the procession, amid the flags of the honor guard, it provides testimony of status. Grandma's original host tablet had been burned to a cinder during the fire, and the black paint on the hurried replacement, carried by two handsome Iron Society soldiers, was still wet. The script read:

Born on the Morning of the Ninth Day of the Sixth Month
in the Thirty-second Year of the Great Manchu Emperor Guangxu.
Died at Midday on the Ninth Day of the Eighth Month
in the Twenty-eighth Year of the Republic of China.
Daughter of the Dai Family, First Wife of Yu Zhan'ao,
Guerrilla Commander from Northeast Gaomi Township,
Republic of China, and Leader of the Iron Society.
Age at Time of Death: Thirty-two.
Interred in the Yang of White Horse Mountain
and the Yin of Black Water River.

Grandma's spirit tablet was draped with three feet of white bunting that lent it graceful solemnity. The Iron Society soldiers carefully placed it in the lesser canopy, then stood at attention beside the opening.

The funeral master shouted, "Great canopy!"

The drum-and-bugle corps struck up the music as a stately procession of sixty-four Iron Society soldiers carried in the large scarlet canopy, on which blue crowns the size of watermelons had been inlaid. The buzzing of the onlookers stopped, until the only sounds in the air were the sad strains of the musicians' pipes and flutes and the anguished wails of mothers whose children had been trampled in the riot.

A solitary, repulsive horsefly flitted around Granddad's injured arm, intent on getting at the clotted dark blood. It darted away when he swatted at it and flew around his head, buzzing angrily. The mournful sound of a brass gong seized his heart and called up a string of tangled memories from the fleeting past.

He was only eighteen when he murdered the monk, an act that forced him to flee his home and wander the four corners of the earth. By the time he returned to Northeast Gaomi Township at the age of twenty-two to become a bearer for the Wedding and Funeral Service Company, he had endured all the torments of the society of man, and had suffered the humiliation of sweeping streets in the red-and-black pants of a convict. With a heart as hard as fishbone and the physique of a gorilla, he had what it takes to become a formidable bandit. He carried with him always the humiliation of being slapped in the home of the Qi-family Hanlin scholar, an incident that occurred in Jiao City in 1920.

Golden rays of blazing light shone down on the musicians in the tilted bandboxes, their cheeks bouncing like little balls as they tooted away, sweat dripping from their faces. People stood on tiptoe to watch the funeral, and the light from hundreds of pairs of eyes settled like anxious moonbeams over real people and papier-mâché figurines inside the circle, over an ancient, resplendent culture, as well as a reactionary, backward way of thinking.

Father was wearing thick white knee-length mourning clothes, tied at the waist by a length of gray hemp, and a square mourning hat covering the shaved part of his scalp. The sour odor of sweat from the crowd and the smell of burned varnish from Grandma's coffin fouled the air and made him weak-kneed. Grandma's pitted coffin had grown hideous beyond belief: it lay on the ground, high at the front end and low in the rear, like a huge muddleheaded beast. Father had the feeling that at any moment it might stand up with a yawn and charge the black-massed crowds. In his mind the black coffin began to billow like a cloud, and Grandma's remains, encased in thick wood and the dust of red bricks, seemed to form before his eyes. She had looked remarkably lifelike when Granddad dug up her grassy grave mound beside the Black Water River and raked up layer after layer of rotted sorghum stalks. Just as he would never forget the sight of Grandma looking up at the bright-red sorghum as she lay dying, he would also never forget the sight of her face as it came into view in her grave.

He relived these spectacular experiences as he carried out his complicated filial obligations to the deceased. The funeral master gave the order: "Move the coffin. . . ."

The sixty-four soldiers who had borne the great canopy rushed up to the coffin like bees. "Heave!" they shouted. It didn't budge, as though it had taken root. Granddad swatted the fly away and stared at the men with scorn in his eyes. He signaled to the officer and said, "Get some cotton ropes. Without them you could struggle with the coffin until sunup and never get it into the canopy!" The officer stared at Granddad with apprehension, but Granddad averted his eyes, looking at the Black Water River, which cut a swath through the black plain. . . .

Two flagpoles, whose red paint had peeled off completely, stood in front of the Qi family home in Jiao City, the ancient, rotting wood standing as a symbol of the family's status. The old man, a Hanlin scholar in the latter years of the Qing dynasty, was dead, and his sons and grandsons, who had shared the good life with him, made elaborate funeral preparations. Although everything was ready, they delayed their announcement of the date of interment. The coffin had been placed in a building at the rear of the vast family compound, and in order to move it out to the street they would have to trundle it through seven narrow gates. The managers of a dozen wedding-and-funeral-service companies had come to look at the coffin and the lay of the land, and all had left hanging their heads, even though the Qi family had promised an astonishingly high fee.

Then the news reached the Northeast Gaomi Township Wedding and Funeral Service Company. Payment of five hundred silver dollars to move a coffin was tempting bait to Granddad and his fellow bearers, and threw them into the confusion of a pining young woman who has been given the eye by a handsome young lad.

They went to see the manager, Second Master Cao, and swore they could put Northeast Gaomi Township on the map with this job, not to mention the five hundred in silver the company would make. Second Master Cao sat stiffly in his wooden armchair without so much as passing wind. The only movement was in his cold, intelligent eyes, and the only sound was the gurgling of the water pipe. "Second Master, it's not for the money!" Granddad and the others argued. "A man only lives once. Don't let the world look down on the people of Northeast Gaomi Township!" At this point Second Master Cao shifted his buttocks and slowly farted. "You men go get some rest," he said. "If you botch the job and some of you are crushed to death, so what? But if you lose face for Northeast Gaomi Township and ruin my business, that's another matter altogether. If you're short of money, maybe I can help you out."

With that, he closed his eyes. But the bearers began to clamor: "Second Master, don't destroy our prestige while furthering the ambitions of others!" Second Master Cao replied, "Don't swallow a scythe if your stomach isn't curved. You think earning that five hundred is going to be easy? Well, there are seven gates in the Qi compound, through which you have to carry a coffin filled with quicksilver! Do you hear me? I said quicksilver! Mull that over in your dog brains for a while, and figure out how much that coffin must weigh." He looked at his bearers out of the corner of his eye, then snorted derisively. "Go on, get out of here," he said. "Let the true heroes earn the real money! As for you, well, little men leave little records. Go out and earn your twenty or thirty yuan, and be happy to carry the paper-thin coffins of the poor!"

His comments went straight to the bearers' hearts like poison arrows. Granddad strode forward before anyone else moved and said loudly, "Second Master Cao, working for someone as stupid as you is goddamned suffocating! A dogshit soldier is one thing, but a dogshit general is another! I quit!"

The hot-blooded bearers echoed his shouts. Second Master stood up, thumped Granddad hard on the shoulder, and said with genuine feeling, "Zhan'ao, now *you're* a man! The seed of Northeast Gaomi Township. The Qi family got where it is by taking advantage of people like us, who earn their living as bearers. If you'll work together and get that coffin out, the reputation of Northeast Gaomi Township is assured. You can't buy glory for any amount of money. But don't forget that, as the descendants of a Qing-dynasty Hanlin scholar, they follow strict decorum. This won't be easy. If you can't sleep tonight, stay up and figure out how you're going to get through those seven gates."

Before the bearers had left the office, two strangers walked in and announced that they were stewards from the Hanlin scholar's home, come to enlist the services of the Northeast Gaomi Township bearers.

Once they had stated their purpose, Second Master Cao asked listlessly, "How much will you pay?"

"Five hundred in silver! You won't see a fee like that many times in your life!"

Second Master Cao tossed his silver water pipe onto the table and sneered. "First of all," he said, "we have all the business we need, and second, we've got money to burn. Maybe you'd better go find someone else."

The Qi family stewards smiled knowingly. "Proprietor," one of them said, "we are all businessmen!"

"Yes," Second Master Cao replied, "we are. And you will have no trouble finding someone to do the job for that fee."

He closed his eyes sleepily.

A quick look passed between the two stewards. The one in front spoke up. "Proprietor, let's not beat around the bush. Name your price!"

"I'm not about to risk the lives of my men for a few silver dollars," Second Master Cao replied.

"Six hundred!" the steward said. "In silver!"

Second Master Cao sat there like a stone.

"Seven hundred! Seven hundred silver dollars! In business you have to deal in good conscience, proprietor."

Second Master Cao's lip curled.

"Eight hundred, then, and that's our final offer!"

Second Master Cao's eyes snapped open. "One thousand!" he said flatly.

The steward's cheeks puffed out like those of a man with impacted wisdom teeth. He stared at the harsh, unyielding expression on Second Master Cao's face.

"Proprietor . . . we don't have the authority. . . ."

"Then go back and tell your boss. One thousand. We won't do it for less."

"All right. You'll have your answer tomorrow."

The steward rode up from the county town on a lathered horse with purple mane the following morning. The date was settled, and a deposit of five hundred silver dollars handed over, the remainder payable when the coffin had been successfully moved.

Sixty-four bearers rose well before sunrise on the day of the funeral, ate a hearty breakfast, and set out for Jiao City, stepping on starlight. Second Master Cao brought up the rear on his black donkey.

Granddad recalled that the sky that day was dotted with morning stars. The dew was icy, and the steel hook he'd tucked into his waistband kept thumping against his hip bone. Dawn had broken when they reached town, and the streets were already packed with people who had turned out to watch the funeral. When Granddad and the others heard whispers from the crowd, they raised their heads and thrust out their chests, wanting to leave a gallant impression. Deep down, however, they were worried.

The Qi compound sported a row of tile-roofed buildings half a block in length. Granddad and the other men followed the family servants through three gates into a garden filled with snow trees and silver flowers, the ground covered with paper money, and the smoke of incense all around. Few families could match that kind of grandeur.

The steward walked up to Second Master Cao in the company of the head of the household, a man of about fifty with a tiny hooked nose high above a broad mouth on a gaunt face. He glanced at the team of men and, with a nod to Second Master Cao, said, "A thousand silver dollars requires an appropriate amount of decorum."

Second Master Cao returned his nod and followed him through the final gate.

When he emerged from the house, his shiny face had turned ashen and his long-nailed fingers trembled. He called the bearers over to the wall and said with a gnashing of his teeth, "We've had it boys!"

"What's the problem, Second Master?" Granddad asked him.

"Men, the coffin's as wide as the door, and on top of it there's a bowl filled to the brim with wine. He says he'll penalize us a hundred silver dollars for every drop we spill!"

They were speechless. The wails of mourners inside the funeral chamber floated on the air like a song.

"What should we do, Zhan'ao?" Second Master Cao asked.

"This is no time for the chickenhearted," Granddad replied. "We'll carry the thing out even if it's filled with iron balls."

"Okay, men," Second Master Cao said in a low voice, "let's go. If you get it out, you're like my own sons. The thousand-dollar fee is all yours. I don't want any of it!"

"No more of that kind of talk!" Granddad said with a quick glance at him.

"Then let's get ready," Second Master Cao said. "Zhan'ao, Sikui, you two man the cable, one in front and one in back. I want twenty of you other men inside, and as soon as the coffin is off the ground, slip under it and prop it on your backs. The rest of you stay out here and move in rhythm as I beat the gong. And, men, Cao the Second is in your debt!" Second Master Cao, normally the tyrant, bowed deeply this time.

The head of the Qi household walked up with a retinue of servants and said, "Not so fast. We need to search you first."

"What sort of decorum is that?" Second Master Cao shot back angrily.

"The decorum of one thousand silver dollars!" the head of the household replied haughtily.

The Qi family servants removed the steel hooks the men had hidden in their waistbands and tossed them to the ground.

Okay! Granddad thought. Anybody can lift a coffin by using steel hooks. A stirring emotion, like that of a fearless man on the way to his execution, surged into his heart. After cinching his pant cuffs and waistband as tight as he could, he took a deep breath and entered the funeral chamber. The mourners—boys and girls—stopped wailing and stared wide-eyed at the bearers, then at the bowl of wine on top of the coffin. The smoky air was nearly suffocating, and the faces of the living were like hideous floating masks. The ebony coffin of the old Hanlin scholar rested on four stools like a huge boat in drydock.

Granddad uncoiled a thick hempen cable and ran it under the coffin from end to end. The tips were finished with loops of twisted white cotton. The other bearers strung thick, water-soaked cotton ropes under the cable and held on to the ends.

Second Master Cao raised his gong. The sound split the air. Granddad squatted down at the head of the coffin, the most dangerous, the heaviest, the most glorious spot of all. The thick cotton rope pulled hard against his neck and shoulders, and he realized how heavy the coffin was before he'd even straightened up.

Second Master Cao banged his gong three more times. A shout of "Heave!" cleaved the air.

Granddad took a deep breath and held it, sending all his energy and strength down to his knees. He dimly heard Second Master Cao's command; dazed though he was, he forced the strength concentrated in his knees to burst forth, fantasizing that the coffin containing the corpse of the Hanlin scholar had begun to levitate and float atop the curling incense smoke like a ship on the ocean. The fantasy was shattered by the pressure of the brick floor on his buttocks and sharp pains up and down his backbone.

The enormous coffin remained anchored in place like a tree with deep roots. Second Master Cao nearly fainted when he saw his bearers crumple to the floor like sparrows that had smashed into windows. He knew they were finished. The curtain had come crashing down on this drama! There was the vigorous, energetic Yu Zhan'ao, sitting on the floor like an old woman holding a dead infant. There was no mistaking it now: the drama had ended in complete failure.

Granddad imagined the mocking laughter of the Hanlin scholar in his tomb of shifting quicksilver.

"Men," Second Master Cao said, "you have to carry it out . . . not for my sake . . . for Northeast Gaomi Township. . . ."

Bong! Bong! This time the sound of the gong nearly tore Granddad's heart to shreds.

Squeezing his eyes shut, he began raising himself up, crazily, suicidally (amid the chaos of lifting the coffin, Second Master Cao saw the bearer called Little Rooster quickly thrust his lips into the bowl on top of the coffin and take a big gulp of wine). With a tremor, the coffin rose up off the stools. The deathly stillness of the room was broken only by the cracking of human joints.

Granddad had no way of knowing that his face was as pale as death. All he knew was that the thick cotton rope was strangling him, that his neck was about to snap, and that his vertebrae were compressed until they must have looked like flattened hawthorns. When he found he was unable to straighten up, it took only a split second for despair to undermine his resolve, and his knees began to buckle like molten steel. The quicksilver shifted, causing the head of the coffin to press down even harder on him. The bowl on top sloped to one side, the colorless wine inside touching the rim and threatening to overflow. Members of the Qi family stared at it wide-eyed.

Second Master Cao gave Granddad a vicious slap.

Granddad would later recall that the slap had set his ears ringing, and that all feeling in his waist, legs, shoulders, and neck seemed to be squeezed out of his consciousness, as though claimed by some unknown spirit. A curtain of black gauze fell in front of his eyes, and he straightened up, raising the coffin more than three feet off the ground. Six bearers immediately slipped under the coffin on all fours and supported it on their backs. Granddad finally released a mouthful of sticky breath. The breath that followed seemed to him warm and gentle as it rose slowly and passed through his throat. . . .

The coffin was lugged past all seven gates and placed in a bright-blue great canopy.

As soon as the thick white cloth rope fell from Granddad's back, he forced his mouth open, and streams of scarlet blood spurted from his mouth and nostrils. . . .

3

DRESSED IN MOURNING CLOTHES, Father stood facing southwest on a high bench and thumped the waxwood butt of his rifle on the ground as he shouted: "Mother—Mother—head southwest—a broad highway—a long treasure boat—a fleet-footed steed—lots of traveling money—Mother—rest in sweetness—buy off your pain—"

The funeral master had ordered him to sing this send-off song three times, since only a loved one's calls can guide the spirit to the southwestern paradise. But he got through it only once before choking on hot, sour tears of grief. Another long-drawn-out "Mom" escaped from his lips, fanned out, and glided unsteadily in the air like a scarlet butterfly, its wings carrying it to the southwest, where the wilderness was broad and the airstream swirled, and where the bright sunlight raised a white screen over the Black Water River. Powerless to scale the translucent screen, the wisp of "Mom" turned and headed east after a momentary hesitation, despite Father's desire to send her to the southwestern paradise. But Grandma didn't want to go there. Instead she followed the meandering dike, taking fistcakes to Granddad's troops, turning her head back from time to time to signal her son, my father, with her golden eyes.

Twenty days earlier, Father had gone with Granddad to dig up Grandma's grave. It was definitely not a good day for swallows, for a dozen sodden clouds, like torn cotton wadding, hung in the low sky, reeking like rotting fish and spoiled shrimp. An ill wind carried a stream of sinister air down the Black Water River, along whose banks the corpses of dogs shattered by muskmelon grenades during the battle with humans the previous winter lay decomposing amid the sallow water grass; swallows migrating north from Hainan Island flew across the river with dread, as frogs below began their mating ritual, gaunt bodies caught up in the passions of love following a winter of hibernation.

Father stood with Granddad and nineteen Iron Society soldiers, all carrying hoes and pickaxes, at the head of Grandma's grave. Golden flowers of bitterweed, the first of the year, dotted the faded black earth of the column of mounds.

Three minutes of silence.

"Douguan, you're sure this is the one?" Granddad asked.

"It's this one," Father replied. "I could never forget."

"Okay," Granddad said. "Start digging!"

The Iron Society soldiers raised their tools, but were reluctant to start. So Granddad took a pickax from one of them, aimed at the mound, which arched up like a woman's breast, and swung with all his might, to bury the tool in the dirt with a heavy thud. He then pulled it toward him, scooping out a chunk of the black earth.

Father's heart knotted up as the pickax split the grave mound, and at that instant he experienced fear and loathing for Granddad's ruthlessness.

"Dig it up," Granddad said feebly.

Forming a ring around Grandma's grave, the soldiers began to chop and dig, leveling the mound in no time. Father's thoughts returned to the night of the ninth day of the eighth lunar month, 1939, when they had buried Grandma. Fires raging on the bridge and torches ringing her body had illuminated her dead face, nearly bringing it back to life, before it was swallowed up by the black earth. Now the likeness was being dug up again, and Father grew tense as the layers were pared away, until he thought he saw Grandma's smile as she kissed death through the dirt separating them.

The Iron Society soldiers stopped digging when the final layer of dirt covering the sorghum was removed and cast pleading looks at Granddad and Father, who saw their noses twitch as the overpowering stench of decay rose from the grave. To Father, who breathed in greedily, it was the odor of the milk he'd suckled at Grandma's breast.

"Clear it away!" Granddad ordered, his black eyes devoid of pity. "Clear it away!"

Reluctantly they bent down and began pulling the sorghum out of the grave. Transparent drops of water oozed from the naked stalks, turned by decay into the glossy red of moist jade.

Deeper and deeper they went, the stench growing stronger. But to Father it was the rich aroma of sorghum wine, intoxicating, dizzying. He wanted to see Grandma as soon as possible, but the prospect also frightened him. The sorghum covering grew ever thinner, yet he felt the distance between him and Grandma increase. The final layer of stalks suddenly rustled loudly, wrenching shouts of alarm from some of the soldiers and striking others dumb with fear. Their faces were ashen, and only Granddad's insistence gave them the courage to peek down into the grave.

Father watched as four brown field voles scrambled up the sides of the unearthed grave, while a fifth one, pure white, squatted on a supremely beautiful sorghum stalk in the middle of the grave. Everyone stared at the brown voles as they scampered away; meanwhile, the white one perched haughtily without stirring, staring back with its tiny, jet-black eyes. Father picked up a dirt clod and hurled it into the grave. The vole sprang two feet into the air, fell back, and scurried madly around the edges. With loathing swelling their insides, the soldiers rained dirt clods down on the white vole until it lay smashed in the middle of the grave.

According to Father, Grandma emerged from the resplendent, aromatic grave as lovely as a flower, as in a fairy tale. But the faces of the Iron Society soldiers contorted whenever they described in gory detail the hideous shape of her corpse and the suffocating stench issuing from the grave. Father called them liars. His senses were particularly keen at the time, he recalled, and as the last few stalks were removed, Grandma's sweet, beautiful smile made the area crackle as though swept by a raging fire. His only regret was how fleeting the moment had been. For, when Grandma's body was lifted out of the grave, her lustrous beauty and delicate fragrance turned into a mist and floated gently away, leaving behind only a white skeleton.

After lifting the body out of the grave, the soldiers ran down to the bank of the Black Water River and vomited dark-green bile into the dark-green water. Granddad spread out a piece of white cloth and told Father to help him lift Grandma's skeleton onto it. Infected by the sound of vomiting in the river, Father felt a spasm in his neck, and hacking sounds erupted from his throat. He hated the thought of touching the pale-white bones.

"Douguan," Granddad said, "you don't think your own mom's bones are too dirty to touch, do you? Not you!"

Moved by the rare tragic look on Granddad's face, Father bent down and tentatively reached out to touch Grandma's pale leg bone, which was so icy it froze his guts. Granddad tried to lift the skeleton by the shoulder blades, but it disintegrated and landed in a heap on the ground. A pair of red ants crawled in the sockets that had once been home to Grandma's limpid eyes, their antennae vibrating. Father threw down Grandma's leg bone, turned tail, and ran, filling the air with howls of grief.

4

AT NOON, the funeral master announced loudly, "Begin the procession," and mourners swept into the fields like a human tide, followed by the Yu family bier, moving slowly toward them like a floating iceberg. Large open tents in which sumptuous road offerings were displayed had been placed on both sides of the road every couple of hundred yards. Cavalry troops led by Five Troubles formed a guard on either side of the road, galloping round and round.

A fat monk in a yellow robe, his left shoulder and arm exposed, led the procession with a halberd from which chimes hung, tinkling as it spun around his body, sometimes flying up in the air toward the onlookers. At least half the onlookers recognized him as the pauper monk from the Tianqi Temple who never burned incense and never chanted the Buddha's name, preferring to drink great bowlfuls of wine and boldly partake of meat and fish. He kept a skinny yet uncommonly fertile little woman, who presented him with a whole brood of little monks. He opened a passage through the crowds by flinging his halberd at their heads, his face beaming.

An Iron Society soldier followed, holding a long pole with a spirit-calling banner woven from thirty-two white strips of paper, one for each of Grandma's years; it fluttered and snapped, though there wasn't a breath of wind. Then came the banner of honor, held ten feet in the air by a strapping young Iron Society soldier, its white silk ornamented with large black letters:

Casket of the Woman Dai, 32-Year-Old Wife of Yu Zhan'ao,
Guerrilla Commander of Northeast Gaomi Township,
Republic of China.

Behind the banner of honor came the lesser canopy, in which Grandma's spirit tablet lay, and behind that, the great canopy encasing her coffin. Sixty-four Iron Society soldiers marched in perfect cadence to the mournful strains of the funeral music. Father, white mourning hood over his head and shoulders, a willow grief-stick in his hand, was being carried by two Iron Society soldiers. His desolate wails were the standard dry variety—his eyes were dry, and blank. Thunder with no rain. This sort of dry wailing was more moving than tearful shrieks, and many of the onlookers were deeply touched by his performance.

Granddad and Black Eye walked shoulder to shoulder behind my father, their solemn expressions belying the conflicts raging inside them.

At least twenty armed Iron Society soldiers surrounded Granddad and Black Eye, their bayonets glinting deep blue under the sun's rays. They in turn were followed by a dozen musicians from Northeast Gaomi Township playing beautiful music, and some men on stilts. Two lion figures brought up the rear, waving their tails and swinging their heads to the antics of a bigheaded child who tumbled over the roadway.

The procession snaked along for at least two li, the going made difficult by the crowds of people jamming the narrow roadway and the need to stop at each roadside tent to pay respects to the spirits; when the coffin was halted, incense was burned, and the funeral master, bronze wine vessel in hand, performed an age-old ritual, all of which combined to keep the procession at a snail's pace.

Three li outside the village, the procession stopped to pay respects to the spirits. As always, the funeral master performed the ritual somberly and conscientiously. All of a sudden a shot rang out at the head of the procession, and the Iron Society soldier holding the banner of honor slipped slowly to the ground, his bamboo pole crashing down on the onlookers by the side of the road. The gunfire caused the crowd to scurry like ants, screaming and wailing like a raging river that has breached its dikes.

As the sound of the rifle shot died out, a dozen or so shiny black grenades came arching out of the crowds on either side of the road and landed at the feet of the Iron Society soldiers, spewing puffs of white smoke.

"Villagers, on your bellies!" someone shouted.

But they were packed so tightly they could barely move, and as the grenades exploded, powerful golden blasts ripped through the sky. At least a dozen soldiers were killed or wounded, including Black Eye, who was struck in the hip. Covering the bleeding wound with his hand, he screamed, "Fulai—Fulai—"

But Fulai, who was about Father's age, was beyond answering, beyond coming to his aid. The night before, when Father had given Fulai the physician's green marble, he'd put it in his mouth as though it were a precious gem and rolled it around with his tongue. Now Father saw the marble anchored in the fresh blood flowing from Fulai's mouth, as green as jade, as green as anything could ever be, emitting a radiance like the legendary fox-spirit that spat out the elixir of life.

A piece of shrapnel hit the jugular vein of the funeral master, and he fell to the ground, his bronze wine vessel crashing beside him and spilling its contents onto the black earth, where it turned into a light mist. The great canopy tipped to one side, revealing Grandma's black coffin.

"Fellow villagers," came another shout, "on your bellies!" Another salvo of grenades. With his arms wrapped around my father, Granddad hit the ground and rolled into a roadside ditch, where dozens of feet trampled on his injured arm. At least half of the Iron Society soldiers had thrown down their weapons and were fleeing helter-skelter. The rest stood mesmerized, quietly waiting for the grenades to explode. Finally, Granddad spotted a man whose face he knew throwing a grenade. It was the Jiao-Gao regiment! Little Foot Jiang's men!

Another salvo of violent explosions. Gunsmoke rolled up and down the roadway, dust flew into the sky, and chunks of shrapnel shrieked in all directions, as people were cut down like harvested grain.

Granddad drew his pistol, awkwardly, and aimed at the bobbing head of the Jiao-Gao soldier. He squeezed the trigger, and the bullet hit the man right between the eyes, popping his green eyeballs out of their sockets like a pair of moth eggs.

"Charge, comrades, get their weapons!" someone shouted from the crowd.

Now that the shock had worn off, Black Eye and his Iron Society soldiers turned their guns on the crowd. Every bullet that left a barrel bit into flesh; every shell passed through at least one body and either embedded itself in another or gouged a lovely curving scar in the black earth.

Granddad scanned the faces of the Jiao-Gao troops. They were struggling like drowning men, and the looks of rapacious brutality hit Granddad like a knife in the heart. One after another, he smashed their faces with awesome precision, confident that he hit no innocent bystanders.

In the village, a bugle sounded the charge, and Granddad saw a hundred or more shouting Jiao-Gao soldiers running toward them, waving rifles, swords, and clubs behind their leader, Little Foot Jiang. In the sorghum field to the south, Five Troubles smacked his dappled horse on the rump and took off at full speed, leading his troops. The Iron Society soldiers re-formed ranks on Granddad's shrill orders and, taking cover behind the cover of funeral flags and memorial tents, fired at Little Foot Jiang's men.

Granddad's Iron Society recruiting exploits had seriously depleted the Jiao-Gao strength; yet the poorly armed soldiers advanced courageously, filled with the spirit of sacrifice, and even as their comrades were cut down by bullets, they charged, brandishing primitive weapons good only for hand-to-hand combat. They came in waves, awesome in their display of defiance as they overran the Iron Society soldiers. As soon as they were within range, the Jiao-Gao soldiers hurled grenades, routing the panicky Iron Society soldiers, who were pursued mercilessly by shrapnel that ripped their flesh.

As he watched the rout of his soldiers, Five Troubles grew anxious and confused. Angrily, he hacked at the men around him, while his horse bit anyone within range, like a dog. He led his cavalry troops onto the road, only to be met by a salvo of wooden-handled grenades lobbed by the Jiao-Gao regiment. Years later, Granddad and Father would recall the practiced way the Jiao-Gao soldiers used their grenades, much as a chess master recalls his defeat at the hands of an inferior opponent who has employed a trick move.

As they retreated toward the Black Water River that day, Father was hit in the buttocks by a reconditioned bullet from a beat-up old Hanyang rifle fired by a Jiao-Gao soldier. Granddad had never seen a bullet wound quite like it. Since the Jiao-Gao regiment was so short of ammunition, they collected their spent cartridges after each battle to make new shells. Whatever dogshit material they used for the bullet, it melted by the time it left the muzzle, and pursued its target like a gob of warm snot.

The latest salvo of hand grenades cut a swath through Five Troubles' cavalry troops, sending the men flying and the horses tumbling. Five Troubles' dappled mount jumped into the air with a pitiful whinny and threw its rider into a shallow ditch beside the road. No sooner had Five Troubles crawled out than he spotted some Jiao-Gao soldiers coming at him with glistening bayonets. After aiming his submachine gun, he opened fire and cut down about ten of them.

But three Jiao-Gao soldiers, gnashing their teeth in anger, buried their bayonets in the chest and belly of the man who had caused the deaths of so many. Five Troubles grabbed one of the heated barrels with both hands and lurched forward. His black eyeballs rolled up and disappeared in his head, and a stream of hot blood emerged from his mouth. The Jiao-Gao soldiers, straining hard, withdrew their blood-drenched bayonets from Five Troubles, who remained standing for an instant before settling slowly into the ditch, where the sun's rays shone down on the fine porcelain whites of his eyes.

The extermination of the cavalry unit shattered the Iron Society soldiers' morale. Those who had fought on stubbornly behind the cover of funeral flags broke and fled to the south, dragging their rifles behind them, and not even Granddad's and Black Eye's commands could hold them. Heaving a long sigh, Granddad wrapped his arms around Father, then took off toward the Black Water River, firing as he ran.

The valiant warriors of the Jiao-Gao regiment collected the Iron Society soldiers' abandoned weapons and mounted the chase, Little Foot Jiang in the lead. Granddad scooped up an abandoned Japanese .38 rifle, threw himself down behind a pile of dung, and pulled back the bolt to send a cartridge into the chamber. His racing heart made his shoulder jerk up and down and caused Little Foot Jiang's head to slip in and out of his sights. So he aimed for the chest, just to be on the safe side. When the rifle fired, Father heard the crack and saw Little Foot Jiang's arms fly out as he fell headlong to the ground. The troops behind him threw themselves down in terror. That was what Granddad was waiting for; grabbing Father by the arm, he ran like the wind to catch up with his retreating men.

Granddad's shot had hit Little Foot Jiang in the ankle. A medic rushed up and bandaged it for him, and, with iron determination, he ordered, "Get moving, forget about me, follow them! I want their weapons! Every last one of them. Charge, comrades!"

Invigorated by Little Foot Jiang's exhortations, the Jiao-Gao soldiers jumped to their feet and mounted an even more furious chase in the face of the occasional round fired their way. The exhausted Iron Society soldiers, not wanting to run anymore, threw down their weapons and waited to surrender.

"Fight!" Granddad bellowed. "Pick up your guns and fight!"

"Commander," a young soldier said, "don't make them madder than they already are. They only want our weapons. Let's give them what they want, so we can all go home and plant our sorghum."

Black Eye fired a shot, and the Jiao-Gao soldiers responded with a fusillade of fire from three submachine guns, wounding three Iron Society soldiers and killing another.

Black Eye was about to fire another shot when a burly Iron Society soldier wrapped his arms around him. "That's enough, Commander," the man said. "Don't provoke those mad dogs."

The Jiao-Gao troops were nearly upon them when Granddad reluctantly lowered his rifle.

Just then a machine gun began barking like a dog from behind the Black Water River dike. An even more brutal fight awaited the Iron Society and Jiao-Gao regiments on the other side of the dike.

5

THE GLOOMY, RAINY AUTUMN OF 1939 was followed by a freezing winter. Dogs that had been shot to death or blown up by hand grenades hurled by Father, Mother, and their martyred friends lay in the soggy marshland, frozen together with fallen stalks of sorghum. Dogs killed by blasts of Japanese muskmelon grenades in the Black Water River and those that had struggled to become pack leaders, only to die cruelly, lay icebound among withered water grasses and weeds along the banks. Famished crows pecked at the frozen corpses with their purple beaks. Like black clouds they soared in the sky between the riverbank and the marshland.

Granddad, Father, Mother, and the woman Liu hibernated in their dilapidated village through the endless winter. Father and Mother were already aware of the relationship between Granddad and the woman Liu, but it didn't bother them. The way she looked after everyone during these trying days was something my family remembered even decades later. Her name was formally added to our "family scroll," where she is listed just below Passion, who follows Grandma, who is second only to Granddad.

It was the woman Liu who had consoled Granddad after Father lost one of his testicles. "Single-stalk garlic is always the hottest," she said. With her encouragement, Beauty, who would become my mother, had aroused Father's wounded, ugly, strange-looking little pecker, thereby ensuring the continuation of our family line.

All this had happened in late autumn, when migrating wild geese often appeared in the sky, and fangs of ice were forming in the marshland. With the arrival of blustery northwest winds, one of the coldest winters in history began.

The shack was piled high with dry sorghum leaves, and there was plenty of grain in the kitchen. To supplement their diet with more nutritious food and keep up their strength and health, Granddad and Father often went dog-hunting. The death of Red had turned the dogs of Northeast Gaomi Township from a roving pack into a bunch of individual marauders. They were never organized again. Human nature once more won out over canine nature, and the paths gouged out by the dogs were slowly reclaimed by the black earth.

Father and Granddad went hunting every other day, bagging only a single dog each time. The meat provided necessary nutrition and internal heat, and by the spring of 1940, Father had grown two fists taller. Having fed on human corpses, the dogs were strong and husky; eating a winter's supply of fatty dog meat was, for Father, the same as eating a winter's supply of human flesh. Later he would grow into a tall, husky man who could kill without batting an eye. I wonder if that had anything to do with the fact that, indirectly, he had cannibalized his own people?

One night a warm southeasterly wind blew, and the next morning they could hear the ice cracking on the Black Water River. New buds the size of rice appeared on weeping willows, and tiny pink flowers exploded onto the branches of peach trees. Early-arriving swallows flew through the air above the marshland and the river, hordes of wild rabbits chased one another in mating rituals, and the grass turned green. After several misty rain showers, Granddad and Father took off their dogskin clothing. Day and night, the black soil of Northeast Gaomi Township was the scene of endless stirrings by a host of living, growing things.

Now that spring had arrived, Granddad and Father felt confined in the shack. They went out to walk along the dikes of the Black Water River, then crossed the stone bridge to visit the graves of Grandma and of Granddad's fallen soldiers.

"Let's join the Jiao-Gao regiment, Dad," Father said.

Granddad shook his head.

"How about joining up with Detachment Leader Leng?"

Granddad shook his head.

The sun shone bright and beautiful that morning. Not a cloud in the sky. They stood speechless before Grandma's grave.

East of the bridge, far off in the distance, they saw seven horses trotting sluggishly toward them on the northern dike. When they got closer, Father and Granddad recognized the freshly shaved foreheads of the Iron Society. Leading them was a swarthy man with a ring of dark moles around his right eye. It was Black Eye, who had already had an illustrious reputation way back when Granddad was living a bandit's life. Back then bandit gangs and the Iron Society went their own ways—well water not mixing with river water—and Granddad had held him in contempt. Then, in the early winter of 1929, Granddad and Black Eye had fought on the dusty bank of the Salty River, with no winner and no loser.

The seven horses trotted up to the dike in front of Grandma's grave, where Black Eye reined in his mount. Instinctively Granddad rested his hand on the handle of his Japanese "tortoiseshell" pistol.

"So it's you, Commander Yu!" Black Eye sat steadily in his saddle.

Granddad's hand shook. "It's me!"

When Granddad challenged him with a dark look, Black Eye chuckled dully and dismounted. He gazed down at Grandma's grave. "She's dead?"

"She's dead!" Granddad said tersely.

"Goddamn it!" Black Eye spat out angrily. "A good woman like that winding up dead as soon as you get your hands on her!"

Flames shot from Granddad's eyes.

"If she'd come with me back then, it wouldn't have turned out like this!" Black Eye said.

Granddad drew his pistol and aimed it at Black Eye.

"If you've got the balls," Black Eye said calmly, "you'll avenge her. Killing me only proves how chickenhearted you are!"

What is love? Everybody has his own answer. But this demon of an emotion has spelled doom for more valiant men and lovely, capable women than you can count. Based upon Granddad's romantic history, my father's tempestuous love affairs, and the pale desert of my own experiences, I've framed a pattern of love that applies to the three generations of my family:

The first ingredient of love—fanaticism—is composed of heart-piercing suffering: the blood flows through the intestines and bowels, and out the body as feces the consistency of pitch. The second ingredient—cruelty—is composed of merciless criticism: each partner in the love affair wants to skin the other alive, physically and psychologically. They both want to rip out each other's blood vessels, muscles, and every writhing internal organ, including the heart. The third ingredient—frigidity—is composed of a protracted heavy silence. Icy emotions frost the faces of people in love. Their teeth chatter so violently they can't talk, no matter how badly they want to.

In the summer of 1923, Granddad lifted Grandma down off her donkey, carried her into the sorghum field, and laid her on his straw rain cape; thus began the tragic "internal-bleeding" phase. In the summer of 1926, when Father was two, Grandma's servant Passion became the third member of a triangle, thrusting her lovely thighs between Granddad and Grandma; this was when the "skinning alive" began. Their love thus moved from the heaven of fanaticism to the hell of cruelty.

Passion was one year younger than Grandma, who turned nineteen in the spring of 1926. The eighteen-year-old girl had a strong, healthy body, long legs, and large, unbound feet. Her dark face featured round watery eyes, a pert little nose, and thick, sensual lips. The distillery was flourishing at the time, and our sorghum wine had taken eighteen counties in nine prefectures by storm. The air was redolent with the aroma of wine. In the intoxicating atmosphere, when the days were long and the nights short, the men and women in my family had enormous capacities for wine. Granddad and Grandma, of course; but even the woman Liu, who had never tasted wine before, was now able to drink half a decanter at one sitting.

Passion, who at first only drank to accompany Grandma, eventually couldn't live without her wine. The alcohol enlivened them and instilled them with the courage to face danger fearlessly and view death as a homecoming. They abandoned themselves to pleasure, living an existence of moral degeneracy and fickle passions. Granddad had become a bandit by then: he coveted not riches, but a life of vengeance and countervengeance, a never-ending cycle of cruelty that turned a decent commoner into a blackhearted, ruthless bandit with great skills and courage to match.

After killing Spotted Neck and his gang, and nearly paralyzing my greedy great-granddad with fear, he left the distillery and began a romantic life of looting and plundering. The seeds of banditry in Northeast Gaomi Township were planted everywhere: the government produced bandits, poverty produced bandits, adultery and sex produced bandits, banditry produced bandits. Word of Granddad's prowess in single-handedly wiping out the seemingly invincible Spotted Neck and his gang at the Black Water River spread like wildfire, and lesser bandits flocked to him. As a result, the years 1925 to 1928 marked a golden age of banditry in Northeast Gaomi Township. Granddad's reputation rocked the government.

This was during the tenure of the inscrutable Nine Dreams Cao, whom Granddad still detested for having beaten him with the shoe sole until his skin peeled and his flesh gaped. His day of vengeance against the Gaomi county magistrate would come.

In early 1926, he and two of his men kidnapped Nine Dreams Cao's fourteen-year-old son in front of the government office. Carrying the screaming little boy under one arm and holding his pistol in the other hand, Granddad swaggered up and down the granite-paved street in front of the official residence. The shrewd, competent enforcer, Little Yan, pursued him with county soldiers, shouting and shooting from a safe distance. Granddad spun around and put his pistol to the boy's temple. "You there, Yan!" he shouted. "Get your ass back there and tell that old dog Nine Dreams Cao that he can have his son back for ten thousand silver dollars. If I don't get it within three days, this kidnap is going to end with a dead kid!"

"Old Yu," Little Yan asked genially, "where do we make the exchange?"

"In the middle of the Black Water River bridge."

Granddad and his two men filed out of town, the boy still under his arm. He had white teeth and red lips, and though his features were contorted by all that crying, he was still a handsome boy. "Stop crying," Granddad told him. "I'm your foster-dad, and I'm taking you to see your foster-mom!" He really started crying then, which tried Granddad's patience. Waving his short, glistening sword under the boy's nose, he threatened, "I said no more crying. If you keep it up, I'll slice off your ear!" The boy stopped crying immediately and was carried along between the two younger bandits with a stunned look on his face.

When they were about five li out of town, Granddad heard hoofbeats behind him. Spinning around to look, he saw a cloud of dust, raised by galloping horses. Granddad ordered the two bandits over to the side of the road, where the three of them huddled together with their hostage, a gun at his head.

The horsemen, led by the shrewd Little Yan, circled Granddad and his men, then headed toward Northeast Gaomi Township, a trail of dust in their wake.

Momentarily confused, Granddad quickly realized what was happening. "Damn!" he said, slapping his thigh. "We're wasting our time with this!"

His two young accomplices asked stupidly, "Where are they going?"

Without stopping to answer, Granddad fired at the retreating horsemen; but they were out of range, and his bullets disappeared into the dust.

Little Yan led his men to our village in Northeast Gaomi Township and straight to our house. He had a speedy horse and he knew the way. Meanwhile, Granddad was running as fast as his legs would carry him. Nine Dreams Cao's son, used to a life of ease and luxury, managed only a li or so before he collapsed. "Finish him off and be done with it," one of the younger bandits suggested. "He's too much trouble."

"Little Yan's going after my son," Granddad said, as he picked up Young Master Cao, hoisted him over his shoulder, and took off at a trot. When the younger bandits urged him to speed up, he said, "We're already too late, so there's no need to go any faster. Everything will be all right as long as this little bastard stays alive."

Back in the village, Little Yan and his men burst into the house, grabbed Grandma and Father, and tied them onto a horse.

"You blind dog!" Grandma railed. "I'm Magistrate Cao's foster-daughter!"

With a sinister smile, Little Yan said, "His foster-daughter is precisely who he told us to nab."

Little Yan and his horsemen met up with Granddad on the road. Hostages on both sides had guns at their heads as they passed so close they could have reached out and touched each other; but no one dared make a move.

Granddad looked up at Father, who was held tightly in Little Yan's arms, and at Grandma, whose hands were tied behind her back.

"Zhan'ao," she said to Granddad, who had a dejected look on his face, "let my foster-dad's son go, so they'll set us free."

Granddad squeezed the boy's hand tightly. He knew he'd have to let him go sooner or later, but not just now.

When it was time to exchange the hostages at the wooden bridge over the Black Water River, Granddad mobilized nearly all the bandits in Northeast Gaomi Township, over 230 of them. Their weapons loaded and ready, they lay or sat around the northern bridgehead.

At midmorning, the magistrate's soldiers arrived, winding their way down from the southern dike of the river. Four of them carried a sedan chair that rocked above them. When they reached the southern bridgehead, Nine Dreams Cao greeted Granddad. With a smile on his face he said, "Zhan'ao, how could the husband of my foster-daughter kidnap his own nephew? If you needed money, all you had to do was ask for it."

"It's not the money. I haven't forgotten those three hundred lashes with the shoe sole!"

Rubbing his hands together and laughing, Nine Dreams Cao said, "It was a mistake, all a mistake! But if it hadn't been for that beating we'd never have met. Worthy son-in-law, you achieved real glory by eliminating Spotted Neck, and I will make that known to my superiors, who will in turn reward you for your deed."

"Who cares about being rewarded by you for my deeds?" Granddad said rudely. His words belied the fact that his heart was softening.

Little Yan pulled back the curtain of the sedan chair, and Grandma slowly emerged with Father in her arms.

She started to walk out onto the bridge, but was stopped by Little Yan. "Old Yu," he said, "bring Young Master Cao out onto the bridge. We'll release them on command."

"Now!" Little Yan called out when both sides were ready.

With a shout of "Dad!" Little Master Cao ran toward the southern bridgehead, while Grandma walked with Father at a dignified pace to the northern side.

Granddad's men aimed their short rifles; the government soldiers aimed long ones.

Grandma and the Cao boy met in the middle of the bridge, where she bent over to say something to him. But, with a loud wail, he skirted her and ran like the wind to the southern bridgehead.

This incident witnessed the end of the golden days of banditry in Northeast Gaomi Township.

In the third month of 1926, Great-Grandma passed away. With Father in her arms, Grandma rode one of our black mules back to her childhood home to make funeral arrangements, planning to be gone only three days and never imagining that heaven would interfere to make that impossible. On the day after her departure, the skies opened up and released a torrential rain so dense that even the wind couldn't penetrate it. Since Granddad and his men could no longer stay in the greenwoods, they returned to their homes, for in such weather even swallows hole up in their nests to twitter dreamily. Government soldiers were kept from going out, but they really weren't needed anyway, since the truce between Nine Dreams Cao and Granddad was still holding. The bandits returned to their homes, stuck their weapons under their pillows, and slept the days away.

Granddad was surprised to learn from Passion that Grandma had braved the violent rainstorm to return to her parents' home to arrange for her mother's funeral. In her loathing for her parents, Grandma had refused to have anything to do with them for years. But as they say, "Strong winds eventually cease, unhappy families return to peace."

The rain sluiced down from the eaves like waterfalls. The murky water rose waist-high, saturating the soil and eroding the bases of walls. Rain-weary, Granddad fell into a state of numbness: drinking and sleeping, sleeping and drinking, until the distinction between day and night blurred, and chaos reigned. More restless than he had ever felt in his life, he scratched the curly black hair on his chest and thighs, but the more he scratched the more they itched. The kang exuded a woman's acrid, salty smell. He threw a wine bowl onto the kang. It shattered. A little rat with a gaping mouth jumped out of the cabinet, gave him a mocking look, and leaped up onto the window ledge, where it stood on its hind legs and cleaned its mouth with its front claws. Granddad picked up his pistol and fired, blowing the rat out the window.

Passion ran into the room, her dark hair a mess; seeing Granddad on the kang with his arms wrapped around his knees, she bent over wordlessly, picked up the shards of the wine bowl, and turned to leave.

A hot flash surged into Granddad's throat. "You . . . stop there . . ." he said with difficulty.

Passion bit her thick lower lip. Her sweet smile suffused the gloomy room with a ball of golden light. The beating of raindrops beyond the window seemed suddenly blocked by a wall of green. Granddad looked at Passion's mussed hair, her delicate little ears, and the arch of her breasts. "You've grown up," he said.

Her mouth twitched, and two cunning little wrinkles appeared in the corners.

"What were you doing?"

"Sleeping!" She yawned. "I hate this weather. How long is it going to rain? The bottom must have fallen out of the Milky Way."

"Douguan and his mom must be stuck there. Didn't she say she'd return in three days? The old lady must have rotted by now!"

"Is there anything else?" Passion asked him.

He lowered his head and, after a pensive moment, said, "No, that's all."

Passion bit her lip again, smiled, and walked out, wiggling her hips.

Darkness returned to the room, and the gray curtain of rain beyond the window was thicker and heavier than ever.

Passion walked back in and leaned up against the door frame, watching Granddad through misty eyes. He felt the soles of his feet and the palms of his hands began to sweat.

"What do you want?"

She smiled demurely. The room was once again filled with golden light.

"Do you feel like drinking?" Passion asked him.

"Will you join me?"

"All right."

She brought in a decanter of wine and sliced some salted eggs.

Outside, the rain beat like thunder, and a chilling air seeped in through the window, causing Granddad's nearly naked body to shudder.

"Cold?" Passion asked disdainfully.

"I'm hot!" he fired back testily.

She filled two bowls with wine, kept one, and handed him the other.

After tossing their empty bowls onto the kang, they just gazed at each other. Two blue flames danced in the golden glow in the room. The golden flames singed his body, the blue flames singed his heart.

"A noble man gets his revenge, even if it takes ten years!" Granddad said icily as he shoved his pistol into its holster.

Black Eye straightened up and walked from the dike down to Grandma's grave. He circled it once, kicked the dirt, and sighed. "People live but a generation, and grass dies each autumn! Old Yu, the Iron Society is going to fight the Japanese. Join us!"

"Join a superstitious society like yours?" Granddad sneered.

"Don't get on your high horse! The Iron Society is protected by the gods. Heaven smiles on us and the people trust us. Being asked to join is an honor." Black Eye stamped his foot at the head of Grandma's grave and continued: "Your black master here is willing to take you on for her sake."

"I don't need your damned pity! One of these days, you and I are going to settle things, once and for all. Our business isn't finished!"

"You don't scare me!" Black Eye patted the revolver on his hip. "I know how to use one of these, too."

A handsome young Iron Society soldier walked down from the dike and stayed his leader's hand. With modest self-control, he said, "Commander Yu, the soldiers of the Iron Society have long respected you, and we'd be honored if you joined us in our mission to keep the country whole. We must put aside our squabbles and drive off the Japanese! Individual scores can be settled later."

Granddad was intrigued by the man, who reminded him of his own valiant young Adjutant Ren, who had died tragically while cleaning his gun. "Are you a member of the Communist Party?" he asked derisively.

"Not the Communist Party," the young man replied, "and not the Nationalist Party. I hate them both!"

"I like your spirit!" Granddad said approvingly.

"They call me Five Troubles."

"I'll remember that," Granddad said.

Father had been standing motionless beside Granddad for a long time, gazing curiously at the shaved foreheads of the Iron Society soldiers. That was their identifying mark, but its significance escaped him.

6

PASSION AND MY GRANDDAD made wild love for three days and nights, until her already thick lips were puffy and swollen. Trickles of blood seeped into the cracks between her teeth, and when Granddad kissed her, the taste of blood nearly drove him crazy. The rain didn't let up during those three days, and when the blue-and-gold light vanished from the room, the rustling of gray-green sorghum, the watery croaks of frogs, and the nibbling sounds of wild rabbits came on the air from the fields. The chilled, fetid air was saturated with a thousand smells.

When Granddad awoke on the morning of the fourth day, he looked at Passion lying beside him and discovered how gaunt and bony she had become; her closed eyes were rimmed with dark-purple circles, her thick lips were cracked and peeling. Hearing the loud crash of a house collapsing somewhere in the village, he quickly dressed and stumbled down off the kang, only to fall flat on his face; he was stunned. As he lay on the floor, his stomach rumbled from hunger. Managing to get to his feet, he called out weakly for the woman Liu. No answer. He went into the room that Passion shared with her, but the only thing lying on the kang mat was a green frog; no sign of Liu.

Returning to the room where he and Passion had spent the last three days and nights, he picked up several squashed slices of salted egg and gobbled them down, shell and all. But they only whetted his appetite, so he went into the kitchen and dug through the cabinet, where he found four mildewed buns, nine salted eggs, two pieces of preserved bean curd, and three withered scallions; he gobbled everything down and finished it off with a ladleful of peanut oil.

The sun's rays spread across the sorghum field like blood. Passion was still asleep, and Granddad looked at her body, sleek as the hide of the black mule. He poked her in the belly with his pistol, and she awoke with a smile, blue flames leaping out of her eyes; but he staggered out into the yard and looked up at the huge, round sun, which was like a damp, newborn infant, still covered with its mother's blood. All around him, rain puddles shone bright red.

The wall separating the eastern and western compounds had come down. Uncle Arhat, the woman Liu, and the distillery hands ran outside to look at the sun.

"Were you in there gambling all this time?" Granddad asked.

"Yes," Uncle Arhat answered, "for three days and nights."

Once the rain had stopped and the sky was clear, the water receded quickly, exposing a layer of soil as wet and shiny as grease. Grandma rode up on her mud-spattered black mule out of the gooey muck of the field, holding Father in her arms. As they picked up each other's scent, the two mules, separated for so long, began to paw the ground, bob their heads, and bray loudly. When they were led up to the feeding trough, they nudged and nibbled each other intimately.

Embarrassed, Granddad took Father from Grandma, whose eyes were red and puffy; she smelled slightly of mildew. "Did you take care of everything?" Granddad asked her.

"We buried her this morning. Two more days of rain and the maggots would have gotten to her."

"That was quite a rain, all right. The bottom must have fallen out of the Milky Way." He turned to my father. "Douguan, say hello to your foster-dad."

"*Foster*-dad? That's a 'bloodless' relationship. Yours is 'blooded,' " Grandma chided him. "Hold him while I go inside and change."

Passion walked outside with a brass basin to get some water. Granddad smiled knowingly, to which she responded with a look of annoyance.

"What's wrong?" he asked softly.

"It's all the fault of that damned rain!" she snapped back.

"What did you say to him?" he heard Grandma ask Passion after she carried the water inside.

"Nothing."

"Didn't you say it was all the fault of that damned rain?"

"No, no, I said that damned rain probably came because the bottom fell out of the Milky Way."

Grandma uttered an "Oh!" Granddad heard the water splashing in the brass basin.

Three days later, Grandma said she was going home to burn incense for Great-Grandma. When she and Father were seated on the black mule, she said to Passion, "I won't be back tonight."

That night the woman Liu went over to the eastern compound to gamble with the hired hands. Golden flames lit up Grandma's room again.

After riding the mule back under the stars, she stood beneath the window and listened to what was going on inside. During the angry tirade that followed, Grandma gouged a dozen bloody lines in Passion's face with her nails and slapped Granddad's left cheek—hard. He just laughed. She raised her hand again, but before it reached his cheek it went limp, and she merely brushed his shoulder. He sent her reeling with a vicious slap.

Grandma burst out crying.

Granddad left, taking Passion with him.

7

THE IRON SOCIETY SOLDIERS freed up one of their mounts so Granddad and Father could ride. Whipping his horse, Black Eye took the lead, while the glib Five Troubles, who hated the Communists and the Nationalists, trotted alongside Granddad. His dappled colt was very young and eager to catch up to the others, but Five Troubles kept a tight rein. Never a man to mince words, he looked back and said, "Commander Yu, I've been doing all the talking. You haven't said anything."

Granddad smiled wryly. "I can barely read two hundred words. I'm an expert in murder and arson, but you might as well take me to the slaughterhouse if you want me to talk about national affairs!"

"Then who do you think we ought to turn the country over to after we drive out the Japanese?"

"That has nothing to do with me. All I know is that no one would dare take a bite out of my dick."

"What would you say if the Communists were in charge?"

Granddad snorted contemptuously out of one nostril.

"How about the Nationalists?"

He snorted out of the other nostril.

"That's what I say. What China needs is an emperor! I've got it all figured out: struggles come and go, long periods of division precede unity and long periods of unity precede division, but the nation always falls into the hands of an emperor. The nation is the emperor's family, the family is the emperor's nation. That's why he governs so benevolently. But if a political party is in charge, everybody's got his own idea, with Grandpa saying it's too cold and Grandma complaining about the heat, and everything's all fucked up."

He reined in his dappled colt and waited for Granddad to catch up. Then, leaning over secretively, he said, "Commander Yu, I've been reading *Romance of the Three Kingdoms* and *Outlaws of the Marshes* since I was a kid, and I know them like the back of my hand. The seat of my courage is as big as a hen's egg, but unfortunately I don't have a wise leader to serve. I used to think Black Eye was one. That's why I left home, to join up with him and do something worthwhile before I got married and settled down.

"Who'd have guessed that he was as stupid as a pig and as dumb as an ox, short on courage and long on bullshit? All he cares about is his little plot of land in Saltwater Gap. Our ancestors had a saying: Birds perch on the best wood, a good horse neighs when it sees a master trainer. After thinking it over, I've concluded that in all of Northeast Gaomi Township you, Commander Yu, are the only true leader. My comrades and I demanded that Black Eye bring you into the society. It's what they call 'inviting the tiger into the house.' When you're one of us, if you can sleep on firewood and drink gall, like the famous king of Yue, you'll gain everyone's sympathy and respect. Then I'll wait for a chance to get rid of Black Eye and nominate you to replace him. With a change in the ruling house, discipline will be tightened. Once we bring Northeast Gaomi Township under our control, we'll move north and occupy Southeast Pingdu Township and Northern Jiao Township, then unite all three areas.

"When that's done, we can set up our capital in Saltwater Gap under the flag of the Iron Society, with you in command. From there we'll send our forces in three directions, taking Jiao, Gaomi, and Pingdu counties, and annihilating the Communists, the Nationalists, and the Japs. With the three capitals in our hands, we can set up our own nation!"

Granddad nearly fell off his horse. He looked with amazement at this handsome young man who was bursting with ideas of statehood, and his insides ached with excitement. Reining in his horse, he tumbled out of the saddle and, since it didn't seem appropriate to kneel before Five Troubles, reached up, grabbed his sweaty hand, and said in a tremulous voice, "Sir! Why couldn't I have met you before this? Why did it take so long?"

"A leader shouldn't talk like that. Let's put our hearts and minds together to do something really important!" Five Troubles said with tears in his eyes.

Black Eye, who was more than a li ahead of them, reined in his horse and shouted, "Hey—are you two coming or not?"

Cupping his hand over his mouth, Five Troubles yelled, "We're coming! Old Yu's cinch broke. We're fixing it now!" He turned to look at Father, who was sitting bright-eyed on his horse. "Young Master Yu," he said, "we've been discussing serious matters. Don't breathe a word of our conversation to anyone!"

Father nodded vigorously.

Granddad felt more clearheaded than ever before in his life. Five Troubles' words were a rag that had wiped his heart clean, until it shone like a mirror; finally, he could see the purpose of his struggles, and he uttered something that even Father, who was sitting in front of him, didn't hear clearly: "Heaven's will!"

Alternating between a gallop and a trot, the horses arrived at the banks of the Black Water River at noon. That afternoon they left the river behind them, and as night was about to fall, Granddad rose up in the saddle to gaze out at the Salty Water River, which was half as broad as the Black Water River and meandered through alkaline plains. Its gray waters looked like dull glass that gave off a murky glare.

8

COUNTY MAGISTRATE NINE DREAMS CAO had used a brilliant stratagem in the late fall of 1928 to wipe out the bandits of Northeast Gaomi Township led by my granddad. Decades later, when Granddad was in the mountains of Hokkaido, this tragic page in history was always before him. He thought back to how smug he had felt as he was driven in his black Chevrolet sedan on the bumpy Northeast Gaomi Township mountain road, an unwitting decoy who had led eight hundred good men into a trap. His limbs grew ice-cold at the memory of those eight hundred men lined up in a remote gulley outside Jinan City to be mowed down by machine guns. While he was roasting fine-scaled silver carp from Hokkaido's shallow rivers, he agonized over the eight hundred deaths. . . .

After making a pile of broken bricks, Granddad climbed over the high wall around the Jinan police station in the small hours of the morning, then slid down the other side into clumps of scrap paper and weeds, frightening off a couple of stray cats. He slipped into a house, changed from his black wool military uniform into some tattered clothes, then went out and merged with the crowds on the street to watch his fellow villagers and his men being loaded onto boxcars. Sentries stood around the station with dark, murderous looks on their faces. Black smoke poured out of the locomotive, steam hissed from the exhaust pipes. . . . Granddad walked south on the rusty tracks.

At dawn, after walking all day and night, he reached a dry riverbed that reeked of blood. The bodies of hundreds of Northeast Gaomi Township bandits were piled up in layers, filling half the riverbed. He felt remorseful, horrified, vengeful. He was fed up with a life that was little more than an unending cycle of kill-or-be-killed, eat-or-be-eaten. He thought of the chimney smoke curling in the air above his quiet village; of the creaking pulley as a bucket of clear water was brought out of the well to water a fuzzy young donkey; of a fiery red rooster standing on a wall covered with date branches to crow at the radiant rays of dawn. He decided to go home.

After spending his whole life in the confines of Northeast Gaomi Township, this was the first time he'd ever traveled so far, and home seemed to be on the other side of the world. Recalling that the train to Jinan had traveled west the entire trip, he thought that all he had to do was follow the tracks east and he'd have no trouble getting back to Gaomi County. When one of the trains came down the tracks, he hid in a nearby ditch or amid some crops to watch the red or black wheels rumble past, bending the curved tracks.

Granddad ate when he could beg food in a village and drank when he came upon a river. Always he headed east, day and night. After two weeks, he finally spied the two familiar blockhouses at the Gaomi train station, where the county aristocracy was gathered to see off their onetime magistrate Nine Dreams Cao, who had been promoted to police commissioner for Shandong Province. Granddad crumpled to the ground, not sure why or how, and lay with his face in the black earth for a long time before becoming aware of the pungent taste of blood in the dirt.

He decided not to go home, even though he had often seen Grandma's snow-white body and Father's strangely innocent smile in the cold realm of his dreams. He awoke to find his grimy face bathed in hot tears and his heart aching. When he gazed up at the stars, he knew how deeply he missed his wife and son. But now that the decisive moment had arrived, and he could smell the intimate aroma of wine mash permeating the darkness, he wavered.

The slap and a half from Grandma had created a barrier between them, like a cruel river. "Ass!" she'd cursed him. "Swine!" An angry scowl had underscored her outburst as she stood there, hands on hips, back bent, neck thrust forward, a trickle of bright-red blood running down her chin. The awful sight had thrown his heart into confusion.

In all his years, no woman had ever cursed him as viciously as that, and certainly no woman had ever slapped him. It wasn't that he felt no remorse over his affair with Passion, but the humiliating verbal and physical abuse had driven that remorse out of his heart, and self-recrimination had been supplanted by a powerful drive to avenge himself.

Emboldened by a sense of self-righteousness, he'd gone to live with Passion in Saltwater Gap, some fifteen li distant. After buying a house, he led what even he knew was a troubled life, discovering in

Passion's deficiencies Grandma's virtues. Now that he'd narrowly escaped death, his legs had carried him back to this spot, and he wanted to rush into that compound and revive the past; but the sound of those curses erected a barrier that cut him off from the road ahead.

Granddad dragged his exhausted body to Saltwater Gap in the middle of the night, where he stood in front of the house he'd bought two years earlier and looked up at the late-night moon high in the southwestern sky. Passion's vigorous, slender body floated in front of his eyes, and as he thought about the golden flames ringing her body and the blue flames issuing from her eyes, a tormenting nostalgia made him forget his mental and physical anguish. He pulled himself over the wall and jumped into the compound.

Keeping a rein on his feelings, he knocked on the window frame and cried out softly: "Passion . . . Passion . . ."

Inside, a muffled cry of alarm, followed by the sound of intermittent sobs.

"Passion, can't you tell who it is? It's me, Yu Zhan'ao!"

"Brother . . . dear brother! Scare me to death, but I'm not afraid! I want to see you even if you're a ghost! You've come to me, I, I'm deliriously happy. . . . You didn't forget me after all. . . . Come in. . . . Come in. . . ."

"Passion, I'm not a ghost. I'm still alive, I escaped!" He pounded on the window. "Did you hear that? Could a ghost make sounds like that on your window?"

Passion began to wail.

"Don't cry," Granddad said. "Somebody will hear you."

He walked over to the door, but before he got there, the naked Passion was in his arms.

For two months, Granddad didn't step outside. He lay on the kang, staring blankly at the papered ceiling. Passion reported talk on the street about the bandits of Northeast Gaomi Township. When he could no longer bear his indelible memories of the tragedy, he filled the air with the sound of grinding teeth. All those opportunities to take that old dog Nine Dreams Cao's life, yet he had spared him. His thoughts turned to my grandma. Her relationship with Nine Dreams Cao had been a major factor in his being duped, so his hatred for Nine

Dreams Cao carried over to her as well. Who knows, maybe they had conspired to lead him into a trap. The news Passion brought made this seem likely.

One day, as Passion was massaging his chest, she said, "Dear brother, you may not have forgotten her, but it didn't take her long to forget you. After they took you away on the train, she went with Black Eye, the leader of the Iron Society, and has lived with him in Saltwater Gap for months." The sight of Passion's insatiable dark body gave birth to repugnance, and Granddad's thoughts returned to that other body, as fair as virgin snow. He remembered, again, that sultry afternoon when he had stretched her out on his straw rain cape in the dense shadows of the sorghum field.

Granddad rolled over. "Is my pistol still here?"

Passion wrapped her arms around him. "What are you going to do?" she asked fearfully.

"I'm going to kill those dog bastards!"

"Zhan'ao! Dear brother, you can't keep killing people! Think how many you've killed already!"

He shoved her away. "Shut up!" he snarled. "Give me my gun!"

She began to sob as she ripped open the seam of the pillow and removed his pistol.

With Father in his lap, Granddad followed Five Troubles on the black horse. Even after gazing for a long time at the dull gray surface of the Salty Water River and the vast white alkaline plains stretching from its banks, his excitement from their stirring conversation still hadn't abated; yet he couldn't stop thinking about his fight with Black Eye on the bank of the river.

With his pistol under his arm, he rode a huge braying donkey all morning. When he reached Saltwater Gap, he tied his donkey to an elm tree at the village entrance to let it gnaw on the bark, then pulled his tattered felt cap down over his eyebrows and strode into the village. Saltwater Gap was a large village, but Granddad walked straight toward a row of tall buildings without asking directions. Winter was just around the corner, and a dozen chestnut trees with a few stubborn yellow leaves were bent before the wind. Though not strong, it cut like a knife.

He slipped into the compound in front of the tiled buildings, where the Iron Society was meeting. On the wall of a spacious hall with a brick floor hung a large amber-colored painting of a strange old man riding a ferocious, mottled tiger. A variety of curious objects rested on an altar beneath the painting—a monkey claw, the skull of a chicken, a dried pig gallbladder, a cat's head, and the hoof of a donkey. Incense smoke curled upward. A man with a ring of moles around one eye was sitting on a thick, circular sheet of iron, rubbing the shaved dome of scalp above his forehead with his left hand and covering the crack in his ass with his right. He was chanting loudly: "Amalai amalai iron head iron arm iron spirit altar iron tendon iron bone iron cinnabar altar iron heart iron liver iron lung altar raw rice forged into iron barrier iron knife iron gun no way out iron ancestor riding iron tiger urgent edict amalai amalai amalai . . ."

Granddad recognized the man as Northeast Gaomi Township's infamous half-man, half-demon, Black Eye.

His chant finished, Black Eye stood up and kowtowed three times to the iron ancestor seated on his tiger. Then he returned to his sheet of iron, sat down, and raised his fists, all ten fingernails turned in and hidden from view. He nodded toward the Iron Society soldiers, who reached up with their left hands to their shaved scalps and covered their asses with their right, closed their eyes, and raised their voices to repeat Black Eye's chant. Their sonorous shouts filled the hall with demonic airs. Half of Granddad's anger vanished—his plan had been to murder Black Eye, but his loathing for the man was being weakened by reverence and awe.

After completing their chant, the Iron Society soldiers kowtowed to the old demon on his tiger mount, then formed two tight ranks in front of Black Eye. Granddad had heard that the Iron Society soldiers ate raw rice, and now he watched as each of them took a bowl of it from Black Eye and gobbled it down. Then, one by one, they walked up to the altar and picked up the monkey claw, mule hoof, and chicken skull to rub on their shaved scalps.

The white sun was streaked with red by the time the ceremony was completed, when Granddad fired a shot at the large painting, putting a hole in the face of the old demon on his tiger. The soldiers broke ranks at the sound of gunfire, took a moment to get their bearings, then rushed out and surrounded Granddad.

"Who are you? You've got the nerves of a thief!" Black Eye thundered.

Granddad lifted his tattered felt cap with the barrel of his smoking gun. "Your venerable ancestor, Yu Zhan'ao!"

"I thought you were dead!" Black Eye exclaimed.

"I wanted to see you dead first!"

"You think you can kill me with that thing? Men, bring me a knife!"

A soldier walked up with a butcher knife. Black Eye held his breath and gave a sign to the man. Granddad watched the blade of the knife hack Black Eye's exposed abdomen as though it were a chunk of hardwood, but all it left were some pale scratches.

The Iron Society soldiers began to chant in unison: "Amalai amalai amalai iron head iron arm iron spirit altar . . . iron ancestor riding iron tiger urgent edict amalai . . . amalai . . . amalai . . ."

Granddad was stunned. How could anybody be impervious to knives and bullets? He pondered the Iron Society chant. Everything on the body was iron—everything, that is, but the eyes.

"Can you stop a bullet with your eye?" Granddad asked.

"Can you stop a knife with your belly?" Black Eye asked in return.

Granddad knew he couldn't stop a knife with his belly; he also knew Black Eye couldn't stop a bullet with his eye.

The Iron Society soldiers came out of the hall armed to the teeth and formed a ring around Granddad, glaring like tigers eyeing their prey.

Granddad knew he only had nine bullets left in his pistol, and that, once he killed Black Eye, the soldiers would pounce on him like mad dogs and tear him to ribbons.

"Black Eye," Granddad said, "since you're so special, I'll spare those pisspots of yours. Turn the bitch over and we're square!"

"Is she yours?" Black Eye asked him. "Will she answer if you call her? Is she your legal wife? A widow is like a masterless dog—they both belong to whoever raises them. If you know what's good for you, you'll get the hell out of here! Don't blame Old Blackie for what happens if you don't."

Granddad raised his pistol. The Iron Society soldiers raised their cold, glinting weapons. Seeing their lips twitch, chanting, he mused, A life for a life!

Just then Granddad heard a mocking laugh from Grandma. His arm fell to his side.

Grandma stood on a stone step holding Father in her arms, bathed in the rays of the sun in the western sky. Her hair shone with oil, her face was rosy, her eyes sparkled.

"Whore!" Granddad railed, gnashing his teeth.

"Ass!" Grandma fired back impertinently. "Swine! Scum! Sleeping with a serving girl is all you're good for!"

Granddad raised his pistol.

"Go ahead!" Grandma said. "Kill me! And kill my son!"

"Dad!" my father yelled.

Granddad's pistol fell to his side again.

He thought back to that fiery red noon in the kingfisher-green sorghum and pictured her pristine body lying in Black Eye's arms.

"Black Eye," he said, "let's make it just the two of us, fists only. Either the fish dies or the net breaks—I'll wait for you on the bank of the river outside the village."

He thrust his pistol into his belt and walked through the ring of stupefied Iron Society soldiers. With a glance at my father, but not at my grandma, he strode out of the village.

As soon as he stepped up onto the steamy bank of the Salty Water River, Granddad took off his cotton jacket, threw down his pistol, tightened his belt, and waited. He knew Black Eye would come.

The Salty Water River was as murky as a sheet of frosted glass reflecting the golden sunlight.

Black Eye walked up.

Grandma followed, with Father in her arms. She wore the same look of indifference.

The Iron Society soldiers brought up the rear.

"A civil fight or a martial fight?" Black Eye asked.

"What's the difference?"

"A civil fight means you hit me three times and I hit you three times. A martial fight means anything goes."

Granddad thought it over and said, "A civil fight."

"Who first?" Black Eye asked.

"Let fate decide. We'll draw straws. The longest goes first."

"Who'll prepare the straws?" Black Eye asked.

Grandma put Father on the ground. "I'll do it," she said.

She plucked two lengths of straw, hid them behind her back, then brought them out in front. "Draw!"

She looked at Granddad, who drew a straw. Then she opened her hand to show the remaining one.

"You drew the long straw, so you go first!" she said.

Granddad drove his fist into Black Eye's belly. Black Eye yelped.

Having sustained the first punch, Black Eye straightened up, a blue glint in his eyes, and waited for the next one.

Granddad hit him in the heart.

Black Eye stumbled back a step.

Granddad drove his final punch into Black Eye's navel with all his might.

This time Black Eye stumbled back two steps. His face was waxen as he pressed his hand over his heart and coughed twice, spitting out a nearly congealed clot of blood. Then he wiped his mouth and nodded to Granddad, who concentrated all his strength in his chest and abdomen.

Black Eye waved his huge fist in the air and swung it hard, stopping inches away from Granddad. "I'll spare you this one, for the sake of heaven!" he said.

He also wasted his second punch. "I'll spare you this one for the sake of earth."

Black Eye's third punch knocked Granddad head over heels, like a mud clod; he hit the hard, alkaline ground with a loud thud.

After struggling to his feet, Granddad picked up his jacket and his pistol, his face dotted with beads of sweat the size of soybeans. "I'll see you in ten years."

A piece of bark floated in the river. Granddad fired his nine bullets at it, smashing it to smithereens. Then he stuck his pistol into his belt and staggered into the wasteland, his bare shoulders and slightly bent back shining like bronze under the sun's rays.

As Black Eye looked at the shattered pieces of bark floating in the river, he spat out a mouthful of blood and sat down hard on the ground.

Cradling Father in her arms, Grandma ran unsteadily after Granddad, sobbing as she called his name: "Zhan'ao—"

9

MACHINE GUNS BEHIND the tall Black Water River dike barked for three minutes, then fell silent. Throngs of Jiao-Gao soldiers who had been shouting a charge in the sorghum field fell headlong onto the dry roadbed and the scorched earth of the field, while, across the way, Granddad's Iron Society soldiers, who were about to surrender, were cut down like sorghum; among them were longtime devil worshippers who had followed Black Eye for a decade and young recruits who had joined because of Granddad's reputation. Neither their shiny shaved scalps, the raw rice steeped in well water, the iron ancestor riding his tiger, nor the mule hoof, monkey claw, and chicken skull shielded their bodies. The insolent machine-gun bullets streaked through the air to shatter their spines and legs and pierce their chests and bellies. The red blood of the Jiao-Gao soldiers and the green blood of the Iron Society soldiers converged to nourish the black earth of the fields. Years later, that soil would be the most fertile anywhere.

Having suffered defeat together at the hands of a common foe, the retreating Jiao-Gao regiment and Granddad's Iron Society were immediately transformed from sworn enemies into loyal allies. The living and the dead were cast together. Little Foot Jiang, wounded in the leg, and Granddad, wounded in the arm, were cast together. As Granddad lay with his head against Little Foot Jiang's bandaged leg, he noticed that his feet weren't all that little, but their stink overwhelmed the stench of blood.

The machine guns opened fire again, their bullets smashing into the roadbed and the sorghum field, where they raised puffs of dust. Jiao-Gao and Iron Society soldiers tried to bore their way under the ground. The topography couldn't have been worse: nothing but flatland as far as the eye could see—not a blade of grass anywhere—and the blanket of whizzing bullets was like a razor-sharp sword slicing the air; anyone who raised his head was finished.

Another interval between bursts. Little Foot Jiang shouted, "Hand grenades!"

The machine guns roared again, then fell silent. The Jiao-Gao soldiers hurled at least a dozen grenades over the dike. A mighty explosion was followed by shrieks and cries, and an arm wrapped in fluttering gray cloth sailed through the air. Granddad shouted, "It's Detachment Leader Leng, that son of a bitch Pocky Leng!"

The Jiao-Gao soldiers lobbed another round of grenades. Shrapnel flew, the water in the river rippled, and a dozen columns of smoke rose from behind the dike. Seven or eight intrepid Jiao-Gao soldiers charged the dike, but they had barely reached the ridge when a burst of fire sent them scrambling back, dead and dying jumbled together, until there was no telling who was who.

"Retreat!" Little Foot Jiang ordered.

The Jiao-Gao soldiers lobbed another round of grenades, and at the sound of explosions, the survivors crawled out of the pile of dead and beat a hasty retreat northward, shooting as they ran. Little Foot Jiang, helped to his feet by two of his men, fell in behind them.

Sensing the danger in retreating, Granddad stayed where he was. He wanted to get out of there, but this wasn't the time. Some of his Iron Society soldiers joined the retreat, and the others were beginning to get the same idea. "Don't move," he said in a low voice.

Gunsmoke curled up from behind the dike, carrying with it the pitiful cries of wounded men. Then Granddad heard a familiar voice shout: "Fire! Machine guns, machine guns!"

It was Pocky Leng's voice, all right, and Granddad's lips curled into a grim smile.

Granddad, with Father beside him, joined the Iron Society. He shaved his forehead and knelt before the ancestor on his tiger mount. When he saw the mended spot where his bullet had made a hole, he smiled to himself. It was as though it had happened only yesterday. Father also had the front of his scalp shaved. The sight of the ebony razor in Black Eye's hand chilled him, for he still had dim memories of the fight that had occurred more than ten years earlier. But Black Eye shaved his scalp without incident, then rubbed it with each of the freakish fetishes—the mule hoof, the monkey claw, and so on. The ceremony completed, Father's body truly felt rigid, as though his flesh and blood had turned to iron.

Granddad was welcomed enthusiastically by the Iron Society soldiers, who, urged on by Five Troubles, staged a revolt, demanding that Black Eye acknowledge Granddad as his deputy.

Once the issue of second-in-command was resolved, Five Troubles then worked on their fighting spirit. He said that a thousand days of military training came to fruition in a single moment. Now that the Jap aggressors were wreaking havoc on the nation, he asked how long the men planned to practice their "iron" skills without actually going out to kill the dwarf invaders. Most of the society soldiers were hot-blooded young men whose hatred of the Japanese was in the marrow of their bones, and the silver-tongued Five Troubles spoke like an orator, making them crave action on the battlefield, to rage potent as an oil fire. Black Eye had no choice but to agree with him. Granddad took Five Troubles aside. "Are you sure your 'iron' skills are sufficient to withstand bullets?" Five Troubles just grinned slyly.

The Iron Society's first battle was small, a brief skirmish with the Gao battalion, a unit of Zhang Zhuxi's puppet regiment. The Iron Society soldiers, who were about to stage a raid on the Xia Family Inn blockhouses, met up with the Gao battalion as it was returning from a raid on grain stores. The two armies stopped and sized each other up. The Gao raiding party, made up of sixty or seventy men in apricot-colored uniforms, was heavily armed. Canvas cartridge belts were slung across the men's chests. Intermingled with the troops were dozens of donkeys and mules carrying sacks of grain. The black-clad Iron Society soldiers were armed only with spears, swords, and knives, except for a few dozen with pistols tucked in their belts.

"What unit are you?" a fat Gao-battalion officer asked from his horse.

Granddad reached into his belt and, as he drew his pistol, shouted, "The one that kills traitors!" He fired.

The fat officer tumbled off his horse, his head a bloody gourd.

"Amalai amalai amalai," the Iron Society soldiers chanted in unison as they launched a fearsome charge. Frightened donkeys and mules broke and ran. The panicky puppet soldiers tried to escape, but the slower ones were hacked to death by the Iron Society soldiers' knives and swords. Those who managed to get away began coming to their senses when they'd run about the distance of an arrow's flight. Quickly forming up ranks, they opened fire—*pipi papa*. But the undaunted Iron Society soldiers, having tasted blood, raised their chant and launched a ferocious charge.

"Spread out!" Granddad shouted. "Crouch!"

His shouts were drowned out by the sonorous chants of men charging in closed ranks, heads high, chests thrust forward.

The puppet soldiers fired a salvo of bullets, cutting down more than twenty Iron Society soldiers. Fresh blood sprayed the air as the shrill wails of wounded soldiers swirled around the feet of their surviving comrades.

The Iron Society soldiers were stunned. Another salvo, and more of them fell.

"Spread out!" Granddad yelled. "Flatten out!"

Now the puppet soldiers mounted a countercharge. Granddad rolled onto his side and jammed a clip into his pistol. Black Eye raised himself halfway up and bellowed, "Get up! Chant! Iron head iron arm iron wall iron barrier iron heart iron spleen iron sheet keep away bullets don't dare approach iron ancestor riding tiger urgent edict amalai . . ."

A bullet whizzed over his head, and he hit the ground like a dog scrounging for shit.

With a sneer, Granddad grabbed the pistol out of Black Eye's trembling hand and shouted, "Douguan!"

Father rolled over next to him. "Here I am, Dad!"

Granddad handed him Black Eye's pistol. "Hold your breath, and don't move. Don't shoot till they're closer."

Then he shouted to his men, "If you've got a gun, get it ready. Don't shoot till they're almost on top of you!"

The puppet soldiers rushed boldly forward.

Fifty yards, forty yards, twenty, ten . . . Father could see their yellow teeth.

Granddad jumped to his feet, guns blazing right and left. Seven or eight puppet soldiers bowed deeply, all the way to the ground. Father and Five Troubles fired with the same degree of accuracy. The puppet soldiers turned tail and ran, offering up their backs as inviting targets. Finding his pistols inadequate for his purposes, Granddad picked up a rifle abandoned by a fleeing soldier and opened fire.

This minor skirmish established Granddad as the unchallenged leader of the Iron Society. The cruel, unnecessary deaths of so many of its soldiers had laid bare the folly of Black Eye's sorcery. From then on they shunned the iron-body ceremony that had been forced upon them. Guns? Those were needed. Sorcery and magic couldn't stop bullets.

Pretending to be recruits, Granddad and Father joined the Jiao-Gao regiment and kidnapped Little Foot Jiang in broad daylight. Next they joined the Leng detachment and kidnapped Pocky Leng.

The exchange of the two hostages for weapons and warhorses fortified Granddad's leadership of the now-awesome Iron Society. Black Eye became superfluous, a man in the way. Five Troubles wanted to get rid of him, but Granddad always stopped him.

Following the kidnappings, the Iron Society became the most powerful force in all of Northeast Gaomi Township, while the prestige of the Jiao-Gao and Leng regiments was silenced once and for all. Peace having settled upon the land, Granddad's thoughts turned to the grand funeral for Grandma. From then on it was a process of accumulating wealth by whatever means, including the appropriation of a coffin and the murder of anyone who got in the way; the glory of the Yu family spread like an oil fire. But Granddad forgot the simple dialectic that a bright sun darkens, a full moon wanes, a full cup overflows, and decay follows prosperity. Grandma's grand funeral would be yet another of his great mistakes.

The machine guns behind the dike roared again. Granddad could tell there were only two of them now, the others obviously taken out by the Jiao-Gao regiment hand grenades.

Granddad's attention was caught by movement among the dozen or so Jiao-Gao soldiers who had been mowed down by machine-gun fire on the dike. A skinny, blood-covered little man crawled in agony up the slope, slower than a silkworm, slower than a snail. Granddad knew he was watching a hero in action, another of Northeast Gaomi Township's magnificent seeds. The soldier stopped halfway up the slope, and Granddad watched him strain to roll over and remove a blood-stained hand grenade from his belt. He pulled the pin with his teeth, then ignited the fuse, sending a puff of smoke out from the wooden handle. Holding the armed grenade between his teeth, he dragged himself up to a clump of weeds growing on the dike. The green-tinted machine-gun barrels were dancing above him, sending puffs of smoke into the air.

Regret was what Granddad was feeling. Regret that he'd been so softhearted. When he kidnapped Pocky Leng, all he'd asked as ransom was a hundred rifles, five submachine guns, and fifty horses. He should have demanded these eight machine guns as well, but his years as a bandit had instilled in him a preference for light weapons over heavy ones. If he'd included these machine guns, Pocky Leng wouldn't have been able to run amok today.

When the soldier reached the clump of weeds, he lobbed his grenade. The crack of an explosion sounded behind the dike, sending the barrels of the machine guns soaring into the air. The grenadier lay face down on the slope, not moving; his blood kept flowing, painfully, agonizingly, and very slowly. Granddad heaved a sigh.

That took care of Pocky Leng's machine guns. "Douguan!" Granddad yelled.

Pinned down by two heavy corpses, Father was playing dead. Maybe I really am dead, he thought, not knowing if the warm blood covering him was his own or that of the corpses on top of him. When he heard Granddad's yell, he raised his head, wiped the blood from his face with his sleeve, and said between gasps, "I'm here, Dad. . . ."

Pocky Leng's troops came pouring out from behind the dike, like spring bamboo after a rain, rifles at the ready. A hundred yards away, the Jiao-Gao soldiers, clearheaded once again, opened fire on the charging troops, the submachine guns they'd gotten from Five Troubles' mounted troops crackling loudly. The Leng soldiers tucked in their heads like a herd of turtles.

Granddad pulled the corpses off Father and dragged him free.

"Were you hit?" he asked.

"I don't think so," Father said after checking his arms and legs.

"Let's get out of here, men!" Granddad shouted.

Twenty or more blood-splattered Iron Society soldiers stood up by leaning on their rifles and staggered off toward the north. The Jiao-Gao soldiers didn't fire at them. And although the Leng detachment fired a few shots, their bullets went straight up in the air.

A shot rang out behind Granddad, and his neck felt as though someone had punched him; all the heat in his body quickly flowed to that spot. He reached up and pulled back a palm covered with blood. When he spun around he spotted Black Eye, whose guts had spilled out onto the ground, his large black eyes blinking heavily—once, twice, three times. Two golden tears hung in the corners of his eyes. Granddad smiled at him, and nodded slightly, then turned and led Father slowly away.

Another shot rang out behind them.

Granddad heaved a long sigh. Father turned and saw a little black hole in Black Eye's temple.

As night fell, the Leng detachment surrounded the Jiao-Gao and Iron Society soldiers, who had waged a desperate fight from the midst of Grandma's funeral procession. Their ammunition exhausted, the two detachments were huddled together, clenching their teeth and staring with bloodshot eyes at the relentlessly advancing Leng detachment, recently fortified by a squad from the Seventh Army. The setting sun lit up the evening clouds and dyed the groaning black earth. Scattered across it were countless sons and daughters of Northeast Gaomi who had grown to adulthood on bright-red sorghum, and whose blood now formed streams that converged into a river. Scavenger birds were drawn to the spot by the smell of blood. Most were circling above the horses—like greedy children, they wanted the biggest pieces first.

Grandma's coffin was pitted with pale bullet holes, having served as cover during the gunfight. The roasted chickens, ducks, pigs, and sheep from the roadside shrines had provided sustenance to the Jiao-Gao soldiers, several of whom now launched a bayonet charge but were mowed down by Leng bullets.

"Hands up! Surrender!" the heavily armed Leng troops yelled.

Granddad looked over at Little Foot Jiang, who returned his gaze. Neither said a word as they raised their hands.

The white-gloved commander of the Leng detachment strode out from his bodyguard and said with a sneer, "Commander Yu, Commander Jiang. Enemies and lovers are destined to meet. Now what do you have to say?"

"I'm ashamed!" Granddad said sadly.

"I'm going to report you for the monstrous crime of disrupting the war against Japan on the Eastern Jiao battlefront!" Commander Jiang said.

Pocky Leng lashed him with his whip. "Your bones may be soft, but your mouth is plenty hard! Take them into the village!" he ordered with a wave of the hand.

The Leng detachment bivouacked in our village that night, after putting their Jiao-Gao and Iron Society prisoners in a shed, where they were guarded by a dozen soldiers armed with submachine guns. The moans of the wounded and the weeping of young soldiers who longed for their mothers, wives, and lovers didn't let up all night long.

Like an injured bird, Father snuggled up in Granddad's arms, where he could hear the beating of Granddad's heart, fast one moment, slow the next, like the music of tinkling bells. He fell into a sound sleep, and dreamed of a woman who resembled both Grandma and Beauty. She stroked his injured pecker with hot fingers, sending bolts of lightning up his backbone. He woke with a start, feeling a sense of loss. The plaintive wails of the wounded floated over from the fields. He didn't dare tell Granddad of his dream. As he sat up slowly, he could see the Milky Way through a hole in the shed roof. Suddenly it hit him: I'm almost sixteen!

At daybreak, the Leng detachment pulled down several tents, from which they removed thick ropes. After tying up their prisoners in groups of five, they dragged them over to the willow trees beside the inlet where the Iron Society had tethered its horses the night before. Little Foot Jiang, Granddad, and Father were tied to the tree nearest the bank. Big Tooth Yu's grave mound lay beneath a solitary tree alongside the inlet. The white water lilies had risen with the water level, their new leaves floating on the surface. Cracks appeared in the dense layer of duckweed to reveal ribbons of green water disturbed by swimming frogs. On the other side of the bare village wall, Father saw yesterday's scars on today's fields; the massacred fragments of the funeral procession lay on the road like a gigantic rotting python. Several Leng-detachment soldiers were chopping up the bodies of dead horses, the stench of dark-red blood permeating the chilly air.

Hearing a sigh from Little Foot Jiang, Father spun his head around and watched as the two commanders exchanged looks of misery, four listless eyes beneath lids heavy with exhaustion. The wound on Granddad's shoulder had begun to fester, and the putrid smell drew red horseflies that had been feasting on the decaying corpses of donkeys and men; the bandage on Little Foot Jiang's foot had unraveled and was hanging around his ankle like a strip of sausage casing. Trickles of black blood oozed from the spot where Granddad had shot him.

It seemed to Father that both Granddad and Little Foot Jiang were trying to say something, but not a word was spoken. He sighed and turned to gaze out over the broad black plain, shrouded in a milky-white mist.

More than eighty soldiers from the Jiao-Gao regiment and the Iron Society were tied to trees. One of Granddad's men was sobbing, and the Jiao-Gao soldier next to him nudged him with his shoulder: "Don't cry, Brother-in-Law. Sooner or later we'll get our revenge against Zhang Zhuxi!"

The old Iron Society soldier wiped his filthy face on his filthy clothes. "I'm not crying over your sister! She's dead, and all the tears in the world won't bring her back. I'm crying for us. You and I are kin from neighboring villages who saw each other every time we looked up, so how did things turn out like this? I'm crying for your nephew, my son, Silver Ingot. He was only eighteen when he followed me into the Iron Society so he could avenge your sister. But before he tasted revenge your men killed him. He was on his knees, but you bayoneted him anyway! You mean, cold-blooded bastards! Don't you have sons of your own?"

The old Iron Society soldier's tears were burned dry by flames of anger. He roared at the ragged Jiao-Gao soldiers, "Swine! You should have been out there fighting the Japanese. Or their yellow puppets!

Why did you turn your weapons on the Iron Society! You lousy traitors! You foreign lackeys . . ."

"Don't go too far, Brother-in-Law," the Jiao-Gao soldier cautioned.

"Who are you calling Brother-in-Law? Did you remember you had a brother-in-law when you were throwing your damned grenades at your own nephew?"

"All you see is one side, old man!" yelled one of the Jiao-Gao officers. "If your Iron Society hadn't kidnapped Little Foot Jiang and demanded a ransom of a hundred rifles, we'd have had no reason to fight you. We needed the weapons to attack the Japanese, to give us a chance on the battlefield, to propel us into the vanguard of the resistance!"

Father, whose voice was changing, felt compelled to enter the fray: "You started it by stealing the guns we'd hidden in the well," he said in a raspy squeak. "We kidnapped him because you stole the dog pelts we'd hung on the walls to dry!"

He coughed up a gob of phlegm angrily and tried to spit it in the face of the Jiao-Gao officer, but it missed its mark and landed on the forehead of a tall, slightly hunchbacked Iron Society soldier, who lashed out as though he'd been shot: "Douguan, fuck your living mother!"

The prisoners laughed, even though their aching arms were turning numb from the ropes and their future was clouded.

But Granddad just sneered and said, "What the hell are you arguing about? We're all a bunch of whipped soldiers."

While the sound of Granddad's words still hung in the air, Little Foot Jiang, his face the color of ashes, fell to the ground. Blood and pus oozed from his injured foot, which had swollen to the size of a winter melon. The Jiao-Gao soldiers, held back by the ropes around them, could only look helplessly at their unconscious commander.

Just then the dapper Detachment Leader Leng strode out of his tent to join his men in inspecting the hundreds of rifles and two cases of wooden-handled grenades they'd captured from the Iron Society and the Jiao-Gao regiment. Twirling his whip, he walked smugly toward the prisoners. Father heard the sound of heavy breathing behind him, and he could picture the angry look on Granddad's face. The corners of Detachment Leader Leng's mouth curled upward, and the fine wrinkles above his cheeks wriggled like little snakes.

"Have you thought about what I'm going to do with you, Commander Yu?" he asked with a giggle.

"That's up to you!" Granddad replied.

"It would be a waste of a good man to kill you. But if I don't, you might kidnap me again someday!"

"Killing me won't close my eyes!"

With a swift kick, Father sent a road apple flying into Detachment Leader Leng's chest.

Leng raised his whip, then let it drop. "I hear this little bastard only has one nut. Somebody come over here and cut off the other one! That'll keep him from biting and kicking!"

"He's just a boy, old Leng," Granddad said. "Whatever you want to do you can do to me."

"Just a boy? The little bastard's got more fight in him than a wolf cub!"

Little Foot Jiang, who had regained consciousness, struggled to his feet.

"Commander Jiang," Detachment Leader Leng said, "what do *you* think I should do with you?"

"Killing me will only bring you trouble, Detachment Leader Leng," Commander Jiang said with bold assurance, but with his face bathed in cold sweat. "The day will come when the people liquidate you for your monstrous crime of slaughtering noble fighters of the anti-Japanese resistance!"

"You can pass the time here until I've had something to eat. I'll deal with you then."

The Leng soldiers sat around eating horsemeat and drinking sorghum wine.

Suddenly the sentry on the northern wall of the village fired a shot and ran into the village. "The Japs are coming—the Japs are coming!"

Detachment Leader Leng grabbed the sentry's sleeve and asked angrily, "How many Japs? Are they real Japs or lackeys?"

"I think they're lackeys. Their uniforms are yellow. A whole line of yellow, running toward the village at a crouch."

"Lackeys? Kill the sons of bitches. Company Commander Qi, take your men up to the wall, and hurry!" he ordered.

Then he turned to two guards with machine guns. "Keep an eye on them," he commanded. "Pop 'em if they act up!" Surrounded by his bodyguards, he ran at a crouch toward the northern edge of the village.

Less than a quarter of an hour later, fighting broke out. The opening salvos of rifle fire were followed by machine-gun fire, and before long the air was filled with the shrieks of incoming projectiles that exploded in the village, sending shrapnel slamming into the village wall and the trunks of trees. Amid the din of shouting came the *jiligulu* of a foreign tongue.

It was real Japs after all, not lackeys. Detachment Leader Leng and his troops put up a stubborn defense, but abandoned their positions after half an hour of fighting and fell back to the cover of toppled walls.

Japanese artillery shells were already falling into the inlet. The anxious Jiao-Gao and Iron Society soldiers stomped their feet and ducked their heads. "Untie us!" they bellowed angrily. "Fuck your living mothers! Untie us! If you came out of Chinese pricks, untie us. If you came out of Japanese pricks, then kill us!"

The guards ran to the stack of rifles and picked up two swords, with which they cut their prisoners' ropes.

Eighty soldiers ran like madmen to the stack of rifles and the pile of hand grenades; then, ignoring the numbness in their arms and the hunger in their bellies, they charged the Japanese, yelling wildly as they ran straight into a hail of lead.

Several dozen columns of smoke rose from the village wall following the exposions of the first salvo of hand grenades thrown by the Jiao-Gao and Iron Society soldiers.

CHAPTER FIVE

Strange Death

1

FULL PURPLE LIPS, like ripe grapes, gave Second Grandma—Passion—her extraordinary appeal. The sands of time had long since interred her origins and background. Her rich, youthful, resilient flesh, her plump bean-pod face, and her deep-blue, seemingly deathless eyes were buried in the wet yellow earth, extinguishing for all time her angry, defiant gaze, which challenged the world of filth, adored the world of beauty, and brimmed over with an intense consciousness. Second Grandma had been buried in the black earth of her hometown. Her body was enclosed in a coffin of thin willow covered with an uneven coat of reddish-brown varnish that failed to camouflage its wormy, beetle-holed surface. The sight of her blackened, blood-shiny corpse being swallowed up by golden earth is etched forever on the screen of my mind.

In the warm red rays of the sun, I saw a mound in the shape of a human figure rising atop the heavy, deeply remorseful sandbar. Second Grandma's shapely figure; Second Grandma's high-arching breasts; tiny grains of shifting sand on Second Grandma's furrowed brow; Second Grandma's sensual lips protruding through the golden-yellow sand . . . I knew it was an illusion, that Second Grandma was buried beneath the black earth of her hometown, and that only red sorghum grew around her gravesite.

Standing at the head of her grave—as long as it isn't during the winter, when the plants are dead and frozen, or on a spring day, when cool southerly breezes blow—you can't even see the horizon for the nightmarishly dense screen of Northeast Gaomi sorghum. Then you raise your gaunt face, like a sunflower, and through the gaps in the sorghum you can see the stunning brilliance of the sun hanging in the kingdom of heaven. Amid the perennially mournful sobs of the Black Water River you listen for a lost soul drifting down from that kingdom.

2

THE SKY WAS A BEAUTIFUL CLEAR BLUE. The sun hadn't yet made an appearance, but the chaotic horizon on that early-winter morning was infused with a blinding red light when Old Geng shot at a red fox with a fiery torch of a tail. Old Geng had no peers among hunters in Saltwater Gap, where he bagged wild geese, hares, wild ducks, weasels, foxes, and, when there was nothing else around, sparrows. In the late fall and early winter, enormous flocks of sparrows flew over Northeast Gaomi Township, a shifting brown cloud that rolled and tumbled above the boundless land. At dusk they returned to the village, where they settled on willows whose naked, yellowing limbs drooped earthward or arched skyward. As the dying red rays of the evening sun burned through the clouds, the branches lit up with sparrows' black eyes shining like thousands of golden sparks. Old Geng picked up his shotgun, squinted, and pulled the trigger. Two sparrows crashed to the ground like hailstones as shotgun pellets tore noisily through the branches. Uninjured sparrows saw their comrades hit the ground and flapped their wings, rising into the air like shrapnel sent flying high into a lethargic sky.

Father had eaten some of Old Geng's sparrows when he was young. They were delicious. Three decades later, my older brother and I went into the sorghum field and engaged some crafty sparrows in a heated battle. Old Geng, who was already over seventy by then and lived alone as a pensioner, was one of our most revered villagers. Asked to speak at meetings to air grievances against the old order, he invariably stripped to the waist onstage to show his scars. "The Japs bayoneted me eighteen times," he'd say, "until you couldn't see my skin for all the blood. But I didn't die, and you know why? Because I was protected by a fox fairy. I don't know how long I lay there, but when I opened my eyes all I could see was a bright-red light. The fox fairy was licking my wounds."

In his home, Old Geng—Eighteen Stabs Geng—kept a fox-fairy memorial tablet, which some Red Guards decided to smash during the Cultural Revolution. They changed their minds and got out of there fast when they saw him kneel in front of the tablet wielding a cleaver.

Old Geng drew a bead on the red fox, knowing exactly which way it would run; but he was reluctant to shoot. He knew he could sell the beautiful, bushy pelt for a good price. If he was going to shoot, it had to be now. The fox had already enjoyed a full life, sneaking over nightly to steal a chicken. No matter how strong the villagers made their chicken coops, the fox always found a way inside, and no matter how many traps they set, it always got away. That year the villagers' chicken coops seemed built solely to store its food.

Old Geng had walked out of the village as the roosters were crowing for the third time and gone straight to a low embankment alongside the swamp in front of the village, where he waited for the chicken thief to show up. Dried-up marsh weeds stood waist-high in the swamp, where a thin sheet of nearly transparent ice, possibly thick enough to bear a man's weight, covered the stagnant water that had accumulated during the autumn rains. Yellow tassels atop imprisoned reeds shivered in the freezing morning air, as powerful rays of light from far off in the eastern sky gradually illuminated the icy surface, which gave off a moist radiance, like the scales of a carp. Then the eastern sky turned bright, staining the ice and reeds the color of mottled blood. Old Geng picked up the odor and saw a tight cluster of reeds part slowly like an undulating wave, then close up quickly. He stuck his nearly frozen index finger into his mouth and breathed on it, then wrapped it around the frost-covered trigger.

The fox bounded out of the clump of reeds and stood on the ice, turning it a bright red, as though it had gone up in flames. Congealed blood covered its pointy little snout; a chicken feather the color of hemp was stuck in its whiskers. It walked with stately grace across the ice. Old Geng cried out, and it froze on the spot, squinting to get a good look at the embankment. Old Geng shivered, closed his eyes, and fired.

Like a little fireball, the fox rolled into the reeds. Old Geng, his shoulder numb from the recoil, stood up under a silvery sky, looking bigger and taller than usual. He knew the fox was hiding amid the reeds and staring at him with loathing. Something suspiciously like a guilty conscience began to stir in Old Geng. He thought back over the past year and the trust the fox had shown in him: it always knew he was hiding behind the embankment, yet it sauntered across the ice as though putting his conscience to the test. And Old Geng had always passed the test. But now he had betrayed this friendship, and he hung his head, gazing into the clump of reeds that had swallowed the fox, not even turning back to look when he heard the clatter of footsteps behind him.

Suddenly he felt a stabbing pain, and stumbled forward, twisting his body, dropping his shotgun to the ice. Something hot squirmed under his pants at the belt line. Running toward him were a dozen uniformed figures armed with rifles and glinting bayonets. Instinctively he yelled in fear, "Japan!"

The Japanese soldiers pounced on him and bayoneted him in the chest and abdomen. He screamed pitifully, like a fox howling for its mate. The blood from his wounds pitted the ice beneath him with its heat. He ripped off his tattered shirt with both hands. In his semiconscious state he saw the furry red fox emerge from the clump of reeds and circle round him once, then crouch down and gaze sympathetically. Its fur glowed brilliantly and its slightly slanted eyes shone like emeralds. After a while, Old Geng felt warm fur rubbing against his body, and he lay there waiting for the razor-sharp teeth to begin ripping him apart. If he were torn to shreds, he'd die with no complaints, for he knew that a man who betrays a trust is lower than an animal.

The fox began licking his wounds with its cold tongue.

Old Geng was adamant that the fox had repaid his betrayal by saving his life. Where else could you find another man who had sustained eighteen bayonet wounds yet lived to tell the tale? The fox's tongue must have been coated with a miraculous substance, since Old Geng's wounds were instantly soothed, as though treated with peppermint oil—or so he said.

3

VILLAGERS WHO HAD GONE TO TOWN to sell straw sandals announced upon their return: "Gaomi has been occupied by the Japanese. There's a Rising Sun at the entrance!"

The panic-stricken villagers could only wait for the calamity they knew was coming. But not all of them suffered from racing hearts and crawling flesh: two among them went about their business totally unconcerned, never varying their routine. Who were they? One was Old Geng, the other a onetime musician who loved to sing Peking opera —Pocky Cheng.

"What are you afraid of?" Pocky Cheng asked everyone he met. "We're still common folk, no matter who's in charge. We don't refuse to give the government its grain, and we always pay our taxes. We lie down when we're told, and we kneel when they order us. So who'd dare punish us? Who, I ask you?"

His advice calmed many of the people, who began sleeping, eating, and working again. But it didn't take long for the evil wind of Japanese savagery to blow their way: they fed human hearts to police dogs; they raped sixty-year-old women; they hung rows of human heads from electric poles in town. Even with the unflappable examples of Pocky Cheng and Old Geng, rumors of brutality were hard for the people to put aside, especially in their dreams.

Pocky Cheng walked around happy all the time. News that the Japanese were on their way to sack the village created a glut in dogshit in and around the village. Apparently the farmers who normally fought over it had grown lazy, for now it lay there waiting for him to come and claim it. He, too, walked out of the village as the roosters were crowing for the third time, running into Old Geng with his shotgun slung over his back. They greeted each other and parted ways. By the time the eastern sky had turned red, the pile of dogshit in Pocky Cheng's basket was like a little mountain peak. He laid it down, stood on the southern edge of the village wall, and breathed in the cool, sweet morning air, until his throat itched. He cleared it loudly, then raised his voice to the rosy morning clouds and began to sing: "I am a thirsty grainstalk drinking up the morning dew—"

A shot rang out.

His battered, wingless felt hat sailed into the air. Tucking in his neck, he jumped into the ditch beneath the wall like a shot, bumping his head with a resounding thud against the frozen ground. Not sure if he was dead or alive, he tried moving his arms and legs. They were still working, but barely. His crotch was all sticky. Fear raced through his heart. I've been hit, he thought. He sat up and stuck his hand down his pants. With his heart in his mouth, he pulled out his hand, expecting it to be all red. But it was covered with something yellow, and his nostrils twitched from the odor of rotten seedlings. He tried to rub the stuff off on the side of the ditch, but it stuck to his skin. He heard a shout from beyond the ditch: "Stand up!"

He looked up to see a man in his thirties with a flat, chiseled face, yellow skin, and a long, jutting chin. He was wearing a chestnut-colored wool cap and brandishing a black pistol. A forest of yellow-clad legs was aligned behind him, the calves wrapped in wide, crisscrossed cloth leggings. His eyes traveled slowly upward past protruding hips, stopping at dozens of alien faces, all adorned with the smug smile of a man taking a comfortable shit. A Rising Sun flag drooped under the bright-red sunrise; onion-green rays glinted off a line of bayonets. Pocky Cheng's stomach lurched, and his nervous guts relinquished their contents.

"Get up here!" Chestnut Wool Cap barked out angrily.

Pocky Cheng climbed out of the ditch. Not knowing what to say, he just bowed repeatedly.

Chestnut Wool Cap was twitching right under his nose. "Are there Nationalist troops in the village?" he asked.

Pocky Cheng looked at him blankly.

A Japanese soldier waved a bloodstained bayonet in front of Pocky Cheng's chest and face. He heard his stomach growl and felt his intestines writhe and twist slowly; at any other moment, he would have welcomed the intensely pleasant sensation of a bowel movement. The Japanese soldier shouted something and swung the bayonet, slicing Pocky Cheng's padded jacket down the middle and freeing the cotton wadding inside. The sharp pain of parted skin and sliced muscles leaped from his rib cage. He doubled over, all the foul liquids in his body seeming to pour out at once.

He looked imploringly into the enraged Japanese face and began to wail.

Chestnut Wool Cap drove the barrel of his pistol into his forehead. "Stop blubbering! The commander asked you a question! What village is this? Is it Saltwater Gap?"

He nodded, trying hard to control his sobs.

"Is there a man in the village who makes straw sandals?" Chestnut Wool Cap softened his tone a little.

Ignoring his pain, he eagerly and ingratiatingly replied, "Yes yes yes."

"Did he take his straw sandals to market day in Gaomi yesterday?"

"Yes yes yes," he jabbered. Warm blood had slithered down from his chest to his belly.

"How about pickles?"

"I don't know . . . don't think so. . . ."

Chestnut Wool Cap slapped him across the mouth and shouted: "Tell me! I want to know about pickles!"

"Yes yes yes, your honor," he muttered obsequiously. "Commander, every family has pickles, you can find them in every pickle vat in the village."

"Stop acting like a fucking idiot. I want to know if there's somebody called Pickles!" Chestnut Wool Cap slapped him across the face, over and over.

"Yes . . . no . . . yes . . . no . . . Your honor . . . don't hit me. . . . Please don't hit me . . . your honor . . ." he mumbled, reeling from the slaps.

The Japanese said something. Chestnut Wool Cap swept the hat off his head and bowed, then turned back, the smile on his face gone in an instant. He shoved Pocky Cheng and said with a scowl, "We want to see all the sandal makers in the village. You lead the way."

Concerned about the dung basket he'd left on the wall, Pocky Cheng instinctively cocked his head in that direction. A bayonet that shone like snow flashed past his cheek. Quickly concluding that his life was worth more than a dung basket and spade, he turned his head back and set out for the village on his bandy legs. Dozens of Japs fell in behind him, their leather boots crunching across the frost-covered grass. A few gray dogs barked tentatively.

I'm really in a fix this time, Pocky Cheng was thinking. No one else went out to collect dogshit, no one but me, and I ran into some real dogshit luck. The fact that the Japanese didn't appreciate his good-citizen attitude frustrated him. He led them quickly to each of the sandal makers' cellars. Whoever Pickle was, he was sure in one now. Pocky Cheng looked off into the distance toward his house, where green smoke curled into the sky from the solitary kitchen chimney. It was the most intense longing for home he'd ever known. As soon as he was finished he'd go there, change into clean pants, and have his wife rub some lime into the bayonet wound on his chest. The great woodwind player of Northeast Gaomi Township had never been in such a mess. Oh, how he longed for his lovely wife, who had grumbled about his pocked face at first, but, resigned at last, had decided that if you marry a chicken you share the coop; marry a dog and you share the kennel.

4

EARLY-MORNING GUNFIRE beyond the village startled Second Grandma out of a dream in which she was fighting Grandma tooth and nail. She sat up, her heart thumping wildly, and, try as she might, she couldn't decide if the noise had just been part of the dream. The window was coated with pale morning sunlight; a grotesque pattern of frost had formed on the pane. Shuddering from the cold, she tilted her head so she could see her daughter, my aunt, who was lying beside her, snoring peacefully. The sweet, even breathing of the five-year-old girl soothed Second Grandma's fears. Maybe it was only Old Geng shooting at wild game, a mountain lion or something, she consoled herself. She had no way of knowing how accurate her prediction was, nor could she have known that while she was sliding back under the covers the tips of Japanese bayonets were jabbing Old Geng's ribs.

Little Auntie rolled over and nestled up against Second Grandma, who wrapped her arms around her until she could feel the little girl's warm breath against her chest. Eight years had passed since Grandma had kicked her out of the house. During that time, Granddad had been tricked into going to the Jinan police station, where he nearly lost his life. But he managed to escape and make his way home, where Grandma had taken Father to live with Black Eye, the leader of the Iron Society.

When Granddad fought Black Eye to a standstill at the Salty Water River, he touched Grandma so deeply she followed him home, where they ran the distillery with renewed vitality. Granddad put his rifle away, bringing his bandit days to an end, and began life as a wealthy peasant, at least for the next few years. They were troubling years, thanks to the rivalry between Grandma and Second Grandma. In the end, they reached a "tripartite agreement" in which Granddad would spend ten days with Grandma, then ten days with Second Grandma—ten days was the absolute limit. He stuck to his bargain, since neither woman was an economy lantern, someone to be taken lightly.

Second Grandma was enjoying the sweetness of her sorrows as she hugged Little Auntie. She was three months pregnant. A period of increased tenderness, pregnancy is a time of weakness during which women need attention and protection, and Second Grandma was no exception. Counting the days on her fingers, she longed for Granddad. He would be there tomorrow.

Another crisp gunshot sounded outside the village, and Second Grandma scrambled out of bed. She, too, had heard rumors that the Japanese would be coming to sack the village, and she was unable to drive away the dark premonition of impending doom. She'd willingly go home with Granddad, even if it meant putting up with Grandma's abuse, for it couldn't be worse than living in Saltwater Gap in constant dread. But Granddad had flatly refused, most likely, I believe, because by then he was cowed by the irreconcilable differences between the two women. He would come to regret this decision, for on the following morning he stood in a yard bathed by the warm rays of the late-October sun and gazed upon the tragic consequences of his mistake.

Little Auntie, awake by now, let out an affected yawn, her eyes shining like small bronze buttons; then she sighed, just as if she were a grown-up. That frightened Second Grandma, whose power of speech momentarily deserted her.

"Help me get dressed, Mommy," Little Auntie said.

As Second Grandma picked up Little Auntie's padded red jacket, she looked with unconcealed surprise at her daughter, who didn't have to be coaxed out of bed for a change. There were wrinkles on her face, her eyebrows sagged, and her mouth was drooping—suddenly she looked like a little old woman. Poor Second Grandma's heart constricted, and the red jacket felt as cold as ice. She called out Little Auntie's pet name, her voice quivering like a frayed zither string: "Xiangguan . . . Xiangguan . . . wait a minute . . . till Mommy warms your jacket over the fire. . . ."

"That's okay, Mommy, you don't have to warm it."

Unable to hold back her tears, and not having the courage to look into her daughter's face, she ran to the stove as though fleeing for her life, and lit a fire to warm the jacket, heavy in her hands. The straw crackled like gunfire and burned itself out as easily as it had caught fire, one stalk after another transformed into a cindery replica of its original shape.

Little Auntie's loud breathing from the inner room brought her out of her daze. She carried the steaming jacket inside, where Little Auntie was sitting up in bed, the deep purple of the comforter contrasting sharply with her delicate white skin. Second Grandma draped the sleeves over Little Auntie's slight shoulders as explosions rocked the village.

They seemed to be coming from beneath the ground: heavy, rumbling noises that shook the paper window-coverings and sent sparrows scurrying into the air, wings flapping. The sounds had barely died out when another barrage followed, and screams and shouts erupted in the village. Second Grandma picked up Little Auntie and hugged her tightly, mother and daughter trembling as one.

The shouts died out for a moment as a deathly still terror settled over the village, broken only by the dull tramping of feet and the occasional bark of a dog or the harsh crack of a rifle. Then, all of a sudden, the village erupted tumultuously, like a river that has broken through its dikes, producing a cacophony of women's shrill cries, children's tortured wails, chickens' loud cackles as they flew up into trees and onto the village wall, and the braying of mules straining at their tethers.

Second Grandma bolted the front door and wedged two poles up against it, then climbed onto the kang and huddled up against the wall to await the coming disaster. She longed desperately for Granddad, but she hated him, too. When he came tomorrow, she'd have a good cry in front of him, then give him hell. The village was immersed in a hail of gunfire, and women's screams came from all directions. Second Grandma knew only too well why they were screaming, for she had heard that the Japanese soldiers were like beasts who wouldn't even spare seventy-year-old women.

The smell of smoke and fire seeped into the room; she heard the crackling of flames, punctuated by the occasional shouts of men. She grew numb with fear when she heard a pounding on her gate and frenzied gibberish. Little Auntie's eyes widened for a moment, then she started to bawl, but Second Grandma clapped her hand over her mouth. The gate creaked and groaned. Second Grandma jumped down off the kang and ran to the stove, scooped out two handfuls of ashes, and smeared them over her face to make herself appear as ugly as possible. She did the same to Little Auntie's face. The gate was about to splinter under the assault, and her eyelids fluttered wildly. Maybe they wouldn't spare an old woman, but they'd surely let a pregnant woman go, wouldn't they? Taking a bundle from the head of the bed, she undid her pants, stuffed it down the front, and retied her belt with a double knot. Little Auntie huddled against the wall, watching her mother's strange behavior.

The gate burst open, one of its broken panels crashing loudly to the ground. Shutting the bedroom door, Second Grandma jumped up onto the kang and wrapped her arms tightly around Little Auntie. The Japanese shouted as they battered down the front door with their rifle butts; flimsier than the gate, it splintered easily, and she heard the poles clatter to the floor. Now that the Japanese were inside, the last remaining obstacle was the paper-thin bedroom door. It was only a matter of whether or not they felt like breaking it down, whether or not they were driven by a desire to seize their prey.

Yet even then she trusted to luck; as long as the door was in place, the dangers would forever remain only in rumors and in her imagination, never becoming a reality. She stared with weak anxiety at the door panels as she heard the heavy footsteps of the Japanese and their urgent conversations. The panels were painted a deep red; the frame was coated with gray dust; and the white wooden bolt was spotted with dark-red stains—the blood of a black-mouthed weasel. Second Grandma remembered how she'd beaten the animal with the wooden bolt and listened to its screeches as its head cracked open like a peanut shell; it rolled on the ground for a moment, its bushy tail swishing back and forth across the powdery snow, before going into convulsions and heaving one final shudder. How she had despised that potent weasel!

On an autumn day in 1931, just as night was falling, she went out to the sorghum field to dig up some bitter greens, and there, at the head of a weed-covered grave mound bathed in the blood-red rays of the setting sun, sat the weasel, its coat golden, its mouth as black as ink. She spotted it while she was squatting down relieving herself. It rested on its haunches, slowly twitching its paws at her, and she reacted as though she'd been struck by lightning: a powerful spasm shot up her back, like a leaping snake. She fell forward, screaming like a madwoman. By the time she'd come to her senses, the field was dark, and bright stars leaped through the black sky, restlessly, mysteriously. She felt her way out of the sorghum field, found the dirt path, and walked back to the village. The fanciful image of the weasel, its golden coat emitting a lustrous sheen like whiskers of grain, appeared and disappeared in front of her eyes, over and over, vivid and real. It was all she could do to contain the screams ready to rip from her throat; some did in fact get loose—she heard them. But they weren't human screams, and she was shocked and frightened by their sound.

Second Grandma's deranged state lasted a long time, leading her fellow villagers to conclude that she'd been possessed by the weasel. She was convinced that it had absolute control over her in some deep, dark place. Whatever it ordered her to do, she did: cry, laugh, speak in tongues, perform strange acts. Whenever the lightning bolt hit her in the middle of her back, it was as though she'd been split in two, and was struggling in a dark-red quagmire filled with the seductiveness of lust and death, sinking beneath the surface, then floating back to the top, only to sink once again. Spotting a rope with which she could pull herself out of the quagmire of lust, she grabbed it with both hands, but it too became part of the quagmire of desire, and she sank helplessly beneath the surface again. Always, the image of the potent, black-mouthed weasel swayed before her eyes, grinning hideously and whisking her vigorously with its tail; each time its tail brushed against her skin, a shout of uncontrollable excitement burst from her mouth. Finally, the exhausted weasel walked off, and Second Grandma crumpled to the ground, spittle drooling from the corners of her mouth, her body lathered in sweat, her face the color of gold foil.

In order to free Second Grandma from her demon, Granddad rode his mule to the market at Cypress Orchid to fetch the Taoist exorcist Mountain Li, who lit incense and burned candles, then drew strange symbols on a piece of paper with a brush dipped in red ink, after which he mixed some dog blood with the incense ashes, pinched Second Grandma's nose shut, and poured the concoction into her mouth. The stuff streamed down her throat and she cried, she tried to scream, she flailed her arms and legs, as the soulful essence oozed out through her pores.

Her condition began to improve after that, and some time later the weasel came to steal a chicken. While it was locked in a desperate struggle with a large yellow-legged, fiery-red rooster, one of its eyes was pecked out by its feathered adversary. It was writhing in agony in the snow when Second Grandma ran into the yard, stark-naked yet oblivious to the cold, holding the white wooden bolt in her hands and bringing it down with all her might on the weasel's shameless, pointed snout. Having gotten her revenge, finally, she stood absently in the snow for quite a while, the bloody wooden bolt still in her hands. Then she bent over and beat her mentor, the weasel, to a pulp. Her madness spent, she turned and went back inside, carrying a residue of hatred with her.

As Second Grandma stared at the dried weasel blood on the white wooden bolt, she was suddenly gripped by a dormant and profoundly disturbing terror; she knew that her eyeballs were rolling wildly, and she heard a terrifying shriek erupt from her throat.

The flimsy door rocked only slightly before it came crashing open, and a golden-hued Japanese soldier, bayonet-tipped rifle in his hands, leaped nimbly into the room. In that shrieking split second, his ratlike features and crafty expression were transformed into the black-mouthed weasel that had died at her hands. His pointy chin, his black mustache above a pointy mouth, and his sly look were the spitting image of the weasel. From a hidden recess of Second Grandma's memory, her derangement resurfaced, stronger and more violent than before. Little Auntie, her ears still ringing from Second Grandma's shriek, was scared witless by the sight of her mother's mouth distorted with hate on her ash-smeared face. Straining with all her might, she broke free of Second Grandma's viselike grip and jumped up onto the windowsill, where she stared at the six Japanese soldiers—the first and the last that she would ever see.

Light glinted off the bayonets as the Japanese soldiers walked up to Second Grandma's kang and stood shoulder to shoulder. To Little Auntie their weasely faces were like sorghum cakes right out of the pan: brown with dark-red edges, warm and beautiful, lovely and inviting. Though she was only slightly frightened by their bayonets, her mother's face terrified her.

The Japanese soldiers grinned, baring their teeth, some even, some bright. Second Grandma, torn between derangement and terror, stared at the soldiers' ominous grins. She shrieked as she wrapped her arms tightly around her belly and pressed up against the wall. One of the soldiers, who must have been about five feet four and somewhere between thirty-five and forty years old, edged up to the kang, removed his cap, and scratched his balding scalp. In pidgin Chinese he said, "You, pretty girl, no be scared. . . ." He leaned his rifle against the edge of the kang, then crawled up clumsily, like a fat, squirming maggot. Second Grandma wished she could crawl into the cracks of the wall.

The tears running down her cheeks formed ruts in the ashes on her face. The Japanese soldier's thick lips parted as he reached out with a coarse, fleshy finger and touched her face, making her skin crawl, as though a slimy toad had wriggled into the crotch of her pants. She shrieked louder than ever, and the soldier grabbed her legs, pulling her toward him, banging her head loudly against the wall. She lay there flat on her back with her belly sticking up like a little mound. The soldier rubbed it with his hand, then, his eyes nearly bursting with anger, drove his fist down into it, hard. Then, pinning her legs with his knees, he reached down and undid her belt. By then she had begun to fight back; struggling to a sitting position, she sank her teeth into his garlic-shoot nose.

The Japanese soldier let out a strange scream and released her belt. Grabbing his bleeding nose, he glared at Second Grandma, as though seeing her in a new light. His buddies roared with laughter as he pulled a grimy handkerchief out of his pocket and held it against his nose. He stood up, his expression swiftly transformed from that of a poet passionately declaiming his undying love into the savage look of a jackal, which suited him better. He picked up his rifle and held the glinting tip of his bayonet against Second Grandma's belly. The final shriek burst from her mouth as she squeezed her eyes shut.

Little Auntie, still perched on the windowsill, read no malicious intent in the old soldier's fleshy round face; in fact, she even tried to grab the curious light reflected off his bald head, and was disgusted with Second Grandma for shrieking like a wild animal. But when she noticed the sudden change in his expression and saw him aim his bayonet at her mother's belly, fear and an overpowering sense of love flooded her heart. She jumped down from the windowsill and rushed up to Second Grandma.

The rat-faced, shrunken-cheeked Japanese soldier who'd been the first into the room said something to his fat comrade, then jumped up onto the kang and dragged him back down to the floor, mocking him with laughter. Still holding on to his rifle, he reached out his other bony yellow hand and grabbed Little Auntie by the hair, tearing her violently from Second Grandma's grasp, as if he were yanking a carrot out of the hard ground. He flung her against the window, then back onto the kang. Little Auntie forced back the sobs in her throat as the color drained from her face. The form and spirit of that part of Second Grandma controlled by the loathsome fanciful image of the weasel was suddenly released, and she flung herself like a she-wolf at the Japanese soldier, who deftly met the charge by kicking her in the belly. Although the force was absorbed by the bundle of clothes, the kick sent her reeling up against the thin connecting wall of the bedroom.

The sobs Little Auntie had been holding back suddenly burst forth, loud and resounding. Second Grandma's head quickly cleared, and the gaunt Japanese soldier standing in front of her was no longer linked to the phantasm of the weasel. His face was thin, the bridge of his nose high, sharp, and hooked, his eyes black and shiny; he looked like an articulate man of wide experience and considerable learning, someone well read and clever. Second Grandma knelt on the kang and pleaded in a sobbing voice: "Mister . . . honorable Commander . . .

spare us . . . please spare us. . . . Don't you have wives and daughters at home . . . sisters . . . ?"

The ratty pouches on the soldier's cheeks twitched a couple of times beneath his black eyes. Although he couldn't have understood Second Grandma's tearful pleas, he seemed to know what they meant, for she saw his shoulders slump briefly in the din of Little Auntie's wails. When Second Grandma glanced furtively at the other five Japanese soldiers, their expressions were all different; but she saw an oily-green, watery softness rolling gently beneath the hard crust of malevolence on their faces. Trying hard to maintain their malicious mockery, they stared at the skinny soldier standing on the kang. He quickly looked away; Second Grandma just as quickly sought out his eyes. Gnashing his teeth as though trying to control some deep emotion, he stuck the tip of his glinting bayonet against Little Auntie's open mouth.

"You, drop your pants! You, drop your pants!" He spoke Chinese as though his tongue were petrified.

At that moment Second Grandma began to crumple under the spell of the weasel again; she saw the Japanese soldier standing on her kang as a gentle, bookish man one instant and the spitting image of the black-mouthed weasel the next. She was racked by loud, spasmodic sobs. The tip of the bayonet was nearly buried in Little Auntie's mouth. A rush of concern for her young and a total disregard for her own well-being snapped her back to her senses. She quickly took off her pants, her underpants, and her shirt, then lay back and said resolutely, "Come on, come on and do it! But don't touch my child! Don't you touch my child!"

The Japanese soldier on the kang withdrew his bayonet and dropped his weary arms. Second Grandma lay there, her naked body the burnt, aromatic color of fried sorghum. A radiant, almost magical ray of sunlight shone between her legs, as though illuminating an ancient, beautiful myth or legend, a fairy grotto, the kindly yet majestic eye of God. As the Japanese gazed at the path through which all mankind must pass, at the same organ possessed by their own loved ones, their eyes glazed over and their faces hardened, like six clay statues. Second Grandma waited for them, her mind a gray void.

I sometimes wonder if Second Grandma might have avoided being ravaged if it had only been one Japanese soldier facing her splendid naked body that day. I doubt it, for a sole virile beast in human form, freed of the need to act like a performing monkey, might have been even more frenzied, shedding his handsomely embroidered uniform and pouncing on her like a wild animal. Under normal circumstances, it is the power of morality that keeps the beast in us hidden beneath a pretty exterior. A stable, peaceful society is the training ground for humanity, just as caged animals, removed from the violent unpredictability of the wild, are influenced by the behavior of their captors in time. Do you agree? Yes? No? Well, say it, yes or no? If I weren't a man myself, and if I were holding the sword of vengeance in my hand, I'd slaughter every last man on earth! If there had been just one Japanese soldier facing Second Grandma's naked body that day, maybe he would have thought of his mother or his wife, and left quietly. What do you think?

The six soldiers didn't budge. They were gazing upon Second Grandma's naked body as though it were a sacrificial offering. None was willing to leave; none dared to. She lay outstretched like a huge dogfish baking under a blazing sun. Little Auntie's voice was hoarse from all her crying, the sound growing weaker, the intervals longer. The once animated soldiers had been subdued by Second Grandma's offering up of her body, her stretching out on the kang like a loving mother in front of her sons, each of whom was thinking about the path he had traveled.

I believe that if Second Grandma had been able to hold out just a bit longer she might have achieved victory. Second Grandma, why, after lying there like that, did you have to get up and start putting your clothes back on? You had barely managed to stick one leg into your pants when the Japanese soldiers began to get restless. The one you'd bitten on the nose threw down his rifle and climbed onto the kang, and as you looked at him in disgust, your derangement took over. Then the skinny Jap who had found the way to subdue you jumped up and kicked his fat buddy away, swinging his fists and growling at his buddies in a language you didn't understand. Then, before you knew it, he was on top of you, gasping like a rooster and breathing foul air into your face.

The black-mouthed weasel flashed before your eyes, and once

again you shrieked madly. But you only stimulated the madness of the Japanese soldiers; your shrieks were met by a concert of shrieks from them.

It was the balding, middle-aged soldier who dragged the skinny one off you. Then he pressed his savage face up to yours, and you closed your eyes in revulsion. You thought you could feel your three-month-old fetus writhing in your belly, and could hear the desperate screeches of Little Auntie, like a rusty knife being drawn across a whetstone. The balding Jap chewed on your face with his daggerlike teeth, as though he wanted to pay you back for biting his nose. Your face was covered with tears, fresh blood, and his thick, sticky slobber. Hot red blood suddenly gushed from your mouth, and a vile stench filled your nostrils. The squirming fetus in your belly produced waves of liver-rending, lung-filling pain; every muscle, every nerve in your body tensed and knotted up, like so many bowstrings. The fetus seemed to be burrowing into some deep recess of your body to hide from a shame that could never be washed away. Anger festered in your heart, and when the Japanese soldier's greasy cheeks brushed up against your lips you made a feeble attempt to bite his face. His skin was tough and rubbery and had a sour taste.

The last one to mount Second Grandma was a short young soldier. Only shame showed on his face, and his lovely eyes were filled with the panic of a hunted rabbit. His body smelled like artemisia; the silvery glint of his teeth shone between trembling, fleshy red lips. Second Grandma felt a rush of pity for him, as she recognized his tortured look of self-loathing and shame under a thin layer of beaded sweat. He rubbed against her body at first, but then stopped and didn't dare move any more. She felt his belt buckle press up against her belly and his body quake.

The soldiers around the kang roared with laughter and shouted derisively at this impotent young soldier. Having gotten his second wind, the skinny one jumped up onto the kang, jerked the young soldier away roughly, and flaunted his own abilities without a trace of shame or embarrassment, making a grand display. Second Grandma felt dead below the neck. Something yellow spun around in her brain, yellow and elliptical. . . .

Afterward, way off in the distance, she heard Little Auntie let out a blood-curdling scream. Struggling to open her eyes, she could not believe what she saw. The young soldier with the lovely eyes stood on the kang and lifted Little Auntie on the point of his bayonet, swung her in a couple of arcs, then flung her away. Like a huge bird flapping its wings, she sailed slowly through the air and landed on the floor next to the kang. Her little red jacket fell open in the sunlight and began to spread out like a piece of soft, smooth red silk, gradually filling the room with undulating waves.

During her flight, Little Auntie's arms froze in the air and her hair stood up like porcupine quills. The young Japanese soldier, rifle in hand, wept clear blue tears.

Second Grandma screamed for all she was worth and strained to sit up. But her body was dead by then. A wave of yellow flashed before her eyes, followed by a green light. Finally, she was swallowed up by an inky black tide.

> Swing your sabers at the heads of Japs!
> The sorghum is red, the Japs come from the east.
> Trampling our soil and disgracing my second grandma.
> Patriotic brethren everywhere, the day of resistance is now!

5

GRANDDAD ARRIVED IN SALTWATER GAP the following morning. He had set out before dawn on one of our two black mules, and arrived just as the sun was climbing above the mountains. Dejection accompanied him on his trip, because of an argument he'd had with Grandma as he was leaving. He ignored the kaleidoscope of gorgeous light on the black Gaomi soil as the sun rose above the mountains, and the crows as they soared into the sky on green wings. The mule, whipped mercilessly by the twisted end of the hempen reins, turned to glare at the man on its back, convinced that it was already moving about as fast as it could go. Puddles of water from the autumn rains stood in the deep ruts left by passing wagons. Granddad, his face livid, passively absorbed the bumps and jolts of the mule beneath him. Field voles hunting for breakfast scurried to safety.

Granddad was toasting the aging Uncle Arhat in the distillery reception hall when he heard rifle and artillery fire from the northwest, and his heart nearly stopped. He rushed outside and looked up and down the street, but when he saw that things seemed normal he went back inside to continue drinking with Uncle Arhat, who was still the distillery foreman. In 1929, the year Granddad was reported murdered and Grandma ran off, the hired hands rolled up their bedding and set out to find work; but Uncle Arhat stayed behind, like a loyal watchdog, to guard the family property, convinced that the dark night was nearly over and that a new dawn would soon be breaking. He maintained his vigil until Granddad cheated death, escaped from prison, and was reconciled with Grandma. With Father in her arms, she followed him from Saltwater Gap back home, where they knocked at the cheerless front gate and roused Uncle Arhat, who, like a living ghost, rushed out of the shed where he'd set up housekeeping. The moment he spotted his master and mistress, he threw himself to the ground, hot tears streaking his leathery old face. He was such a decent, devoted man that Granddad and Grandma treated him like their own father, giving him a free hand in all distillery-related matters, including expenses, no matter how high they ran; they never once questioned him.

The sun was high in the southeast sky when more bursts of rifle fire erupted, and Granddad knew it was coming from somewhere near Saltwater Gap, perhaps from the village itself. Anxious and impatient, he went to get the mule to set out right away, but Uncle Arhat urged him to wait. Uncle Arhat made sense, but Granddad was too restless to stay put, walking in and out of the building as he waited for news from the hired hand Uncle Arhat had sent to investigate. Just before noon, the breathless man returned, sweaty-faced and mud-spattered, to report that the Japanese had surrounded Saltwater Gap at daybreak and that it was impossible to know what was going on there. He'd hidden in a clump of reeds some three li away, where he'd heard demonic cries and wolfish howls and seen thick columns of smoke rising from the village. After the man left, Granddad poured some wine, tipped back his head, and drained the cup, then ran to get his pistol, which he had hidden in a hole in the double-layer wall.

As he rushed outside, he bumped into seven or eight ragged, pale-faced refugees from Saltwater Gap, leading a popeyed, shedding old mule with two baskets slung over its back. A torn jacket with loose padding covered the one on the left; in the one on the right squatted a boy of about four. Granddad examined the boy's skinny neck, his enlarged head, his fleshy, fanlike ears, as he sat peacefully in the basket, not a care in the world, whittling a white willow switch with a nicked knife so rusty it had turned red. Wooden curlicues flew from the basket. Granddad asked his parents about the situation in the village, never taking his eyes off the child, particularly his large ears, which symbolized good luck, longevity, and great fortune.

The adults vied with one another to describe the actions of the Japanese soldiers in their village. They had managed to escape because their son, who had started bawling the previous afternoon, demanded to be taken to visit his maternal grandma. No threats or promises could get him to change his mind, and they finally gave in and, early the next morning, readied their mule. When the first shots were fired, they were one step ahead of the Japanese, who put the village under siege. Granddad asked about Second Grandma and my little auntie Xiangguan, but they shook their heads and fidgeted, anxious looks on their faces.

The boy in the basket lowered his busy hands to his belly, raised his head, and said weakly, his eyes closed, "Why aren't we moving? Waiting to be killed?" His parents froze for a moment, perhaps pondering the prophetic possibilities of what he'd said, then awoke to the reality of their situation. The mother looked numbly at Granddad as the father slapped the mule's rump, and the squad of refugees skittered off down the road. Granddad watched their retreating backs, especially the boy with the big droopy ears. His premonition would prove accurate, for twenty years later the little bastard would become a demonic zealot in this sinful spot known as Northeast Gaomi Township.

Granddad ran to the western wing, where he opened the hole in the double-layer wall to get his pistol. It was gone, but he could see the outline of the spot where it had lain. Something funny was going on here. He turned, and there stood Grandma, a contemptuous grin on her face. Thin eyebrows curved downward on her dark, gloomy face. Granddad glared at her and demanded, "Where's my pistol?"

Her upper lip twitched as two blasts of cold air snorted from her nostrils. With a final disdainful look she turned, picked up a feather duster, and began dusting the kang.

"Where's my pistol?" Granddad thundered.

"How the hell should I know?" she retorted, mercilessly beating the poor bedding.

"Give me my pistol," Granddad said, trying to keep his anxieties under control. "The Japanese have surrounded Saltwater Gap," he said in a low voice. "I have to see how they are."

Grandma spun around angrily and said, "Then go! It's none of my damned business!"

"Give me my pistol."

"How should I know where it is? Don't ask me."

Granddad pressed up close. "You stole my pistol and gave it to Black Eye, didn't you?"

"That's right, I gave it to him! And that's not all. I slept with him, and I loved it! It was wonderful! One hell of a time!"

Granddad's mouth split into a grin and he uttered a single "Ah!" as he clenched his fist and hit her squarely in her nose, from which dark blood spurted. She shrieked and crumpled to the floor like a toppled column. As she struggled to her feet, he drove his fist into her neck. The second punch, a real powerhouse, sent her flying into a chest against the wall.

"Slut! Filthy bitch!" Granddad lashed out through clenched teeth. Bad blood stored up over the years coursed through his veins like a poison. He was thinking back to the untold shame of being knocked down by Black Eye, and to how often he'd imagined Grandma lying beneath the wolfish man, moaning and panting and crying out shamelessly; with his guts writhing like snakes, and his body as hot as the midsummer sun, he grabbed the date-wood bolt from the door and took aim at Grandma's blood-smeared head as she tried to get to her feet, vital and tenacious as ever.

"Dad!" Father ran in screaming, grabbed the door bolt, and held on for dear life. His shout saved Grandma's life for sure. So instead of dying at the hands of Granddad, she would one day die from a Japanese bullet, and her death would be as glorious and as brilliant as ripened red sorghum.

Grandma crawled over to Granddad, wrapping her arms around his knees and rubbing his muscular legs. She raised her gloomy face, soaked with tears and blood, and said, "Zhan'ao—Zhan'ao—elder brother—dearest elder brother, kill me, go ahead and kill me! You can't imagine how it hurts to see you go, you'll never know how badly I want you to stay. With all the Japanese out there, I fear you'll never come back. No matter how great you may be, it's just you and your gun, and even a tiger is no match for a pack of wolves. It's that little bitch's doing, it's all her fault. You were never out of my mind when I was with Black Eye, and I won't let you go to your death! I can't live without you. Besides, my ten days aren't up yet, not till tomorrow. She's robbed me of half of you. . . . All right, go if you have to. . . . She can have one of my days. . . . I hid your beloved pistol and thirty-one bullets in the rice vat. . . ."

With her face buried in his legs, he was filled with remorse, especially since Father was lurking fearfully behind the door. Despising himself for being so brutal, he bent down, lifted up Grandma, who was nearly unconscious, and carried her over to the kang. He decided not to go to Saltwater Gap until first thing the next morning. Let heaven watch over mother and daughter and keep them from harm!

Granddad rode his mule from the village to Saltwater Gap, a distance of only fifteen li, although it seemed like miles. Even though the black mule ran like the wind, it wasn't fast enough for Granddad, who whipped it mercilessly with the hempen reins. Dirt clods flew in all directions behind the mule's hooves, a thin layer of dust hung in the air above the fields, and the sky was filled with rivers of meandering black clouds; a peculiar odor drifted over on the wind from Saltwater Gap.

Oblivious to the sprawling bodies, human and animal, Granddad went straight to Second Grandma's and rushed into the yard, his heart sinking as he saw the broken gate and smelled the stench of blood. He despaired when he saw the bedroom door, barely hanging on its hinges. Second Grandma lay on the kang in the same position she'd assumed when offering up her body to protect Little Auntie. . . . Xiangguan was sprawled on the dirt floor in front of the kang, her face puddled in her own blood, her mouth open in a silent scream.

Granddad let out a roar, drew his pistol, and stumbled to the still-panting black mule, which he smacked on the rump with his pistol, wanting to fly to the county town to avenge the murders on the Japanese. He didn't realize he'd taken the wrong road until he became aware of a patch of withered yellow reeds standing silently and solemnly in the morning sunlight. As he swung the mule around and headed off to town, he heard shouts behind him, but he kept beating the mule wildly without a backward glance. With each blow, the mule bucked, but the more it protested the angrier Granddad became. He was taking his fury out on the poor animal, which bucked and twisted so violently it finally threw its rider into last year's sorghum.

Granddad climbed to his feet like a wounded beast and aimed his pistol at the narrow head of the lathered mule, which stood rigidly, its head lowered and its rump covered by goose-egg-sized lumps and streaks of dark blood. Granddad leveled the gun with his shaky hand. Just then our other mule came flying down the road out of the red sunrise, Uncle Arhat on its back. Its hide shone as though covered with a coat of gold dust.

Uncle Arhat, exhausted, jumped down off the mule and took a couple of tottering steps before nearly collapsing. Placing himself between Granddad and the black mule, he reached out and forced down the hand holding the pistol. "Zhan'ao," he said, "come to your senses!"

As he looked into the face of Uncle Arhat, Granddad's seething anger turned into simmering sorrow, and tears slid down his face. "Uncle," Granddad said hoarsely, "both of them, mother and daughter . . . It's horrible. . . ."

Overcome by grief, he squatted on the ground. Uncle Arhat helped him up and said, "Manager Yu, a noble man can wait a decade to seek revenge. You should be back there taking care of arrangements so the dead can rest in peace."

Second Grandma wasn't dead. She gazed into the staring eyes of Granddad and Uncle Arhat as they stood beside her kang. Seeing her thick, heavy lashes, her dimming eyes, bloody nose, gnawed cheeks, and swollen lips made Granddad's heart feel as though it had been cleaved by a knife, the searing pain mixed with an agitation he couldn't drive away. Droplets of water began to ooze from the corners of her eyes, and her lips trembled slightly as she uttered a weak cry: "Elder brother . . ."

"Passion . . ." Granddad groaned.

Uncle Arhat backed silently out of the room.

Granddad leaned over the kang and dressed Second Grandma, who cried out when his hand brushed against her skin; she began to rant, just as she had years earlier when possessed by the weasel. He pinned her arms down to keep her from struggling, then slid her pants up over her dead, soiled legs.

Uncle Arhat walked in. "Manager Yu, I'll borrow a wagon from next door . . . take mother and daughter back to get better. . . ."

He searched Granddad's face for a reaction. Granddad nodded.

Uncle Arhat picked up two comforters and ran outside, where he spread them out on the bed of the big-wheeled wagon. Granddad cradled Second Grandma, one arm under the nape of her neck, the other under the crook of her legs, as if she were a priceless treasure. He walked past the smashed gate out into the street, where Uncle Arhat waited with the wagon. He had hitched one of the mules to the wagon shafts; the poor mule whose rump Granddad had beaten bloody was tied to the rear crossbar. Granddad laid the now-screaming Second Grandma onto the bed of the wagon. He knew how badly she wanted to be strong, but he also knew she didn't have the will.

Now that he'd taken care of Second Grandma, he turned to see Uncle Arhat, his weathered face streaked with an old man's tears, walking up with the corpse of Little Auntie Xiangguan. Granddad's throat felt as if it were in the grip of a pair of metal tongs. He coughed violently, racked by dry heaves. Gripping the axle to support himself, he looked skyward and saw in the southeast the enormous emerald fireball of the sun bearing down on him like a wildly spinning wagon wheel.

Taking the body of Little Auntie in his arms, he looked down into a face twisted by torment; two stinging tears fell to the ground.

After laying Little Auntie's corpse next to Second Grandma, he lifted a corner of the comforter and covered the girl's terror-streaked face.

"Get up on the wagon, Manager Yu," Uncle Arhat said.

Granddad sat impassively on the railing, his legs dangling over the side.

Uncle Arhat flicked the reins and started out slowly, the axles of the wagon turning with difficulty. Long-drawn-out groans emerged from the dry, oil-starved sandalwood, followed by loud creaks that sounded like death rattles as the wagon bumped and rolled out of the village and onto the road heading toward our village, from which the scent of sorghum wine rose into the air. Although Second Grandma looked as if she had been rocked to sleep by the bumpy ride, her misty gray eyes remained open. Granddad put his finger under her nose to see if she was breathing. Weak, but he could feel it; that put him at ease.

A vast open field all around, a wagon of suffering passing through, the sky above as boundless as a dark ocean, black soil flat as far as the eye could see, sparse villages like islands adrift. As he sat on the wagon, Granddad felt that everything in the world was a shade of green.

The shafts of the wagon were much too narrow for our big mule, the spoked wheels much too light. Its belly was squeezed so uncomfortably between the shafts that it wanted to start running; but Uncle Arhat controlled the metal bit in its mouth, so it could only nurse a silent grievance and raise its forelegs as high as possible, as though it were prancing. Mumbled, sobbing curses tumbled from Uncle Arhat's mouth: "Fucking swine . . . fucking inhuman swine . . . slaughtered the whole family next door, ripped open the daughter-in-law's belly. . . . Depraved . . . Unborn baby looked like a skinned rat. . . . Potful of soupy yellow shit . . . Fucking swine . . ."

The black mule tied to the back of the wagon plodded along behind, its head bowed, although it was impossible to tell whether the look on its long face was one of indignation, anger, shame, or capitulation.

6

FATHER RECALLED THAT THE MULE-DRAWN WAGON carrying Second Grandma and the corpse of Little Auntie Xiangguan arrived in our village at noon. A strong wind from the northwest raised clouds of dust on the roads and rustled leaves on the trees. Dead skin peeled from his lips in the parched air. When the wagon, one mule in front and another at the rear, appeared in the village, he ran like the wind to meet it. Uncle Arhat was hobbling along beside the bumping, creaking wagon. The mules, Granddad, and Uncle Arhat all had a gummy, dust-covered residue in the corners of their eyes. Granddad sat on the railing, holding his head in his hands like a clay idol or a wooden icon. The scene sucked the words right out of Father's mouth. At a distance of about twenty yards from the wagon, his sensitive nose detected an inauspicious odor emanating from the wagon. Frightened, he turned and ran back home, blurting out to Grandma, who was anxiously pacing the floor, "Mom, Dad's back, the mule's pulling a long wagon, dead people in the back."

Grandma's face fell. After a momentary pause, she rushed outside with him.

The wagon wheels ground to a bumpy halt, creaking one last time as the wagon stopped just beyond the gate. Granddad climbed down slowly and stared at Grandma with bloodshot eyes. The sight frightened Father; Granddad's eyes reminded him of the cat's-eye stones on the banks of the Black Water River, whose colors were forever changing.

"Well, you got your wish!" Granddad snarled at Grandma.

Not daring to defend herself, she timidly approached the wagon, Father on her heels, and looked into the bed. The folds of the comforter were filled with black earth, revealing the lumpy outlines of whatever was underneath. She picked up a corner, but let it drop as though her fingers were scalded. Father glimpsed Second Grandma's smashed, pulpy face and Little Auntie's rigid, open mouth.

That open mouth called up all sorts of pleasant childhood memories for Father. He'd frequently gone to Saltwater Gap to spend a few days, against Grandma's wishes. Granddad had told him to call Second Grandma "Second Mom," and since she treated him like her own son, he thought she was just wonderful. She occupied a special place deep in his heart, and seeing her was like coming home. Little Auntie Xiangguan had a mouth as sweet as honey that was forever filling the air with gentle shouts of "Elder Brother." This dark-skinned little sister was one of his favorites, and he was fascinated by the fine, nearly transparent fuzz on her face; most of all he loved her bright eyes, like shiny buttons. Yet, just when they were at the peak of enjoyment, Grandma would send someone over to drag him home, and he would look down at her from his perch in the arms of the messenger on the mule and feel terribly sad. He wondered why Grandma and Second Grandma hated each other so.

Father thought back to the time he'd gone to weigh the dead baby, a couple of years or so earlier. He'd accompanied Mother to the place called Dead Baby Hollow, some three li beyond the village. Since township tradition forbade the burial of babies under the age of five, the tiny corpses were abandoned out in the open. Traditional birthing customs were followed back then, and only the most rudimentary medical treatment was available, so the infant mortality rate was particularly high, and only the strongest survived.

I sometimes think that there is a link between the decline in humanity and the increase in prosperity and comfort. Prosperity and comfort are what people seek, but the costs to character are often terrifying.

When Father went to Dead Baby Hollow with Grandma, she was obsessed with the Flower Lottery, a small-scale form of gambling in which you neither fly too high nor fall too hard, which had captivated the villagers, the women in particular; since Granddad was enjoying a stable, prosperous life, the villagers chose him as the society head and banker. Placing the names of thirty-two flowers in a bamboo tube, he publicly drew out two a day, one in the morning and one at night. The herbaceous peony or the Chinese rose, maybe the common rose, maybe the prickly rose. The gambler whose flower was picked earned thirty times the amount she'd bet. Women caught up in the Flower Lottery devised all manner of methods to guess which name Granddad would draw. Some poured wine down their daughters' throats in anticipation of babbled visions in their drunkenness. Others forced themselves to dream for the answer. Going to Dead Baby Hollow was Grandma's unique and appalling method.

It was so dark that Father couldn't see his hand in front of his face. Grandma had wakened him in the middle of the night, startling him out of a deep slumber and making him feel like screaming at her for frightening him like that. "Don't make a sound," she had whispered.

"Come with me to guess the flowers." With his natural curiosity and the promise of a good mystery, Father was immediately awake and eager to go. Quickly putting on their boots and caps, they tiptoed past Granddad and slipped out of the yard and the village. Because they proceeded with caution and walked very quietly, their passage went unnoticed even by the village dogs. Grandma was holding Father's left hand, leaving his right hand free to carry a red-paper lantern; she was holding him with her right hand, leaving her left hand free to carry her special scale, on which the names of thirty-two flowers were carved.

As they walked out of the village Father heard a southeast wind whistling through the sorghum fields and rustling the broad green leaves; he could smell the Black Water River far off in the distance. After groping along for a li or so, he grew accustomed enough to the dark to distinguish between the brown road surface and the waist-high sorghum by the roadside. The soughing of the wind through the stalks added to the mystery of the dark night, while the screeches of an owl on one of the trees out there cast a patina of terror over the enigma of the dark night.

The owl was perched in a large willow tree directly above Dead Baby Hollow. Had it been daytime, Grandma and Father would have been able to see the growths of blood-red beards on the trunk of the tree, which stood in the middle of a marshy plot of land. Father sensed the owl's green eyes flashing solemnly amid the willow branches. His teeth chattered and chills snaked from the soles of his feet all the way up to the crown of his head. He squeezed Grandma's hand, feeling that his head was about to explode from the terror building up inside it.

A sticky odor clung to the air above Dead Baby Hollow. White drops of rain the size of brass coins fell to the ground, gouging out scars in the impenetrable blackness. Grandma tugged on Father's hand as a sign for him to kneel down, and as he did so his hands and legs touched wild grasses growing in crazy profusion in the marshy land; the coarse, needlelike tips of leaves jabbed his chin, upsetting the harmony in his soul. He felt countless pairs of dead babies' eyes boring into his back and heard them kicking, squirming, laughing.

Bang bang crack crack. Grandma was striking a flint against a piece of steel. Gentle red sparks illuminated her trembling hands. When the tinder caught fire, she blew on it, and a weak glimmer of light began to spread. She lit the red candle in the paper lantern, from which a ball of red light emerged like a lonely specter. The owl's song stopped as dead babies formed ranks to surround Father, Grandma, and the lantern.

Grandma made a search of the marshy hollow while dozens of moths slammed into the red-paper covering of the lantern in her hand. Her bound feet made walking difficult on the wild grasses and the soft ground. Father was curious to know what she was looking for, but didn't dare ask. He followed her silently.

A rolled-up straw mat lay amid a clump of thick-stemmed, broad-leafed cocklebur. Grandma handed Father the lantern, laid her scale on the ground, then bent over and picked up the mat. In the red light of the lantern her fingers looked like squirming pink worms. The mat fell open to reveal a dead infant wrapped in rags. Its bald head was like a shiny gourd. Father's knees were knocking. Grandma picked up the scale and hooked it to the rag shroud. Holding the scale in one hand, she adjusted the weight with the other. But with a loud rip the rag gave out and the tiny corpse fell to the ground, followed by the weight, which landed on Grandma's toe, and the scale, which flew over and hit Father on the head. He yelped in pain and nearly dropped the lantern. The owl let out a hideous laugh, as though mocking their clumsiness. Grandma picked up the scale and jammed the hook through the baby's flesh. The horrifying sound made Father's skin crawl. He looked away, and by the time he'd turned back, Grandma was moving the weight across the arm of the scale, notch by notch, higher and lower, until it was in perfect balance. She signaled Father to bring the lantern closer. The scale glowed red. There it was: "peony."

When they reached the village Father could still hear the owl's angry screeches.

Grandma confidently put her money on "peony."

The winner that day was "winter sweet."

Grandma fell gravely ill.

As Father looked at Little Auntie Xiangguan, he recalled that the mouth of the dead infant also gaped; his ears rang with the songs of the owl, and he yearned for the moist air of the marshy land, since his lips and tongue were parched by a dry northwest wind that sent dust swirling in the sky.

Father saw how Granddad was looking at Grandma, darkly malevolent, like a bird of prey about to pounce. Her back hunched suddenly as she bent over the bed of the wagon and began thumping the comforter, her face covered with tears and snot: "Little sister . . . dear little sister . . . Xiangguan . . . my baby . . ."

Granddad's anger softened in the face of Grandma's anguish. Uncle Arhat walked up beside her and said softly, "Mistress, don't cry. Let's take them inside."

Grandma picked up Little Auntie Xiangguan's body and carried it into the house. Granddad followed her with Second Grandma.

Father stayed on the street to watch Uncle Arhat lead the mule out from between the shafts of the wagon, its sides rubbed raw by the narrow shafts. Then he untied the other one from behind the wagon. They shook themselves violently, filling the sky with fine dust clouds, before Uncle Arhat led them into the eastern compound. Father fell in behind him. "Go home, Douguan," Uncle Arhat said, "go on home."

Grandma was sitting on the floor stoking a fire in the stove, on which a half-filled pot of water stood. As soon as Father slipped into the room, he spotted Second Grandma lying on the kang, eyes open, cheeks twitching ceaselessly. He also saw Little Auntie Xiangguan lying across the top of the kang, a red bundle covering her hideous countenance. Once again he thought back to that night when he had accompanied Grandma to Dead Baby Hollow to weigh the dead infant. The braying of the mules in the eastern compound sounded incredibly like the owl's screeching. Soon, Xiangguan would be lying in Dead Baby Hollow to feed the wild dogs. He had never dreamed that the dead could look so hideous, yet he could barely resist removing the red bundle to stare at Xiangguan's repulsive face.

Grandma walked into the room with a brass basin full of hot water and placed it beside the kang. "Go outside!" she said, giving Father a shove.

Reluctantly, resentfully, he went into the outer room and heard the door shut behind him. Unable to control his curiosity, he stuck his eye up against a crack in the door to see what was happening inside. Granddad and Grandma were kneeling beside the kang undressing Second Grandma. When they flung her clothes to the floor, her soaked pants landed with a loud thud. The nauseating stink of blood assailed Father's nostrils. Second Grandma flailed her arms weakly as ghastly sounds emerged from her mouth.

"Hold her arms down," Grandma pleaded. Both Grandma's and Granddad's faces were blurred in the rising steam from the brass basin.

Grandma took a steaming sheepskin towel and wrung it dry, the excess water dripping loudly into the basin. The towel was so hot it scalded her hands, even when she flipped it from one to the other. After shaking it open, she placed it on Second Grandma's soiled face. Poor Second Grandma twisted her neck, and screams of terror, owllike screeches, filtered up through the towel. When Grandma removed the towel, it was filthy. She swished it in the basin, then wrung it dry, and slowly wiped down Second Grandma's body.

Less and less steam rose from the brass basin, while beads of condensed steam dotted Grandma's face. "Dump the dirty water," she said to Granddad, "and bring me some clean water."

Father ran out into the yard to watch Granddad. His back was bent as he staggered over to the low wall of the privy to dump the water on the other side. Father ran back and put his eye up to the crack in the door again. By now Second Grandma's body was glowing like polished sandalwood. Her protests were low and labored, no more than agonized moans. Grandma had Granddad lift her up so she could remove the kang mat. Then she took a clean one and spread it over the kang. After Granddad laid Second Grandma back down, Grandma put a big wad of cotton between her legs and covered her with a sheet. "Little sister," she said softly, "sleep, go to sleep. Zhan'ao and I will stay with you."

Second Grandma closed her eyes peacefully.

Granddad went out to dump some more water.

While Grandma was washing Little Auntie Xiangguan's body, Father slipped rashly into the room and stood in front of the kang. Grandma saw him but didn't chase him away. As she wiped the dried blood from Little Auntie's body, pearllike strands of tears fell from her eyes. When she was finished, she leaned her head against the bedroom wall and didn't move for a long time, as though she, too, were dead.

At sunset Granddad wrapped Little Auntie's body in a blanket and held it in his arms. Father followed him to the door. "Go on back, Douguan. Stay with Mom and Second Mom."

Uncle Arhat stopped Granddad at the southern-compound gate. "Manager Yu," he said, "you go back, too. I'll take care of it."

Granddad returned to the doorway, where he held Father's hand and watched Uncle Arhat walk out of the village.

7

ON THE TWENTY-THIRD DAY of the twelfth month in 1973, Eighteen Stabs Geng celebrated his eightieth birthday. Waking at the crack of dawn, he overheard the weak, sickly voice of an old neighbor woman—"Yongqi . . ."—and the gravelly voice of a man—"Feeling better, Ma?" The old woman replied, "No, I'm dizzier when I wake up than when I go to bed. . . ."

Eighteen Stabs Geng strained to sit up by resting his hands on the icy mat. He, too, felt dizzy this morning. A cold wind whistled outside, driving snow flurries against the murky paper on the window. He threw his moth-eaten dog pelt over his shoulders, reached out for his dragon-head cane leaning against the wall behind the door, and stumbled out the door. The yard was covered by a thick blanket of snow, and as he gazed at the crumbling earth wall all he could see was a sea of silvery white, dotted here and there with sorghum husks.

The snowfall showed no sign of letting up. He turned back, a sense of the survivor's good fortune in his heart, but when he raised the lids of the rice and flour vats with the head of his cane, both were empty. Last night's eyes hadn't tricked him. His stomach had not been visited by food for two days now, and his useless old intestines twitched and twisted. It was time to swallow his pride and ask for some grain. Although his belly was empty and he was shivering from the cold, he knew that getting grain out of the hardhearted branch secretary was not going to be easy. He decided to boil some water to warm his belly before going out for a showdown with that bastard. He raised the lid of the water vat. No water, just chunks of ice.

It dawned on him that he hadn't lit the stove for three days, and that it had been ten days since his last visit to the well. He went into the yard and scooped up twenty or thirty gourdfuls of snow, which he dumped into his cracked, unscrubbed pot. Then he looked around for some firewood, but there was none. So he went into the bedroom, tore a handful of straw from the mat covering the kang, and hacked up some woven sorghum cushions and a block of straw with his cleaver. He knelt down and started a fire with his flintstone. Matches that used to sell for two fen a box now required a ration coupon, which he didn't have, and he couldn't afford matches that didn't require a coupon. He was a penniless old bastard.

Tongues of red flame began to lick out of the black hole in the stove, so he pressed up close to warm his freezing belly. The chill melted away, but his back was as cold as ever. After quickly stuffing more straw into the stove, he turned his back to the fire. The chill melted from his back, but ice re-formed on his belly. A body cold on one side and warm on the other only increased his misery, so he concentrated on feeding straw into the stove to get some water boiling. With a bellyful of hot water, he could stand up to that little bastard, and if he couldn't squeeze any grain out of him, at least he'd take him away from his toasty stove for a while.

As the fire began to die out under the pot of water, he shoved the last handful of straw into the greedy, gaping black mouth of the old Kitchen God and prayed it would burn slowly. But the fuel flared up and burned like mad, with no sign of progress in the pot. So he jumped up, more nimbly than even he thought possible, and dashed into the bedroom, where he ripped out the last few handfuls of straw from under the kang mat, and stuffed them into the stove hole, a desperate attempt to melt the ice in the pot. Then, with brutal determination, he shoved his little three-legged stool into the stove hole and jammed his nearly bald broom down the black throat of the Kitchen God, which belched once or twice and vomited clouds of dense black smoke. Turning pale with fright, he frantically fanned the air around the stove, which kept swallowing, then spewing clouds of smoke. A loud crackle preceded the harsh, glowing flames from the stool and the broom, as he paused to catch his breath. Stung by the smoke, his old eyes shed tears like gummy mucus, which coursed down his leathery face.

The water in the pot began to sizzle like chirping cicadas—music to his ears—and a childlike grin spread across his face. However, when the fire began to dim, his smile was quickly replaced by a look of panic. Jumping to his feet, he searched for something, anything, to burn. The beams and crossbars would work, but he wasn't strong enough to pull them down. Suddenly he remembered the story of Iron Crutch Li, one of the Eight Immortals, who incinerated his own leg. According to legend, Iron Crutch Li stuck his leg into the stove and listened to it crackle. "Dear brother," his wife had said, "you'll make yourself a cripple." And just as she had forecast, the leg was ruined. Of course Geng knew he was no immortal, and even without burning his leg he could barely take a step. But, gimp or no, he was going to make his way to the branch secretary's home and demand some grain.

Finally, as the fire in the stove was about to die, Geng's gaze fell upon the spirit shrine set into the wall, and the black tablet it held. He reached up with his dragon-head cane to knock it loose. Dust flew and fear gripped his old heart as a profound misery suddenly penetrated the marrow of his bones. He picked up the ash-covered fox-spirit tablet, to which he'd made offerings for thirty-six years, and flung it into the belly of the stove. Hungry flames began licking the tablet, which sizzled and spat out juicy, dark-red drops . . . scorching the flesh of the red fox that had diligently licked the eighteen wounds on his body with its cool, glorious tongue. Nothing would ever shake his belief that there was something miraculous about the fox's tongue, since his wounds had been free of infection even after he'd crawled back to the village.

Although he was sure that his miraculous salvation portended good fortune in his future, it somehow never came. Eventually he became a pensioner, protected by the "five guarantees" of food, clothing, medical aid, housing, and burial, and knew that his good fortune had finally arrived. But even that soon vanished, as he was neglected by everyone, including the little bastard who had been squatting in the basket over the mule's back whittling a willow switch years earlier—the current branch secretary, who would probably be provincial secretary by now had he not been responsible for the deaths of nine people during the Great Leap Forward. The little bastard had canceled his eligibility for the "five guarantees."

The wooden tablet burned as slowly as a living fox, and as the blood-red tongues of flame baked away, he heard the water in the pot seethe and boil.

After scooping up the scalding water with the cracked gourd, he quickly sipped a mouthful and sent it coursing down to his stomach. He shuddered, then swallowed another mouthful. Now he was an immortal.

By the time he'd drunk two gourds of the hot water, his body was sweaty, and the lice, rejuvenated by the warmth, began to squirm and crawl around. Now he was hungrier than ever, but at least his strength had returned. Supported by his dragon-head cane, he walked out into the snowy landscape, shards of white jade cracking beneath his feet, his mind as clear as a bright August sky. The street was deserted, except for a black dog that stopped every so often to shake the snow off its back.

He followed the dog to the home of the little bastard, whose shiny black gate was closed tight. Fiery winter-sweet blossoms atop the wall drooped down like bright-red droplets. Absentmindedly admiring them, he walked up the stone steps, breathed deeply, and knocked on the gate. A dog barked, but there were no human sounds. Suddenly gripped by fury, he leaned against the wall to steady himself, raised his dragon-head cane, and pounded the hasp of the shiny black gate. The dog on the other side roared and howled.

Finally the gate opened. A bright-eyed, pudgy little dog darted out and charged at him, but quickly retreated when Old Geng waved his cane in its face. Next out was a fair-skinned middle-aged woman. "Oh, it's you, Master Geng," she said genially when she saw Eighteen Stabs standing at the gate. "What can I do for you?"

"I want to see the secretary," he answered hoarsely.

"He went to a meeting at the commune," she said sympathetically.

"Let me in," he said weakly. "I want to ask him what right he had to make me ineligible for a pension. I was bayoneted eighteen times by the Japs, but they didn't kill me. Did I go through all that just so I could starve to death at his hands?"

"Master Geng," the woman said awkwardly, "he's not home, honest. He went to a meeting at the commune early this morning. If you're hungry, come in and have something to eat. We don't have much, but there are plenty of yam cakes."

"Yam cakes?" he said icily. "Not even your dog eats yam cakes!"

The woman was losing patience. "I won't force you to eat them. He's not home. He's in a meeting at the commune. That's where you'll find him!" She pulled her head back in and slammed the gate shut. He raised his cane and pounded on the gate again, but was so weak he nearly crumpled to the ground. As he shuffled through the foot-deep snow on the street, he mumbled, "Go to the commune. . . . Go to the commune. . . . Sue the little bastard. . . . Sue him for oppressing decent folk, sue him for holding back my grain." Even after he'd walked a long way, he could still smell the delicate fragrance of winter sweets amid the falling snow; he stopped and turned, then spat in the direction of the shiny black gate. The winter-sweet blossoms waved in the falling snowflakes like crackling tongues of flames.

It was nearly dusk by the time he reached the commune gate, whose steel ribs were as big around as his thumb; each was tipped with a barb. He could see through the spaces that the snow on the ground in the commune yard was black and filthy. People in new clothes and new caps, with large heads, fleshy ears, and greasy mouths, were scurrying back and forth. Some carried debristled pigs' heads—the tips of the ears were blood-red—others carried silvery ribbonfish, and still others carried recently slaughtered chickens and ducks. He banged his dragon-head cane against the metal ribs, raising a loud clatter; but the people inside were too busy to give him anything but chilly glances before continuing on their way. He shouted angrily, tearfully, "Your honor . . . leader . . . I've been treated unjustly. . . . I'm starving. . . ."

A young man with three fountain pens in his coat pocket walked over and said coolly, "What's all the racket about, old-timer?"

Seeing all those pens in the young man's pocket, he assumed he'd caught the attention of a ranking official, so he knelt down in the snow, grabbed hold of two metal ribs in the gate, and said tearfully, "Eminent leader, the production-brigade branch secretary has held back my grain rations. I haven't eaten for three days, I'm starving, eighteen stabs by the Japs didn't kill me, now I'm going to starve to death. . . ."

"What village are you from?" the young man asked him.

"Don't you know me, eminent leader?" he asked. "I'm Eighteen Stabs Geng."

The young man laughed. "How am I supposed to know you're Eighteen Stabs Geng? Go home and see your brigade leader. The commune organizations are on holiday."

Old Geng banged on the metal gate for a long time, but no one else paid him any attention. Soft yellow light shone down from the windows in the compound, in front of which feathery snowflakes swirled silently. Firecrackers exploded somewhere in the village, reminding him that it was time to send off the Kitchen God to make his report in heaven. He wanted to go home, but as he took his first step he fell headlong to the ground, as though shoved. When his face hit the snow, it felt amazingly warm, reminding him of his mother's bosom—no, it was more like his mother's womb. His eyes were closed in the womb, where he swam in complete freedom, with no worries about food, clothes, anything. He was indescribably happy; the absence of hunger and cold brought him extreme joy.

The golden rays of light from the commune windows and the fiery-red winter-sweet blossoms at the home of the branch secretary lit up the world like rapidly licking flames, and the glare blinded him; snowflakes swirled like gold and silver foil as each family sent off its Kitchen God on a paper horse to soar up to heaven. With all that light streaming down on him, his body felt hot and dry, as though he'd caught fire. He quickly stripped off his jacket—hot. Then he took off his padded pants—hot. Took off his padded shoes—hot. Took off his felt cap—hot. Naked, just as he had emerged from his mother's womb—hot. He lay down in the snow, the snow scalded his skin; he rolled around in the snow—hot, so hot. He gobbled up some snow, it burned his throat as though it were filled with sunbaked pebbles of sand. Hot! So hot! Rising from the snow, he grabbed the metal ribs of the gate, but they scalded him, and he couldn't pull his hands off the gate. The last thing he wanted to shout was: Hot! So hot!

The young man with the pens in his pocket came out early the next morning to shovel snow. When he casually raised his head and glanced at the gate, his face paled with fright. What he saw was the old man from last night who'd called himself Eighteen Stabs Geng, stark naked, his hands stuck to the gate, like the crucified Jesus. His face had turned purple, his limbs were spread out, his staring eyes were fixed on the commune compound; hard to believe he was a lonely old man who had died of starvation. The young man made a careful count of the scars on his body. There were eighteen, all right, no more, no less.

8

POCKY CHENG WAS FINALLY SET FREE by the Japs after leading them to all the village sandal workshops, each of which they blew up. "Are there any more?" Chestnut Wool Cap asked sternly.

"No," he asserted, "honest, there aren't."

Chestnut Wool Cap looked over at the Japanese, who nodded. "Get the hell out of here!" he said. Cheng backed up a dozen or so steps, bowing and scraping, then nodding over and over, as he spun around to get out of there as fast as his legs would carry him. But they were so rubbery, and his heart was pounding so hard, that he froze on the spot. The bayonet wound in his chest throbbed, and the mess in his crotch had turned sticky and cold. As he leaned against a tree to catch his breath, he heard ghostly sobs and screams from the houses around him. His legs buckled as he slid to the ground, his back scraping the dry, brittle bark of the tree. Clouds of smoke filled the sky above the village, the residue of exploding hand grenades, I suppose.

After lobbing hundreds of black muskmelon grenades through overhead windows and doors, the Japanese encircled the sandal workshops while muted explosions tore them apart, making the ground tremble as thick smoke rose from the windows, accompanied by the pitiful screams of those who had survived the blasts. The Japanese soldiers then stuffed straw into the windows, muting the shrieks inside until you had to strain to hear them. With Pocky Cheng as their guide, the Japanese blew up twelve workshops. He knew that three-fourths of the village men made straw sandals and slept in those workshops, so there was little chance any of them could have survived. The enormity of his crime hit him suddenly. Without his lead, the Japanese would never have found the workshop in the remote corner of the eastern section of the village; it was one of the biggest, employing twenty or thirty men, who spent their nights there weaving sandals and joking with one another. The Japanese lobbed over forty grenades into that workshop alone, blasting the roof off the building, which, following the last explosion, became a flattened graveyard. A single willow pole that had supported the roof stood alone in the mud like a rifle barrel pointing to the crimson sky.

He was afraid. He was racked with guilt. All around, familiar, newly dead faces denounced him. He began to defend himself: The Japs forced me at bayonet-point. If I hadn't led the way, they'd have found the workshops on their own. The murdered villagers glanced at one another in stupefaction, then left quietly. As he gazed at their mangled bodies, he felt like a man soaking in an icy pool, freezing inside and out.

After dragging himself home, Pocky Cheng discovered his beautiful wife and thirteen-year-old daughter lying in the yard, naked, their intestines spread out around them. Everything turned black, and he keeled over. He felt dead one minute, alive the next. He was running after something, heading southwest. A red oval cloud floated in the rosy southwest sky, where his wife, his daughter, and hordes of villagers were standing, men and women, young and old. He ran as though his feet had wings, chasing the slow-moving cloud, his face raised skyward. The people in the cloud spat at him, even his wife and daughter. He hastily defended himself, but the spittle continued to rain down on him. He watched the cloud rise higher and higher in the sky, until it turned into a bright, blood-red dot.

For his beautiful, fair-skinned young wife, marrying a man with pockmarks had been a disgrace. But at the village inn he played his woodwind every night, making it weep and cry, and nearly breaking her heart. It was his woodwind she'd married. Over and over he played it, until she grew tired of it; and his pocked face, which had repulsed her from the very beginning, now became unbearable. So she ran off with a fabric peddler, but Pocky Cheng went after her and dragged her back, spanking her until her buttocks were swollen and puffy: a battered wife, kneaded dough. From then on, she put her heart and soul into domesticity. First she had a little girl, then a little boy, who was now eight. Regaining his senses, Pocky went looking for the boy, and found him, stuffed in the water vat, head down, feet up, his body as rigid as a pole.

Pocky Cheng tied a rope to the top of the door frame, made a noose in the end, then stood on a stool, stuck his head through the noose, and kicked the stool out from under himself. A teenage boy happening on him reached up with his knife and cut the rope in two. Pocky Cheng crashed to the ground.

"Uncle Pocky!" the boy fumed. "Haven't the Japanese killed enough of us? Why do their job for them? You can't get revenge unless you're alive!"

Pocky Cheng complained tearfully to the boy, "Chunsheng, your auntie, Little Orchid, Little Pillar, they're all dead. My whole family's gone!"

Chunsheng walked into the yard, knife in hand, and when he returned his face was as white as a sheet and his eyes were red. "Uncle," he said as he helped Pocky Cheng to his feet, "let's join the Jiao-Gao regiment! They're at the village of Two Counties recruiting soldiers and buying horses right now."

"But my house, my belongings?" Pocky Cheng said.

"You crazy old man! You just tried to hang yourself. Who'd have gotten your house and belongings then? Let's go!"

It was especially cold in the early spring of 1940. All the villages in Northeast Gaomi Township lay in ruins. Those who had survived were like marmots in burrows. The powerful Jiao-Gao Regiment was beset by the miseries of hunger and cold. From commander to common foot-soldier, the gaunt, thin men all shivered in their unlined jackets. After making camp in a tiny village not far from Saltwater Gap, they lay atop the battered wall when the sun came out to pick lice off their bodies and soak up the midday heat. All day long they conserved their energy; then, at night, they nearly froze in the cold. They were afraid that if they weren't killed by the Japs the weather would do them in.

Pocky Cheng was their most fearless fighter, a lionhearted man who had earned the complete trust of the commander, Little Foot Jiang. Hand grenades were his weapons of choice. In battle he would rush to the front line, close his eyes, and hurl one grenade after another at the enemy. Even if they were only six or seven yards away, he refused to take cover; yet, strange as it sounds, with shrapnel flying around him like locusts, he was never hit.

Commander Jiang called a meeting of officers to grapple with the problems of cold and hunger. Pocky Cheng rashly burst in on them, a stern look on his face. "What do you think we should do, Old Cheng?" Little Foot Jiang asked him.

Pocky Cheng held his tongue.

A bookish squad leader volunteered, "Holing up here in Northeast Gaomi Township is the same as waiting to die. We should go to the cotton factories in Southern Jiao County to get some clothes. And since there's plenty of yams there, food won't be a problem, either."

Commander Jiang took a mimeographed newspaper from his shirt and said, "According to news reports, the situation in Southern Jiao is grimmer than here. The rail brigade was wiped out by the Japanese. By comparison, Northeast Gaomi Township is ideal for guerrilla activity. The land is broad, the villages are few and far between, and the Japanese and their puppet troops are weaker here. Since most of last year's sorghum crop hasn't been harvested, we have more places to hide. All we have to do is solve the problems of food and clothing. The chance to attack the enemy will come as long as we stick it out."

A gaunt-faced officer said, "Where are we going to find any cloth? Or cotton wadding? Or food? Except for sorghum that's sprouting buds, we've got nothing to eat. And that alone could wind up killing us! I say we pretend to surrender to the puppet-regiment commander, Zhang Zhuxi. That way, we could get our hands on some lined clothes and stock up on ammo, then pull out."

The bookish squad leader jumped angrily to his feet. "You want us to become a bunch of traitors?"

The officer defended himself: "Who asked you to become a traitor? I said *pretend* to surrender! Back in the Three Kingdoms period, that's what Jiang Wei did, and so did Huang Gai!"

"We're resistance fighters. We don't bow our heads when we're starving, and we don't bend our knees when we're freezing. Anybody who wants to give allegiance to the invader and cast off his moral courage will do so over my dead body!"

Not to be intimidated, the other officer said, "Is it the mission of resistance fighters to starve or freeze? No, we must be flexible and resourceful. Tolerance must be one of our stratagems. The only way we'll win this war of resistance is by conserving our strength."

"Comrades," Commander Jiang said, "that's enough bickering. If you have something to say, take your turn."

"I've got a plan, Commander," Pocky Cheng spoke up.

When Little Foot Jiang heard Pocky Cheng's plan, he rubbed his hands in delight and complimented him profusely.

On the night when Pocky Cheng's plan was implemented by the Jiao-Gao regiment, they ran off with over a hundred dogskins my father and granddad had nailed to the crumbling village walls, and stole the rifles Granddad had hidden in the dry well. Having carried out this phase of their plan, they went out to hunt dogs for some needed nutrition, as well as the warmth of the skins.

That spring, as a freezing cold settled over the land, there appeared in the broad expanse of Northeast Gaomi Township an army of intrepid "dog soldiers" who fought a dozen or more battles, major and minor, with the Japanese and their puppets. That included Zhang Zhuxi's Twenty-eighth Battalion, who trembled in their boots whenever they heard the barking of dogs.

The first battle occurred on the second day of the second month, by the old calendar—the day, according to legend, when the dragon raises its head. The Jiao-Gao regiment, dogskins draped over their shoulders and rifles in their hands, slipped into Ma Family Hamlet, where they surrounded the Ninth Company of Zhang Zhuxi's Twenty-eighth Battalion and a squad of Japanese soldiers. The enemy's headquarters was in Ma Family Hamlet's onetime elementary school, which consisted of four rows of blue-tiled buildings surrounded by a high wall of blue bricks and barbed wire.

The commander of the puppet Ninth Company was a brutal man from Northeast Gaomi with a deceptively gentle smile. Since the onset of winter, he had begun a campaign to accumulate bricks, stones, and lumber to build new quarters for his company. As a result, his personal worth, all of it ill-gotten, increased dramatically. The locals despised him.

Ma Family Hamlet was in the northwest corner of Jiao County, bordering on Northeast Gaomi Township, about thirty li from the Jiao-Gao regiment headquarters. The two hundred Jiao-Gao soldiers waited until nightfall to set out from the village, dogskins draped over their shoulders, fur on the outside, tails dragging between their legs, and the multicolored fur shining brightly in the fading sunlight. It was a beautiful, bizarre army of underworld demons on the march.

Their commander, Little Foot Jiang, wore a huge red dogskin—it had to have been Red, the dog from our family—and as he walked at the head of his troops, the fur on his pelt waved in the wind. The bag hanging over Pocky Cheng's chest was stuffed with twenty-eight hand grenades.

Cold stars filled the night sky when they slipped into Ma Family Hamlet. A couple of dogs barked in friendly welcome, and a mischievous young soldier answered them in kind. An order from the front swept through their ranks: No more barking! No barking! No barking!

They took up positions a hundred yards outside the main gate, where bricks and rocks were piled in readiness for springtime construction.

"Pocky," Little Foot Jiang said to Pocky Cheng, who was sticking close to him, "let's get moving!"

"Number Six, Chunsheng, you two follow me," Pocky whispered.

He removed the bag of hand grenades to lighten his load. After tucking one grenade in his waistband, he handed the bag to a tall soldier and said, "When we've made it to the gate, bring this to me."

With stars spreading their weak light over the ground and a dozen or so lit carriage lanterns hanging from the barracks, it looked like dusk in the compound. Two puppet sentries patrolled the gateway, casting long shadows on the ground. An aging black dog ran out from behind the piles of bricks and stones, followed by a white dog, then a spotted one. They snarled and rolled on the ground, their profiles merging as they approached the gateway. In the shadows of a woodpile no more than a dozen paces from the gate, the dogfight turned nasty. From a distance it looked like three mutts fighting over a choice morsel of food.

Commander Little Foot Jiang watched the masterful performance conceived by Pocky Cheng, and was reminded of the benumbed, cowardly man who had shown up to join the army, sniveling at the drop of a hat, like a useless old woman. Pocky and his comrades continued their dogfight ruse in the shadows as the distracted sentries stood shoulder to shoulder and listened. One picked up a rock and threw it at the dogs. "Mangy damned mutts!"

Pocky Cheng yelped like a dog hit by a rock, and Commander Jiang had to stifle a laugh, it sounded so much like the real thing. The Jiao-Gao soldiers had been practicing their barking since the assault plan for Ma Family Hamlet was first drawn up. Pocky Cheng, a Peking-opera buff and woodwind player, had wonderful breath control and a loud, booming voice, not to mention a lively tongue; he easily became the regiment's champion "dog."

Growing impatient, the sentries moved cautiously up to the woodpile, where the dogs were really getting into it. Rifles ready, bayonets fixed, they were only three or four steps from the woodpile when the dogs stopped barking and began to whine, as though afraid.

The sentries advanced another slow, cautious step.

Pocky Cheng, Number Six, and Chunsheng jumped up, fur shimmering in the dim yellow glow, and charged the sentries like bolts of lightning. Pocky Cheng smashed his grenade down on the head of one; Number Six and Chunsheng buried their bayonets in the other's chest. Both crashed to the ground like sacks of cement.

The Jiao-Gao soldiers looked like a frenzied pack of dogs as they charged the enemy barracks. Pocky Cheng, who had retrieved his bag of hand grenades, ran like a madman toward the tiled buildings.

Rifle fire, exploding grenades, shouts, and the screams of Japs and their puppet allies shattered the winter calm at Ma Family Hamlet. The local dogs were barking like crazy.

Pocky Cheng lobbed twenty grenades into a window, and the pathetic cries of the Japanese inside reminded him of the day years earlier when they had hurled their grenades into the sandal workshops. But instead of satisfying his sense of vengeance, this re-enacted scene caused him such anguish that his heart felt as though it were being sliced open.

This was the most intense battle fought by the Jiao-Gao regiment since its formation, and it ended with the most brilliant and complete victory anywhere in the Binhai region, for which a special committee bestowed a commendation upon the entire regiment. The dog soldiers were caught up in wild joy, until two occurrences caused them great distress: First, the store of weapons and ammunition that fell into their hands after the battle was allocated to the Binhai Independent Battalion. Commander Jiang knew that the special committee's decision was the right one, but his soldiers grumbled with resentment, and when battalion soldiers came to collect the weapons, looks of shame covered their faces. Second, Pocky Cheng, who had so distinguished himself in the battle at Ma Family Hamlet, was found hanging from a tree at the head of the village. All the evidence pointed to suicide. From the back he looked like a dog, but from the front a man.

9

THERE WERE NO MORE SCREAMS from Second Grandma after Grandma washed her body with hot water. A gentle smile graced her scarred and battered face the day long, but blood kept flowing down below. Granddad called in every doctor in the area, and all sorts of medicinal potions were tried.

The last doctor was someone Uncle Arhat brought over from the town of Pingdu, a man in his eighties with a silvery beard, a broad fleshy forehead, and long curved fingernails. A comb made from a bull's horn, a silver ear pick, and a bone toothpick hung from the buttons of his mandarin robe. Granddad watched him lay a long finger on Second Grandma's pulse, and when he was finished he crossed her left hand over her right and said, "Make preparations for the funeral!"

Granddad and Grandma felt miserable, but they saw the old doctor out and did as he said. She stayed up to make a set of burial clothes, while he sent Uncle Arhat to the carpentry shop for a coffin.

The next day, with the help of neighbor women, Grandma dressed Second Grandma in the newly made clothes. No resentment showed on Second Grandma's face as she lay stiffly on the kang in a red silk jacket, blue satin pants, a green silk shirt, and red satin embroidered slippers, a gentle smile on her face, her chest rising and falling, frailly yet tenaciously.

At noon Father spotted a cat as black as ink pacing the ridge of the roof and letting out blood-curdling screeches. He hurled a broken piece of brick at the cat, which sprang out of the way, landed on one of the roof tiles, and pranced off.

When it was time to light the lamps, the distillery hands walked up with the coffin and laid it down in the yard. Grandma lit a soybean-oil light with three wicks, because it was a special moment. Everyone stood around waiting anxiously for Second Grandma to breathe her last. Father hid behind the door staring at her ears, which in the lamplight looked like amber, and were just as transparent, evoking a sense of mystery that danced in brilliant color in his heart. At that moment he knew that the black cat was stepping on a roof tile again, that its black eyes were flashing, and that it was rending the darkness with obscene screeches. His scalp burned, his hair seemed to stand up like porcupine quills.

Suddenly Second Grandma's eyes snapped open; and although her gaze was fixed, her lids fluttered, her cheeks twitched, and her thick lips quivered—once, twice, three times—followed by a screech more hideous than that of a cat in heat. Father noticed that the golden light from the soybean-oil lamp had turned as green as onion leaves, and in that flickering green light, the look on Second Grandma's face was no longer human.

"Little sister," Grandma said, "little sister, what's wrong?"

A stream of epithets poured from Second Grandma's mouth: "Son of a whore, I'll never forgive you! You can kill my body, but you can't kill my spirit! I'll skin you alive and rip the tendons right out of your body!"

It wasn't Second Grandma's voice, Father was sure of that, but the voice of someone well over fifty.

Grandma shrank from the force of Second Grandma's curses.

Second Grandma's eyelids fluttered as rapidly as lightning; one minute she was screaming, the next cursing, the sound shaking the rafters and filling the room. Her breath was glacial. Father saw that from the neck down her body was as stiff as a board, and he wondered where she found the strength to scream.

Not knowing what to do, Granddad told Father to summon Uncle Arhat from the eastern compound. Even there you could hear the terrifying screams.

Uncle Arhat walked into the room, glanced at Second Grandma, and quickly led Granddad outside by the sleeve. Father followed them. "Manager Yu," he said softly, "she's already dead. She must be possessed."

He'd barely gotten the words out when he heard her curse him loudly from inside: "Arhat Liu, you son of a whore! No easy death for you! Skin you alive, rip the tendons out of your body, cut off your prick. . . ."

"Wash her with river water to exorcise the demon," Uncle Arhat said after a thoughtful pause.

Second Grandma's curses kept coming.

When Uncle Arhat walked inside with a jug of filthy river water, he confronted waves of laughter. "Arhat, Arhat, pour it, pour the water, your auntie's thirsty now!"

Father watched one of the hired hands force a funnel into Second Grandma's mouth, and another pour the water, which eddied momentarily, then disappeared so fast it was impossible to believe it was actually emptying into her stomach.

Second Grandma quieted down. Her belly was as flat as ever, but her chest heaved, as though she were gasping for air.

Everyone breathed a sigh of relief.

"Okay," Uncle Arhat said, "she's old now!"

Once more Father sensed the patter of paws on the overhead tiles, as though the black cat were on the prowl again.

Second Grandma's rigid face parted in a bewitching smile. She screamed once or twice before a stream of turbid water gushed from her mouth. The fountain rose straight up, at least two feet in the air, then came straight down, fanning out as the drops splashed like chrysanthemum petals on her newly made funeral clothes.

Second Grandma's fountain trick sent the hired hands running from the room in fright. "Run," she shouted, "run, run, you can't get away, the monk can run but the temple will never get away!"

Uncle Arhat looked imploringly at Granddad, who returned the look, as Second Grandma's curses grew more spirited again. Now they were accompanied by spasms in her arms and legs. "Jap dogs," she cursed, "Chinese dogs, in thirty years they'll be everywhere. Yu Zhan'ao, you can't get away. Like a toad that eats a blister beetle, the worst is yet to come for you!"

Her body arched like a bow, as though she wanted to sit up.

"Oh no!" Uncle Arhat gasped. "A sitting corpse! Quick, give me a flintstone."

Grandma tossed him the flintstone.

Somehow Granddad found the courage to pin Second Grandma down so Uncle Arhat could press the flint down over her heart. It didn't work.

Uncle Arhat began to back out of the room. "Uncle," Granddad said, "you can't leave now!"

"Mistress," Uncle Arhat said to Grandma, "bring me a spade, quick!"

Once Second Grandma's chest was pressed down by the spade, her body grew still. She was left in the room to suffer alone, as Grandma, Granddad, Uncle Arhat, and Father went into the yard.

"Yu Zhan'ao," Second Grandma shouted from inside, "I want to eat a yellow-legged rooster!"

"Take my gun and shoot one!" Granddad said.

"No," Uncle Arhat said. "Not now. She's already dead!"

"Quick, uncle," Grandma said, "think of something!"

"Zhan'ao," he said, "I'll go get the Taoist at Cypress Orchid Market!"

In the early hours of dawn, Second Grandma's shouts nearly ruptured the window paper. "Arhat," she fulminated, "you and I are enemies who cannot live under the same sky!"

As Uncle Arhat walked into the yard with the Taoist, her curses turned to long sighs.

The seventy-year-old Taoist wore a black cassock with strange markings on the front and back. A peach-wood sword was slung over his back, and he carried a bundle in his hands.

Granddad went out to greet him and recognized him immediately as Mountain Li, the Taoist who had exorcised Second Grandma's weasel spirit years before. He was skinnier than ever.

With his sword the Taoist cut the paper out of the window so he could look into the room. As he withdrew his head, the blood drained from his face. Bowing to Granddad, he said, "Manager Yu, I'm afraid my power is inadequate to deal with this evil."

Filled with terror, Granddad pleaded, "Mountain, you can't leave. You must drive it away. You will be amply rewarded."

He blinked his demonic eyes and said, "All right, the Taoist will take a drink of courage and bang his head against the golden bell!"

To this day the legend of how Mountain Li exorcised Second Grandma's demon still makes the rounds in our village.

In the legend Mountain Li, his hair a wild jumble, performs a dance of exorcism in the yard, chanting as he twirls his sword in the air, while Second Grandma lies on the kang tossing and turning, screaming and cursing.

Finally, the Taoist tells Grandma to bring him a wooden bowl, which he fills half full with clear water. He takes a potion out of his bundle and dumps it into the water, then stirs it rapidly with the tip of his wooden sword, chanting all the while. The water gets redder and redder, until it is the color of blood. With a greasy, sweaty face, he jumps into the air, falls to the ground, and begins foaming at the mouth. Then he loses consciousness.

When the Taoist came to, Second Grandma breathed her last. The stench of her decomposing body and rotted blood floated out through the open window. When her body was put in its coffin, all the mourners held goatskin chamois soaked in sorghum wine over their noses.

Some people say that when she was placed in the coffin she was still cursing and kicking the lid.

10

FOR TEN YEARS I had been away from my village. Now I stood before Second Grandma's grave, affecting the hypocritical display of affection I had learned from high society, with a body immersed so long in the filth of urban life that a foul stench oozed from my pores. I had paid my respects at many gravesites before coming to that of the woman whose short but magnificent life constitutes a page in the most heroic and most bastardly history of my hometown. Her eerie, supernatural death had awakened in the souls of Northeast Gaomi Township a mysterious emotion that germinated, grew, and became strong, flowing slowly through the memories of village elders like a sweet scarlet syrup that fortified us and made us capable of facing the world of the future.

On each of my previous visits to the village, the power of that mysterious emotion was revealed in the drunken eyes of those old-timers. Comparisons are always risky, but when I approach them logically, I discover to my horror that in my ten years away from the village I have seen eyes like that only in the fragile heads of pet rabbits, turned red by boundless desire. There are, it appears, two separate human races, each evolving in accordance with its own value system. What frightens me is that my eyes, too, have taken on that crafty look, and that I have begun to utter only the words that others have spoken, themselves repeating the words of still others. Have I no voice of my own?

Second Grandma leaps from her grave holding a golden-hued mirror, the deep lines of a mocking grin tilting the corners of her full lips. "You're no grandson of mine. Look at yourself!"

Her clothes flutter, and everything is the same as when she was put in her coffin, yet she is younger and lovelier than I had imagined; the messages carried by her voice prove that she is infinitely more thoughtful and profound than I. Her thoughts are liberal, dignified, and richly resilient, yet serene and firm, whereas mine float tentatively in the air like the transparent membrane of a reed flute.

I look at my reflection in Second Grandma's brass mirror. As I'd feared, the clever look of a pet rabbit shines in my eyes; words that belong to others, not to me, emerge from my mouth, just as the words emerging from Second Grandma's mouth on her deathbed belonged to others, not to her. My body is covered with the seals of approval of famous people.

I am scared to death.

"Grandson!" she says magnanimously. "Come home! You're lost if you don't. I know you don't want to, I know you're scared of all the flies, of the clouds of mosquitos, of snakes slithering across the damp sorghum soil. You revere heroes and loathe bastards, but who among us is not the 'most heroic and most bastardly'? As you stand before me now, I can smell the pet-rabbit odor you brought with you from the city. Quick, jump into the Black Water River and soak there for three days and nights—I only hope that when the catfish in the river drink the stench that washes off your body they won't grow rabbit ears!"

Second Grandma returns swiftly to her grave. The sorghum stands straight and silent; the sun's rays are wet and scorching hot; there is no wind. The grave is covered with weeds whose fragrance fills my nostrils. It is as though nothing has happened. Off in the distance I hear the high-pitched songs of peasants tilling their fields.

The sorghum around the grave is a variety brought in from Hainan Island; the lush green sorghum now covering the rich black soil of Northeast Gaomi Township is all hybrid. The sorghum that looked like a sea of blood, whose praises I have sung over and over, has been drowned in a raging flood of revolution and no longer exists, replaced by short-stalked, thick-stemmed, broad-leafed plants covered by a white powder and topped by beards as long as dogs' tails. High-yield, with a bitter, astringent taste, it is the source of rampant constipation. With the exception of cadres above the rank of branch secretary, all the villagers' faces are the color of rusty iron.

How I loathe hybrid sorghum.

Hybrid sorghum never seems to ripen. Its gray-green eyes seem never to be fully opened. I stand in front of Second Grandma's grave and look out at those ugly bastards that occupy the domain of the red sorghum. They assume the name of sorghum, but are bereft of tall, straight stalks; they assume the name of sorghum, but are devoid of the dazzling sorghum color. Lacking the soul and bearing of sorghum, they pollute the pure air of Northeast Gaomi Township with their dark, gloomy, ambiguous faces.

Being surrounded by hybrid sorghum instills in me a powerful sense of loss.

As I stand amid the dense hybrid sorghum, I think of surpassingly beautiful scenes that will never again appear: In the deep autumn of the eighth month, under a high, magnificently clear sky, the land is covered by sorghum that forms a glittering sea of blood. If the autumn rains are heavy, the fields turn into a swampy sea, the red tips of sorghum rising above the muddy yellow water, appealing stubbornly to the blue sky above. When the sun comes out, the surface of the sea shimmers, and heaven and earth are painted with extraordinarily rich, extraordinarily majestic colors.

That is the epitome of mankind and the beauty for which I yearn, for which I shall always yearn.

Surrounded by hybrid sorghum, whose snakelike leaves entwine themselves around my body, whose pervasive green poisons my thoughts, I am in shackles from which I cannot break free; I gasp and groan, and because I cannot free myself from my suffering I sink to the depths of despair.

Then a desolate sound comes from the heart of the land. It is both familiar and strange, like my granddad's voice, yet also like my father's voice, and like Uncle Arhat's voice, and like the resonant singing voices of Grandma, Second Grandma, and Third Grandma, the woman Liu. The ghosts of my family are sending me a message to point the way out of this labyrinth:

You pitiable, frail, suspicious, stubbornly biased child, whose soul has been spellbound by poisonous wine, go down to the Black Water River and soak in its waters for three days and three nights—remember, not a day more or a day less—to cleanse yourself, body and soul. Then you can return to your real world. Besides the yang of White Horse Mountain and the yin of the Black Water River, there is also a stalk of pure-red sorghum which you must sacrifice everything, if necessary, to find. When you have found it, wield it high as you re-enter a world of dense brambles and wild predators. It is your talisman, as well as our family's glorious totem and a symbol of the heroic spirit of Northeast Gaomi Township!